An architect by profession, CHARLES BELFOURE has published several architectural histories, two of which have won awards from the Maryland Historical Trust. He was also given grants by the Graham Foundation and the James Marston Fitch Foundation for architectural research. A graduate of the Pratt Institute and Columbia University, he taught at Pratt as well as at Goucher College in Baltimore, Maryland and his area of specialty is historic preservation. He has been a freelance writer for the *Baltimore Sun* and the *New York Times*.

By Charles Belfoure

The Paris Architect
House of Thieves

HOUSE OF THIEVES

CHARLES BELFOURE

Allison & Busby Limited
12 Fitzroy Mews
London W1T 6DW
allisonandbusby.com

First published in 2015.

This paperback edition published by Allison & Busby in 2016.
Published by arrangement with Sourcebooks Inc.

A CIP catalogue record for this book is available from
the British Library.

10 9 8 7 6 5 4 3 2 1

ISBN 978-0-7490-1903-7

Typeset in 10.5/15 pt Adobe Garamond Pro by
Allison & Busby Ltd.

The paper used for this Allison & Busby publication
has been produced from trees that have been legally sourced
from well-managed and credibly certified forests.

Printed and bound by
CPI Group (UK) Ltd, Croydon, CR0 4YY

For Chris

CHAPTER ONE

It was a perfect day to rob a bank.

The rain outside hammered the pavements like a monsoon. The river of delivery wagons, double-decker omnibuses, and carriages of all description that usually flowed in an unending torrent along West Thirty-Third Street had been reduced to a trickle. In place of the rush of pedestrians along the pavement, a few men with umbrellas hurried by the plate glass windows of the Manhattan Merchants & Trust Bank. Customers would hold off coming to the bank until the downpour stopped – and that wasn't going to happen for hours.

All of which meant fewer witnesses.

Stick Gleason looked down the barrel of his Colt Navy revolver at the people lying face down on the shiny, white marble floor, then glanced over at Sam Potter, who was standing guard inside the massive oak-and-glass double doors of the front entrance. Potter nodded: things were going well. Though they both wore white muslin masks that hid their faces, Gleason knew Potter was smiling at him.

The woman on the floor in front of him started to whimper, reminding him of a hunting dog he'd once owned. When the dog wanted out of his crate, he'd give a high-pitched whine until Gleason couldn't stand the noise any longer and freed him. Gleason could only see the top of the woman's scarlet-coloured hat, which had a slanted brim with a sort of high mound on top, like a beehive covered with yellow and green cloth flowers. Must have been a society lady.

'Keep quiet, ma'am. We'll be through in just a few minutes,' Gleason said in a soothing tone, tapping the top of her hat with the barrel of his Colt. She shut up immediately.

He was getting anxious himself. 'Come on, Red. How much longer?'

'Goddamn you, I told you never to rush me,' Bannon said angrily, the words muffled by his muslin mask. He continued to pour the nitroglycerinee drop by drop from the small glass vial into the joints of the bank vault's hinges. Beads of sweat slipped down his forehead, sliding over his eyebrows and into his eyes, making him blink uncontrollably. He kept wiping them away with his left hand.

It was dead quiet in the bank. Then Gleason heard a faint noise building quickly toward a screech, like a boiling tea kettle about to blow.

'Listen, woman, I told you.'

An ear-piercing scream exploded out of the society lady's mouth. Bannon flinched – and Stick watched in horror as the glass vial slipped from his fingers and fell to the marble.

The blast was like a white-hot fireball of a meteorite, streaking from the vault room to the front windows of the bank, incinerating everything in its path. Bannon was vaporised in a millisecond, along with Gleason, the society lady, four bank tellers, two customers, and the entire wood-and-marble interior of the banking hall. Potter was propelled like a rocket into West

Thirty-Third Street and through a shopfront window directly south across the road.

A delivery driver and his bay horse lay dead and bloody amid the wreckage of a dray wagon. A cast-iron electric light pole was bent parallel to the street. Windows and shopfronts on the south side of West Thirty-Third Street were blown in too, leaving black holes that seemed to gape out at the newly silent street in astonishment.

James T. Kent, standing under an umbrella on the flat roof of the eight-storey Duckworth Building directly across from Manhattan Merchants & Trust, watched as a great plume of black smoke billowed up from West Thirty-Third Street, drifting past him and blending into the grey sky. The street below was a mass of confusion, with people running toward the building from all directions. The clanging of fire wagons could be heard in the distance. *There won't be any need for them,* Kent thought. The blast had sucked the oxygen out of the space, which meant no fire.

From his vantage point, the men on the street looked like ants scurrying in and out of the blasted opening of the bank. *They'll find no bodies,* he thought. *Only tiny pieces of human flesh and bone.*

'Poor bastards,' said Ben Culver, a short, stout, broad-shouldered man.

'It was the nitro,' Kent said, not a shred of emotion in his voice. 'Handling it is like trying to hold quicksilver – almost impossible. But still better than using dynamite. Remember Maritime National? The cash, negotiable bonds, and stock certificates, all burnt to ashes by the blast. It took Red hours to sweat out that nitro from a dozen sticks of dynamite. He said blowing the vault would be the easy part.'

'We'll never replace Bannon, Mr Kent.'

'No, we won't. Red was the best cracksman in New York.' Kent took a cigar out of his gold case with his black-gloved hand and tapped it idly against his palm.

'These vaults are too damn hard to blow in the daytime, Mr Kent. Bank jobs are just too risky anyhow. The Company has to . . .'

'Diversify?'

'Yeah, that's it.'

'I agree,' said Kent with a smile. 'What do you suggest?'

Kent was a tall, thin man in his early forties, with greying hair and a commanding presence. He always wore a black frock coat with matching waistcoat and pearl-grey trousers, all ordered from Henry Poole & Co., the best tailor in London. He had schooled Culver, whose previous wardrobe could charitably be described as loud, in dress. A gentleman, he'd said, must always be so well dressed that his clothes are never observed at all.

Culver valued this advice almost as much as his cut from their jobs. These days, he was as elegantly clothed as his employer, though the juxtaposition of his battered and meaty red face with his fine, tailored outfits frequently struck one as very odd.

'The army's stopped guarding President Grant's grave in Riverside Park,' he said, brimming over with his excitement at offering a new business proposition. 'They just have a night watchman. They haven't started building the real tomb over it either, so we could snatch the body and hold it for ransom. Like they did with A. T. Stewart back in '78. His widow forked over twenty thousand dollars for the body. For a department store king! Think how much we'd get for a United States president.'

'I can find only two things wrong with your plan,' Kent said amiably. 'First, I served proudly under Grant in the war. And second . . . it's incredibly stupid.'

He smiled and patted Culver on the shoulder, as if to lessen the sting of his words. A disappointed expression twisted Culver's

10

face, and he looked down at his expensive, black patent leather shoes – the ones Kent had advised him to purchase. Culver wasn't the brightest, but he was absolutely the most loyal employee of the Company, and Kent genuinely liked him.

'I know those men had families,' he said, pulling out his tan pigskin wallet and removing ten one-hundred-dollar bills. 'Please divide this among them.'

'That's very kind of you, Mr Kent.'

Kent extracted his Gorham solid-gold pocket watch from his waistcoat and frowned. 'The annual board of directors meeting for the Metropolitan Museum is at eleven. I'd best get going.'

CHAPTER TWO

'John, you should be damn proud of this boy of yours.'

John Cross turned and stared at his son, who stood next to him in the entry foyer of Delmonico's. It was hard to believe that this was the same toddler he'd once played with on the beach at Long Branch or taken to Central Park to sail boats. George was strikingly handsome. He had inherited his mother's dark complexion and straight black hair and was at least three inches taller than his father. The twenty-two years of his son's life blurred together in Cross's mind. When had his boy grown into a man?

'Thanks, Stanny. He turned out all right, I suppose.'

Stanford White, a six-footer with red hair and a thick brush of a moustache, roared with laughter. Beside him, Charles McKim, normally a very reserved fellow, also burst out laughing. White's enthusiasm was always infectious.

Cross had met White and McKim many years ago, when they all worked for Henry Hobson Richardson as apprentice architects. Stanny and Charlie remained his closest friends, and he was particularly happy that they were there for his son's graduation party.

'Graduating from Harvard, captain of the baseball team. Not

too shabby,' said McKim. 'In fact, I'm jealous. I sat on the bench when I played there.'

'Yes, congratulations, Georgie. So, are you following in the old man's footsteps and taking up architecture?' White asked, giving Cross a wink.

'No, sir. Unfortunately, I didn't inherit my father's artistic talent. I'm going to be a mathematics teacher at Saint David's this autumn.'

'George has been teaching part-time for the Children's Aid Society downtown since the winter. Then next year, after Saint David's, full-time at Columbia graduate school. On his way to becoming a brilliant professor,' Cross said, voice full of pride.

'Not a bad place to begin your teaching career,' said McKim. 'Saint David's is the poshest school in town.'

As White nodded with approval, his face broke into a sly smile. 'Ah, behold. The beautiful Helen of Troy.'

Cross's wife, Helen, walked up to join the men. She was mesmerizing in a crimson evening dress from Worth of Paris; a lovely pearl-and-diamond necklace set off its deep décolletage, and a pair of large diamond festoon earrings framed her high cheekbones. Few women in New York society could challenge her beauty and charm. At parties and balls, men swarmed around her like bees to honey, making Cross proud and nervous at the same time. Having a beautiful wife was a double-edged sword – Helen was the object of pride *and* possible scandal. But he knew he didn't have to worry about Stanny, whose preferences for female companionship tilted toward those below the age of fifteen.

Helen gave the group a steely look. 'You gentlemen are blocking the way of Georgie's guests. Take your masculine good fellowship into the grand dining room, please. John and Georgie, you stay where you are.'

White bowed, took her hand, and kissed it. 'Whatever Helen of Troy commands.'

Cross looked out, past the glass-front double doors of the restaurant. 'Do you think she'll come?'

Helen rolled her eyes. 'When she says she's going to do something,' she snapped, 'she always follows through. For heaven's sake, don't worry.' She straightened George's white tie, brushed a bit of lint from his white silk waistcoat, and then ran her hands along the shoulders of the black cutaway tailcoat. Satisfied, she rose on her tiptoes and kissed him on the cheek.

'Later, I want you to be sure to talk to Granny – and Mary Morse.'

'Oh, Mother.'

For the next twenty minutes, the trio greeted more guests. Finally, Cross nodded toward the doorway and said in a low voice, 'Here she is.'

On Fifth Avenue, directly in front of Delmonico's, a shiny black brougham pulled by two sleek chestnut horses in a gold-trimmed harness drew to a stop. The driver and attendant were dressed in gold and navy-blue livery and black top hats. The attendant hopped down from the box and opened the passenger door.

In the dusk of the warm July evening, a short, rather stout woman in a beautiful black silk brocade evening gown stepped out, holding on to the white-gloved hand of the attendant. She stepped onto the pavement into the circle of bright light cast by the new electric street lights, which had recently replaced their much dimmer gaslight predecessors. The glow of the light reflected in tiny sunbursts off her tiara of diamond garlands and her dog-collar necklace of hundreds of tiny diamonds on a band of deep purple satin. As she rearranged her black lace shawl over her shoulders, a crowd gathered on the pavement to gawk at her.

Cross watched as she marched with regal ease and confidence

through the glass doors of the restaurant. She moved as if she owned Delmonico's. And in a way, she did.

Caroline Astor was the undisputed queen – or despot, some felt – of New York society. She alone determined who belonged and who did not. If a person failed to meet her approval, he or she was condemned to social death.

In 1886, New York society had only two parts: old and new. The old, known as the Knickerbockers, were the descendants of the original Dutch founders of New Amsterdam, nicknamed for the knee-length breeches they once wore and headed by families with names like Schuyler, Schermerhorn, Van Cortlandt, and Van Rensselaer. There was also an old English flank of founders led by the Livingstons and the Phillipses. The rigid Knickerbocker social code demanded absolute propriety and strict conformity. They religiously obeyed this code, even dwelling in identical brownstone houses the colour of chocolate sauce, driven by the paralysing fear that they would be thought different and would thus become the subject of gossip.

Then there were the new, a *nouveau riche* class made up of millionaires who had made their fortune from businesses such as railroads, steel, or horse carts. Dirty, undignified pursuits, the Knickerbockers sniffed. The new displayed their wealth with outrageous extravagance, building luxurious mansions and amassing yachts, jewels, and clothing – luxuries universally condemned as vulgar by the old moneyed class. But undaunted, these parvenus came from all over America to New York City, where they stormed the walls of the Knickerbocker aristocracy.

Caroline Astor was a proud Schermerhorn, but she straddled the world of old and new by marrying the grandson of John Jacob Astor, a German-born fur trader who had become America's richest man. Helen Cross was a distant, relatively poor member of the Schermerhorn clan. John Cross, a distant and equally poor Livingston relative, helped cement the Knickerbocker connection. 'Aunt' Caroline liked them both and watched over them like a mother hen, and they had been taken under her wing and safely ensconced in 'new' New York society. She even insisted on paying for Helen's wardrobe and jewellery. They lived modestly, however, in a wide three-storey brownstone house at the corner of Madison Avenue and East Thirtieth Street and had only four servants. Cross likened his lifestyle to the architectural scale he used in his drawings; he lived at one hundredth the full-scale life of the Astors.

But to her credit, Caroline had opened doors to the advantages and privileges of society, to him and especially to George, and John's other two children, Julia and Charlie. Thanks to her connections, Cross's architectural practice prospered. But Cross knew that if there were the tiniest hint of scandal about anyone in his family, she'd cut them off in a second and would have nothing to do with them again. These were the ironclad rules of their world. One malicious whisper could annihilate a family's reputation and banish them from society forever. Completely shunned – people who were once your closest friends would never talk to you again, even to your children.

'Aunt Caroline, thank you so much for coming,' said Helen, meeting her at the door, arms outstretched. Helen was one of the very few people Aunt Caroline ever publicly hugged. She gloried in the fact that such an incredibly beautiful woman was a Schermerhorn.

'Tonight I must attend a tiresome charity performance at the Academy of Music,' said Aunt Caroline, 'but I knew I had to stop by to see Georgie. Where is that handsome boy of yours?'

'Aunt Caroline,' said George, stepping forward, taking her hand with both of his and kissing her cheek.

'Here's a little something for my class of '86 man,' she said, handing him a small box wrapped in silver paper. George unwrapped the present in front of her, knowing she would want to see his reaction.

Others had made their way to the foyer, eager to curry favour with Mrs Astor. White, one of her architects, hovered about with Charles Crist Delmonico, the grandnephew of the founder who controlled the restaurant dynasty and had made it the best restaurant in the city.

Nestled in a wad of cotton was a magnificent gold pocket watch and chain. George pulled it out, eyes wide in wonder. Instead of the usual incised decoration, the tiniest of diamonds and rubies formed a sinuous, vine-like design on the watch's cover and sides. The inside cover featured a similar raised motif in a vortex swirl, with a large diamond at the centre. The back of the watch was engraved: 'To George, Harvard Class of 1886, From Aunt Caroline.' Helen's and John's eyes met; their first reaction was not pride but fear. *What if George lost such a beautiful gift?*

Beside them, White let out a whistle. 'That's incredible.'

'You know that workmanship, Mr White. I had Louis Comfort Tiffany design it specifically for Georgie,' Mrs Astor said.

White had just completed a commission for the Tiffany family, constructing a huge mansion of golden-brown brick at the corner of Madison Avenue and Seventy-Second Street.

'This is a work of art. Thank you so much.' George bent to hug his aunt, who bear-hugged him right back.

'It's a pleasure, my dear boy. And now I must be off.' Before anyone could bid her goodbye, Aunt Caroline turned, the train of her gown sweeping around, and marched triumphantly back to her carriage. Dozens of people were waiting to get a look at her and, more specifically, to see what she was wearing, for Caroline Astor also dictated New York fashion. If she decided to wear a Chinese coolie's straw hat to dinner, Fifth Avenue's shops would be flooded with them the next day.

As John and Helen stood at the front door, waving goodbye, Charles Crist Delmonico said, beaming with delight, 'Ladies and gentlemen, dinner is served in the grand dining room.'

Only Caroline Astor could have persuaded Charles Eliot, president of Harvard University, to stop by to say a few words at George's graduation party. Eliot had been travelling through New York from Boston the day after commencement and couldn't say no, especially to such an immensely rich donor. Besides, George had been both an academic and athletic star at Harvard, so Eliot was pleased to visit.

So that he might leave in time to catch his train to Washington, Eliot spoke briefly before the meal started. He rose to his feet at the end of the long dinner table, a slight and unassuming man in his fifties, with a long nose and bushy sideburns, the leader of America's greatest university. The cacophony of the celebration was instantly silenced.

'Ladies and gentlemen, George Cross exemplifies the kind of man Harvard produces. During my tenure at the university, I've seen a change in the Harvard man's character. His sense of personal honour and self-respect has increased. Drunkenness has decreased. It still troubles me to see vices born of luxury and self-indulgence on the rise. But this doesn't touch George Cross. Not only does George exemplify academic brilliance, but he's also a man of great character and determination – as he showed last year at the Polo Grounds, when he drove in the winning run in the ninth inning against Yale.'

The dining room erupted into wild cheering and applause, and George shyly rose and waved to his admirers. President Eliot shook his hand, bowed to the crowd, and left the room, a signal that the eating and drinking could begin. Because Helen and many other ladies were present – and because Caroline Astor had paid for the dinner – it was not a wild male bacchanal that such an occasion might have prompted, but rather a luxurious society event. More than one hundred diners sat at a table that stretched the length of the room. Down its centre ran a deep trough bordered by high banks of beautiful summer flowers. In the trough swam three white swans, which glided up and down its length, oblivious to the diners on either side. The eight courses, served on silver, included consommé á l'Impériale, Maryland terrapin soup, red snapper, canvasback duck, fillet of beef, cold asparagus vinaigrette, a dish of sherbet to cleanse the palate, and then a saddle of mutton, truffled capon, and fresh vegetables of all kinds, followed by desserts and candies. Claret, Burgundies, Madeira, and champagne flowed into the guests' glasses as from a spigot; in the background, an eight-piece musical ensemble played on and on, light sounds to enliven but not disrupt the burble of conversation.

The party came to an end at about 2:00 a.m., when Cross found his son saying goodbye to Stanford White, always the very last to leave.

'George, your mother and I are going now,' Cross said, clapping his son on the shoulder. 'It was a wonderful party. Please be in touch in a few days.'

'Thank you so much for tonight, Father. I'll never forget it.' George clasped his father's hand, smiling.

'Helluva party, Georgie, old boy,' Stanny shouted as he left the restaurant with John and Helen. 'The night's still young, and I know a place on East Forty-Fifth that's just beginning to heat up.'

'We're not going anywhere with that blackguard,' Helen hissed into Cross's ear as they made their way to a carriage on Fifth Avenue.

Cross just sighed. He had long since given up trying to change his wife's stubborn opinion of Stanford White's sybaritic character, especially his taste in women.

His guests gone, George walked downstairs to the restaurant's open-air street cafe, settled into one of the carved wooden chairs, and lit a cigarette. After almost six hours in the dining room, the night air felt cool and refreshing. Fifth Avenue was deserted, and the pure silence soothed George after the hours of unending noise. He leant back and closed his eyes, savouring the triumphant evening.

'Beautiful night, isn't it, George?'

The voice came from directly behind him. George smiled and swivelled around, expecting to see an admiring classmate. Then his face turned pale, and the cigarette dropped from his lips.

James T. Kent sat at a table a few yards away, dressed in elegant evening attire, smoking a cigar and sipping a glass of white wine.

'Just dropped in for a nightcap before heading home after the theatre. But now that I'm here, maybe I could have a word with you. It's about a matter of some delicacy.'

George rose from his seat and started toward the low wrought iron fence that enclosed the pavement cafe. But a short, broad-chested man stepped out of the shadows, moving to cut off his exit.

'I think you remember my business associate, Mr Culver.'

Culver smiled at George but said nothing.

'Why don't we take a little trip?' said Kent.

CHAPTER THREE

Oh, he floats through the air
With the greatest of ease,
This daring young man
On the flying trapeze;
His actions are graceful,
All girls he does please,
My love he has purloined away . . .

Kent got such pleasure out of seeing his men enjoy themselves. He hadn't realised Freddy Dugan had such a wonderful baritone voice. If he hadn't become an extortionist, the man could've made it on the stage.

Kent and ten of his employees were standing inside the new cable car power plant, currently under construction on the East Side. It was a huge brick and stone structure with tall, arched windows and a cavernous central room, where steam machinery would be installed to pull the coils of steel cables that wound and twisted beneath the city streets. Cable cars were the latest fad in New York, and the wise bet said they would soon replace the horse cars entirely. Kent saw it as a great investment. A cable car didn't have to be fed. It could work all day, and most importantly, it didn't deposit tons of shit and an ocean of piss onto the streets. When the Brooklyn Bridge had opened three years before, cable cars had been installed, and they'd been a great success. And they were still the future.

The present object of his men's delight, George Cross's body, was swinging like a giant clock pendulum above the cement floor, bound and suspended upside down at the end of a thick rope whose other end was looped over a steel roof truss twenty feet above the men's heads. Culver held the end of the rope, and Tommy Flannigan pushed George's body, sending him in a wide arc. Back and forth he went. Kent's men sang and roared with laughter at each swing. Kent had never seen them have so much fun sober. When George threw up his banquet from Delmonico's, they whooped and howled.

Finally, Kent walked over to the swinging body and raised his hand, signalling for silence.

'For a mathematician, George,' Kent said as the boy swung by, 'I thought you'd have a better head for numbers.' He pulled out a cigar and lit it, drawing in and exhaling the smoke with great pleasure. 'Figuring in compounded interest, what you owe me is forty-eight thousand dollars. Quite a bit of money. Let me put it another way. A master carpenter makes about a thousand dollars a year. You owe me forty-eight years of a carpenter wages.'

'For God's sake, cut me down, Jim.'

'I know you love to gamble, George. But if you lose, you *have* to pay up. I warned you about the interest that was accruing on your debt, but you ignored me. And you can't say I haven't been patient. Or generous. I gave you the opportunity to forgive the whole thing by putting the fix on the Harvard–Columbia baseball game . . . but you didn't come through, my boy. I lost on that bet, and I lost heavily. You're lucky I didn't add it to your total.'

'I tried! I swear I did! But you can't throw a game when no one else is in on it,' George cried.

'I can't have you stiff me, George. It's bad for business. If people see that I let you slide, they won't have any respect for me, and they'll try to stiff me too.'

'Give me one more chance, please,' pleaded George.

Kent watched George swing. Then he signalled Flannigan to bring the body to a halt. Flannigan grabbed George on each pass to slow him down until the boy hung there, slowly turning around and around like a slab of beef on a hook. Kent motioned for Al Carney, a mountain of a man with broad shoulders and fists the size of hams, to come over.

'George, Al here once fought John L. Sullivan and lasted almost five rounds. Five rounds against the great John L. Imagine that. There was an article about it in the *Police Gazette*.'

Carney's jowly face flushed red with embarrassment as he approached the hanging body. Then his fists let loose as if he was bashing a body bag in a gym. George cried out at each blow.

'I'm most sorry to have to do this to a society gentleman,' Kent said, his tone sincerely apologetic. 'But you have to understand, George, that I live in a world that also has a strict code of rules. Just like in New York society, when one breaks the rules, one must be punished. And as you may well imagine, that punishment can be . . . severe.' He gave a sly smile. 'Let me introduce you to Abe Gibbons. In his former life, Abe was a butcher.'

A lanky, grey-haired man of about fifty walked over and placed a long knife to George's throat. Carney continued to punch, ignoring him; the ex-boxer was enjoying himself too much to stop.

'They'll find pieces of your body from the Bronx to Cape May, George.'

'Please – no!' screamed George.

'There's no one you know who can pay off the debt?' Kent asked, more irritated than curious. 'What about your family?'

'My family doesn't have that kind of money. My father's just an architect.'

Kent's brow wrinkled, and he motioned for Carney to cease his pummelling.

'I didn't know your father was an architect. What does he design?'

'Office buildings. Like the Chandler Building on East Fourth.'

'Indeed? That's a very handsome building. What else?' Kent sounded genuinely impressed.

'Empire State Life Assurance on Nassau Street. Saint Mary's Church. Lots of big houses up on Madison Avenue and Riverside Drive.'

Kent turned and walked slowly across the power plant. He made a wide arc, returned to George's hanging body, and nodded at Gibbons, who lunged at George.

'God help me!' George screamed.

With a slash of the knife, the thick rope was severed. George fell hard and landed on his head with a groan that echoed throughout the empty plant. The men howled with laughter.

Kent walked over to Culver, who, relieved of holding the rope, was leaning against a wall, smoking a cigarette and enjoying the festivities.

'You remember George Leslie, don't you, Mr Culver?'

'Sure. The king of bank robbers. Planned the Manhattan Savings job on Bleecker in '78. Got away with two *million*.'

'Wasn't he an architect?'

'That's what they say. I heard that he could read them building drawings of banks, could even draw 'em up himself.'

'And didn't they find him dead up in Yonkers?'

'Yep, said he was fooling around with one of his men's girls. The man was a genius. Shame to die because of a goddamn woman,' Culver said, shaking his head.

Writhing in pain on the concrete floor, George yelled, 'Just get it over with! Kill me and be done with it, you bastard.'

'A *Harvard* man,' Kent murmured, smirking. He turned to Flannigan.

'Mr Flannigan, you're going to take George on a little vacation.'

Visibly disappointed, Gibbons sheathed his blade.

'Yes, sir,' muttered Flannigan.

'What are you going to do to me?' George shouted.

Flannigan took hold of George's feet.

'Wait,' said Kent.

Kent pulled out a handsome leather wallet from George's inside pocket. He opened it, examined the contents, removed a card, and then returned the wallet. He nodded to Flannigan, who began dragging George out of the power plant.

'Mr Culver, first thing tomorrow morning, I want you to deliver a message.'

CHAPTER FOUR

John Cross sat in the upper deck of the Fifth Avenue omnibus, the air already baked by the hot July sun. His eyes were vacant, his mind elsewhere as he mulled the strange events of the past two hours. He had never gotten new work in so peculiar a manner.

At around 9 a.m., a rough-looking man came into the office, asking to see him. The fellow had very crooked teeth but was dressed better than Cross, who felt himself taken aback when the man entered his private office. The clothes and the man seemed entirely at odds; it was like a pig wearing evening dress to the opera. The man explained that his boss admired Cross's work and would like to talk to him about designing a building. Because he was going out of town, however, they had to meet that day, at 11 a.m.

The economic boom of the 1880s had set off an enormous amount of construction in New York City. Cross had received his share of this new work entirely by word of mouth. Men he knew from the Union and Knickerbocker Clubs, the riding club, his Harvard classmates, gentlemen from Saint Thomas Episcopal and Newport – they all recommended him. But this fellow certainly didn't belong to that set.

The other requirement for the meeting was even odder. They

were to meet in Saint Patrick's Cathedral on Fifth Avenue. This intrigued Cross. Perhaps the project was work for the Archdiocese, which oversaw a lucrative group of churches, parochial schools, and convents. Though he was a society High Episcopalian, he didn't mind designing for the Roman Papists, as his mother-in-law called them. Churches were a plum commission. Cross had designed just one, a Protestant church, early in his career, and he was eager for another opportunity.

The man tipped his expensive top hat and left. Cross left at once, walking from his office on Broadway and Eighth Street to Fifth Avenue, where he caught the omnibus. He enjoyed the ride; from the top, he had a grandstand view of the city.

Fifth Avenue was the backbone of his world. Its staid three- and four-storey brownstone buildings passed before his eyes, an unending line of high stoops, wrought iron railings, and striped canvas awnings extended out to block the summer sun. Cross watched as servants scurried in and out and families emerged from behind tall double doors of wood and glass. Broughams, hansoms, and victorias driven by men in top hats and black cutaway coats stood by the kerbs, waiting for their owners. Dray carts carrying goods of all kinds slowly made their way up the avenue, making deliveries from house to house.

At Madison Square, where Fifth Avenue and Broadway collided then separated, the building style shifted and became a mix of commercial and residential. The Fifth Avenue Hotel, currently the city's most fashionable, stood on the left. The spire of the Marble Collegiate Church towered above Twenty-Ninth Street. Then, on the left, came a familiar sight: William Backhouse Astor II's wide brownstone house. Aunt Caroline's home. To the south was a large walled garden that connected to her brother-in-law John Jacob Astor III's house.

The previous summer, Cross had stood in the garden with the Astors, looking over the high wall at President Grant's funeral procession. Now, as he passed Aunt Caroline's house, he smiled at its modesty. It was really only an extra large brownstone building, but that was the way it was supposed to be: unpretentious, dull, and respectable.

As the horse-drawn omnibus slowly rattled along on the cobblestones, halting to pick up and drop off passengers, Cross glimpsed the cathedral. Just north of Fiftieth Street, Saint Patrick's was complete but for its two spires, finally under construction after a hiatus of almost eight years. Its architect was James Renwick Jr., a man Cross greatly admired. Both were in the New York chapter of the American Institute of Architects. When he got the commission, Renwick had travelled around Europe for more than three years, observing and sketching twin-spired churches. Finishing Saint Patrick's soaring towers would complete a magnificent design that rivalled the cathedrals of the Old World.

The Knickerbockers, Protestant to the core, were shocked that such a huge Catholic church could be built on Fifth Avenue. It dwarfed nearby elite Protestant churches like Saint Thomas and Fifth Avenue Presbyterian. Weren't there laws against such a thing? the Knickerbockers protested. The fact that the church was paid for with the nickels and dimes of Irish immigrants, the same trash that washed the Knickerbockers' floors and dishes, was even more galling. There was talk of building a Protestant cathedral on the West Side to put the Catholics in their place.

Sighing, Cross shifted his gaze. The daily promenade by the fashionable had begun. Men in elegantly tailored frock coats accompanied by women in beautiful walking dresses with tasselled parasols filled Fifth Avenue's pavements. 'Shoddyites', the Knickerbockers called these 'fashionable' new people. *They dress magnificently,* Cross thought, *making up in display what they lack in taste and education.* He recognised a client but made no effort to wave to him.

In front of the cathedral, Cross got off the omnibus and walked inside. He'd been to the church many times, and on each visit he marvelled at the nave's breathtaking vaulted ceiling, supported by rows and rows of Gothic arches. It ended at an altar in a full-height semicircular apse, lit by tall windows of stained glass. He felt as if he were in France. It was amazing how the thick stone walls of the church kept the interior so cool and refreshing, even on such a miserably hot day.

Most men hated what they did for a living – it was just a means to pay the bills – but Cross genuinely loved being an architect. He was proud that he'd chosen the right path in life and dreamt of being the best architect in the city (although he knew there was a lot of competition). He wanted someday to design something as magnificent as this cathedral, something that people would use for centuries after he was gone from this earth. Cross felt he had the talent to do it. He ran his hand over the cool stone of a column and smiled. *Yes,* he thought, *one day I'll do something truly great.* He turned and looked around for his new client.

His odd visitor had told him that a Mr Kent would be waiting for him in the rear pew on the north-west corner. *It seems so mysterious,* Cross thought again, shaking his head. He walked towards the corner and saw a distinguished-looking man. He appeared to be about forty, clean-shaven, with swept-back hair and a sharp, almost hawk-like nose. Most encouraging, he looked like a very prosperous client.

'Mr Kent?'

'It must be a wonderful thing to be an architect, Mr Cross,' Kent said, eyes fixed on the nave ceiling. 'To think, you design and draw every square inch of a church like this. You decide what it will look like, down to the tiniest detail. Like that decoration atop that cluster of columns holding up the arch.'

Cross took an instant liking to this fellow.

'Yes, it is wonderful,' he said.

Kent stood and extended a hand, which Cross shook. 'James T. Kent. Thank you for coming on such short notice.'

'I'm glad to meet you, sir. I'm told you have a building you want designed?'

'Mr Cross, although I do very much admire your work, I'm afraid you were brought here on a pretence.'

A frown replaced the smile on Cross's face.

Kent continued. 'I'll get to the point. This meeting involves a personal matter. I'm afraid that your son George has been doing business with me for the last year or so. Now he finds himself in serious financial difficulty. You see, he owes me a great deal of money.'

'He – how much money?'

'Please sit down, Mr Cross.'

'How much?'

'About forty-eight thousand dollars.'

Cross stood for a moment, dumbfounded, and then slumped into the pew as though someone had clubbed him. He rubbed his hand over his mouth, unable to speak. 'I don't believe you,' he finally forced out.

'I'm afraid you must, Mr Cross. George will tell you himself that it's forty-eight thousand dollars – and that he has no way of paying it back.'

'How could he owe you that much, for God's sake?'

'Of course, I suppose you don't know. George has a serious gambling habit, sir, and in very ungentlemanly places. The Bowery, the Tenderloin – you will see my meaning.'

'No, no. That can't be,' Cross said through tightly clenched teeth.

'Parents are always the last to know their children's shortcomings.'

Cross stood, furious. 'Who are you, scoundrel?'

'A businessman, sir. Who expects to be paid back.'

'You're a criminal who took advantage of my son. There's no way he can pay you.'

'Then George is going to die, Mr Cross.'

Cross sat back down, gazing in stunned silence at the padded leather kneeler of the pew. 'You can't threaten me,' he said at last, defiantly.

'It's not a threat, Mr Cross. It's an ironclad guarantee. George will die if he does not pay me back.'

'He's only twenty-two! He just graduated from Harvard. He—'

'And you must be very proud of him – at least until now,' Kent said with a smile.

'I won't let you kill him, do you hear me?' Cross said, his voice rising above the accepted volume for the hushed solitude of a church. A woman praying over her rosary in a nearby pew gave him a disapproving look. Now he understood why Kent had wanted to meet him in a public place, and he clenched his fists.

'I know you won't,' Kent said. 'You're going to pay George's debt for him. You'll even pay the interest, which is accruing as we speak.'

Cross laughed derisively. 'Do you really suppose I've got forty-eight thousand dollars?'

'No, but you know where to get it – and more.'

'What the hell are you talking about?'

'You're a successful architect, Mr Cross. You've designed mansions for the rich, office buildings for all kinds of big companies and banks. Places that hold things of great value.'

31

'You damn fool, you expect me to go and rob them?'

'Not at all. I expect you to help *me* rob them.'

'You're mad.'

'Am I? If you don't, pieces of George's body will be found floating around the island of Manhattan tomorrow. I give you my word on that. But for the present, George is my guest.'

'That's a lie! He went home last night.'

'Then how do I come to have this?' Kent smiled and handed a slip of paper to Cross, who let out a groan when he saw what it was – George's membership card to the Union League Club. 'Impressive that someone so young is a member of the most prestigious club in the city, Mr Cross. Myself, I belong to the New York Club.'

Cross stood, grabbing Kent by the lapel of his frock coat. 'You're bluffing. I'll go to the police about this, and you'll be thrown in prison, you damn rogue.'

Unruffled, Kent gently removed Cross's hand. 'I urge you not to do that, Mr Cross. It will mean death for your son. In fact, I'll kill him in front of you and then kill you. Please believe me. I trust you'll understand that it's best you cooperate and pay back the debt. Then the whole matter will be settled. But until you agree, George will remain with me.'

'You can go to hell!' Cross shouted and stomped out of Saint Patrick's, the echo of his footsteps bouncing off the white marble walls.

On Fifth Avenue, he stood in a daze in the middle of the pavement. A flood of pedestrians from either direction swept around him, like a stream around a boulder. His mind spun. He felt as if he were being sucked into a vortex, a horrible nightmare. If only he could wake up in his bed, begin the day anew, realise with a sob of relief that none of this had happened.

It can't be. This had to be some practical joke by George and his friends. *That's it!* Cross thought with a mixture of anger and happiness. It was a joke, and he had been taken in. His son was alive and safe. Perhaps Stanny was behind the charade. If so, he'd curse his old friend up and down for putting George up to such a thing.

A feeling of relief swept over Cross. His breathing returned almost to normal, and he started walking south. But when he came to Forty-Ninth Street, he stopped abruptly.

Suppose this wasn't a joke.

A man in a derby and dark grey frock coat collided with his back. 'Damned idiot,' the man muttered, stepping around him. Cross took no notice. With a sinking feeling, he replayed the events of the morning in his head. It was too cruel and elaborately staged to be a joke. But if it was all true – Kent wasn't bluffing – he couldn't stand by and let his son be murdered. He'd give his life in a second to save George or Julia or Charlie. The thought of losing his children was too horrible to bear.

Cross walked blindly, covering block after block as if in a trance. He crossed streets without looking, lucky not to be run over by the parade of wagons and carriages. All the while, his mind raced with terrible images of how Kent would murder George. How had his son gotten into such a fix?

In that instant, Cross realised he knew as much about George as one of these strangers next to him on the pavement. His son wasn't what he seemed. His handsome, charming façade masked deviant, illicit behaviour. Cross had thought he'd been a model father. Well, the joke was on him. If what Kent had told him was true, then he'd failed miserably. His knees almost buckled under him, nearly sent him to the ground right there on Fifth Avenue. *A son's faults are his father's faults,* his mind repeated numbly.

He realised he couldn't face this alone, but he couldn't tell Helen. At heart, she was a weak-willed, status-obsessed woman who'd collapse into hysterics if he told her what their son had done. Cross kept walking, passed Aunt Caroline's house at Thirty-Fourth Street – and stopped dead in his tracks. Of course – he had the Astors, the most powerful force in the city, on his side. Surely they could save George.

Cross started sprinting up to the front porch but halted midway. What was he thinking? The thought of knocking on Caroline's door and telling her what had happened filled him with shame. George's dishonour would repulse her, and knowing Caroline, she'd slam the door on his family. If her son, Jack, had found himself in this kind of fix, it was merely a matter of writing a check and keeping the whole thing secret. But being poor, distantly related Schermerhorns and Livingstons only went so far. Society people walked on eggshells their whole lives to avoid the merest whiff of scandal. Cross had seen lives shattered by a mere whisper, no matter how untrue. And if it *was* true . . .

No, he couldn't go directly to Caroline. But perhaps he could reach out to someone in her circle of influence, a person he wasn't tied to by blood. Cross walked to the bottom of the front path and thought for a while. Then he walked slowly downtown to Madison Square, oblivious to the scorching sun that beat down upon him. Continuing on Broadway, he stopped in front of the recently finished Lincoln Building at Fourteenth Street. The office of Thomas Griffith, the Astors' most trusted attorney, was located there. Griffith, the city's paragon of the legal profession, would tell Cross what to do, and he'd never breathe a word to the Astors.

Finally feeling a small measure of relief, Cross entered the towering, ten-storey limestone building.

CHAPTER FIVE

Even if it hadn't been a sweltering July night, Cross wouldn't have been able to sleep. He was still too shaken and frightened by the day's revelations.

After tossing and turning for hours, he finally gave up and rose. Thankfully, he and Helen had separate bedrooms. If they'd slept in the same bed, his wife would have known immediately that something was wrong. Cross usually slept like a rock.

Putting on his dark green silk dressing gown, Cross sat on the sofa in the parlour and smoked until dawn's light streamed in through the gap in the heavy velvet drapes hanging over the tall windows. He couldn't get his mind off what George had done. It didn't seem possible that Kent was talking about his son. Did George really live in a secret world, one unfathomable to Cross?

Of course Cross knew what gentlemen of his class did when away from the prying eyes of their families. Stanford White was the supreme example of a gentleman's penchant for extracurricular activities, and Cross was no saint himself. But even those debaucheries followed class boundaries. You'd never see White on the Bowery or in a Chinatown gambling den.

President Eliot's words from George's graduation party rang in

Cross's ears: '. . . *vices born of luxury and self-indulgence on the rise.*' At the time, Cross had thought with self-righteous satisfaction that Eliot's words didn't apply to his boy. He'd seen high-society fathers destroy their sons with money, yachts, racehorses, and anything else they wanted – gifts that killed the boys' ambition. Despite his own past, Cross had avoided this path. Yes, he came from a society family with all the Knickerbocker advantages: elite private schools, summers in Newport and the Berkshires, riding, shooting, European tours, servants, balls. He'd gone to Harvard too. But then, defying the Knickerbocker business tradition, he went to Paris to train in architecture at the École des Beaux-Arts. After apprenticing for one of America's greatest architects, Henry Hobson Richardson, he'd set up his own practice. Cross had had a real goal in life. In turn, he wanted to set an example for his son. To his delight, George had great dreams too – to become a mathematician and teach, perhaps as a professor at Harvard. What the hell had happened?

None of that matters, Cross told himself. What mattered was keeping George alive. Speaking to Thomas Griffith yesterday had set Cross's mind somewhat at ease, if only because it allowed Cross to share his desperate burden.

To Cross's surprise, Griffith, a taciturn, granite-faced man of seventy, had turned ashen when he'd heard Kent's name. Kent, he explained to Cross, was a well-bred, Princeton-educated man from a wealthy mercantile family in Baltimore. Rumour had it that he'd originally trained to be a doctor. His connections at the highest levels of business and government in New York made him a man of great influence and power. Even Tammany Hall, the political machine that ran the city, did what he told them to do.

Kent was a man to be feared. Although he was already so rich he didn't need the money, he ran an extensive crime organisation that committed any kind of depravity that would turn a profit.

His gang was nicknamed 'Kent's Gents' because they dressed like society gentlemen, down to their gold-capped walking sticks, which were used more frequently for beating people to death than strolling about.

The attorney made Cross repeat the conversation they'd had at Saint Patrick's word for word. Then, with a terrified look on his face, Griffith told Cross that they had to move quickly or George would indeed be killed. Kent did not make idle threats.

At these words, Cross groaned as if he'd been punched in the stomach and dropped his head, tears welling up in his eyes. Griffith went to the telephone on his office wall and asked for police headquarters on Mulberry Street. He was immediately connected to Thomas Byrnes, chief inspector of the New York City Police Department. From his tone, they seemed to be good friends. Griffith explained that he was calling on a matter of great urgency, and Byrnes agreed to see him first thing the next morning.

Cross had breathed a great sigh of relief when he heard the policeman's name. Byrnes was a ruthlessly efficient Irish cop who had transformed the New York City police, weeding out corruption and modernising investigations with innovations like mugshots, which created a photographic gallery of known criminals. Before Byrnes's arrival, the New York underworld had seen the city's police force as a joke. But all that had changed. Wall Street, for instance, had always been a rich hunting ground for criminals, who preyed on bank messengers, robbing them of the bonds, securities, and cash they carried from bank to bank. Byrnes declared that Fulton Street, the northern boundary of Wall Street, would be a 'dead line', below which all criminals would be arrested on sight. He was true to his word, and robberies on Wall Street soon dropped to zero.

Byrnes, Cross realised, was the only man who could save his son.

* * *

It was 6 a.m. He heard Colleen, their maid, moving about in the kitchen on the ground floor, lighting the fire in the cast-iron stove and getting ready to set the table for breakfast. Mrs Johnston, the housekeeper, and Mrs O'Shea, the cook, would be down soon. Cross hadn't eaten anything since yesterday's meeting with Kent. Now, he found that his appetite had returned.

As Cross walked into the centre hall to the stairs, he heard the telephone ring. Odd to get a call so early in the morning.

'It's for you, sir,' said Colleen in her chipper Irish brogue as she passed him on the staircase.

Cross picked up the receiver in the kitchen.

'Good morning, Mr Cross,' a man's voice said. 'We wanted to let you know that we just made an ice delivery.'

The phone clicked off. Cross turned to look at the refrigerator on the far wall of his kitchen, a thoroughly modern room with the latest in newfangled technology, befitting an architect. The refrigerator was clad in dark walnut and lined with cork insulation; it had extra shelves and a space at the top to hold a block of ice weighing about two hundred pounds. A little door in the back faced another matching door that Cross had cut into the outside brownstone wall on the Thirtieth Street side. The iceman could place the ice directly in the refrigerator without coming into the kitchen. But Mrs O'Shea usually placed a card in the kitchen window to tell the iceman when ice was needed. It was odd that he would call the house.

Cross slowly walked to the refrigerator and opened it. He saw nothing unusual on the shelves, just the ordinary perishable foodstuffs. Cheese and lettuce. Puzzled, he opened the door of the top compartment – and stepped back with a gasp. Inside, encased in a block of ice, was the severed head of a man. After a few seconds, Cross recognised Thomas Griffith, the Astors' attorney. Griffith's eyes were wide with terror. His severed flesh was tinted bluish, the lips purple, his white hair floating above his skull like he was under water.

Heart pounding, Cross wheeled, made sure no one else was in the kitchen, and quickly pushed the door of the refrigerator shut. At that moment, the telephone rang again. He ran to it before Colleen could answer from upstairs.

'Mr Cross? We must apologise. We delivered the wrong ice to you this morning. But don't worry. We'll replace it right away.'

Cross slammed the receiver against the holder and fell to the slate floor like a building collapsing in on itself. Crumpled and hyperventilating, he stared at the refrigerator in horror. As if from very far away, he heard the doors at the back open and then the sound of blocks of ice being moved about. The telephone rang for the third time. Cross stared at the dark oak telephone box for a long moment. Then he slowly reached for the receiver.

'Good morning, Mr Cross. Please meet me at the Dakota today at 3 p.m. Apartment 7G.' Cross recognised the voice of James Kent, who hung up abruptly.

Mrs O'Shea, a gaunt Irish woman in a dark grey dress and white apron, came into the kitchen, humming to herself.

'Why, Mr Cross, whatever are you doing down here this early?' Without waiting for his answer, she went right to the refrigerator and opened the top compartment to check the ice, as she did every morning.

The block of ice was crystal clear.

CHAPTER SIX

'When you present your calling card to the butler, Julia, you must wait to see if the lady of the house will receive you. If the butler tells you, "She's not at home to callers", that's perfectly acceptable. Don't take it as a slight. Leaving your card fulfils your obligation. Now, if she does receive you, never stay for more than thirty minutes. And never pay a call before two or after four.'

Helen Cross delivered her lecture in a stern schoolteacher's voice. Her daughter wrinkled her brow, took the calling card from her mother, and examined it.

'No lady *ever* leaves just her own card on the first visit. She must always include her husband's,' Helen continued.

'This is so complicated, Mother. Why must I know all this absurd social arithmetic?' Julia asked, her tone a combination of scorn and amusement.

Her grandmother, a slender and graceful Knickerbocker matriarch who still retained her beauty after seventy years, took Julia by the shoulders and looked her in the eyes. 'My child, calling cards are the alpha and omega of social intercourse. You *must* remember this.'

'You won't get your own cards in your first season, mind. Your name will be on mine,' Helen said. 'It seems complicated, but you'll soon learn the rules. We all had to go through this.'

'The most important rule to remember is that an unmarried woman never receives a gentleman caller without her mother or a chaperone present.' Granny spoke with an earnestness that startled Julia. 'A chaperone knows the world; a young girl doesn't.'

Aunt Caroline Astor placed her arm around Julia. 'Remember, my dear, you're a Schermerhorn. We're held to a higher standard.'

'Why yes, of course, Aunt Caroline.'

'You'll have the most brilliant coming-out ball in the city. At my place, of course. I'll see to *everything*.' Aunt Caroline spoke confidentially to Helen, who beamed with delight. That meant that from now on, Caroline would pay for Julia's wardrobe. To Julia, she added, 'You'll be the most beautiful debutante of the season.'

'So much work to be done. We must make the list of guests, and then I'll make a personal call on every one,' said Helen, who didn't consider this task work. She looked forward to seeing all two hundred people in advance of this, a truly special occasion in her life. A daughter's coming-out meant that the mother had decided she was ready to be accepted by the world as a fully mature woman – and more importantly, ready to receive homage from rich, eligible men.

'What about me? Where's my invitation?' asked Charlie Cross, Julia's ten-year-old blonde brother, sliding down the black walnut banister of the front staircase in the entrance hall of the Cross home, where the women stood.

'You, little boy, are not coming,' said Julia with a frown.

'I wouldn't want to come to your dumb party. I bet no one shows up,' Charlie said, dismounting before he collided with the ornate newel post. He leapt to the floor with the agility of an acrobat.

'Charlie, aren't you going to play in Madison Park?' his mother asked.

'On my way,' yelled Charlie as he crashed through the front doors.

Julia's mentors were content to stay in the entrance hall, a wide, graceful space that ran the length of the house to the back stairs used by the servants. Its ten-foot-high walls were adorned with flowered brocade wallpaper and dark walnut wainscoting. A heavy, carved walnut hallstand with coat hooks, a large mirror, and a built-in seat dominated the space.

Granny pointed at the silver calling card stand next to the seat.

'The cards are left in the stand. You'll fill out this ledger stating when your visitors' cards were presented and by whom. It must *always* be up-to-date.'

'Remember that a guest *must* pay a personal call within two days of a dinner party. For all other entertainments, leaving a card with the butler will do,' Aunt Caroline added emphatically.

'I understand,' said a bewildered Julia. 'May I go upstairs, please, Mother?'

'Yes, dear. We'll start the list tonight.' Helen spoke excitedly, like a child looking forward to her birthday party.

The women watched as Julia ran up the stairs.

'She's inherited your beauty, Helen, and that's important. A girl's beauty assures her brilliant future,' Aunt Caroline said. 'It's the most important possession a girl can have.'

'But Julia, I think, has an independent streak,' Granny said. She spoke disapprovingly, as if her granddaughter had done something reprehensible. 'A girl *has* to conform. She must. And she needs a good chaperone.'

'Hush, Mother. Julia would never do anything untoward. She's only seventeen.'

'But what's this talk about her going to college? To Vassar?' Granny spoke incredulously, her tone bordering on panic. 'A girl like her doesn't need college. She's already too educated. Men don't want a wife cleverer than they are.'

Colleen stepped out of the front parlour and curtsied. 'Tea is served, madam,' she chirped.

'Thank you so much,' Helen said. Granny frowned. Helen knew what was bothering her – Granny would think that Helen should have left off the 'so much' or not even said a thank-you. Her mother thought familiarity with servants was vulgar and unwarranted. While servants were indispensable to society people, they had to know their place. This was why Americans were largely held to make terrible servants – they were too independent, expecting to have all sorts of *rights*. Absolutely the best way to run a household, Granny always said, was with dumb and subservient Irish servants, a spinster English housekeeper, or – if the house was big enough – an English butler.

The women settled into their chairs in the parlour, and Helen poured tea from a gleaming silver tea set on a mahogany tea table. Smiling, she passed a plate stacked with iced lemon cakes. Her front parlour, accessible through panelled sliding doors off the entrance hall, was 'the best room' and served as the stage for important family events, as well as for entertaining. There, the lady of the house demonstrated her family's cultural refinement through her selection of the paintings and lithographs that adorned the blue damask walls. Like all society ladies, Helen had a fear of empty space. She filled every square inch of wall and floor with bric-a-brac. The deep-purple Belter chairs with their round backs, the scarlet velvet sofa, the flowered rug, the forest-green drapes on the tall front windows – even the design of the lace doilies on the backs of the chairs was an aesthetic choice. She was proud of her parlour. It had to be the height of fashion, for soon it would be Julia's courting arena.

'Did you read, Caroline, that forty thousand workers have gone on strike in Chicago? It seems they want an eight-hour workday.' Granny shook her head, appalled as ever by the changing times. 'Fifteen thousand marched in Union Square to support them.'

'All the meat packers, cigar makers, and leather workers in Chicago on strike. It's unbelievable. They already have a ten-hour day. Those fools should be grateful. It used to be twelve. I suppose that next they'll want Saturdays off.' Caroline huffed. 'William says the owners may call in Pinkertons to deal with them.' A private army of policemen, the Pinkertons were detectives hired by rich businessmen to solve crimes and especially to put down strikes and labour protests the local authorities could not deal with. Considered much smarter than the regular police, the Pinkertons used brute force and bullets to get results.

'I hope they do. They know how to handle anarchists,' Granny said with a smile.

'Then there's this talk of home rule for Ireland,' Caroline said. 'Every day, the front page of the *Tribune* has an article about the debates in Parliament.'

'If the Irish we get as servants are any indication, it's madness to think they can rule themselves,' Granny said. 'They're no better than children.'

'My Irish servants have gotten along rather well,' said Helen, smiling. She knew what her mother would say next.

'You let your help walk all over you, Helen. It's a disgrace.'

'I just happen to remember that they're human beings, Mother.'

'When his mistress enters the room, a servant is supposed to turn away and avert his eyes,' Granny said indignantly. 'Yours speak to you without being spoken to first!'

'I'm glad to have the respect and loyalty of my servants,' Helen said, reminded again how lucky she was that her mother still lived in her own massive brownstone house on East Twenty-Fifth Street.

Caroline gracefully changed the subject. 'Ellen Thackeray was a guest at President Cleveland's wedding reception last month. She said his bride, Frances Folsom, looked absolutely radiant in white lace.'

'That man's old enough to be her father,' Granny said.

There was a noise in the hall. *John coming down the stairs,* Helen thought. She rose and intercepted him in the entry hall before he made it to the front door.

'John, I thought you were ill. You said you weren't going to the office today.'

She'd known something was wrong from the instant she'd laid eyes on her husband that morning. It was as though all the blood had drained from his face. Normally a robust man, he seemed listless and lethargic, unable to focus on her words.

'Helen, I must go out,' John said.

But she blocked his path. 'You look terrible, John. Go back to bed. I'll have Colleen bring you some tea.'

'Goddamn it, I don't need any tea. I have an appointment, and I can't be late!' Cross shouted.

His harsh tone made her jump out of his way. She watched in alarm as her husband grabbed his hat and stormed out the door. What could possibly be wrong?

CHAPTER SEVEN

'Mr Cross, I want you to know that I'm not angry at you for what you did. But I will be less lenient if something like that should happen again.'

Kent reminded Cross of a schoolmaster sitting in his wood-panelled office, reprimanding a recalcitrant student. Cross himself sat stiffly, balanced on the edge of the sofa, watching Kent pour tea. Aunt Caroline would have envied the quality of the silver. In a multi-tiered stand on the tea table were a variety of pastries, but Cross had lost all appetite since the delivery of the ice that morning.

The Dakota was like a huge European château, a riot of steep gables, turrets, finials, and dormers clad in olive-coloured stone and salmon-coloured brick. Its sheer enormity was amplified by its position on the Upper West Side, surrounded by vacant lots and shacks. It gave the impression of a mountain that had risen out of nowhere. From Central Park, it reminded one of a fortress in the middle of an enchanted forest, like in a fairy tale.

Despite its far-flung location, it had quickly become a highly fashionable place to live. Kent's apartment was magnificent. He and Cross sat in a beautiful library lined with floor-to-ceiling bookshelves. A vista of Central Park stretched across the tall windows behind them.

'How many lumps do you take?'

'Two, no milk.'

Kent handed him his cup and settled back in his green overstuffed velvet armchair. He sipped his tea with a look of great pleasure.

'Quite a place, Mr Cross, hmm? Like living in a palace without having to own it.'

Cross didn't reply.

At that moment, the front door to the apartment opened. A short, elegantly dressed woman with chestnut-coloured hair followed by three small children walked past the open door of the library.

'Mr Cross, meet my wife and children,' Kent said in a jolly voice. 'Hello, Millicent. How was the outing?'

'Oh, wonderful. The children so loved the ponies.'

Cross rose and smiled at the beautiful woman, who beamed back at him.

'It's such a pleasure, Mr Cross,' Millicent said.

'Mr Cross is a new business associate. And these rascals are Bill, Henry, and Abigail.'

The children, all of whom were well dressed and well mannered, bowed to Cross and then raced off in three different directions.

'If you'll excuse us, my dear, Mr Cross and I have business to discuss. Tonight at dinner, you must tell me all about your day. I wish I'd been there.' Kent followed his wife out, closed the sliding doors, and returned to his seat. 'I'm so glad we were able to come to an understanding, Mr Cross,' he said. 'I'm sure we can do business together.'

'Nothing is to happen to my son,' Cross said.

'Or Helen, Granny, Charlie, and Julia – as long as you keep our agreement.'

Cross was visibly shaken. After this morning, he knew what this man was capable of. Kent would kill his entire family without batting an eye. He was sure of it.

'I enjoy doing business with a family man,' Kent said amiably. 'There's so much collateral.'

'Where is George?'

'In very pleasant circumstances. I'll notify him that his debt is forgiven, but I won't tell him of our arrangement. Don't worry – if you keep your end of the bargain, he'll never know. George will be back in his apartment in a few days. I just hope he can deal with his "little weakness". You do know there are hundreds of gambling dens in New York City besides mine. But that's your problem now.'

Cross blinked. In all the confusion, he hadn't thought about that.

'Let me explain how our business arrangement will work,' Kent said, setting down his teacup. 'You will choose buildings you've designed that contain articles of great value – cash, stock certificates, gold, merchandise such as expensive clothing, fine linen, silverware, and jewellery. You will help me plan each robbery by giving me drawings of these places and telling me where items worth stealing can be found. And after each robbery, the value of the goods will be deducted from George's debt.'

'Promise me that, once it's paid back, I'm free of this.'

'Why, of course. I don't think you're cut out for a life of crime, Mr Cross.' Kent gave him a wink. 'But you are a talented architect. That Chandler Building – and those tall arches! I envy your talent. I wish I could do something like that.'

Cross was silent. Coming from this merciless bastard, it hardly felt like a compliment.

'The next step will be for you to take some time – one week, say – to choose a building. Then we will meet to discuss whether your plan is feasible. It takes a criminal eye to evaluate these things,' Kent said. 'You'll want to pay off the debt immediately, of course. But for our first effort, let's choose something modest. And bring copies of the drawings. I understand that with the new blueprinting process, it will be easy for you.'

Kent was sharp. Only a few years ago, copies of architectural drawings had to be traced over by hand, a long and tedious process. But with the introduction of blueprinting, all that had changed. Now, a photosensitive coating could be applied to a sheet of paper, which would be placed behind the original linen drawing. The contraption was put in a wood frame that sat out in the sun, developing a perfect image on the paper like a photograph.

'Yes,' Cross said, nodding. 'I can bring you your own copies of the drawings.'

'From now on, it's better to meet elsewhere. You'll be told where to go and when.' Kent rose from his chair. The meeting was over. 'Please don't think me rude, but I have a Presbyterian Hospital board meeting in an hour over on East Seventy-Second,' Kent said apologetically as he escorted Cross to the foyer. 'But before you go, you must see my latest treasure.'

He led Cross to a large oak table with carved legs and removed a heavy sheet of paper, revealing what looked like a very old, yellowed parchment.

'An early eighth-century illuminated manuscript from France. Isn't it magnificent?'

Though Cross didn't give a damn, he pretended to be impressed out of courtesy. After taking a respectful amount of time to examine the gold-leaf-flecked pages, he nodded and walked toward the library doors.

'Henceforth, Mr Cross, you must learn to think like a criminal. Coming from your background, that may be difficult,' Kent said as he slid open the panelled doors.

'It didn't seem to be an obstacle for you.'

Kent gave a roar of laughter. 'I suppose Griffith told you all about me. True, Princeton didn't give me much training for my line of work. You're a Harvard man?'

Cross nodded.

'A satisfactory school, but they have no eating clubs, unlike Princeton. So uncivilised,' he said. 'Do take a look around the building before you go. You'll find it most interesting.'

'I walked through right before it opened. The architect, Henry Hardenbergh, is a friend of mine. It's a remarkable building,' Cross said softly, looking up at the ceiling. 'The best apartment building in the city. I wish I had done it.'

CHAPTER EIGHT

In the courtyard of the Dakota, Cross drew a deep breath and looked up at the four seven-storey-high stone walls surrounding him. He felt like a mouse trapped in a box.

At the corner of Seventy-Second Street, he walked across Eighth Avenue into Central Park. The Transverse Road that cut across the vast green space was filled with carriages. It was the time of day when, rain or shine, society people paraded themselves. Various conveyances, pulled by teams of sleek horses with two men in full livery atop the box, travelled back and forth on the carriage drives. Every day without fail, hordes of onlookers lined the roadways of the park to watch the Knickerbockers, the parvenus, and the famous pass by in an unending procession. Pure vanity, not fresh air, was what brought the society women to Central Park each afternoon. Cross paid them no mind. Instead, lost in thought, he veered off on one of the winding paths through the trees.

George was safe, he told himself, and that was all that mattered. He could do nothing to stop his own involvement with Kent; no one was coming to rescue him. Griffith had been murdered before his meeting with Byrnes in the police department. Cross was on his own.

He had no choice but to become a criminal in order to save not only George's life, but the rest of his family's as well. With his loved ones in danger, he shouldn't be doubting what he had to do. And still – still he wavered. Was it out of some conviction that resorting to crime went against all that he believed? It wasn't a matter of faith. Cross hadn't been brought up in a religious family – society people went to church every Sunday, Easter, and Christmas because it was expected of them, but it was all for show.

Was he afraid? Did he make a moral objection to committing crime as cover for this fear? *Yes*, Cross thought. He secretly knew this to be true. Deep down, he *was* a coward. More than twenty years ago, during the Civil War, he faced the decision of whether to fight. He hired a substitute to serve in his place. Not to pursue business or a professional career, like the other men of his class, but because the thought of being ripped apart by a volley of rifle or artillery fire in some far-off field terrified him.

War had seemed a noble and abstract concept to him. Then he saw Matthew Brady's photographs of the dead on the battlefield. No one had ever shown the cruel reality of war in such a way. The illustrated papers depicted only the victorious, marching to glory. Brady's pictures were unbelievably real, a harsh image of bullet-ridden corpses rotting in the sun. That was someone's son or brother lying there, Cross had thought, the soldier's eyes and mouth wide open and frozen in shock, hundreds of flies buzzing about the open wounds. Cross's mind transposed his own face onto one of the corpses, and he actually shook with fright.

It was his father who told him of the substitute law. He was secretly overjoyed. Though he put up a pretence of wanting to fight, his father, a successful businessman who didn't give a damn about slavery and saw the great profit to be made from the war, browbeat him into hiring a substitute. Cross was saved because his father could afford the three-hundred-dollar payment. But his older brother, Robert, refused to sit out the war. He volunteered immediately.

While the war raged, Cross gave his choice no mind. But the Union won, and the returning warriors were admired and worshipped. His brother and the others had probably been scared to death. Yet they chose to serve. Robert had even won a medal for gallantry in action, which made Cross feel even more like a coward. Ever since, a sense of shame had dogged his heels. And he was still a coward; he had proved that with his vacillations. But no matter how scared he was, he *had* to do this. Even if it meant getting himself killed.

He needed to clear his mind and determine which place to rob. He came to the edge of the lake's south dog-leg and sat on the grass bank, watching the fleet of snow-white swans gliding along the still surface. Forming a list of past projects in his head, Cross tried to visualise each one, tried to remember who the client was and where the building was located. But he'd been in practice for fourteen years; there were more buildings than he could recall with any clarity. All the offices, the apartments, Saint Mary's Church on West Sixty-Fourth Street, train stations in the suburbs, the Exchange Hotel, Manhattan Hospital and Dispensary, and scores of houses and cottages. He would have to go back to the office to refresh his memory.

Cross made his way back through the trees to the Transverse Road, following it east until he came to the wide stone steps that swept down from the Mall to Bethesda Terrace. There, the great fountain stood by the edge of the lake. It was an unbearably hot July day, and dozens of people refreshed themselves in the fine spray carried off the fountain by the breeze. Children stood at the edge, splashing the water at one another. A few ragged urchins, contrary to park rules, were wading. Some society ladies holding brightly-coloured parasols to keep the heat at bay had even gotten out of their carriages to stroll the Terrace.

Cross stood at the top of the stairs, staring at the scene. Central Park had actually become the democratic meeting ground that its architects, Olmsted and Vaux, intended it to be. Below him, the wealthy rubbed elbows with the lowest of the low, immigrants from the Lower East Side and the Bowery. His class was never this close to such people, not unless they were shining shoes or washing floors. At any time they liked, the men and women of Cross's class could travel to the Berkshires, Newport, or Long Branch for fresh air and nature. But the convenience of Central Park drew them in. For the poor, Central Park was their oasis, easily reachable by horse car or elevated train. There, they could stretch out on the grass for a few hours before returning to the squalor of their everyday lives. Cross saw the park as a masterpiece, a work of art. Everything, save the large rock outcroppings, had been designed and placed by man.

With a sigh, Cross descended to the Terrace and circled the fountain. He was making his way back up when someone called his name. Turning, he saw an old client, William Cook.

'Playing hooky from work, old boy?' Cook was a short man in his early fifties, not fat but exceedingly well fed. A member of the new rich, he'd made tens of millions in the shoe business in Saint Louis. His wife had then forced him to move to New York to breech the walls of Aunt Caroline's high society. Many of the city's millionaires were originally from the Midwest or West Coast. Like the tens of thousands of poor immigrants who streamed through Castle Garden in the Battery, these wealthy people descended upon the city each year, seeking a new life.

While Cook was a 'shoddyite', dressed in only the best suits, he was a good, decent man. He only flaunted his wealth as offensively as he did because he wanted to please his social climber of a wife.

'Hello, Bill. Yes, you've caught me. But why aren't you at work?'

'We're shutting up the house and taking the steamer to the cottage at Newport tonight. Alice loves that place you designed for us, John. I think she likes it more than the one you did in the city.'

'That's kind of you to say.'

The 'cottage' Cross had designed for the Cooks on Bellevue Avenue in Newport was a twenty-four-room, wood-framed house covered with shingles and surrounded by deep porches. Cross considered it one of the best things he'd done. He loved when a client told him how much they appreciated his work.

'Of course, I wanted to take a stroll in the park before we left. Nice thing about having a home on Fifth Avenue: Central Park is your front yard! I love walking about the place. Lot of good lookers on parade, if you know what I mean,' Cook said and winked.

'Helen and I will be coming up later this month. I'll give you a call. We can meet at the casino,' Cross said, waving goodbye as he trotted up the stairs.

'That would be awfully jolly,' Cook called.

Cross looked back and smiled. The new rich, Granny complained, were always using vulgar British phrases like that.

On Fifth Avenue, Cross walked along the inside of the low stone wall separating the park from the wide pavement. He stopped at East Seventy-Eighth Street and surveyed the Cook mansion from behind the trunk of an elm tree. He smiled when he saw the huge Renaissance Revival mansion.

The house looked impenetrable from the outside because a dry moat surrounded it on all four sides. After his first trip to England, Cook had become crazy about castles and moats and wanted one like a child covets a toy for Christmas. A real moat was out of the question for his new city mansion, but Cross had cleverly provided one without water, a stone-lined ditch that was fifteen feet wide and twenty feet deep. It actually had a practical purpose; it accommodated two stories of kitchens, storage rooms, and servants' quarters below the street level, with windows even. To Cook's delight, his architect added iron-and-wood drawbridges to span the moat to the front door and to the rear service entry. At night or when the house was empty, the drawbridges were raised, creating a wide, deep, protective chasm between the pavement and the house. But best of all, Cook felt that the unique design meant that he didn't need a night watchman while he was away.

Yes, this will do nicely, Cross thought.

CHAPTER NINE

Though he was a prisoner, George had to admit the jail was magnificent. Especially the views. To the south, you could see Kaaterskill High Peak; to the north, South Lake and North Mountain. George and his jailer, Tommy Flannigan, were taking a stroll along the front of the Kaaterskill Hotel, the finest in the Catskill Mountains. A four-hundred-foot-long building with three-storey columns, it boasted six hundred rooms with steam radiators, running water, and electric service bells.

'You know what I like best about this place, Georgie? The air. It's so cool and refreshing. Not like bein' in that steam bath in Manhattan. I thought it might be more pleasant for us to spend some time together out here.'

'Yes, it feels wonderful,' George said. He hadn't given the weather a second's thought. It wasn't as important as knowing whether he would live or die.

It was a shrewd move on Kent's part, bringing him up there. If he'd kept him captive in Manhattan, George could have escaped and been on the next boat to China. But in the Catskills, one hundred and thirty miles north of the city, he was in the middle of a wilderness with no place to run to.

'Look at the size of this joint, will you? You know that it all got built on account of a fight over fried chicken?'

'What?'

'The owner, George Harding. He was staying over at the Catskill Hotel and wanted his daughter to have fried chicken, but they wouldn't give it to her because it wasn't on the day's menu. They told him to go build his own hotel if he wanted fried chicken. And that's what he did,' said Flannigan with a braying laugh.

The sound reminded George of a jackass.

As they walked back to the main lobby, George watched Flannigan out of the corner of his eye. For years, he'd terrorised victims in the Five Points and the Bowery. Once, when he was arrested, the police found a price list for services in his pocket: nineteen dollars to break an arm; fifteen dollars to bite off an ear; ten dollars to break a nose and jaw; twenty-five dollars to stab or shoot in the leg. But for all these horrible acts of violence, Flannigan had a soft streak, and he'd been George's constant sympathetic companion for the previous two days. George could see that the genial bear of a man was downhearted about having to kill him.

'Come on, Georgie,' he said, slapping George on the back with his big paw. 'Things will work out. From what I hear, Mr Kent may let the debt slide.'

'After you break my arms and legs and poke out my eyes.'

'Oh no, Georgie. I'd never do that to you. I've always had a hard time beating the hell out of really handsome guys like you. Seems like destroying God's best work.'

'That's very noble of you, Tommy,' George muttered.

The two men entered the hotel lobby, which was crowded with families waiting to check in and out. Since its opening in 1881, the Kaaterskill had become a fashionable destination for New York society. Like a Madrid bull, Flannigan rammed and pushed the well-dressed customers aside to get to the front desk. George waited in a sitting area, looking over a copy of the *Tribune*. Soon, he realised, his death might be a front-page article. Most murder victims in New York City were found floating in the East or Hudson Rivers, their bloated bodies bumping against the bulkheads of the wooden piers lining the island. He could imagine the police going to his home and asking his father to identify his rotting corpse. His family would be crushed. *It'd be better,* George thought grimly, *for my body to completely disappear.* Then no one would discover the ugly circumstances of his downfall. Kent was a gentleman – of a sort. Perhaps he would be amenable to such an arrangement.

'Mr Cross.'

George looked up to see Mary Morse, a pretty, blue-eyed brunette in a navy-blue walking dress and matching hat. Next to her was a small woman in her fifties, with beady eyes and an expressionless face. *The chaperone,* thought George. Every girl of Mary's set had one who followed her like a shadow.

'Hello, Miss Morse.'

The lack of enthusiasm in George's voice brought a look of disappointment to Mary's face. She had hovered about him at his graduation party like a fly around horse manure – to his annoyance.

'It's so nice to see you here,' she said brightly. 'We're stopping for a few days before travelling to Newport. This afternoon, we're going on a walk in the Catskills to visit the waterfall. It's most beautiful. I do hope you might join us. Mrs Rampling, my mother's great-aunt, will be with me.'

Mrs Rampling gave George the iciest of smiles. There would be no monkey business on her watch.

'I'm sorry, Miss Morse, but I've made other plans,' George said. 'Maybe later this week, if you're still here, I could call on you.'

'Oh yes! We're in room—'

'Holy shit, I had a helluva time fightin' my fuckin' way up there to get the goddamn key. Oh, hello there,' said Flannigan, trotting up to them.

'Miss Morse, this is Mr Flannigan . . . a friend of mine,' George managed.

'Damn glad to meet ya,' Flannigan said, thrusting his broad red hand towards Mary. She shook it gingerly, as if it were dipped in blood. 'And who's this other gorgeous dove?'

'Mrs Rampling,' snapped the chaperone, stepping back. Clearly she had no intention of touching Flannigan.

'Hey, what do you say we all have a drink in the bar, huh? I'm buying.'

'Miss Morse was on her way to take a walk in the mountains, Mr Flannigan. Maybe another time,' George said.

'Sure. What's your room number? I can come by later to get you.'

'I already asked them, but unfortunately they've made plans for later.'

'Oh, that's a goddamn shame.'

'Miss Morse, maybe we'll run into each other again.' George bowed and dragged Flannigan away by the arm.

'Good-looking babe, George. Were you making time with her? I hope I didn't butt into anything.'

'No, Tommy. In fact, you rescued me, and I'm eternally grateful,' George said, laughing.

Mary was like all the girls in his world. Marriage was their only vocation; it was what they were brought up for. With his looks and family background, he was a prime candidate – or victim – for their machinations.

Flannigan and George walked to their room on the sixth floor of the east tower, the best spot in the hotel. The room was large but not fancy. It had plain white walls, two beds, a chest of drawers, and a bright carpet. A green recamier stood in the corner; George flopped down onto it, rubbing his hands over his face. His mind was racing. When – and how – had his life changed?

George knew the answer. He could picture the winter night he'd first stepped through the door of Pendleton's, the most exclusive den of iniquity in the city. Some Harvard upperclassmen had taken him during the Christmas holidays in '84. At Pendleton's, gentlemen of the highest pedigree could gamble, drink, and seduce chorus girls, free from the disapproving eyes of Aunt Caroline's New York society. Tucked away in a brownstone building on East Forty-Fifth Street, the interior of the club was lavishly designed, with walnut-panelled walls, marble floors, and crystal chandeliers. In private gambling rooms, one could play faro, poker, baccarat, or roulette. Liquor and food flowed freely. It was as if George had opened a trapdoor and walked down a staircase into a magical world of enchantment and pleasure.

Being a mathematician, George had an innate talent for gambling. He loved everything about it – analysing the probabilities, calculating odds, counting cards, the throw of the dice. But it was the incredible rush of excitement when he won that thrilled him most. Pure euphoria. The sensation was even more pleasurable than sex, another pastime he was introduced to at Pendleton's. Soon, gambling became an obsession. It was all he could think about or wanted to do. At every second, he felt the uncontrollable urge to bet. He had no willpower, no control over his actions; the desire had taken hold of him, like a puppeteer manipulating the wires of a marionette.

At Pendleton's, George met James T. Kent. They took an instant liking to each other. Kent was one of George's own: a rich, dashing figure with a great deal of charm and intelligence. And the man knew how to enjoy himself.

If Pendleton's was the apogee of pleasure houses, however, below it swam a multitude of grimy, low-life establishments. Along the Bowery and Broadway were sleazy dance halls, whorehouses, and gambling dens that catered to the scum of the earth. In addition to games of chance like keno, dice, and craps, they offered wagers on cockfights, prizefights, dogfights, ratting, and horse racing. In addition to its opium dens, Chinatown had its own native gambling called fan-tan and pai gow.

George discovered these places by pure accident. A Harvard professor persuaded him to volunteer in the industrial school of the Children's Aid Society, and to George's delight, he discovered he had a gift for teaching. He loved working with children. But the mission was located in one of the city's vilest neighbourhoods – the Lower East Side, which averaged four gambling dens per block. Like a little boy in a confectioner's shop, George couldn't help himself. And he could never walk away from the table when he was ahead – he had to keep playing.

In the fall of '85, his luck turned. A long losing streak began, one he couldn't pull himself out of. George found himself deep in debt, constantly chasing his losses. He drained his inheritance from his grandfather, which was meant to pay for his graduate studies at Columbia. It felt like he was running on an endless railroad track, trying to catch up with the last car of the train. He'd reach out and almost grab on, but then the train would accelerate at the last second and pull away, leaving him deep in debt again.

After a particularly catastrophic loss on a horse named Grey Ghost, George approached Kent for credit. That day began his fatal descent. Kent gladly extended loans and credit to him. For a while, some of George's luck returned, allowing him to repay Kent. This opened the door to more loans, and more again. Then the losing streak returned with a vengeance. It had continued until the day of George's reckoning at Delmonico's.

A knock sounded at the door.

'Damn you, Mary Morse. I don't want to go for a walk,' George growled.

'Maybe they want that drink,' Flannigan said, moving to open the door. Then, 'Christ Almighty, Pretty Kitty McGowan, what the hell are you doing here?'

In the doorway stood a ravishingly beautiful woman with jet-black hair, a dark complexion, and large brown eyes. George thought she could have been described as Creole.

'On special assignment, Tommy. Here, take this double eagle and sample the goods in the bar.' She deftly flipped up a coin. With equal dexterity, Flannigan snapped it out of the air and left the room.

'Kitty,' gasped George. 'Oh, Kitty.' He ran over to her and took her in his arms. 'Oh God, it's good to see you.'

Kitty held George for a long time, burying her head against his chest. Finally, George took a step back and looked at her. Even amid all the fashionable ladies in the lobby, she was by far the most beautiful and elegant. No one would've suspected she was among the most desirable whores in New York, the darling of every scion, captain of industry, bank president, and Wall Street stockbroker.

George had met Kitty at Miss Jennie's, a discreet and handsomely furnished brothel that catered exclusively to the society set. The tinkling sound of a piano added a sophisticated note to its air, and champagne sold for ten dollars a bottle. The girls were clean, refined, and trained in the art of conversation. On Friday and Saturday nights, only clients in evening dress with bouquets of flowers were admitted. And, above all, Miss Jennie's was honestly run. In some of New York's brothels, called panel houses, a man would emerge from behind a detachable panel in the wainscoting and steal a man's wallet from his trouser pocket while he was busy with a girl. Such a thing would never happen at Miss Jennie's. Nor did her girls use knockout drops to rob clients.

George was drawn to Kitty immediately. He didn't mind that other men coveted her too. In a short time, she paid George the highest compliment a whore can pay – she had sex with him without compensation in her off hours. The two soon fell in love with each other.

'Georgie, Kent sent me. I have wonderful news. He said to tell you he's calling off the debt. You're free, my love.'

CHAPTER TEN

'Take a deep breath and hold it.'

Mrs Johnston yanked hard on the laces of the corset, and Julia
Cross groaned as the air was pushed out of her body. The English
housekeeper, a stout old woman with beefy forearms, tied the corset
as expertly as if she were wrapping a parcel.

'There,' chirped Helen Cross. 'You have the perfect figure for a
princess gown. Long and narrow.'

'Perfect,' Mrs Johnston agreed. 'Next, you'll need the camisole
trimmed in lace and ribbons, and the petticoat with the ruffle along
the bottom edge.'

Helen beamed with pride as the housekeeper continued to dress
her daughter. She had waited a long time for this moment. No
longer would Julia wear her hair long and unpinned; it would be
piled stylishly atop her head. In place of loose-fitting skirts hemmed
six inches above her ankles, her dresses would be long and tapered,
sweeping the floor. Above all, she could wear jewellery – as long
as it had not been given to her by an unmarried man. Julia would
finally be leaving her gawky, girlish days behind.

The housekeeper fastened a wire bustle atop Julia's buttocks.
'Now for the dress,' Mrs Johnston said. Julia stepped into a

beautiful, cornflower-blue gown, which the housekeeper rapidly fastened up at the back. Her mother stood behind her and looked at her in the mirror.

'You're a real beauty, Julia,' she said, hugging her from behind. She lifted Julia's flowing hair and coiled it on top of her head. 'I'll get some pins.'

Fifteen minutes later, with the aid of eighteen hairpins, Helen had transformed Julia's hair. 'Next week, you'll attend your first private teas. So many people to see. You know, the Beekmans' son just finished West Point,' Helen said, smiling at Mrs Johnston. The housekeeper also knew the social cachet of a West Point man from a Knickerbocker family.

'May I keep this on? Just for a bit, to get used to it?' Julia asked. Helen nodded.

'I have to finish some writing. But I'll be down for tea,' Julia said. Helen watched as her daughter skipped out of the room, her playful gait at odds with her new grown-up look. By the ironclad rules of society, she was supposed to be raising her daughter as her mother had raised her. But Helen refused to practise the benign parental neglect expected of her class. Her mother had told her that she must see her children only on occasion and be 'reasonably' acquainted with them. Helen defied her and fostered a close relationship with George, Julia, and Charlie. She'd made sure her husband did the same.

Julia's coming-out did not mean Helen was losing a daughter, of course. There was no rush to the altar; her daughter was only seventeen. Still, the whole journey was to be undertaken with great care. For Julia to have the highest value on the society matrimonial market, even the tiniest hint of scandal must be avoided. *The girl is lucky to have Aunt Caroline to give her counsel*, Helen thought. Caroline would help Julia avoid the misfortune of her own daughter's poor decisions.

Emily, Caroline's eldest, had fallen in love with James Van Alen, heir to millions from investments in the Illinois Central Railroad. An eccentric Anglophile who pretended to speak with an English accent, Van Alen was dubbed totally unsuitable by the Astors. William Backhouse Astor II, Caroline's husband, publicly stated that they would have nothing to do with the Van Alens. The groom's father, a Civil War general, challenged Astor to a duel; Astor backed out and apologised. The marriage took place, and the unhappiness began. After a succession of long, empty years, Emily died in 1881 while giving birth to her third child.

Caroline's own marriage, Helen knew, was an elaborate façade. Astor was content to let her spend his millions, but he'd pushed her out of his life long ago. He carried on with prostitutes and showgirls on his yacht, the aptly named *Light of the Harem.* Caroline, a master of ignoring unpleasant matters, pretended he was a loving and devoted husband but went to great lengths to keep him from her balls and dinners.

Her own marriage, Helen had to admit, followed similar rules.

As she often did when entering her bedroom, Julia got a running start and flopped onto her bed. This time, she let out a loud yelp. The corset jammed up under her newly full breasts, and the bustle rammed into the lower part of her back. Immediately, she jumped up again.

Sadness came over her in a wave. The adult way of dressing, she realised, ruled out relaxing and playing. She couldn't slide down the banister in this thing. Julia perched awkwardly at her roll-top desk, the corset forcing her to sit ramrod straight, the bustle keeping her at the edge of the seat. But her new posture didn't deter her from commencing her daily two hours of writing. She was working on a novel, a tale of love and adventure very much influenced by the work of Sir Walter Scott.

Julia was glad her parents hadn't listened to Granny and had her tutored at home. To their credit, they both wanted her to attend a day school – the elite and expensive Miss Spence's, where she could make friends with girls from her own class and get a first-rate education. There, she discovered her passion for literature and writing. In Granny's prehistoric world, too much education was dangerous; ladies only needed 'ornamental knowledge' to win a husband. To placate Granny, Helen made sure Julia had lessons in painting, sketching, needlework, piano, and, most importantly, dancing. Now that she was coming out, the latter skill was essential.

There were other lessons too. Since all the men of her class were mad about horses and especially about racing, Julia had the requisite equestrian training from an early age. She went riding in Central Park – always sidesaddle, never astride – at least two times a week. Because her family spent every summer in Newport and the Berkshires, expertise in archery, lawn tennis, and croquet was also required. A girl should be proficient – but never good enough to beat a man.

In the past month, Julia had begun rigorous schooling in the intricate rules of etiquette. A dinner never starts earlier than nine, she was told. Sherry is always cooled but not red wine. Don't let two brown or white sauces follow each other in succession. Then there was the strict code of behaviour. Two essential rules had been drilled into her: restrain all emotional outbursts in public, and any hint of scandal means disaster, for once a girl is talked about, she's done. Break these and it meant social extinction, Granny and her mother preached.

An eager student, Julia loved school. Now that colleges for

women like Vassar and Wellesley existed, she eagerly looked forward to higher education. She wasn't sure if she'd be allowed to go – many Knickerbockers thought college was a colossal waste of time for society girls. Learning Greek wouldn't help her do important things like needlework, keeping the servants in line, or determining whether a room had been properly dusted.

'Why even bother?' Granny always said. 'A woman's body is not equal to a man's, so it stands that her brain isn't equal either.'

But Julia didn't want to be ornamental. Her mother was against college, but she could tell her father was on her side. As an architect, he had an innate thirst for knowledge and beauty, which she'd inherited.

Immersed in a description of her heroine's faithful nanny, Julia didn't notice Charlie stealing into the room until he plopped down on her bed.

'Why are you dressed like that?' he asked.

'From now on, I dress like an adult, little boy.'

'What a bore.'

'And adults prize their privacy. So get out, you little beast.'

'I can't. I've to stay clear of Father.'

'And why is that?'

'He's in a very peculiar mood.'

CHAPTER ELEVEN

Helen Cross watched as her husband absent-mindedly picked at his saddle of lamb. It was usually his favourite dish. But tonight, in thirty minutes, he'd eaten one bite. He'd not said more than five words to her in that time either, but that was quite normal. Monks, who'd taken a vow of silence, talked more than she and John did at supper.

'Mrs O'Shea's going to be upset to see all that food you've left on your plate.'

As was the custom of the Knickerbockers, except for Sunday and holiday meals, the Crosses took the evening meal by themselves in the formal dining room. Children younger than eighteen ate downstairs in the kitchen with the servants.

Black walnut panelling covered every square inch of the walls and ceiling of the dining room. The light of the four-armed, electric chandelier hanging above the table reflected off their expensive Wedgwood dinnerware and gave the white linen tablecloth a warm glow.

Cross dropped his fork on his plate with a clatter. 'Helen, I'm not a child who has to be told to clean his plate.'

A long moment of silence followed, interrupted only by the

ticking of the antique brass clock on the sideboard. Helen dabbed her lips with her napkin and stared at her husband.

Six months after they married, they both realised they had nothing in common. In their world, this was normal. After a year, they retreated to different universes. Helen had hoped it wouldn't happen, but it was a natural occurrence, really, like the coming of winter. It had happened to her parents. Now, it was the same for her. Though she'd lost her husband's love early on and was resigned to the fact, sometimes, after all these years, it still pained her.

'I suppose you're going out tonight,' she said. 'You usually do when there's nothing on the social calendar.'

'Let's not get into this, Helen. I'm in no mood.'

'You could stay home and spend some time with me.'

'I spent time with you last night,' snapped Cross.

'That was across a ballroom at the Merricks'. And the night before, from the opposite end of a dinner table at the Linden-Travers'.'

'Goddamn it, Helen, I told you: let it go. I'm a damn good husband who provides for his family.'

'You are a good provider, yes. But there's more to being a husband than that.'

'Like what?' shouted Cross. 'You have everything you want.'

His gaze slid to the wall. He'd designed a pass-through panel behind the sideboard; it allowed the maid to slide trays of food through from the kitchen. Tonight, Mrs O'Shea was behind it. He knew she was listening in.

'It's true that I have every dress and bauble I might want. But did you ever think of my feelings? That perhaps I desire affection and attention more than I do another Dupret gown?'

'Really?' Cross asked, amused. 'Affection? More than a Parisian gown?'

'Yes! You and I, sitting in the parlour *by ourselves*, you asking me how I'm feeling or how my day was or what I'm reading. Is that so inconceivable?'

'Helen, for God's sake. I always ask you about your day.'

'No! You ask about running the house – preparing the meals, getting your underwear washed and folded, dealing with the servants, reminding you which social functions we're to attend. But you never ask about *me*.'

'Stop this foolishness, now. I'm in no mood,' thundered Cross, rising from his chair. 'I won't allow it.'

Helen stared down at her empty plate. 'Just a tiny gesture of affection,' she murmured.

'Then find yourself a better husband.' Cross walked to the sliding doors of the dining room and opened them. 'Yes, I am going out tonight. I'll be back late.'

'Here we are, sir: 158 Hester Street. Billy McGlory's joint.' The carriage driver opened the door and added, as Cross was stepping out, 'If you're going slumming tonight, sir, then Milligan's Hell on Broome is the place. The waiter girls there spread their legs as wide as the mighty Mississippi. Can take you there, if you'd like.'

A look of shock came over Cross's face, followed by disgust. 'No, thank you,' he said politely, slapping the fare down into the driver's gloved hand.

Although it was nine o'clock at night, Hester Street was awash with pedestrians. In his neighbourhood, the pavements were empty by seven, except for cats and the occasional stray dog. Cross surveyed the line of buildings on the north side of the street, which were still lit by old-fashioned gaslights. Five- and six-storey brick tenements crowded together, the ground floors given over to shops of every description. Nearly everyone had a Hebrew-sounding name on the awnings or the windows – Liebman, Pinsky. Every open upper-storey window was filled with human faces, flushed and sweaty, hoping for relief from the oppressively humid July evening. People filled the pavements and the street as well from gutter to gutter, stopping at the kerbside pushcarts to examine their goods and haggle with the vendors over the price. Wagons and carriages had to inch their way through the crowds, the drivers cursing constantly at pedestrians to move out of the way.

Cross looked down at the gutter and discovered he was standing in a pool of oozing, blackish-brown filth. Stepping up to the kerb to scrape the mess off his shoes, he saw an unconscious drunk sprawled out no more than six feet away. His jacket and trouser pockets had been turned out. The crowds of boisterous people, many of them men and women arm in arm, stepped over him as if he were a piece of litter.

Strange that McGlory's music hall would be such an unassuming building. Cross had expected something much fancier, a grand entry, perhaps. To his right, he heard the sound of a scuffle. Walking toward an obscured doorway, he was shocked to see a man holding a filthy handkerchief over a well-dressed fellow's nose. In the next instant, the latter collapsed, unconscious. With the help of another man, the thief took his wallet and began to strip off his clothes. The crowds continued to swarm along the pavement, completely ignoring them.

Stunned, Cross stumbled toward the dingy double doorway of 158 Hester Street. As he reached the door, two men burst out, dragging a third man by his armpits. They heaved his body out into the middle of the street like a sack of flour and strode back inside. Trembling, Cross entered and found himself in a narrow, unlit corridor. Like a blind man, he felt along the walls for almost twenty feet until he saw a crack of light beneath an opaque door. Opening it, he was astonished to see a huge dance hall, brightly lit, with dozens of tables and chairs and a bar the length of a city block. The hall was two stories high; a balcony lined with curtain-covered cubicles ran along two sides. There had to be at least five hundred men in the space, all shouting and laughing above the screeching music played by a piano, cornet, and violin trio off to the side. Young girls in garish make-up and short red-and-white dresses moved through the crowd, singing and carrying trays of drinks. Their skirts exposed their legs up to their plump thighs.

At almost every table, even cheaper, more tawdry-looking women sat in the laps of men, arms around their necks, laughing and kissing them full on the lips. To Cross's astonishment, one woman drained a large stein of lager in one try.

Did Kent really want to meet me here? Cross thought wildly. Shoving his way past the throng and weaving through the maze of tables, he finally found an empty seat. The second he settled down, two harpies were upon him. One plopped into his lap, and to his horror, Cross realised it was a man very unconvincingly dressed as a woman. His face was powdered white, his rouged cheeks as red as cherries.

'Buy me a drink, handsome,' said the degenerate. Though Cross did not reply, two drinks appeared in front of him as if from nowhere. The fake female grabbed one of the drinks and disappeared into the crowd.

'Two dollars,' a voice called out. To avoid any problems, Cross paid.

'How about some quarters in my stocking for good luck?' said the other woman, stretching a shapely, gartered leg in front of Cross. Again, he immediately obliged. She had hair the colour of a Florida orange and seemed to be a genuine female. Pleased at his quick response, she whispered in his ear, 'Why don't we go up to a private box, for a special cancan exhibition?' and she motioned toward the curtained alcoves lining the balcony.

Cross looked up and saw a man in evening dress buttoning his fly as he left one of the cubicles. 'That's very tempting, young lady, but I'm here for a business appointment,' he said apologetically. The constant noise and loud music were giving him a pounding headache.

The whore leant over and wrapped her arms around Cross. 'Surely a real gentleman like yourself can spare a little time for me.'

In the next instant, the slut was yanked off him. A moon-faced man with a broken nose and a handlebar moustache roughly shoved her away by the wrist. 'Mr Kent will see you now, Mr Cross. If you'll come this way,' he said in the same polite tone Caroline Astor's butler would have used. He then grabbed the woman's other wrist and pulled a wallet from her hand. 'And I believe this belongs to you, sir.' He handed him the wallet and slapped the woman in the face. The blow was so hard, so punishing, that she fell, the back of her head slamming against the damp, sawdust-covered floor.

CHAPTER TWELVE

The man escorted Cross through the smoke and cacophony of the dance hall to a rickety wooden staircase leading to the basement. In the low, dimly lit passage, Cross almost scraped his head on the underside of the floor joists. They reached a door that opened into a large room with newly plastered walls. At least ten men sat around a long oak table filled with liquor bottles, growlers of beer, and glasses. Cross spotted Kent, who stood and spread his arms in warm welcome, as if he were meeting a long-lost relative.

'Boys, meet John Cross. Our new business consultant.'

Murmurs of polite welcome rose through the swirl of cigar and cigarette smoke that enveloped the room. Cross cringed at the sound of his name. Then he sank into an empty chair directly across from Kent and looked around the table. He'd never met any of these men at the Union League or the Knickerbocker Club. They were a mean-looking bunch, the scars of a rough and unhappy life permanently etched on their faces. One man's face looked as though it had been beaten with a cat-o'-nine-tails; another's was so pockmarked that it looked as if someone had hammered drawing pins into it. One man with a missing ear was nervously sticking a stiletto into the wood table, again and again, tiny, jabbing blows. Most of the noses present had been broken.

Oddly, though, all the men were fashionably dressed in frock coats, waistcoats, and pinstriped trousers – most likely from Cross's own tailor, Brooks Brothers. Some had gold-topped canes by their sides.

At first, the only person Cross recognised was the man who'd paid a visit to his office. Then, to his surprise, he saw the man who'd held the handkerchief over the face of the fellow in the street. Some of the men were welcoming; a few remained expressionless, seemingly suspicious of the newcomer.

Sitting next to him was a gimlet-eyed hulk of a man with bright red hair. He was fingering a set of brass knuckles. Cross could see blood on them. A short, meek-looking man rose from his seat and handed Cross a shot of whisky.

'Wet your whistle, Johnnie,' he said.

Cross smiled and took the shot in a single swallow. His new friends nodded in approval. It was a good way of breaking down the barriers between them.

The man with the handkerchief smiled at him. 'I believe I saw you on the street earlier tonight.'

'Yes, I do recall seeing you. You seemed busy.'

'I had a client.'

'Pig McGurk's the best chloroform man in the city,' said the skinny bald man next to him, slapping Pig on the back.

'Chloroform?' Cross asked.

'Yep. I can sneak up behind anyone, place a hanky of 'form over their face, knock 'em out, and strip 'em clean. Ten seconds or less.'

'Each of these gentlemen brings a special talent to our company.' Kent sounded as if he was boasting about his children. 'Like you, Mr Cross. I believe you have something to share with us.'

From the side pocket of his frock coat, Cross removed a folded set of blueprints and flattened them out on the table so that Kent, who was sitting across from him, could see. He was about to speak but hesitated.

It bothered him that so many people were in on Kent's scheme. He'd thought they'd be speaking alone. The expression 'no honour among thieves' came to mind. Then he remembered the ice delivery, and he knew that none of these men would dare betray Kent.

'This is the Cook mansion. It's one of the first built on upper Fifth Avenue, on the corner of Seventy-Eighth Street.' He showed the group the front elevation sheet, which displayed how palatial the house was, with its steep slate roof and tall chimneys, taking up half of the Fifth Avenue block. Cook owned the rest of the block, all the way up to Seventy-Ninth Street, allowing for a large open space behind the house for a yard and carriage access.

'That's a beautiful house. Indoor toilets, I bet,' said McGurk.

'You better believe it! Imagine, living in a place like that and taking a shit out in an outhouse!' exclaimed the man with the missing ear.

'Hey, isn't that the house that has the big, wide ditch all around it?' asked another man.

Cross paused, smiled politely, and said, 'That's exactly the house.'

'Then how the hell are we getting in there?' countered the man.

'That ditch is called a dry moat, and I designed it, including the drawbridges. They are lowered and raised by a new type of electric motor and steel cables – the same kind they used on the Brooklyn Bridge,' Cross answered, a note of pride in his voice. 'I know how to operate them. So no one will see us from the street. We'll work in the rear. I'll lower the bridge, and then you'll break in through the back door.'

The men all nodded their heads in admiration and exchanged smiles.

'Wait – after we crack this place, won't they know you used the bridge, since you thought of it?' asked McGurk.

The men stopped smiling and looked at Cross. All of them were thinking the same thing – if Cross was picked up by the police, he'd squeal on them in a second.

'Mr McGurk,' said Cross, 'there were scores of workmen

involved in constructing this building, plus all the servants who've seen how the bridges work. They'll be the prime suspects. And there's one more important point you have to understand – they'd *never* suspect a gentleman.'

Kent smiled at this last observation.

'Now, let's move on,' said Cross. 'Here's the sub-basement. Right next to the wine room is a large vault that holds the silverware, chinaware, and, in an adjoining room, all the linens. The Cooks have an unusually large English silver service by Garrard and complete sets of real Dresden and Sèvres china. There are very expensive sets of embroidered Irish and Belgian lace linens in this separate cedar-lined room.' Cross pointed to a space in the middle of the plan. 'The door to the vault is hidden behind a wall rack of bottles. It swings out on hinges.'

'Combination lock on the vault?' Kent asked.

'No, just a padlock that can be pried off with a crowbar.'

The gang had risen from their seats and were hunched over the plans. Cross wondered if any of them besides Kent could actually read them. Most of his rich, well-educated clients couldn't decipher the drawings. But intent on making a good first impression – and stealing the most he could, the better to repay George's debts – Cross laid out the second-floor plan on top of the basement plan.

'The second floor contains the family's private spaces – the bedrooms, study, a sitting room where they gather informally.'

'That's goddamn amazing, a big place like this for one fuckin' family,' said a rotund man in a dark-grey frock coat with an elegant pearl-grey waistcoat.

'In Mrs Cook's bedroom is a safe. It holds all her jewels.'

'The woman has her own bedroom?' McGurk said.

'Yes, all husbands and wives have separate bedrooms.'

McGurk and his colleagues exchanged smiles at this arrangement.

'The family's up in Newport now, and a society woman never

takes all her jewellery with her. She leaves the best for the social season that begins in mid-November. I happen to know that Mrs Cook has a Cartier tiara. Five large diamonds, each mounted with a freshwater pearl. It'll be there.'

'And the safe?' Kent asked. 'Behind a painting?'

'That's where you'd expect it to be. So I put a false front of a safe behind a painting. The safe is actually right here.' Cross pointed to a solid square drawn in the corner of the bedroom.

'What's that?' asked Kent.

'It's a Roman marble statue of Diana, goddess of the hunt. I put a small portable safe in its base with a removable panel at the back.'

'The lock?'

'That has a combination lock. But the safe's not anchored to the floor. You can take it with you.'

Grinning, the gang members started chattering among themselves, excited at the potential of such a big robbery. Cross looked down, conflict roiling in his belly. The Cooks had been excellent clients; they were down-to-earth and kind-hearted, unlike most of the society folk he dealt with. Bill Cook had grown up dirt poor on a Missouri farm and had never forgotten his humble beginnings. Last month, he'd been kind enough to remember Charlie's birthday and had sent him an expensive present.

But Cross had no choice. The Cooks would survive. George might not.

And he had one more surprise for Kent's men.

'This room next to Mrs Cook's bedroom is her dressing room. Here's the closet for her clothes.'

'Christ, that's as big as her bedroom,' said the red-haired man with the brass knuckles.

'It's bigger than this room we're in now,' Cross agreed, eliciting whistles and a few 'holy shits' from the gang. 'It has to be, because society ladies change their clothes at least four times a day.'

'Four times a day? Holy hell, my wife don't even change her underwear every day,' said a man with unusually large ears and a pointy nose. He looked like an elf from a children's book.

'Morning dresses, afternoon dresses, tea dresses, riding habits, blouses, skirts. But the most expensive items are her evening dresses and ballgowns, which are in this cedar-lined closet here. Mrs Cook's are from Worth's, the very best fashion house in Paris. Twice a year, she orders a completely new set of gowns and accessories. They're made from the most expensive silks, satins, brocade, velvets, and lace money can buy. The rest of the closet is filled with hats, shoes, gloves, silk lingerie, and furs.' Cross tapped his finger on the dressing room image for dramatic emphasis. '*This* will be your biggest take, even more than the jewels and silver.' He looked up to see Kent smiling appreciatively at him.

'Very impressive, Mr Cross,' he said. Many around the table raised their glasses in response.

But then a tall, physically imposing man with a haggard but handsome face rose. Cross had noticed him earlier, twisting a length of what looked like piano wire in his hands. He slammed his fist, which sported a large diamond ring, down hard on the table.

'How can we trust this goddamn swell?' he cried. 'We don't know this guy from Adam. Suppose he's a Pinkerton?'

'For Christ's sake, calm down, Brady!' one of the men yelled.

The smile vanished from Kent's face, and he turned to look at the dissenter. 'We can trust him because I said we can, Mr Brady.' Kent's voice was icy. The man scowled but backed off. 'One question, Mr Cross,' Kent said, the smile returning to his face. 'Did the Cooks leave any staff behind?'

'No, they went to Newport with the family. And no watchman.'

Cross didn't want to wait for any more questions. He wanted to get the hell out of there. 'Well, gentlemen, it was a pleasure to meet you,' he said, picking up his hat from the table. 'You will no doubt want to examine the drawings further and discuss things, so I'll get out of your way. Goodnight to you all.'

He was almost to the door when Kent intercepted him.

'Just a moment, Mr Cross. Culver here will get you a carriage. I don't believe the Lower East Side is quite your milieu.' Kent waved his gold-topped cane toward Culver. 'Let's wait in here, shall we?'

Kent led Cross into another room, filled with what were probably the hall's excess tables and chairs. Most were damaged. As they waited, a slow trickle of ragged, dirty men and women entered. A blind beggar wearing black glasses and carrying a cane sat down at a table. He took off the glasses and began counting coins and paper money from a tin can. Another filthy-looking wretch wearing a leg prosthesis limped in – and took off the false limb, exposing a perfectly healthy leg. When he saw Cross's expression, Kent started laughing.

'Billy McGlory is kind enough to let these unfortunates do their day's accounting here.'

'But that man can see as well as I can. And that man there is no cripple!' exclaimed Cross.

'Welcome to my world, Mr Cross,' Kent said, laughing uncontrollably. As more fake cripples straggled in, he continued to speak, tapping his palm with the head of his cane. 'We're off to a good start,' he said. 'You did very well, made a good impression on the boys. We'll go over your drawings and start to prepare. Preparation is everything in this game, Mr Cross.'

'Where's my son?' Cross demanded, his patience worn thin. His voice drew curious glances from the cripples, but they quickly returned to their money.

'You delivered the goods tonight. I will keep up my end of the bargain and deliver George. He'll be home by late tomorrow morning.'

When Culver appeared at the door, Cross started toward him. But Kent blocked his way with his cane.

'Before you go, there's one more small favour I'll ask of you.'

It was Ned Brady's habit to stop at the Hurdy Gurdy for a drink on the way home. Being a regular, he was given his own private cubicle at the back of the bar. Though he had a common-law wife at home, many women vied for his attention and affection. He was a strapping, good-looking man, generous with money. Only a select few were allowed his company, however.

But tonight, Brady desired no female companionship. He finished his shot of rye and left. As he walked west on Stanton Street, a filthy white-and-brown dog leapt from the shadow of a doorway. It attacked his leg viciously. Enraged, Brady shook the mutt off – and saw a ragged old man in his seventies standing nearby.

'Get your fuckin' mutt off me, you goddamn fool.'

'Barleycorn knows a mean man when he sees 'im,' the old man snarled.

Brady walked up to the man and smiled.

'You've got yourself a smart dog, then.'

'Barleycorn's damn smart.'

In a fraction of a second, Brady lunged at the man. He had a loop of piano wire around his neck before the old fellow could blink. With his powerful fists, he effortlessly pulled on both ends of the wire, garrotting the man until his face turned grey-blue and his eyes bulged out.

With a sick thud, he dropped to the pavement.

'You're right. I *am* mean,' Brady said to the dog. It whimpered and cowered back in the corner of the doorway.

CHAPTER THIRTEEN

'Add three more to the two you already have. How many is that?'

The nine children in the spartan classroom looked at George with blank expressions. When he'd first met his pupils, he'd been stunned. They were filthy, emaciated, and often seemed deaf and dumb. More like feral animals than children, and so different from his younger brother, Charlie. At first, George thought they were orphans, but he'd soon learnt that almost all of them had been thrown out into the streets when their families could no longer support them. They were left to fend for themselves, stealing or working as bootblacks and newsies. The girls sold shoelaces and matches in the streets. Some worked in sweatshops, making envelopes or twine.

Before they came to the lodging house, all the children were homeless, forced to sleep in basements or alleys, to sprawl across steam gratings in the Five Points and the Bowery. Dr Caldwell, the school's director, said that twenty thousand more roamed the streets of New York like rats. None of them had ever celebrated a Christmas or a birthday; most didn't even know when they had been born. To George, their reality came as a cruel shock.

'What about you, Tim? How many?'

The scrawny, freckle-faced child stared at the caramels that sat before him. Instead of toothpicks or matches, George used sweets for his arithmetic lessons. These wretches didn't have the tiniest of pleasures. He meant to kill two birds with one stone. Chewing gum, liquorice sticks, and boiled sweets became teaching tools.

Tim knit his brow and moved his lips, silently counting.

'Five?'

'As a reward for Tim's academic brilliance, the class may now eat today's lesson,' George said.

Smiles broke out, and the children began unwrapping the caramels and popping them into their mouths. Initially, when George gave them sweets, he expected them to devour every piece at once. He was surprised to see that most saved some to eat later. This, he discovered, was a survival instinct they'd learnt on the streets.

It gave George great pleasure to see his class enjoy their treats. The longer he taught, the more it pained him that these children had absolutely nothing in life – no mother or father, no prospects for a bright future. It made him feel ashamed that he'd been given so much. And so, every week, George had come down by train from Cambridge to teach the urchins arithmetic. They weren't stupid. No, it was as if their minds were frozen on account of their mistreatment and neglect. Sometimes he tried to do something special for them, taking them on excursions to Central Park, the wax museum at Eden Musée, or a puppet show on Fourteenth Street. Dr Caldwell had objected, but George convinced him the trips had a sound educational purpose.

'I'll see you next week,' George said to his class with a wave of the hand, and the children bounded out of the classroom.

On his way out, he smiled at Miss Cavendish, the secretary, who blushed at such a handsome man's attention. The Children's Aid

Society building on East Broadway was a massive brick-and-stone edifice designed by a friend of his father's, Calvert Vaux. It held dining facilities, classrooms, and dormitories for destitute children. Some people had even complained that it was too fancy for street urchins.

George walked north on Ludlow Street toward the Third Avenue Elevated Railroad. His new home at the Bradley, an apartment house on West Fifty-Ninth Street, right across from the park, awaited him. As a gift, Granny had paid the eighteen-hundred-dollar annual rent, even though she disapproved of apartment houses, calling them glorified tenements. They were just a fad, she said, because Anglo-Saxons would never share the same roof with strangers.

As he walked, George's thoughts kept returning to the day before. Something wasn't right. For Kent to forgive his debt – it seemed unthinkable. He'd been sure he was going to die, had even resigned himself to the fact. But there he was, back in the city as if nothing had happened. Kitty couldn't give him any details about Kent's decision, and to his dismay, Kent had flatly refused to talk to him.

It was frustrating. George wanted to tell Kent that he'd give him a percentage of his salary each week in appreciation for what he'd done. When he'd dropped him off at the kerb, Flannigan had warned him to stay away from Kent's joints. George couldn't understand the reprieve, but he thanked God that his family hadn't found out. The shame would have destroyed them.

A block before Delancey Street was a basement dive called the House of Hell, a low-life gambling den George had frequented many times. He stopped by the staircase leading down to the basement and stared at the crude sign of a tiger above the battered wooden door, which meant the dump was a faro house. There was paper money in his trouser pocket. He pulled it out. Six dollars.

George bolted down the stairs – but stopped midway and climbed back up to the pavement. He closed his eyes, breathing heavily.

At times like this, he couldn't understand the universal forces at play. It was like he was made of pure iron, not flesh and blood, and the dive was a giant magnet, pulling him towards it with an unearthly power. He grasped the railing tightly, as if to prevent his body being yanked back down into the cellar. But there was no magnetic force emanating from the dive. The pull was coming from his brain, which was commanding his body to slap his six dollars on the green felt of the faro table. George wanted to feel that indescribable sensation of suspense in placing his bet, then the pure exhilaration of winning. He would never tell Kitty this, but the thrill was absolutely wonderful, more satisfying than any orgasm. With his mastery of numbers, he knew he could beat the house. Gambling was just a series of mathematical probabilities that had to be analysed.

Feeling himself beginning to perspire, George tightened his grasp on the railing. Then, taking a deep breath, he let go and bolted down the pavement. He didn't look back. If he did, he knew he'd be lost.

Charlie Cross was determined to get the Crandall mini steam engine.

The gifts from his birthday last month had been disappointing, to say the least. He didn't give a damn about learning the value of money from card games like the 'Amusing Game of the Corner Grocery' or the 'Game of Banking.' He'd been hoping for the engine or one of those new safety bicycles. The only decent present, a Mike Kelly baseball bat, had come from George.

The Crandall mini steam engine. That was something special. You could actually sit on the thing and ride around. While looking at the sports pages of the *Tribune*, Charlie had seen an advertisement for the toy. It was sold at a shop off Pearl Street and the Bowery, which, the ad emphasised in bold black letters, was conveniently located near the Second Avenue Elevated Railroad.

Having been on the Third Avenue line many times with his friends, Charlie felt he was ready to take the Second Avenue Elevated train on his own. The one good thing about his parents was that they trusted him and gave him free rein to roam about the neighbourhood. On foot, he and his pals had ventured all the way up to the park, as far south as Union Square, and east and west to each of the rivers.

He took his time on his way to the Thirty-Fourth Street and Second Avenue station, stopping to look in shop windows, buying liquorice, playing with a stray cat, and examining junk abandoned by the kerb. On the downtown train, he knelt on a seat, looking out at the buildings as they rushed past. He loved being so high off the ground. The colours and lettering styles of the signs that covered almost every square foot of the building façades captivated him.

As his stop at Chatham Junction approached, Charlie turned to face his fellow passengers. Dressed in odd clothing and chattering in strange languages, they were nothing like the people on Fifth and Madison Avenues. He found them as fascinating as characters in a storybook. One old man, dressed all in black with a broad-brimmed hat, had a full, snow-white beard that flowed down to his chest and a long, single curl of hair hanging from each ear. Farther down the car, there was even a Chinaman in a scarlet-and-gold quilted jacket.

At Chatham Junction station, where the Second and Third Avenue elevated rail lines crossed and formed a dramatic double-decker set of tracks, Charlie scampered down the long stairway to the street. He began walking east in search of Pearl Street and the Bowery but soon found himself completely lost. Confused, he rounded a building and was astonished to see the stone towers of the Brooklyn Bridge looming above him. He'd never seen anything so tall. It dwarfed the buildings around it, even the church steeples.

The net of cables attached to the bridge's towers reminded him of giant spiderwebs. A flood of people, horses, and wagons was crossing the bridge in both directions. Convinced he had gone the wrong way, Charlie turned north and kept walking until he reached the corner of Baxter and Worth Streets. It was as if he had walked onto another planet. The pavements in front of the ramshackle two- and three-storey buildings were choked with people and strewn with foul-smelling rubbish. Instead of cobblestones, the streets were a mash of churned rubble and horse manure. Two-wheeled delivery wagons and pushcarts fought their way along. Charlie stared in amazement at the wide eyes of a dead horse lying in the gutter, covered with green flies. Above him, a withered old woman leant out of a second-storey window and emptied a white porcelain-enamelled chamber pot onto the pavement. The pedestrians dodged the airborne filth without batting an eye.

The shops along Baxter Street were unlike the neat and tidy ones in Charlie's neighbourhood. Dark and dilapidated places, they displayed their stock in boxes and on long plank tables on the pavement. Most of it seemed to be used clothing. Their owners continually accosted passers-by, trying to physically drag them inside. Peddlers pushed rickety carts, calling out their wares. A fat woman smoking a long clay pipe was selling apples and gingerbread. Charlie was amazed to see little girls younger than him hawking wilted flowers and socks. Men without arms and legs sat on the pavement, selling shoelaces and buttons.

It was about ninety degrees, and the stink of the place was making Charlie dizzy. He leant against a building. Its surface was coated with mouldy, greenish slime. A greasy rat scurrying through the filth of the gutter stopped in front of Charlie and fixed him with its beady black gaze.

'Those are some real fancy duds you have on.'

Two boys a couple of years older than Charlie were standing perhaps three feet away. They wore filthy, torn canvas shirts and tattered black trousers that stopped a few inches above their bare feet. Their faces and feet were smeared with dirt; it looked as if they'd been down a coal chute. Charlie dropped his chin to his chest to see what they were referring to. To please his mother, he had agreed to wear a velvet jacket and lace collar in the style made so popular by the story *Little Lord Fauntleroy*, which had just come out. At ten years old, Charlie had graduated to wearing long pants and refused to wear Lord Fauntleroy shorts or get his hair curled. The jacket was a compromise.

'Hey, we'll show ya somethin' neat,' said one of the boys, smiling broadly and gesturing for Charlie to follow him into an adjacent alleyway filled with rubbish. Charlie was about to politely decline the invitation, but before he could say a word, the larger of the two put his filthy hand on the back of Charlie's neck, his grip as tight as a vice, and shoved him into the alley. A few yards in, Charlie tried to twist away, but the boy's accomplice struck him full in the face. Down he went, and the two boys began to kick and pummel him. He was too shocked to utter a sound. As he lay on his back, stunned, he felt his attackers undressing him.

'This stuff's real velvet. And the shoes don't have no holes in 'em.'

Like a carcass being picked over by vultures, Charlie was stripped to his underwear in seconds. He heard the scuffling of the boys' footsteps as they ran. His head was pounding with pain, and there was an excruciating ache in his stomach. He tried to fight back the tears, but they poured out in torrents. Pulling himself up from the filth of the alley, he grabbed on to a nearby rain barrel and tried to steady himself.

Out of the corner of his eye, he saw an older boy striding confidently towards him, holding each of his assailants by their ears. The thieves were howling in pain.

'Give 'em back,' the boy said, lifting his arms up to stretch the boys' ears even farther. They screamed in agony, dropping the clothing and shoes on the ground.

'Kick 'em in the balls,' the boy said.

Charlie shook his head. He didn't understand. 'Balls?'

'Yeah, balls.' With great agility, the boy swung his leg and kicked one of the boys between the legs. 'Go ahead,' he ordered.

Forgetting his pain, Charlie got a running start and kicked each of the thieves with all the force he could muster. Still holding them by the ears, the older boy smashed their skulls together with all his might. There was a loud crack, like someone splitting open a coconut. The boys collapsed to the ground and then stumbled away down the alley, clutching their heads.

'Let me help you.' The boy held out Charlie's trousers so he could step into them.

'Thank you,' peeped Charlie.

'So, what brings you to the Five Points today?'

CHAPTER FOURTEEN

Cross sat in a carriage at Fifth Avenue and Eightieth Street, waiting to begin the Cook robbery. It was 2 a.m. on a moonless July night.

'You'll find the experience most interesting,' said Kent, who was seated next to him.

Interesting? Terrifying, perhaps. Cross could hardly prevent himself from shaking with fear. His shirt was soaked with sweat.

Sitting across from Cross and Kent were Culver and Brady, the roughneck who'd been so reluctant to trust him. Brady toyed constantly with a length of piano wire, scowling at Cross all the while. The gang had a hierarchy of sorts, Cross had come to realise. Culver, the trusted right-hand man, and Brady, the henchman, were the two top members and thus sat in the boss's carriage.

Along the surrounding streets were scattered enclosed delivery wagons of all types – milk, grocery, bakery, lumber. They would transport the loot. Development on Fifth Avenue above Seventy-Sixth Street was just beginning, with construction proceeding in a chequerboard manner. With its many vacant lots, the area still had a desolate feel. It was deserted at night and rarely patrolled by the police, which was fine with Cross. No one was around to see them.

Kent, who had been puffing on a cigar, exhaled, filling the carriage with the thick, sweet aroma of a Havana premium. He pulled out his pocket watch.

'It's two-fifteen, gentlemen,' he said. His jolly tone reminded Cross of Charlie, bounding into their bedroom to tell them it was Christmas morning.

Kent, Brady, and Culver got out of the carriage. The plan was for two men to leave each wagon at one-minute intervals with one man remaining to drive. They would meet at the rear of the house. Other men would serve as lookouts.

Cross froze as if he were glued to his seat. His mind ordered him to get out of the carriage, but his body wouldn't obey.

'Time to go, Mr Cross. It's your debut performance tonight,' said Kent. 'We can't be late.'

Cross did not budge. Brady reached into the carriage, grabbed Cross by the lapels, and yanked him out. 'Move,' he said with a snarl.

'Please don't be embarrassed, Mr Cross. Everyone gets stage fright on their first night,' exclaimed Kent, beckoning Cross to come with a wave of his arm.

Cross's legs felt like gelatine, and he thought he was going to collapse. Somehow, though, he made it to the back of the mansion. A grand wrought-iron gate was connected to the low fence that surrounded the fifteen-foot-wide dry moat. To Cross's surprise, the gate lock had already been picked.

Cross swallowed hard, took a deep breath, and slowly walked over to a paving stone right next to the gate. He placed all his weight on the side of it, and up popped the stone, revealing a little compartment below that contained what looked like the inner workings of a clock. His accomplices smiled at one another. He knelt down and turned a lever to the right.

The iron-and-wood drawbridge that covered the rear door slowly lowered with just a low murmur of cables and pulleys.

Everyone at once noticed a light come on at the far end of the basement level at the bottom of the moat. Cross stooped down and switched the lever to stop the bridge. It was only halfway down, at a diagonal to the face of the house. Kent and his men stood motionless, their eyes fixed on the light. Half a minute passed, then the light went out.

Brady turned an accusing eye on Cross and laughed, his voice harsh in the silence.

'I told you this little shit couldn't be trusted.'

'It's a servant,' Cross said in a calm voice, knowing exactly what room it was.

'Take care of it,' Kent said to Brady in a matter-of-fact tone. He might have been telling him to shine his shoes.

Cross saw the smirk on Brady's face and knew what would happen next. 'You can't,' he yelled, grabbing the arm of Kent's well-tailored frock coat. Kent's eyes slowly travelled from his sleeve to Cross, who flushed with embarrassment, realising his faux pas. But he couldn't keep silent. 'No one's to be hurt!' he cried.

As Brady raised his fist to punch Cross in the face, Kent lifted a hand in silent command.

'I'm afraid that's going to be difficult, Mr Cross. We certainly can't call the job off. You can see the position I'm in.'

With Brady's hand still raised, Cross gathered his nerve. 'Just let me peek in the window.'

'What the hell good will that do?' Brady sneered.

'Maybe he didn't hear anything. Listen, I set up this job. You can at least give me ten minutes.'

Kent nodded, though his eyes were sceptical. 'All right, but you're wasting your time, Mr Cross . . . and mine.'

Brady bristled with anger at his boss's decision but didn't protest.

But Cross stopped and realised he had no way of getting down into the moat. No one brought ladders or ropes because he didn't think they'd be necessary. Then he remembered that the grey granite walls that lined the moat were rusticated – they had deep, wide joints between the stones that could act as hand and footholds. Cross swung his body over the iron fence and slowly climbed down the wall as if it were a ladder. When he reached the stone floor, he crept over to below the window and craned his neck until his eyes peered just over the very edge of the sill. The lower sash had been raised about a foot, allowing the servant to get some air in the cramped room. Cross let his eyes adjust to the darkness of the interior. He raised up further, until his entire head was through the opening.

The room was a typical servant's abode, with barely any furniture and no rug. Servants were not allowed to display personal items, and with its bare, white plaster walls, the space resembled a prison cell. Directly below Cross was a cast-iron bed. A young man in a white nightshirt slept soundly on his back. Cross had no idea why he was in the house. The entire domestic staff of city mansions always went to Newport in the summer.

He crouched back down and crawled away from the window, then sat against the stone wall of the house. He needed time to think. Kent waited impatiently above.

'Do you keep a bottle of that stuff on you?' Cross asked in a hushed voice to McGurk, who was standing next to Kent.

'The chloroform? Never leave the house without it,' he said with a smile, patting the side pocket of his jacket.

Cross extended his arms and beckoned for McGurk to toss down the bottle, which he did.

'Mr Culver, will you please go to the carriage and get the whip and the sponge in the horse's water bucket?'

Culver was puzzled by the request but trotted off. After a few minutes, he was back with the whip and sponge.

'What the fuck are you doing, swell? Time's a-wasting,' Brady hissed from the pavement above.

'Go to hell, you blackguard,' Cross said, surprising himself with his nerve. He looked up at Kent and spoke directly. 'You're not going to kill him.'

Taking the oblong yellow sponge, he squeezed it out. With his penknife, he cut a slit in the end and inserted the long handle of the carriage whip into the space. He emptied the entire bottle onto the sponge. A pungent smell rose up in the warm night air.

Cross crept back and slowly threaded the carriage handle through the open window. Leaning his whole body into the opening, he lowered the sponge to the sleeping man's face, covering his nose. Two minutes passed. Cross pulled his head back and whispered up to McGurk, 'Is this long enough?'

McGurk chuckled. 'With the shot you gave 'im? He won't wake till tomorrow evening.'

Cross pulled the carriage handle out and climbed back up the wall. 'All right, let's get to it,' he said to Kent, almost like an order.

Cross finished lowering the bridge. After Culver jimmied open the rear door, Cross took them first down to the sub-basement, where they easily yanked off the padlock and entered the vault. He stood aside while they cleaned out the space, placing everything in canvas sacks. They worked quickly and efficiently, a well-oiled team. Even Brady threw himself into the effort. The vault was bare in minutes, the loot transported quickly across the drawbridge and piled into the wagons that waited in the back yard.

Throughout the process, Kent stood, smoking a cigar and observing. He seemed to be enjoying every second of the experience and was a good leader, like a general at the front of his troops' charge into battle. His men respected that. And his eyes were sharp. As one man came out, Kent grabbed his arm. He reached into the man's jacket pocket, produced a bottle of wine, and ordered him to put it back.

Once the last of the loot was removed, the gang reassembled in the kitchen, and Cross led them up the servants' stairs to Mrs Cook's bedroom. Once inside, they stood in stunned silence, gaping at the walls.

'Holy hell,' McGurk whispered.

The walls of Mrs Cook's bedroom were beautifully carved, gilt boiserie that sparkled in the light of the huge crystal chandelier. Cross hadn't designed this room. The interior was purchased from a Louis XVI palace in France and reassembled upon arrival in New York. At the far end, a gargantuan, ornately carved four-poster bed sat on a high platform fronted by a gilded balustrade, draped by a canopy of scarlet silk and dark-green velvet.

'A family of ten could sleep in that goddamn thing,' McGurk said.

Eager to get the men's attention back to the job at hand, Cross pointed out the safe in the base of the statue of Diana. Two men eased it out and onto the maroon and gold carpet. Then a man brought in two lengths of wood, which were placed under the safe. They carried it out of the bedroom as though on a litter. They'd obviously done this many times before; it was all so amazingly fast.

Next came Mrs Cook's clothes. Ball and evening gowns, furs, coats, dresses, riding habits, and hats of all description were swept from the closets and stuffed into more canvas sacks. Scores of shoes, scarves, gloves, silk petticoats, chemises, even whalebone corsets were taken. Then Cross escorted them to Mr Cook's bedroom. The closets of London-tailored clothes were also stripped bare. The thieves reminded Cross of a horde of locusts, devouring a crop and leaving not a speck of grain behind.

As the robbery progressed, Cross realised that, to his surprise, he wasn't scared. Out in the carriage, he had been a nervous wreck, sweating like a pig. But once inside, he'd been so swept up in the excitement of the event that he actually had a feeling of giddy elation, like he'd drunk a bottle of champagne. He was alive with energy; an electrical current seemed to flow through his body.

The men worked in total silence. The gregariousness of that night at McGlory's had vanished, and not one word was exchanged. As they continued to scoop up more articles in Cook's bedroom, a great crash was heard from an adjacent room, like something breaking on the floor. The men froze. Almost at once, each man pulled a gun out of his side jacket pocket. Cross, who also stopped dead in his tracks, was momentarily fascinated at the variety of weapons drawn – derringers, short barrel revolvers, big Colt Navy revolvers, a western six-shooter.

A few seconds of deafening silence passed until McGurk slowly walked toward the wood-panelled door and pushed it wide open. Every man held their breath until he shined his lantern in to see a calico cat on the fireplace mantel and a Chinese vase lying in pieces below on the stone hearth. The cat jumped down and rubbed and purred against McGurk's trouser leg. Laughter broke out, then the gang went back to work. McGurk picked up the cat, rubbed under its chin, and set it down gently. The room was Cook's private study, his inner sanctum, where he went to escape his wife and the world. In went the gang and out came his rare sixteenth-century duelling pistols and his beloved collection of ancient and medieval swords.

With an air of great satisfaction, Kent smoked and watched. Then he strolled around, taking a slow tour of the second floor. The long hallway was lined with green onyx stone and lit by five bronze chandeliers. At one end, it connected with a monumental staircase of grey marble. Eyes sweeping the space critically, Kent ordered that a Flemish tapestry depicting a battle from Ancient Rome be carted away, along with two suits of armour that had been brought over from a Scottish castle. A man was even sent back to Mrs Cook's bedroom to roll up her rug.

Finally, Kent came over to Cross and placed his hand on his shoulder. 'Does Cook collect manuscripts?'

When Cross shook his head, a look of disappointment came over Kent's face. Sighing, he looked up at the coffered wood ceiling of the study. Even this was decorated in gold leaf.

'A private palace, this. The workmanship is amazing. One day, Mr Cross, I'll have a place like this too. And you're going to design it. Millicent will love it.'

Cross, whose heart normally leapt at the thought of a new commission, grimaced.

'These paintings,' Kent said abruptly. 'Any true masterpieces – Titians, Rembrandts?'

'No, they're all by popular French salon painters. Like that military scene over there – it's by Meissonier,' Cross said, gesturing to a huge painting of Napolcon on horseback, directing his troops from a hilltop.

'Too bad they're so damn big. There's no room for them in the wagons.'

Cross laughed. 'To a society man, the bigger a painting, the more valuable it must be.'

Culver signalled to Kent: they were finished. He and Cross walked towards the monumental staircase but paused when Brady called out to them.

'Kent!'

'Go on. I'll meet you in the back,' Kent said to Cross, who started down the stairs.

Brady was standing by a door at the end of the second-floor hall. 'Look what I found,' he said, yanking a skinny teenage girl out of the doorway. She had bright red hair and blue eyes and was dressed in a plain cotton nightgown. She shook violently in Brady's grasp, eyes wide in fright.

'I heard crying – found her hiding on the third-floor rear staircase.'

'Come here, young lady,' Kent said in a kind, paternal voice. 'Tell me, are you and the fellow downstairs the only ones in the house?'

The girl nodded.

'You know what happens to little girls who lie, don't you?'

'They go to hell. But I'm telling the truth, sir,' she said, voice trembling.

'And why are you here?'

'I forgot to bring Mrs Cook's cat with us,' she said, lowering her head in shame. 'Jamie came back with me to get him, and we decided to spend the night. Please don't tell her I forgot him. She'll be so cross with me.'

'It's all right. I promise I won't tell anyone.' Kent reached out to stroke her hair, smiled at Brady, and walked away.

CHAPTER FIFTEEN

'The house wins again.'

George stared at the green-felt faro table and the blue-ivory check that represented his twenty-five-dollar losing bet. The dealer, who sat behind the table with an assistant who tracked the house's card count, met his eyes, looking for a sign that he would continue to bet. But George turned and walked away from the table, Kitty on his arm.

He was down four thousand. Two hours ago, he had been ahead seven.

Less than a week after his debt was forgiven, George had caved in and resumed gambling. He couldn't help himself; the gambling dens reeled him in like a helpless fish. He fought with all his might, but it was useless. With college finished, George devoted more days to teaching. Doing so put him in constant proximity to the scores of gambling joints on the Lower East Side. Walking by them every day was torture. He was like a starving man walking by rows and rows of restaurants, smells of delicious food wafting out to tantalise him.

His brief hiatus had been hell. Like a drunk on the wagon, his body seemed to go through withdrawal. Smoking, pacing back and forth in his apartment, and going for long walks in Central Park were no help in shaking off the malaise. Even while making love to Kitty, he thought about the tables. But there would be no income until the autumn, when he started teaching at Saint David's. The only money George had on hand was his weekly trust fund allowance, which he needed for living expenses. If he blew that, he'd have to live off Kitty – or worse, go to his parents. Inevitably, they would start asking questions.

One morning, he leapt out of bed and, without really thinking, took the graduation watch Aunt Caroline had given him to a pawnbroker on East Forty-Fourth Street, along with a few other valuable trinkets, such as a gold cigarette case. With a one-thousand-dollar stake burning a hole in his pocket, George's willpower vanished into thin air. Kitty begged him to stop with all her might, but it was like trying to halt a runaway locomotive. George could not be swayed.

Because Kitty insisted on going with him, George went to a respectable house instead of the low-life joints, which had the lower stakes he preferred. Chamberlain's, a first-class gambling house that catered to society men, looked no different from the other brownstone mansions off the side streets of Broadway. The interior was magnificently furnished with expensive furniture, marble fireplaces, frescoed ceilings, and plush velvet carpets. Its front parlour was given over to the entertainment of guests, while the rear parlour was reserved for gambling. A large dining room beyond the rear parlour provided free meals, cigars, and liquor to the well-dressed patrons. Faro, the most popular game in the city, was played fairly in these first-class houses. George knew he wouldn't be cheated.

They sat down on a recamier in the front parlour, and Kitty laid her head on his shoulder.

'I can lend you some money to keep playing.'

'No. You've given me too much already,' George said. He kissed her cheek.

'Bad night, George?' asked a rotund, Havana-puffing man as he walked past.

'Just wasn't my night, Senator.'

Chamberlain's boasted the most exclusive clientele in the city. Like Senator Philip Merrill of New Jersey. Two Congressmen, a city councilman, and an ex-governor were in attendance. The house's most frequent customers, though, were Wall Street speculators. They were in the enviable position of being able to lose five thousand in a night and then make eight thousand from deals the following day.

Merrill was standing next to Ned Chamberlain, the middle-aged proprietor. As the senator walked away, Chamberlain leant in and spoke confidentially to George. 'I'm sorry about tonight, Mr Cross,' he said apologetically. 'I hope we can come to an understanding about tonight's setback. You're the last person I'd like to see something happen to.' He bowed slightly and walked off.

Kitty shot a glance at George, who remained silent. 'You have to ask your aunt for some money, Georgie.'

George looked at her in astonishment. 'For Christ's sake, Kitty, I could never do that. The shame it would bring on my family! They'd be ruined.'

'Ruined? That's all you goddamned society people care about – your good name.'

'You don't understand. You think society people live in a world of luxury and pleasure? Well, it comes at a price. There's an incredibly rigid code of behaviour we have to obey, and if we break one single rule, we're subject to something worse than physical torture or death: expulsion from society. Forever. No forgiveness.'

Kitty shook her head slowly from side to side. 'You people just don't know how good you have it.'

'And you just don't understand,' George said, giving her a playful kiss on the cheek.

'It's 4 a.m. Come back to my place,' she said, changing the subject abruptly.

'No. I have to go home and get cleaned up for class. I promised the students we'd go to Battery Park, and I can't let them down. Not after everyone else already has.'

'I have to work this evening,' said Kitty, 'but I could come over to your place at two.'

'I'll be at the Windsor Palace.'

Kitty sat up and clutched George's arm. 'For God's sake, Georgie, you can't go back there.'

'They have a chuck-a-luck game going on, and I can win. I know I can,' George said, determined. He had just been introduced to the dice game, which had become very popular on the Bowery. 'I'll put down a fiver and let it ride.'

'No, my love. Don't. Stay home and wait for me. I can cook you your favourite breakfast in the morning. Beefsteak and kidneys.' She stroked his hair, gazing at him.

Kitty knew she could have any man in New York. She could be showered with wealth and diamonds, feted and adored. But she chose George. He didn't think of her as a mere sex object; he actually enjoyed her company. To Kitty, their conversations were the best part of their romance – long, engaging rambles about everything under the sun. Sometimes they'd talk into the night so enthusiastically that they'd forget about making love. They had gone to the Museum of Natural History and the theatre at Niblo's Garden and strolled the promenade at Far Rockaway, arm in arm. Never was George embarrassed to be seen with her. *Not like my clients*, Kitty sometimes thought bitterly, who would avert their eyes if they happened to pass one another on the street. To them, she was still a whore, no matter how beautiful and poised she appeared. It delighted her that George was so non-judgemental.

And never once did he ask her to give up her work. There was the practical side, of course – he couldn't support her yet, so she had to earn a living, making in one night what he would be making in a month as a teacher. And there was something very erotic to George that other men coveted his girl. George was never ashamed of what she did for a living, nor was she; in fact, she enjoyed it. Kitty was refreshingly open and comfortable about sex, and she knew how to give pleasure to a man. To the society girls George knew, sex was an unpleasant obligation in a well-arranged marriage. When it came to immorality, his world was unforgiving. He told her once about a classmate of his sister Julia's who had been hounded out of society because she sat beside a gentleman in a carriage instead of opposite. Her family was ruined. Even the slightest mention of sex in polite company was deeply inappropriate; a woman who exposed her ankle was dubbed a harlot.

But all this ostensible propriety, Kitty knew full well, was an elaborate façade. Men of George's class engaged in the most deviant sexual practices, sometimes with girls as young as ten. George had seen his father's friend, Stanford White, entertaining one no more than thirteen at Miss Jennie's. Half the buildings between Fifth and Seventh Avenues and Twenty-Fourth and Fortieth Streets were used for immoral goings-on, a veritable sexual playground for the rich and powerful. Sometimes it seemed that every society gentleman was a part of this secret world of indecency and vice. Kitty remembered a client telling her that a gentleman wouldn't be a real gentleman if he didn't have a dark secret, be it women, gambling, or little boys.

With the ample income she earned at Miss Jennie's, Kitty had acquired a nice apartment on East Nineteenth Street. It was there that George had noticed her sketches on the walls. He urged her to keep drawing, telling her she had real talent, and he told her about the Art Students League at Fifth Avenue and Fifteenth Street. Kitty took classes in her spare time, and her drawing did improve. Her new-found talent thrilled her, filled her with pride. George loved and *cared* for her as a real person, she'd think sometimes as she filled a blank sheet of paper with images, black lines moving across the expanse of white. It was this quality that had won her heart. One day, she hoped, they would travel to California, to a place where she had no past, and they'd start a new life together. Kitty loved George so much. Watching him destroy himself with his sickness was killing her.

'Please don't go out tonight, Georgie. Remember, you promised to wait up and pose for me.'

George leant over, kissed her cheek, and nodded. He saw Kitty to the door of her apartment. In the carriage, he called out to the driver, 'Fifty-Ninth and Seventh.'

But after a few minutes, he thumped the roof of the carriage and shouted, 'Do you know the Windsor Palace on the Bowery?'

CHAPTER SIXTEEN

Julia liked to think of it as a raging river of well-dressed society women, flowing endlessly from Twenty-Third to Fourteenth Streets. Every day, enormous numbers of ladies in a rainbow array of velvets, silks, brocades, and satins, all wearing large hats topped with flowers and feathers, travelled along Ladies' Mile, the city's prime shopping district. Huge department stores lined block after block, their plate glass windows full of wonderful things to buy – from pet monkeys to French silk stockings to Peruvian hat feathers. Broadway, the spine of the district, was packed with carriages of all varieties, horse-drawn trolleys, and hordes of pedestrians crossing back and forth between them.

With her mother by her side, Julia was swept along in the current of shoppers. At Broadway and Nineteenth Street, they extracted themselves and entered the arched entrance of Lord & Taylor. The building, with its diagonal tower at the corner and a mansard roof (since childhood, her father had taught her architectural terms), had been built with cast iron. Julia's father loved cast iron and used it on his own buildings, but he said some critics thought it a false material that only pretended to be stone. Still, whenever Julia walked past a cast-iron building, she rapped her knuckles on a column to hear the metallic sound.

Inside, they went into the double-height shopping space on the main floor. Although Julia's coming-out gowns had already been ordered from Worth's, there was still a whole new adult wardrobe to be selected. Dresses for mornings, afternoons, and evenings needed to be bought, each with dozens of accessories. The choices were daunting, and Julia felt a wave of envy for men, whose clothes were not meant to attract attention. A man who would dare wear a purple waistcoat, say, would be branded an outcast. But for society women, uniformity was a grave sin. Their wardrobes had to stand out and dazzle. The more extravagant, the better.

Julia was glad that her mother was there to guide her. She knew Helen was considered a great beauty, and her choice of clothes was admired by all. Julia was also happy that Granny had not accompanied them. Since beginning preparations for her coming-out, Julia had been bombarded by advice from Granny. Last night, she proclaimed, 'Unless very, very well acquainted, a man who grins at a lady when he tips his hat is not a gentleman of good breeding.'

Julia and Helen liked to tackle one shop a day instead of racing up and down Broadway. Yesterday, they had shopped at Arnold Constable. Tomorrow, a day at B. Altman was planned. After making some selections on the main floor of Lord & Taylor, they took the steam lift to the upper levels. Each floor was a riot of femininity, with shop girls waiting on well-dressed women at counters and wrapping desks and running back and forth with parcels and change. Little Lord & Taylor boys in white shirts followed behind the female shoppers, carrying their purchases. There was hardly a man to be seen.

Mother and daughter patiently examined the wares, moving steadily up to the fifth floor with their bag boy. Finally, they descended to the luxurious reception room on the main floor where they ran into many friends and had tea while a woman played Brahms on the piano.

On the way out, Helen realised she had left her gloves in the reception room and left Julia to wait outside the main entrance. Amid the flow of humanity up and down Broadway, Julia noticed a boy on a safety bicycle, the new kind with identically sized wheels. He slowly rode south – then accelerated and intentionally ran into an elderly woman crossing the street, knocking her over. His bike tipped. The boy got up, yelling and cursing at the woman for her carelessness. In a second, a crowd of people gathered, blocking Julia's view. Straining to see, she made out a young man in his twenties, wearing a grey three-piece suit. He walked to the edge of the crowd, where a man was craning his neck, trying to see the commotion. In a fraction of a second, he stole the man's wallet from his trouser pocket. The young man walked slowly along the perimeter of the crowd and stole a wallet from another distracted man; an instant later, he stuck his hand in a woman's blue velvet handbag and removed a leather change purse. He worked with lightning speed. Then he walked south on Broadway, casually as if he were taking an afternoon stroll. Julia was mesmerised, unable to believe what she'd just seen.

Helen came up behind her. Julia kept her eyes glued on the man.

'Mother, I just ran into Lavinia Stewart, and she asked me to go to Macy's with her and her mother to look at a dress. I'll take a hansom back home. Will that be all right?'

'I suppose. I wanted to pop into W & J Sloane to look at a rug for Charlie's bedroom. Don't be late for supper, dear.'

Julia kissed her mother and disappeared into the crowd. Breathless, she walked quickly down Broadway; soon, she was just twenty feet behind the man. A sense of giddy excitement swept over her. A great admirer of Dickens, she had read *Oliver Twist* three times, fascinated by the story of Fagin and his gang. But while she'd read about pickpockets, she'd never seen one.

Near Broadway and Fifteenth Street, the boy on the bicycle reappeared and ran into an elderly man. A crowd formed, and the young man went to work. Julia stood in the doorway of a shop and watched, grinning from ear to ear. When he finished, she kept following. The pavements were packed with shoppers. She knew she blended in with the crowd and wouldn't be noticed, even if he turned around.

The young man made his way to the Fourteenth Street station of the Sixth Avenue Elevated Railroad. The station, built of iron and covered with steep roofs capped by iron cresting and finials, straddled Fourteenth Street like a huge crab. As Julia followed, she passed through dappled patterns of sunlight and shadow thrown onto the street by the lattice-like train tracks above.

Although her family's main means of transportation were carriages, her father had taken her and her brothers for rides on the Third Avenue Elevated Railroad. The whole experience was thus quite familiar. Staying a healthy distance behind the pickpocket, she paid the off-peak fare of ten cents and went into the waiting room, an elegantly appointed space done in black walnut and stained glass. Soon the rumble of an approaching train began to vibrate the station like an earthquake tremor, and dozens of waiting passengers went out on to the platform. The pickpocket was taking an uptown train. Julia hid behind one of the slender cast-iron columns that held up the platform roof, but she could still see the man.

The train's steam engine screeched and hissed as it pulled into the station. Julia took a seat at the opposite end of the pickpocket's car. The train lurched forward and picked up speed. Keeping one eye on the man, Julia looked out the window. The thing she liked most about riding the elevated train was that you passed within a few feet of the apartment windows on the buildings lining the avenue, so close that she felt she could reach out and tap the inhabitants on the shoulders. It was better at night, of course. Then the apartments were lit up and you could secretly observe the intimacy of people living their lives: eating, reading, arguing. She'd see a mother feeding a baby, two lovers holding hands on a sofa. It was like going to the theatre, but with dozens of miniature stages stacked together. Julia was so caught up that she almost missed the pickpocket's stop at Thirty-Second Street.

After disembarking, the pickpocket walked down Sixth Avenue and stopped just south of Thirtieth Street, in front of a three-storey brick building painted bright yellow. He went in, greeting the two men who were coming out. Julia cautiously approached the building, worried that he'd suddenly reappear. From the kerb, she saw that the building was called the Haymarket Dance Hall. A sign by the door stated that women were admitted free, while men paid a twenty-five-cent admission. She went to the entrance to look inside, half expecting to see Fagin and his boys gathered around a table. Music emerged from within, and she stepped aside to let by a fat, middle-aged man holding the arm of a garishly dressed woman with rouge on her cheeks.

A man in a black frock coat and grey trousers walked up to her and smiled. 'What do ya say . . . two dollars . . . for an hour? That's more than fair for a classy looker like you.'

'I have no idea what you're talking about,' Julia said.

'All right, three, then.'

When Julia didn't reply, the man shrugged his shoulders and walked on. Confused, Julia stepped up into the doorway to get a better look.

'I wouldn't go in if I were you,' said a voice directly behind her.

Startled, Julia spun around to face the pickpocket. Up close, she saw that he was in his early twenties and surprisingly handsome, with penetrating blue eyes. Regaining her composure, Julia put on a look of indignation. 'Why ever not? The sign says women can enter for free.'

Her reply made the pickpocket laugh out loud. 'You're not that type of woman.'

Baffled by his answer and angered by his laughter, Julia stiffened her spine and added ice to her voice. 'Sir, I never talk to complete strangers on the street.'

'But I'm not a stranger, am I? You've been following me since Fifteenth Street.'

'That's absurd.'

'You sat in the same car on the elevated train.'

'You're terribly mistaken.'

'You'd be a rotten undercover detective – you're too beautiful. I spotted you a mile away.'

Taken aback by the backhanded compliment, Julia paused, then went on the attack.

'You're a thief,' she said in a shrill, accusatory tone. 'I saw you.'

'So you caught me. Why not turn me over to the police? Look, here's your chance.' The pickpocket pointed to a barrel-chested policeman strolling down Sixth Avenue, twirling his truncheon. 'Go ahead.'

Tongue-tied, Julia looked down at the slate pavement as the cop passed by.

'Dandy John Nolan's my name,' said the pickpocket, tipping his bowler hat and grinning. Granny's admonition from last night came immediately to mind, and Julia looked away.

'Sir, we've not been formally introduced by our mothers.'

'Who's been feeding you that malarkey? Listen, you've come all the way up here. Let me buy you a beer. You seem real

112

interested in what's going on inside. I'll show you. Come on.'

Julia looked at the handsome young man and then at the double doors of the Haymarket Dance Hall, perplexed. If Fagin was in there, she was determined to see him. She wasn't going to be afraid. Besides, didn't writers need to experience all aspects of life?

'I have never tasted beer,' she said softly.

'Then you're in for a treat. It's the nectar of the gods.' Nolan flashed her a smile, which Julia shyly returned. He held out his arm, and she hesitated for a moment, then took it.

Together, they went inside.

CHAPTER SEVENTEEN

'This is a gold mine, Jimmy. A goddamn gold mine.'

Kent watched Bella Levine pick through the stack of gowns and dresses heaped on the plank floor of the warehouse.

'These are from Paris! *Paris*, Jimmy. The very best of the best. Look, see how they're stitched with real silver and gold threads?' She was beside herself with excitement.

Levine, a mountain of a woman who weighed more than three hundred pounds, let out a whoop of delight and flopped down face first onto the huge pile of clothes.

'I'm swimming in dough, Jimmy. Where d'you get this stuff?' she asked, caressing a green silk brocade gown. 'This is better'n finding Captain Kidd's treasure.'

Kent smiled and blew a ring of cigar smoke into the stagnant air of the warehouse. 'Yes, Bella, I've discovered a gold mine.'

A professional thief with a great deal of stolen goods at hand is still poor. He can't sell them or take them to merchants on the open market without arousing suspicion. He needs a fence to dispose of stolen goods, and Bella Levine had owned New York City's best fencing operation for the last ten years. Bella handled millions of dollars in loot – for a hefty fifty per cent fee, of course.

But Kent knew it was worth it. Bella was honest and, above all, reliable. She and her husband lived in an opulently furnished three-storey brownstone house on East Twenty-Sixth Street from which she ran her fencing operation. Her business made her very rich and enabled her to bribe judges, police officers, and district attorneys into leaving her alone. She regularly entertained the city's power fraternity, including Tammany men, with eight-course dinners at her home. Bella was the city's foremost female criminal and greatly admired by other well-known female thieves like Kid Glove Rosey and Little Annie.

Kent appreciated her discretion. Unlike his former fence, Black Lena Kleinschmidt, who was arrested after wearing a stolen diamond ring to a party, Bella never kept stolen goods. She was wealthy enough to buy things as nice as the Vanderbilts'. Items to be fenced were never brought to her home but were examined at a warehouse tucked away on 448 Broome Street. The interior of the cast-iron building resembled the Arnold Constable department store: five floors crammed with every conceivable type of goods. Once, Kent had seen a dinosaur skeleton.

'And this silver!' Bella exclaimed, pointing to the goods on the floor. 'That isn't American stuff. It's English, the absolute best.'

'I'm glad you like my goods. Maybe because of the quality, you'll take forty-five per cent this time?'

A menacing scowl replaced the smile on Bella's face. Normally, she had a jolly personality as large as her immense body. Now, she resembled an angry bull elephant. She rose with difficulty from the heap of clothes and waddled over to Kent.

'Forty-eight. Then if you bring me more quality stuff, maybe forty-five. Maybe.'

'Don't worry, my beautiful dove. There's a lot more where this came from.'

Culver stepped off the freight lift and motioned to his boss.

'Excuse me, Bella,' Kent said. She was too engrossed in the piles of men's evening dress to hear. 'Didn't I tell you not to disturb me?' Kent snapped at Culver.

'Bald Jack's been picked up. By Byrnes.' Culver spoke in a quiet, worried voice, hoping Bella wouldn't overhear.

'What for?' Kent asked indignantly.

'Killing that bank messenger four years ago.'

For years, banks had been in the foolish habit of sending messengers through the streets with substantial amounts of cash and securities. As the banks were too cheap to provide armed escorts, these men were easy prey for sneak thieves. Stealing from them yielded smaller amounts than could be had from vaults, but it was usually an easy job; the messengers always gave up the money without a fight. Save one Union Trust man who carried a pistol. He would have killed Bald Jack Sanders if Kent's man hadn't killed him first. Bald Jack had no choice in the matter. There had been no witnesses that day on Hudson Street, Kent recalled grimly. Someone must have informed on Bald Jack to win a lighter sentence.

'Is he in the Tombs?' Kent asked, referring to the city's main prison on Centre Street.

'No. Byrnes is taking no chances. He has him in Blackwell's Island. They're to ship him up to Sing Sing until the trial.'

Kent lit a Havana and began to pace the warehouse in wide circles. If it had been anyone else, the solution would have been easy: have Bald Jack killed in prison. But the man was his top earner. An expert sneak thief, he consistently brought in more money than anyone else in the organisation (Kent hated the word *gang*). He was fearless and robbed anything from anybody. In his finest professional moment, he'd hijacked four flatbed trailers loaded with carriages from the New York Central Railroad at Tarrytown.

'Is he in the old or new part of Blackwell's?'

'The new addition, the one they finished in the spring.'

Bella approached them. 'What are you fellows whispering about? Bald Jack?'

Kent wasn't surprised. Bella knew everything that went on in the city a day before anyone else.

'Go and see Hummel,' she said.

Abe Hummel may have looked like a deformed dwarf, but he and his partner, William Howe, were the most powerful criminal lawyers in New York. Since the early 1860s, Howe and Hummel had represented thousands of criminals. Once they got 250 out of 300 prisoners in Blackwell's released on a technicality. Their client list included entire gangs, like the Whyos and the Sheeny Mob, and celebrities like P. T. Barnum and Edwin Booth. Howe and Hummel were so effective that many gangs and criminals, including Bella Levine, kept them on a five-thousand-dollar annual retainer.

Kent went immediately to their office, located at Leonard and Centre Streets across from the Tombs, for a consultation.

'You've got a problem here, Jim,' Hummel said. He sat behind his desk, obscured by a haze of cigar smoke. 'Byrnes won't budge on this. He wants your man hanged.'

'How much will it take to change his mind?'

'That's not gonna work this time. And bribing the guards is out.'

Kent stared out of the window at the Tombs. True to its name, it looked like an Egyptian mausoleum, framed by four massive stone columns trimmed with carvings of acanthus leaves. *Such an impressive and palatial building*, he thought, *to house the scum of the earth*. It had an execution yard between an inner and outer building, linked by a bridge of sighs across which the condemned took their last walk.

The Tombs usually housed New York's most serious criminals. It was unusual for Byrnes to move Bald Jack to Blackwell's, an island in the middle of the East River. But despite its formidable appearance, there had been many successful escapes from the Tombs. *Byrnes is being very careful indeed*, Kent thought, drumming his fingers idly on the desk.

'His cell is in the new addition, you say?'

Hummel nodded.

'I'll need to know the number,' Kent said, rising from his chair.

CHAPTER EIGHTEEN

'Welcome to my house.'

'This is incredible!' Charlie cried.

Charlie's rescuer, Eddie Mooney, had graciously invited him to visit his home. He stood before the open hatch to a huge, unused steam boiler in an abandoned factory near the corner of Cherry Street and the East River. Together, they crawled inside an iron-lined compartment furnished with an old mattress, a table, and a chair. It was big enough to stand. Eddie lit a candle, throwing a spooky light against the rusty walls.

'Pretty cosy, eh?'

'I'll say. And it's all yours?'

'Yep. Until they tear down the building, which'll probably be never,' Eddie said. 'Have a seat.'

Charlie had been so grateful to his rescuer that he'd given Eddie three dollars of the money he'd saved for the Crandall steam engine. Eddie, touched by this gesture, offered to buy Charlie a drink. To his amazement, Charlie didn't drink beer or whisky, so he treated him to a sarsaparilla.

Eddie plopped down on his bed and pulled out a sack of tobacco. He rolled a cigarette for himself and his guest. He didn't dare think that Charlie didn't smoke. Everybody he knew smoked. He didn't want to offend the boy. Smiling, he lit Charlie's cigarette.

Charlie inhaled, coughed, and gagged a bit. 'It's marvellous that your parents let you live here,' he said when he was able to speak.

Eddie, who was skinny and buck-toothed, with a prominent cowlick of greasy hair, shot him a puzzled look. 'My parents? I ain't seen 'em in five years. They kicked my ass out onto the streets when I was seven.'

'Why'd they do that?'

'Couldn't afford to keep me, what with the five other tykes. My ol' man was a worthless ass drunk, and my ma was a drunk and a two-bit whore to boot. Every kid I know down here got kicked out like that. What about you? Your parents kick you out yet?'

'Well, no, not yet,' said Charlie, surprised by the question.

'I used to sleep in doorways, cellars, on old barges. Slept in a carriage in a stable for a month before they found me. But I've had this place almost two years now. I got me a real padlock for the hatch so no one can take it away.'

Charlie was distracted, replaying their conversation in his mind. 'What's a whore?'

'A woman who fucks a stranger for money,' Eddie said. It struck him as an odd question, like asking 'What planet do we live on?' He smiled at his young guest. 'Charlie, old boy, there's a lot of learning I gotta teach ya.'

'So who takes care of you?' Charlie asked, still puzzled.

'I take care of myself,' Eddie said indignantly. 'I work as a newsboy . . . and some other things, to scrape up money.'

Charlie had seen newsboys all over the city. They weren't much older than him, ragged-looking waifs standing at the entrances to elevated stations, on busy street corners, and in front of the department stores on Ladies' Mile, yelling out, begging people to buy their papers.

'How much can you make?' he asked. He'd never earned a nickel of his own; he had to beg his parents for change or wait for birthdays and Christmas.

'On a good day, fifty cents. That's after overheads like buying the papers and paying for selling space. Mine's the Hanover Square Elevated Station – lot of Wall Street swells there. I do a good business. I used to pay this older kid, name of Mikey Harrigan, protection money, but he took half my profit. So last year when I got to be big, I got a lead plumbing pipe and beat the shit out of him. No more protection money,' Eddie said.

Charlie was old enough to understand that he was related (in a distant way) to the Astor fortune. Somehow, though, Eddie's entrepreneurialism impressed him far more.

'It's getting late,' Eddie said. 'I gotta go down to Park Row and get my evening papers from the folding room at the Sun. That's my rag. Come along with me.'

As Eddie locked up his abode, he patted the old boiler affectionately.

'I'll tell ya, it's a lot better living here than at the Newsboys' Lodging House. You can get a bed and meal for six cents each, but you know what they do? If you stay there a month, they ship your ass off to Kansas or some fuckin' place out west. Make you work on a goddamn farm like you're a nigger slave or somethin'. Can you imagine? You'd never make it back to New York. And New York's the best place in the world to live. You know that too, huh, Charlie?'

They walked up to Madison Avenue and headed east, Eddie chattering like a magpie.

'I used to clean pigsties. Then I shovelled coal for a while. Tried factory work, making twine and paper collars, but I couldn't stand being cooped up all day, and the pay was shit. A fella with the Little Daybreak Boys on the waterfront found me a place in the gang as a lookout on robberies. I crawled through the portholes of the ships docked at the piers to steal shit for 'em. But then I got too big to fit through, so I left.'

The boys approached a grocery stand on the corner of Madison Avenue and Rutgers Street.

'Ya hungry, Charlie?' Before Charlie could answer, Eddie pulled him inside a doorway. 'Well, I'm gonna show you a trick. See that old man in the apron? You go up to him and ask what's the best way to City Hall. Then pretend to be confused and ask him to repeat it.'

Charlie felt a flush of excitement surge up his back. He casually strolled up to the man, who could see by his clothes that he wasn't the usual filthy guttersnipe. The old man was straining to see if the kid's mother was behind him when Charlie asked for directions. With the man's back turned, Eddie helped himself to generous amounts of fruit from the stand, stuffing them inside his tattered shirt. He crossed the street and continued up Madison Avenue. A moment or two later, Charlie caught up with him.

'Good job. Have a peach.'

Charlie bit into the ripe fruit, wiping the juice from his mouth with his sleeve. It seemed to taste more delicious because it was stolen.

At the newspaper office, Eddie pushed his way through dozens of other newsboys to get his papers. They all seemed to know and like him. Charlie was proud to be with someone so popular. The two boys took the Second Avenue Elevated train downtown to the Hanover Square station. During the ride, Eddie opened *The Sun* and scanned the pages.

'You know,' he boasted, 'I can read and write real good. And I

122

can read big words too – like parliament.' A moment later, he cried out, 'Look, a man got bit by a rabid dog on Avenue A. That's what'll be our hook. Murders, animal attacks, fires, robberies. Those all sell papers. So you yell out, "Man killed by rabid dog".'

Charlie looked down at the article. 'It says he was just bit. We'd be lying.'

'Don't worry. He'll be dead before the week's out. The newspaper business, Charlie, is nothing but lies.'

Eddie and Charlie each took a position at the bottom of the uptown and downtown stairs to the Hanover Square station and hawked their papers. As the crowds rushed by, Charlie screamed out the headline. To his delight, pennies were thrust into his hand until every paper was sold. When Eddie was finished, they met by the entrance to the nearby Hanover Bank.

'Here you go,' Charlie said, proudly pouring his money into Eddie's hands.

'Hey, you're a born newsie.'

'I have to get home, but I'll meet you at your place tomorrow morning,' Charlie said and bounded up the station steps.

Eddie watched Charlie as he left and could see that he was beside himself with joy, which made Eddie feel happy and sad at the same time. That always happened when he thought about Harry, his little brother, and Charlie reminded him of Harry. Thinking about the fun times they'd had made Eddie feel so good, but then he would descend into a deep sadness.

Harry had been thrown out of the house at the same time as Eddie. Together, they fended for themselves on the streets. Harry would serve as lookout while Eddie lifted items from a shop or warehouse. Sometimes, Harry would even squirm inside an open window and do the stealing himself. They were quite a team. But

Harry wasn't as strong as Eddie, and the street life wore him down. He was sick all the time, coughing up blood and getting such bad night sweats that his body would shake convulsively, as though he were in a carriage moving over cobblestones.

Three years ago, they'd had one of the coldest winters on record. Shivering, Eddie woke one morning from a bed of rags at the bottom of a basement staircase off an alley. His feet and fingers felt numb. He gave Harry a gentle shake, but his brother didn't stir. Pulling the filthy, torn blanket away, Eddie discovered that his brother had frozen to death. Harry was stiff as a board, his eyes staring up at the sky.

That morning, Eddie did something he hadn't done for years: cry. He sobbed for hours, hunched over by the side of his brother's body. He knew he couldn't call the police or a doctor. If he did, he'd wind up in an orphanage for sure. So he waited until dark, and then he wrapped his little brother up, carrying him to the front of a Methodist church a few blocks away. He knew the congregation would give Harry a real burial.

Walking away from Harry's body was one of the loneliest things Eddie had ever done. The feeling of that horrible day stayed with him always.

CHAPTER NINETEEN

'You're telling me that the debt is only reduced by six thousand dollars?'

'Mr Cross, you and George don't seem to understand the concept of compound interest. There's fifteen per cent interest accruing weekly on the principal.'

'Fifteen per cent a week? That's usury, you bastard!' Cross yelled. 'A damned Hebrew wouldn't charge that much!'

Brady came up from behind and grabbed Cross by the neck, placing his knee against Cross's buttocks and bending his back like an archery bow.

'That silver and linen was worth twenty thousand dollars, easily. The clothing had to be forty thousand dollars!' Cross cried, ignoring the choking pressure of Brady's stranglehold.

'The fence we use to dispose of the goods gets a fifty per cent cut, Mr Cross. The actual take from the robbery is thus greatly reduced,' Kent said in a patient voice. 'But don't worry – you'll soon learn the economics of our business.'

Brady released Cross, who fell forward, gasping.

'Goddamn it, Kent,' he rasped out. 'This is an outrage. I planned this robbery and get a pittance in return.'

'Why don't you complain to your congressman?' Brady said, erupting in laughter.

'You know the alternative, Mr Cross. And I know you don't want that,' Kent said softly.

Cross slumped down in a chair. They were in the basement room at McGlory's, but this time only Culver and Brady had joined Kent.

'Do you remember a very short, bald gentleman, Mr Cross? From the robbery?'

Cross looked up at Kent, puzzled. 'Yes, I do.'

'That was Bald Jack Sanders, a very valuable member of our organisation,' Kent said.

Cross chuckled in spite of himself. 'Why do you people in the netherworld have such colourful names? In architecture, we don't have monikers like Charming Charlie McKim or Racy Richard Morris Hunt.'

Kent ignored the question. 'Bald Jack has been arrested – and that means trouble for you.'

'Me?'

'Bald Jack saw you at the robbery. Under duress, he might give you up.'

'He might, but if he does, I can give you up.'

Kent smiled and took a sip of whisky. 'I know you won't do that. Like I said before, family men come with a lot of collateral.'

As he stared at Kent, Cross's mind raced, trying to sort out the various possibilities. Why was Kent trying to bluff him?

'Bald Jack is being held in the Blackwell's Island prison, in addition I've learnt it was designed by your friend from the Dakota, Henry Hardenbergh.'

Cross burst out laughing. 'Give me the telephone, then. I'll ring him up and say, "Oh, hello, Henry. I need your help springing a crook from prison".'

'I was thinking along those lines,' Kent said.

'Is it my imagination, or is James T. Kent showing loyalty toward a fellow human being? You must really like this man if you're willing to take such a risk instead of just having him killed.'

'For a society man from Harvard, you show exceptional shrewdness. But for your own good, I insist you help me.'

'For ten thousand off the debt.'

'Four thousand.'

'It's very kind of you to meet me on such short notice, Henry.'

'Not at all, John. I'm happy to help.'

'I was down on Wall Street and saw your Astor Building. The entrance is wonderful. I wanted to see how you detailed that arch, the one with the columns? And that attic gable with the diaper-patterned terracotta facing.'

'Thank you, John. That job came out well,' Hardenbergh said, giving a brusque nod. He was a touch uncomfortable, Cross saw. After all, the building had been commissioned by the Astor family, and Cross was an Astor relative. Though there had been many referrals over the years, Cross had never gotten any work directly from the Astors.

'I have to be uptown for a dinner, so I can't stay. But Maxwell here will be glad to assist you.'

Maxwell, a draftsman in his mid-twenties, nodded, his face expressionless. Cross guessed he was irritated as hell to be kept after work.

Hardenbergh placed his top hat on his head, waved, and departed.

It was just after six, and there was no one left in the large, open studio. The poor illumination cast by the gaslight fixtures made it useless for architects and their draftsmen to try to work into the evening. Cross had recently installed electrical fixtures in his office and had seen a real improvement in the light level – to the dismay of his employees, who now had to work late.

'These are the Astor Building drawings,' Maxwell said, pulling out the drawer of a flat file. He lifted a stack of thirty-by-forty-inch linen sheets, placed them on a table, and stood off to the side.

Cross flipped through them until he found the sheet he wanted. Pulling it from the pile, he turned to the draftsman and gave him an absent smile. 'Maxwell, old man, do me a favour and go downstairs to that saloon on Forty-First. Get me a sandwich and a growler of beer.' He handed Maxwell a five-dollar bill. 'And keep the change for yourself.'

Maxwell's eyes lit up like bonfires. The four dollars' worth of change was a dollar more than his average pay per day. 'Thank you so much, sir,' he cried and flew out the door.

Cross immediately went back to the flat file, found the drawer labelled Blackwell's Island Prison, and pulled it out. He flung the stack of drawings on the table and quickly sifted through them to the site plan showing the whole layout of the prison, all the way to the East River. Taking some sheets of tracing paper off a desk, he placed one over the drawing and started working. Flipping through more drawings, he traced the parts he needed. Fifteen minutes later, he was finished. He had just replaced the prison drawings and was back at the table, looking over the Astor details, when Maxwell returned with his food and drink.

CHAPTER TWENTY

'You sure you want to do this?' Nolan asked, removing his derby and scratching his head.

'I'm absolutely sure,' Julia said. 'I'm dying to see it. Please.'

This was the second time Julia had met Nolan in the Tenderloin since their introduction at the Haymarket Dance Hall the previous week, and she felt like Alice, falling down the rabbit hole into Wonderland. Somehow she had stumbled into an exciting world of fantasy and revulsion. Even the name of the neighbourhood, 'the Tenderloin', had a magical sound.

At their first meeting, Nolan had showed her what a concert saloon was. Men would come to meet ladies of the evening – Nolan had explained them too – to dance and make friends. Julia thought the music was tinny but quite entertaining, and the whole joint – another term learnt from Nolan – was gay and lively. The owner, William McMahon, was a genial, well-dressed gentleman who didn't allow swearing or close dancing and forbade the girls exposing their ankles. Huge behemoths of men called bouncers threw any rowdy customers into the gutter.

The curtained-off cubicles at the side of the hall, Julia was told, were for private dances, in which some girls performed naked.

There was a secret tunnel from the hall to an adjacent hotel for more intimate liaisons, Nolan added.

At home, Julia hadn't gotten a wink of sleep. Her head was swimming, awash with the incredible sights she'd seen. The next morning, she decided to shelve her old novel and start a new one, based on the new world she'd discovered. To meet Nolan again, she told her mother she was going out with her school friend, Lavinia. She delighted in coming up with these lies. As a writer, she realised, she had a great talent for altering the truth.

'Shouldn't we be going? You said it starts at one on the dot,' she said.

Nolan frowned, seemingly unsure. But when he saw Julia's pretty face and looked into her brown eyes, the size of silver dollars, he relented. 'It's on Twenty-Seventh Street.'

The Tenderloin had its own specific geography, she learnt. West Twenty-Eighth Street was for high-end gambling, West Twenty-Seventh Street for low-end. West Twenty-Ninth Street was exclusively row houses for the ladies of the evening. She and Nolan passed the Cairo Dance Hall, where they'd gone the day before yesterday. Julia didn't think it was as nice as the Haymarket. The Cairo, Nolan told her, was a clip joint – it watered down the drinks.

All the streets had saloons. They'd visited two: the Star and Garter, and the Ruins. Each had a long bar to the side with a mirror behind it, sawdust-covered floors, a pot-bellied stove, and chromolithographs of prize fighters and plump nude women on the walls. All women had to be escorted, and if you had two beers, a free sandwich lunch was offered, which Julia found delicious but quite salty. In her society world, a saloon was considered low class. But it was really a club, she learnt, a second home for the men who played cards or pool and argued about politics and sports. In a way, it was no different from her father going to the Union League or Knickerbocker clubs.

Nolan was delighted to show her the sights and had proudly escorted her by the arm into dance halls and saloons. On the streets, he pointed out colourful local characters like Dan the Dude, a knockout drop artist – although Julia didn't quite understand what that was yet. Nolan was also flattered to be asked about his profession, and Julia laughed delightedly when she discovered that he'd been trained in a Fagin school right out of *Oliver Twist*. Nolan spilt trade secrets about how to distract a mark and then pull a wallet or purse. The bicycle trick she'd seen was taught to him by one Crazy Bob, who had even trained his dog, Whisky, to snatch purses!

Nolan hadn't hesitated to show her anything – until now. They stopped at the Last Hope. From the outside, it looked like any other saloon. 'Here we are,' he said.

'Lead the way, Mr Nolan,' Julia chirped. They addressed each other as mister and miss because, as etiquette dictated, they hadn't known each other since childhood.

Nolan smiled and took her by the arm. They strode into the saloon, past the patrons with their shot glasses and mugs of beer. The men and women looked up, surprised by the sight of Julia, who wore a stylish blue afternoon dress.

When they reached the rear of the first floor, Julia gasped, 'Just like Ancient Greece.'

In front of her was a wooden amphitheatre that stretched down into the basement. The benches were filled almost completely with men, some of whom had gaudily dressed women at their sides. Nolan paid the attendant four dollars and guided Julia down the steep steps. They found seats near the arena floor. Men called out greetings to Nolan, who raised his derby in return, proud that they were admiring Julia.

The wall surrounding the arena was about four feet high and lined

131

with zinc sheets. The floor was packed earth and gave off a damp, mouldy smell. Off to the side stood a man in a green three-piece suit. He held an excited fox terrier on a leather leash.

'How does this work?' Julia asked above the din of the spectators.

'Fifty in a twenty-minute limit and three-to-one odds on Sampson, the mutt.'

'What should we bet?' asked Julia, removing a bill from her red and gold embroidered purse. 'I've got a five,' she said, handing it to Nolan.

He caught the attention of a bookie standing at the top row behind them and nodded. 'Get ready!' he yelled.

A gate opened at the side of the arena wall. In one fluid motion, two burly men set a large wooden box on the dirt floor and opened a front flap. Out came dozens of rats, scurrying like mad around the arena. The men pulled the box in and closed the gate. At that moment, a whistle blew. The man in the green suit released the dog and climbed over the wall, taking a seat.

The fox terrier ran into the mass of rats, grabbed one by the neck, sank his white teeth into him, shook him violently, and flung the dead carcass away. Then he attacked another, and another. At each kill, the crowd roared with delight. The dog killed systematically, with great discipline. He didn't waste a second chasing the rats about. The spectators cheered raucously, urging Sampson on.

Seated on a bench near the floor was a man holding a pocket watch. A man next to him held a slate, on which he made a chalk mark for each kill. As the tally mounted, the crowd went into a frenzy. The dirty grey rats formed a vortex in the arena, colliding with one another, leaping over the dead bodies of their comrades. The man holding the watch yelled out, 'Ten minutes left! Twenty-nine kills.'

Julia found herself screaming Sampson's name. At five minutes left and forty-one kills, the volume of the cheering increased fourfold. The dog kept attacking without the tiniest sign of fatigue. Julia thought dizzily that he must be enjoying himself. But some rats evaded him, scattering here and there, making him race around the arena to run them down. Only three remained, and they were determined to live. Sampson sat back and waited for one rat to run right into him. Two left. The dog chose his first victim and went in for the kill.

'One minute!' yelled the timer, and the crowd went mad. The last rat was not only fast but wily, as if he knew the remaining time. In a burst of speed, Sampson caught up with him and hurled his body to the ground as the timer yelled out, 'Time!'

Some of the crowd was ecstatic; others were angry and disgusted. Julia and Nolan threw their arms up in victory. 'We won fifteen dollars!' Nolan yelled.

Sampson's handler had him back on the leash. He paraded him in front of the cheering crowd like a gladiator in a Roman arena. The white curly fur around the terrier's mouth was bloodstained, but Sampson was triumphant. To the delight of his fans, he stopped, picked up a dead rat, shook it, and threw it to the floor.

A few moments later, Julia and Nolan found themselves back on the pavement of West Twenty-Seventh Street.

'That was exciting, Mr Nolan,' Julia said breathlessly. 'Thank you for taking me.'

'Would you believe the record is one hundred in fifteen minutes, Miss Cross?'

'One hundred in fifteen minutes? That's amazing!'

'I must be honest: I didn't know if you'd like it.'

'Oh, Mr Nolan, rats are evil. Did you know that they spread the Black Death in the fourteenth century? The plague killed half of Europe!'

It was a hot July afternoon, and Julia was fanning herself.

'Would you like something to drink, Miss Cross? Perhaps a cold sarsaparilla?'

'No, I must be getting back. I told my mother I was at the Natural History Museum with Lavinia.'

'I suppose you did get to see some animals.'

Julia gave an unexpected burble of laughter. 'And they weren't stuffed.'

'I had a wonderful time, Miss Cross.'

'Next Tuesday at 10 a.m.?' Julia asked, shaking his hand and smiling.

CHAPTER TWENTY-ONE

Sitting in a rowing boat in the East River across from Blackwell's Island at 2:00 a.m., Cross was surprised by how cool and refreshing the air was.

A strong wind swept up the river. In Manhattan, the August night had been unbearably hot and humid; to feel the wind was a sweet relief. All day, he'd dreaded this moment. He hadn't bothered to ask whether he would accompany Kent's men tonight. He knew his presence would be mandatory.

The three men sat in a long rowing boat tied to an overhanging tree. They were hidden in the shadows on the banks of the river at Long Island City, less than a thousand feet from Blackwell's. To avoid detection by people on Manhattan's piers, it was safer to approach from the less-populated Queens County side in the east.

'Here they come,' Brady whispered, nodding to a passing guard boat. 'It won't be back for another two hours.'

The steam-powered prison patrol boats continuously circled the twelve-mile-long, cigar-shaped island. As this one passed, a barrel-chested man named Wild Jimmy Coogan untied the line and began rowing them to the island. The prison, a forbidding stone fortress topped with castle-like crenellations, was located near the southern end of the island, just north of the smallpox and municipal hospitals. Coogan expertly guided them across, taking advantage of the speedy south current. Cross guessed he must have been a seaman before embarking on a career in crime. To Cross's relief, they encountered no other boats. No one said a word during the trip, and only the sound of the oars cutting softly through the water could be heard.

From the middle of the river, the men could see a few lights on in the prison.

Coogan continued rowing until they were fifty yards away from the sloping granite sea wall that circled the island.

'What now, Mr Engineer?' whispered Brady.

Cross took out his tracings. It was a moonless night and hard to read. He struck a match and looked up at the sea wall.

'I'm an architect, not an engineer,' he whispered indignantly.

'Goddamn you, which way?' Brady snarled, punching Cross hard on his right arm.

'Head about twenty yards to the south,' Cross said, trying not to grimace from the pain. After a minute, he called out, 'That's it.'

A circular opening in the sea wall appeared before them, and Coogan steered towards it. If it had been high tide, they never would have seen the sewer tunnel, which sloped up almost 150 feet to the new addition at the prison's south end. When Kent told Cross about Hardenbergh's addition, Cross had remembered an article he'd seen in the trade journal *American Architect and Building News*. Back at his office, he'd looked it up. Instead of having a slop bucket in each cell for the prisoners to relieve themselves, the men had unenclosed toilets that dumped into waste lines between the two hundred back-to-back cells. During the day, a huge cistern on the roof of the addition periodically flushed the lines into a sewer tunnel, which dumped into the river. The addition had been designed according to the wishes of the Prison Reform Society, a do-gooder group that lobbied the state legislature for more humane prison conditions.

To Cross's surprise, Hardenbergh's drawings showed no iron gate over the opening. The state had skimped on money, he guessed, and never installed it. All the better. They wouldn't have to saw off a padlock.

About ten feet from the opening, Brady grabbed Coogan's arm and pointed along the top of the sea wall. They saw a single light by the edge, coming toward them from about twenty feet away. It swung to and fro as it moved.

'It's a guard,' Brady hissed, and the men immediately crouched low in the boat. With several powerful stokes of the oars, Coogan slid the craft inside the opening as the guard stopped directly above them. They froze and waited, listening to the river lap against the walls of the tunnel. With an oar, Coogan steadied the boat, keeping it from drifting out of the tunnel.

After five minutes, Brady nodded, and the men started to gather their equipment. Without the gate, there was no place to tie up the boat. It took several minutes to concoct a mooring. The distinct sound of streaming water interrupted their work. Brady raised his hand as the signal to halt, and the men froze again, struggling to meet one another's eyes in the darkness.

Outside the tunnel, they saw a thin jet of liquid falling from above the opening. The stream began to taper off, and someone said, 'Ah.' A minute later, a cigar butt was tossed into the water. Brady and Coogan exchanged smiles. Brady lit a lantern and ordered Cross to lead the way.

The diameter of the tunnel was only four feet, but it was big enough to bend over and walk through. Past the point at which high tide rinsed the tunnel clean, a powerful putrid odour hit them like a shovel to the face.

'Keep your mouths open and you won't smell it,' whispered Cross.

Looking down, he realised he shouldn't have worn his good shoes.

The tunnel sloped at a very steep angle. Good for drainage but tiring for walking. About fifty feet from the prison, they heard a rumbling.

'Brace yourselves and don't let go of the bag!' Cross yelled.

A few seconds later, a wall of brown water crashed into them.

'Christ, I'm covered in shit!' Coogan screamed as the torrent swept around his waist.

'Goddamn you, Cross,' Brady hissed, clutching the bag of tools to his chest.

'How the hell should I know when they flush the lines?' Cross snapped, thinking he shouldn't have worn his Brooks Brothers trousers either.

Stinking and angry, the men kept walking until they reached the exterior prison wall. They climbed through a hatch into a plumbing cavity in the addition, a towering three-storey space filled from top to bottom with waste lines from each cell. The space was barely four feet wide. Cross pulled the drawings from inside his soaking shirt. Brady raised the lantern.

'He's in cell twenty-four, second tier,' whispered Cross. He started pacing off a small distance to his right, trying to find the actual position of the cell as displayed on the drawing. 'Right up there.'

Using the labyrinth of piping like a ladder, Brady began climbing up to the cell, his dirty canvas bag of tools bouncing against his side. When he grabbed for an upper piece of lead pipe, it pulled out of its joint and crashed to the cement floor. The sound reverberated through the space like a pistol shot. The men froze, waiting for a reaction.

The minutes passed like months. Cross's wet body was drenched in sweat. He tried to imagine how he would explain his presence. Nothing he thought of was very convincing. He could see the front-page article in the *Tribune*, imagine the ruin that would befall his family.

Yet there was nothing but silence. Brady, still above them, took another route to the second tier. Coogan followed. To provide ventilation, each cell had a two-foot-square grille made of wide bands of iron; it looked like the weave of a basket. Above them, in the roof over the cavity, ventilators drew in fresh air. Hardenbergh was no fool; he knew the grilles could be escape routes, and he took great care in detailing their anchorage to the massive stone walls. Huge bolts and iron plates secured them to the inside face of the cavity wall. There was no way a prisoner could unfasten them from inside the cell, but from the outside, it was a simple matter of unbolting – as Brady was about to do with the huge wrench he'd brought along.

'Sanders, we're here to get you out,' he whispered through the vent grille.

'I'll keep watch by the bars while you work,' a voice said.

Brady placed the spanner on the first bolt and threw his weight on the handle. The bolt loosened with a tiny squeak. He quickly attacked the other three. Once loosened, he unscrewed them, placed them in his bag, pulled out the vent, and handed it to Coogan, who was perched on the pipes. The shiny, round pate of Bald Jack appeared in the opening. Being skinny and small, he squirmed through without difficulty.

'Good evening, Mr Brady,' whispered Bald Jack. He wore a grey-and-black-striped prison uniform of rough wool but otherwise looked much the same.

As Brady and Coogan helped Bald Jack keep his balance on the piping, a head of red hair appeared. 'Who the fuck is this?' hissed Brady, watching the man wriggle his shoulders and arms through the opening.

'That's Gordon, my cellmate,' Bald Jack said. 'This isn't the Fifth Avenue Hotel. I don't get my own goddamn room.'

'And I'm coming too. Ya ain't leaving me behind,' Gordon snarled. He bulled his way through to his waist, and then Bald

Jack and Brady pulled him the rest of the way out.

Brady carefully inserted the vent into place and tightened the bolts.

'They'll think we vanished into thin air,' said Bald Jack with a smile.

'Let's move,' said Coogan, leading the way down.

'Who the hell is he?' asked Cross, who had been waiting for them at the bottom of the plumbing cavity.

'Never you mind,' said Brady, who took the lead as they moved back into the sewer tunnel.

'Holy shit, it stinks,' Gordon said.

'Shit smells like shit,' said Coogan with a smile.

The five men splashed through the tunnel to the boat. Brady scanned the sea wall for guards. Satisfied, he gave Coogan the signal to shove off.

'You know, the grub wasn't bad in there. Ya got a pound of meat for dinner every day,' Bald Jack said, looking back at the prison as they rowed away.

'And a whole quart of vegetable soup,' added Gordon.

'We can turn around and take you back if you liked the place so much,' said Coogan.

'Shit no. You know the worst part of bein' in there? They *made* you go to evening school,' Bald Jack said.

Brady laughed. 'Hell, let's take 'em back. You would've finally learnt to read and write at the age of forty.'

The rowing boat silently made its way back across the river. To Cross's relief, there wasn't a boat to be seen. Just a few hundred yards more, and they'd be safe on the Queens side.

'So what were you in for, Gordon?' Brady asked.

'Got caught robbing Saint Jerome's Rectory on East Forty-Seventh Street.'

'Tough break,' Brady said sympathetically. 'Lotta silver in those places.'

'You bet. When I get back to Manhattan, I'll get set up, maybe go back to the same place and try again.'

'That's a real smart idea. They won't expect you to hit it twice in a row,' said Brady, nodding in approval.

They reached the bank of the river and tied up. As he stepped out of the boat, Gordon laid his hand on Bald Jack's shoulder. 'It was real white of ya to let me come along, and I won't forget it. You should look me up at the Black and Tan on Bleecker. That's my joint.'

'Sure thing, Gordie,' said Bald Jack, extending his hand.

As Gordon reached out to take it, Coogan and Brady grabbed him from behind and flung him face down into the river. They held him under, Cross watching in horror as the man struggled with all his might to free himself, arms and legs flailing, splashing against the dark water. After two agonising minutes, his body went completely still. Bald Jack watched impassively as Brady tugged the floating body by the back of the collar, gently guiding it into the fast-moving current. The black-and-grey form was carried away silently into the night.

'You bastards!' screamed Cross, his voice shattering the silence.

In a second, his own head was underwater. Gulping down what seemed like a gallon of river water, he felt hands forcing him down, down. He flailed his arms in panic.

Suddenly, he was released. He stumbled to the riverbank, coughing and gagging.

'It's late. Time to go home, Cross,' said Brady, watching him with impassive eyes.

CHAPTER TWENTY-TWO

'There's a fellow out front who wants to see you, Mr. Cross. Says he's your brother.'

Cross put down his pencil. He'd been working on a design for an office building on Broadway and Spring Street. Like his former master, H. H. Richardson, he would make a rough sketch of an idea and then hand it off to his assistants to refine and develop. But an avalanche of work had descended upon the office in the last month, and he was behind. He hadn't even started the design for the new orphan asylum up in Westchester.

When he did sit down to work, he couldn't keep his mind off of Gordon's body, floating away into the night. It wasn't so much the image of his corpse as the fact that Cross had watched him be murdered. Brady and Coogan had done it with such ease, such absolute lack of emotion. Still, Gordon's death had a positive side. It had almost completely erased his anxiety over getting caught for the Cook robbery – what was a little jail time when he could be dead?

Cross approached the office reception room slowly, trying to see if it really was his brother or one of Kent's men with a message. A week after the jailbreak, he'd received a call telling him he had a week to prepare the next job. Had Kent's men come early?

But no. Standing there was Robert, his older brother, someone he hadn't seen in years. Cross smiled when he saw how fit and well Robert looked. His full head of dark hair was showing some grey, but he still cut an imposing figure. Cross looked up to his older brother still, even though their father thought Robert a failure. He'd dropped out of Harvard after one year and drifted around the East Coast until the outbreak of the Civil War. He joined the Union Army, rising to the rank of captain and winning a medal at Gettysburg. His heroism had made Cross proud but at the same time ashamed for having sat out the war.

'Robert,' Cross cried, and every draftsman lifted his head and looked up. They embraced, and Cross found that he had tears in his eyes.

'You blackguard, I haven't seen you in three years,' Robert said. 'Before you start jabbering on about your architecture, tell me how Helen and the children are.'

'Fine, just fine. George graduated, Charlie's ten and constantly in motion, and Julia's about to make her debut.'

'Already? She was so little when I last saw her.'

'All grown up. Though she can't stand wearing a corset.'

'I can't wait to see them all. How's the beautiful Helen?'

'Running around like mad, preparing for Julia's coming-out ball.'

Robert checked his pocket watch. 'It's getting close to noon. Stop slaving away on those drawings and come out to lunch with me.'

'You're in luck. I'm meeting George at Delmonico's on Fourteenth Street for lunch. And you're coming too,' Cross said, almost giddy with happiness. 'He'll be surprised as hell to see you.'

Seeing his brother was the best medicine he could have

imagined. Growing up, Cross had adored his big brother, who always welcomed his company, unlike many older brothers who would tell their younger siblings to get lost. Robert was a far bigger influence in his life than his aloof father, often giving him advice on how to play baseball or ride a horse, how to avoid getting bullied by classmates at prep school, and on the best methods to woo the opposite sex. Robert had the knack of knowing when something was troubling his brother and would immediately offer counsel on how to deal with sadness, disappointment, or anger over a particular problem. It bothered Cross that they had drifted apart over the last few years.

As it was a beautiful August day, they decided to walk from Broadway and Grand Street up to the restaurant. Robert had always been a good listener, and now he asked his brother insightful questions about his business. Because they had time on their hands, he graciously asked if there were any of Cross's buildings nearby. There were, and the brothers took a detour toward a publishing company at Lafayette and Bond Streets.

'Damn, Johnny,' Robert said, staring up at the façade. 'I wish I had talent like yours. To figure out all that decoration on those arches? That's really something.'

Ever since he was a boy, Cross had loved his older brother's praise. This time, the words gave him pause – the admiration suddenly reminded him of Kent's.

'Does Aunt Caroline ever throw you work?' Robert asked with a sly smile.

'Lots of referrals, but no real Astor work.'

'Always keep on the old girl's good side, Johnny,' Robert said. 'Remember how she said I was acting common when she caught me smoking that cigar?'

'In her formal parlour! And you were ten,' Cross said, laughing.

144

They turned north onto Fifth Avenue. Before Cross could ask about his brother's life, Robert said, 'The thing I envy most about you is your family. Sometimes I wish I had one.'

'Nonsense. There's still time.'

'Not pushing fifty and in my line of work.'

'What are you doing now? Last I heard, you worked for the Remington Arms Company.'

'I'm a Pinkerton man.'

'Since when?'

'About two years ago. I ran into a man from my old regiment who was a Pinkerton. Said that with my military background, he could get me a job, and he did, in Buffalo. That's where I've been all this time. But they transferred me to New York last week.'

'Do you like the work?' To Cross, being a detective sounded exciting and romantic, though in recent years, the working classes had come to think of the Pinkertons as a ruthless mercenary army used to break strikes. But society people loved them, for they kept the commoners in their place.

'I've finally found my calling,' said Robert, nodding. He slapped his brother on the shoulder and resumed walking.

'And you're based in New York permanently?' Cross couldn't keep the excitement from his voice.

'Yes. I've been promoted to the main office. I'm staying at the Hotel Brunswick for now. Perhaps you can help me find an apartment?'

'Of course. That's wonderful, Rob. I can recommend a few places.'

'Wonderful. I've been assigned a very interesting case, you see. A rich fellow named Cook – of Cook Shoes, out of Saint Louis? Perhaps you've heard of him. Had his place on Fifth Avenue completely cleaned out a few weeks ago. Never seen so thorough a job. The criminals strangled an unfortunate servant girl who happened to be there. The police found her body in the river.'

Robert looked to his side, but Cross wasn't there. He turned and saw his brother, standing still as a statue in the middle of the pavement.

'What's wrong, Johnny?' Robert asked, alarmed.

At first, Cross didn't answer. He just stared off into space. His head was swimming; he thought he was going to faint.

Concerned, Robert walked up to him.

'I never saw anything about it in the papers,' Cross whispered, trying to pull himself together.

'Cook was embarrassed. He didn't want any publicity. That's why they called us in.'

'Any leads?'

'Not one. Come on, I'm starving. I could eat a bear.'

This would be the first time since the graduation party that he'd seen George – and the first time since he'd found out about his debt. Despite his anguish regarding his son's secret life, Cross had been looking forward to it. His anger towards his son had diminished, and he was slowly beginning to forgive him. *A son's faults are the father's faults*, he kept reminding himself. And every time he thought of leaving Kent, he saw his son's corpse.

But Kent's warnings about his son's 'weakness' haunted him. Although Cross was closer to his son than most society fathers, a wide gulf still yawned between them. Though he might wish it otherwise, and while he desperately wanted to believe George was staying out of trouble, he really had no idea if the boy had kept gambling.

Down deep, he didn't want to know. The thought terrified him. He pushed it away, viciously sublimating it. *Like Aunt*

Caroline, he thought grimly. *Always ignoring anything unpleasant.*

So, after all these weeks, the sight of George did not brighten Cross's spirits. The news his brother had delivered crushed him; his mind reeled. While his son and brother chattered away, he kept thinking of the girl's body, floating in the water. Just like Gordon.

Had she been like Colleen, the Crosses' servant girl? Pretty and sweet-natured, straight off the boat from Ireland? Girls like that spent their entire lives bent over washtubs and ironing boards, but incredibly, they still had a cheerful outlook on life. They were happy just to be in America. Cross thought back to that night in the carriage, watching Brady play with the length of piano wire. It wasn't a nervous affectation.

Cross hadn't touched his terrapin soup or the lamb chops. He swallowed hard and looked over at George, laughing and happy.

'John . . . John. Are you still with us, old man?' Robert asked.

Cross snapped out of his trance. 'Why yes, yes, of course. What were you talking about?'

'That it's incredible George played in the Polo Grounds in front of all those people.'

'He's too modest to tell you he hit the game-winning home run against Yale.'

'Damn, I wish I could've seen that. And against those bastards from Yale too!'

But as Cross watched them speak and exchange easy smiles, his whole feeling towards his son shifted with the abruptness of a switch being thrown. He'd been fooling himself all this time. His family's calamity was the result of George's foolishness. Cross stared at his son, the brilliant Harvard academic scholar. It was all a façade, shielding a terrible secret. At that moment, there was not a shred of fatherly love in him. He felt like reaching across the table and throttling George. A father wasn't supposed to hate his own

147

son. Cross hated *himself* for feeling this way, but he couldn't help it. He averted his eyes.

'Now that I live in New York,' Robert was saying, 'we can go to the Polo Grounds to see the Giants.'

'Charlie's going to love that,' said George.

'Robert,' said Cross. His voice was unusually loud and halted the conversation. 'Please come to dinner tomorrow night to meet the rest of the family. George, I hope you can make it.'

'I'm sorry, Father. I've made plans.'

Cross glared at his son. An uneasy silence fell upon the table. A waiter came to take dessert orders and serve the coffee and brandy. Robert tried to resurrect the conversation, to no avail. After Cross saw his brother off in a carriage, he hailed one for himself.

'I'll drop you off uptown, George.'

'I wasn't heading that way, but—'

'Get in,' Cross snapped.

They sat in silence as the horses clip-clopped up Fifth Avenue. Progress through the morass of afternoon traffic was slow. As he stared at his son, anger built up within Cross like red-hot magma in the throat of a volcano. He took a deep breath and turned his head to look at the stream of pedestrians on the pavement. Not one of them, he thought, could have as great a burden as the one he shouldered at that moment.

'So you have plans for tomorrow. Do they involve numbers?'

'No, Father. I don't have to teach.'

'What about numbers on playing cards? The five of diamonds, the three of spades?'

Cross saw the puzzled look on George's face change to panic. His son shifted his body uncomfortably on the leather bench seat of the carriage.

'Even as a child, you had an affinity for numbers. You could do

148

the most complicated puzzles, add large sums in your head. I was so damn proud of you. I knew you'd become a scholar – and you did.' Cross spoke without looking at George. His gaze was fixed on the passing shopfronts along the street.

'Yes, I was always fascinated by numbers,' George said, his eyes full of worry and suspicion.

'I suppose there's one number that's of particular fascination – forty-eight thousand.'

For a second, Cross thought George would throw open the carriage door and bolt. But the boy froze in his seat and looked his father straight in the eye.

'I have a gambling debt of forty-eight thousand dollars,' he said in a loud, clear voice.

Instead of exploding in anger, Cross was actually pleased by his son's candour. He could tell George was shaken down to his boots, but he was fighting hard to put up a brave front. It was impressive.

'You *did* have a gambling debt of forty-eight thousand dollars. I paid it. Mr Kent and I have reached an agreement that ensures no harm will come to you.'

George's brave façade crumbled. His hands covered his face. He bent over as though the shame had punched him in the stomach.

'No one in the family knows of this – and they never will.'

Still bent double, George began to sob. 'I'm so sorry, Father. I—'

'I don't understand how you got mixed up in this. You're an adult, and I respect that. I would not attempt to meddle in your personal life. But you can never gamble again, George. It's over. It has to be!'

George looked up at his father. 'Thank you so much,' he said in a trembling voice. 'You don't know how grateful I am. I'm so sorry for what I've done to you.'

Cross could see the shame and embarrassment breaking his son in two. It was painful to watch, but he had no intention of letting up. 'It's what you've done to *yourself*. You don't know how close you came to destroying your life – and your family's. You have a brilliant academic career ahead of you, George. I won't allow you to throw that away. We'll put this behind us, but I *forbid* you to gamble again. You must promise me, son.'

'Yes, yes. Of course. I know what I did was foolish. I swear to you, it won't happen again. I swear.'

When the carriage reached the corner of Fifty-Ninth Street and Fifth Avenue, George reached over and hugged his father, pulling him close. Cross embraced his son, tears filling his eyes. He didn't want to let him go. It was like George was six years old again. He wanted to hold him, to protect him from all the bad things in life.

As George walked away, he turned and waved to his father. Cross's anger towards his son vanished. He loved George with all his heart. He would do anything to save him.

George walked to the north side of the street and into Central Park. Running off the stone path, he stumbled into the undergrowth, fell to his knees, and threw up his lunch. His head was spinning. He turned onto his back, looking up through the canopy of trees at the cloudless sky.

His worst fear had been realised – his father had discovered his secret. He wished Kent had killed him that night in the power plant. The shame and humiliation of what had happened ate away at George's insides like a horrible pain, the likes of which he'd never felt in his life. In their world, fathers and sons weren't supposed to be close, but George and his father were, which made the revelation all the more unbearable.

He was lucky, George knew. A tyrannical father would have

exposed him and cast him out of the family forever. Instead, his father had forgiven him. He was even giving him another chance – as long as he gave up gambling.

George wanted to keep his promise with all his heart, but he knew it was almost impossible. There was an illness inside him. He hadn't attempted to explain that to his father in the carriage; he knew people didn't understand, that they thought gambling a moral failing. But it was a sickness, he thought wildly, one that caused men and women to destroy themselves like a drunk or drug addict would. He didn't know if he had the strength to withstand it.

Where did my father get forty-eight thousand dollars? he wondered, staring up at the trees. His first thought was Aunt Caroline, but he knew his father could never go to her; such a request would have meant certain expulsion from her world. Did his father borrow from friends or clients, sell the house on Madison, or even place a bet? The amount was easily three years of his income as an architect.

Wherever he'd gotten the money, George swore he'd pay him back – after he wiped out the nine thousand he still owed.

CHAPTER TWENTY-THREE

'Charlie, meet my friend, Injun Sam Kelly.'

Charlie, who had never met an Indian, stared at the boy, looking for some trace of Indian blood. But he seemed to be completely white, a pale, blonde-haired boy of about eight. He wore a man's plaid shirt that hung past his knees.

'Glad to know ya, Charlie. Call me Sam.'

'So what have ya been up to?' Eddie asked the boy.

'Doin' lookout work for the Whyos,' Sam said, voice brimming with pride.

'The Whyos are the toughest gang in town, next to Kent's Gents,' Eddie told Charlie. 'When they're robbing a shop at night, Sam here keeps an eye out for the cops.'

'Also been robbin' Protestant churches.' As an aside to Charlie, Sam said, 'We're all Irish down here, so we hate Protestants.'

'That's way better than what you used to do – pretending to be the kid of that wop organ grinder on Mulberry and gathering up the pennies people threw at him,' Eddie said, smiling at the memory.

Sam rolled his eyes – then lit up with an idea. 'Say, I know a warehouse at the end of Grand where there's boxes full of bridles and horse stuff. We can get in real easy. What d'ya say? We sell it and split it three ways.'

'Later. Charlie and me's goin' uptown to do a little wranglin'.'

Carrying a large canvas US Post Office mailbag and a wooden truncheon, Eddie led Charlie along Twelfth Avenue. Charlie had freed up his whole afternoon by telling his parents he'd be at dancing class. Last Thursday, he'd supposedly attended drawing lessons. Charlie's new-found interest in the arts had delighted his parents. Praising his enthusiasm, they'd given him money – which Charlie had promptly pocketed for other ventures. *Science classes at the Museum of Natural History will be next*, he thought, smiling.

'It's coming up on the right. All these places along the docks are good huntin',' Eddie said with an air of authority. 'But I've had the best luck here.'

They stopped in front of an abandoned four-storey brick warehouse, once used to store cargo unloaded from the ships that docked across the street. Eddie pointed to the arched entry that no longer had a door, and they entered. Inside was an open space, the planked floor completely covered with debris and broken glass. The tall windows allowed enough daylight for the boys to see their way around.

Eddie positioned Charlie near the rear wall and handed him the club. 'When I tell you, start banging this club like crazy all over the floor,' he whispered.

Eddie walked to a door in the rear wall and out into a tiny yard. Near the corner of the building, a small basement window with missing glass stood open. Spreading the mailbag wide, he covered the entire opening. 'Start banging!'

At the signal, Charlie began to pummel the floor with the club. The sound was like pistol reports, echoing throughout the building.

Eddie heard the scurrying of tiny feet and high-pitched squeaking from the basement below. Then objects started hurling themselves into the bag from the window opening with great velocity, as if someone was throwing rocks.

The bag filled up fast, until it looked like a single, vibrating mass.

'Stop!' Eddie yelled. He yanked the bag to an upright position and pulled the drawstrings tight. Dozens of grey rats with long, pink tails raced past his feet into the yard.

Club in hand, Charlie ran to the back. 'There must be a hundred in there,' he said, delighted.

'I dunno. I sure as hell ain't putting my hand in to count 'em. Rat bites hurt like hell, and you can get rabies from 'em. Start foaming at the mouth like a mad dog.'

Eddie tied the drawstrings around the neck of the bag, ensuring there would be no escapees. The bag was pulsating with rats, struggling in a mad frenzy. He took the club from Charlie and started beating on the canvas. 'That'll keep 'em in line,' he said.

The boys took hold of the bag and dragged it through the warehouse and on to the pavement.

'We don't have far to go. The place is just a few blocks up, on West Twenty-Seventh,' he said.

'How much do you think we'll get?' Charlie asked eagerly.

'The going rate is twelve cents a head, and I ain't gonna take a penny less.'

Taking a rest every block, the boys finally made it to a saloon whose front was painted a bright blue. They dragged the bag through an alley on the left-hand side to a rear yard.

'Wait here, and I'll get Nardello.'

Eddie eventually returned with a lean, swarthy man who had greasy black hair. 'Put 'em in the corral for the count,' he ordered.

At the rear of the yard was a walled enclosure of wood boards almost four feet high. At the bottom was a sliding panel, which Nardello opened with his foot.

'All right, let 'em out.'

Eddie untied the drawstrings, shoved the bag into the opening, and kicked the rear until every rat was out.

'Eleven cents a head.'

'Fuck you and the horse you came in on. Twelve, you dago bastard. Look at the quality there. Nice and fast,' Eddie yelled.

Charlie gaped at him. He had never seen a child talk to an adult in such a manner.

'Twelve, then. So I can get rid of your ass.'

Eddie hung over the top of the wall and began counting with his index figure, jabbing at the air.

Nardello did as well.

'I got forty-eight,' said Nardello.

'I got fifty-three,' snapped Eddie.

'Fifty, then,' Nardello said. Eddie nodded.

The man counted six one-dollar bills into Eddie's palm, and the boys exchanged triumphant smiles.

'We're about to start. If you want to watch, I'll let you in for free,' Nardello said.

'Nah, we gotta get downtown to get our papers,' Eddie said, placing three dollars in Charlie's hand.

As Charlie and Eddie came out of the alley, Julia and Nolan entered through the front door of the saloon.

CHAPTER TWENTY-FOUR

George hated cooking for himself. His bachelor apartment on West Fifty-Ninth Street had a small kitchen off the parlour, but he rarely set foot in it. If Kitty didn't fix him a meal at her place, he'd eat in a restaurant or buy a sandwich. He could always go home to eat – his mother begged him constantly to come for dinner – but that would mean facing his father, and he just couldn't bring himself to do it. He'd thought the shame would diminish with time, but it had increased instead. Over and over, he relived the confrontation with his father. He felt physically sick every time he thought of it.

He loved his father more than anything. John Cross had spent many hours talking and playing with him. He was always there to help George when he was troubled. Although he was busy with his architectural practice, he never used it as an excuse not to spend time with his son. He was like that with Julia and Charlie too. All three children had a close bond with their parents, unlike most of George's friends, whose nannies were more like their mothers.

Dodging his father meant not seeing his brother or sister, and this, too, gave George a profound feeling of emptiness. He enjoyed discussing literature with Julia and baseball with Charlie. He'd promised to take his little brother to the Polo Grounds to see a

Giants game this summer, and he wasn't going to let him down. He resolved to call him when he got home.

The question of where his father had found forty-eight thousand dollars to pay his debt was also deeply troubling. This weighed on George, a mystery he couldn't solve. His determination to repay his father had become all consuming – and this intensified his gambling sickness. But he kept losing.

'Why, George Cross, haven't seen you in a coon's age. How's my Harvard man?' a voice behind him called out.

George spun around to face Jack Bacon, a collector for Turk Holden, who owned the Silver Slipper gambling den on Houston Street.

'Good to see you, Jack,' said George, resisting the overpowering impulse to start running in the other direction. 'What are you doing in this neighbourhood?'

'Just conducting a little business for Holden,' the broad-chested thug replied. 'You know, Georgie, why don't you come with me? You might find it fun.'

'Well, Jack, I was just . . .'

'It'll only take a few minutes. Come on, old boy, keep me company,' he said in a cheerful tone.

Jack took hold of George's elbow and steered him along Fifty-Sixth Street. While they walked, Jack chattered on about baseball and how well Brooklyn was doing, rattling off the season's statistics and scores. He led George to a well-to-do apartment house. On the fifth floor, Jack knocked on a door.

A well-dressed, middle-aged woman answered. A look of sheer terror convulsed her face when she saw Jack.

'Good afternoon, Mrs Todd. Is William about?' he asked in the politest of voices.

'No, I'm sorry. He . . .'

Jack placed his shovel-sized hand in the centre of the woman's forehead and shoved her violently to the floor. He walked through the doorway, turned, and beckoned George to follow him, smiling broadly.

The apartment was well furnished. The spacious parlour had a grand round table in the centre, adorned with ornaments and a sculpture. Jack deliberately walked into it, sending it crashing to the ground. The woman cried out.

'Oops. So clumsy of me. My apologies.' Still smiling, he reached over and pulled a glass-fronted bookcase forward. It hit the floor with a resounding crash. While the woman wailed, Jack went from room to room in the apartment, looking under beds and in closets. George followed behind, unsure what else to do.

Sitting deep in the rear of the kitchen pantry, Jack found a paunchy, bald man of about fifty.

'So good to see you again, William,' Jack said, yanking the man out by his ankle.

'I'll have something for you tomorrow, I swear! I swear!' William screamed.

Jack kicked the man full in the face, if he were punting a football. Then he kicked him repeatedly in the stomach while William's wife screamed continuously from the front parlour. Pulling William upright, Jack leant him against the kitchen wall and pummelled his face until blood splattered in all directions. William screamed for mercy, reaching desperately into his pockets to produce some money, but Jack was unmoved. He started working on his midsection.

Pressed hard against the opposite wall, George stood cringing at the sight.

Mrs Todd came rushing into the kitchen to intervene, but as she approached Jack, he swung out his left arm and swatted her to the polished wooden floor with no more effort than he would have taken to strike a fly.

Growing tired of the effort, he let go of William, who slumped to the floor, and looked around the kitchen. Taking a knife from the kitchen counter, Jack placed the blade inside William's left nostril and flicked up. Blood gushed like a geyser. Jack stood over him, viewing his handiwork, then shook his head and cut the other nostril. Satisfied, he kicked William hard in the groin as a parting gesture.

'I'm coming back tomorrow, and you better have my six hundred dollars, William. If you don't, I'm going to have to hurt you,' Jack said over his shoulder as he walked towards the door. To the right of the entrance, an expensive-looking vase sat on a console table. Jack grabbed it and smashed it against the wall.

At the door, George stopped and turned to view the carnage. Husband and wife were screaming in agony; blood covered the kitchen floor. It looked as though someone had slopped a bucket of red paint from one end of the room to the other. George felt faint. He steadied himself against the foyer wall, trying to breathe. An instant later, he started violently as Jack slapped his paw on his shoulder, guiding him down the iron and stone stairs.

'Now, like I was sayin', Jeffries of Brooklyn is just as good a player as anyone the Giants got.'

CHAPTER TWENTY-FIVE

Cross didn't want to go to the Lees' dinner party, but he and Helen had already accepted the invitation. A popular saying held that if a man who had accepted a dinner invitation died, his executor had to take his place.

Handwritten invitations on thick, white vellum arrived a full three weeks before the event. At the same time, flowers had been ordered, a French chef had chosen the menu, and Mrs Lee had purchased a new silver service. Society parties were expected to be a show of magnificent ostentation, and the hostesses never failed to live up to this obligation.

The Crosses' carriage pulled up to the Lee mansion the customary thirty minutes prior to the eight o'clock meal time. Located on the corner of Fifth Avenue and Sixty-First Street, the house was a wide, four-storey, French Empire model with an English basement. *A dull, uninspired design*, Cross thought. Footmen outfitted in black-and-gold livery stood by the red carpet that ran from the kerb to the front door, opening the carriage doors and bowing to the guests, all of whom were dressed the same: men in white tie and tails, women in light summer evening gowns with long gloves. Honoria Lee, a middle-aged woman whose beauty had barely faded over the years, stood in the gilt-panelled reception hall, greeting her guests.

'Helen, how beautiful you look,' she gushed. It pleased Cross that instead of his wife having to flatter, she was always flattered herself. 'And, John. So lovely to see you. Go and see who you're escorting.'

Cross walked to a table where small white envelopes inscribed with the names of the gentlemen guests were arranged. Locating his, he opened it to find a card: Elizabeth Burnham. The wife of an insurance company owner, she was beautiful, with raven hair and piercing blue eyes, but exceedingly insipid and dull. It would be like talking to a rock all evening. Still, in society, beauty excused a great many failings. And it was bad form for a gentleman to complain about his escort. Cross strolled into the drawing room, a palatial space adorned with Chinese vases full of red roses, mahogany panelling, a white marble floor, and a sparkling crystal chandelier.

A crowd had assembled around the Tarletons, the guests of honour, who had recently arrived from London. Everyone in Cross's set was a rabid Anglophile, loving every intricacy of British aristocratic life, from cricket to pheasant shooting to tweed suits. Sir Henry was regaling the crowd with descriptions of the renovation to Castle Twickham, his ancestral home. Tarleton, John understood, was one of the few British elites who still had a substantial fortune. Many British lords had seen their riches frittered away by prior generations and had had to sink to the humiliating state of marrying young American heiresses – 'dollar princesses', the press called them – who might rejuvenate their fortunes and save their estates.

Sir Henry and his plump wife, Deidre, were basking in the glow of New York society's admiration. They interrupted their boasting to meet Helen, with whom the couple was immediately captivated.

On the outskirts, Cross milled about, nodding to people he knew, paying compliments to ladies, and conducting an informal architectural survey of the house. He enjoyed appraising the proportions, detailing, and finishes of all the houses he was invited into.

He felt a tap on his shoulder, and there was Stanford White.

'Hello, Stanny. I knew you'd be here. You did their place in Newport, I recall?'

'Oh yes. And I never turn down a good meal,' White said, patting his belly. It had grown considerably since the two men had worked together at H. H. Richardson's office.

'What are you currently working on?' Cross asked.

'Christ, I just came from Columbia Bank, a job I did on Fifth Avenue and Forty-Second. They want alterations to the banking hall. Idiots. It's fine the way it is.'

Cross nodded. All of White's buildings were special. Though he envied his friend's incredible talent, he had long ago acknowledged that he could never surpass him as a designer. The bank building was unique and original – all Stanny's work was. Done in the Classical Revival style, it had a pair of balconies covered by flat roofs and supported by slender Ionic columns, which gave the big building a wonderful sense of lightness.

'Where'd you put the vault?'

'They wanted it in a sub-basement. That's where the safety deposit boxes are.'

'Is the vault all steel or encased in cement?'

'Steel.'

'Did you put in one of those new alarm systems?'

'It's just an electric line connecting to a police precinct. Why? You got a bank project?'

'Ah, yes . . . I'm looking into any new vault systems,' Cross said.

He added in a low voice, 'Maybe I could look at your drawings?'

Avery Lee, their host, approached. Beside him was a man sporting a magnificent waxed moustache.

'Gentlemen, this is Count Sergei Aleksandrov, of the court of the Czar in Saint Petersburg. I'm privileged to have him as my house guest.'

Both men bowed, impressed by the man's aristocratic bearing. The count was the very model of what an aristocrat should look like – very tall, lean, and strikingly handsome.

'Count, these are two of New York's finest architects. Perhaps they might design a home for your visits to America?'

'That would be wonderful. Much more pleasurable than imposing on friends or living in a hotel,' the count said in perfect but heavily accented English. Bowing, he excused himself.

'Stanny, John, have you heard about these robberies in the city?' Lee growled as soon as the count was out of earshot. 'It's unbelievable. A whole mansion cleaned out! Where the hell are the police?'

Cross stared down at the polished marble floor.

'What do you make of it, Mr Cross?' Lee asked.

A butler called out, 'Madame, dinner is served,' saving Cross from having to answer. He and the other men in the room scurried about like mice, looking for the women they had been assigned to escort. As per strict custom, Mr Lee led the way into the dining room with Lady Tarleton. The rest of the guests followed, with Mrs Lee and Sir Henry entering last. On the dinner table sat twenty-four place cards, arranged to ensure that husbands and wives were well separated and that the guest of honour, Sir Henry, sat to Mrs Lee's right.

Cross thought the table impressive, even by New York standards. Down its centre and raised a few inches above the white embroidered damask tablecloth was a continuous sheet of plate glass. Beneath it, dozens of tiny electric lights glowed, giving the cut-glass bowls of carnations spaced every three feet a magical aura. Each seat had a setting of Sèvres china, laid with ten pieces of engraved silver from Gorham that included a fork for oysters, a fork for fruit, and separate knives for bread, fish, and meat. Five different kinds of glasses for the sparkling water, wines, champagne, hock, and claret flanked the setting.

Cross pulled out a chair for Mrs Burnham and then seated himself, unfolding his napkin, which held a dinner roll. Next to his plate was the usual small party favour – tonight, a silver cigarette case. His dinner companion found a jewelled brooch. Cross examined the handwritten menu, inscribed on gilt-edged vellum. Chesapeake Bay oysters on the half shell to start, chicken consommé a l'Italienne, Spanish mackerel á la Maître d'Hôtel served with hock, soft shell crab farcies with Johannisberger sparkling wine, and perdrix aux truffes. Honoria always put forth a good spread. French chefs were more prized than jewels in New York society, and the Lees had one of the finest. Everything was cooked at home instead of catered, which made a vast difference in quality.

Cross set about engaging Mrs Burnham in conversation. He decided to set the bar high and work down to banalities about the weather.

'Do you think Parliament will grant home rule to Ireland, Mrs Burnham?'

'I . . . wouldn't really know, Mr Cross.'

A footman appeared at his left with a plate of oysters. All dinner parties were served à la russe. The footmen stood by the side of each guest, offering him or her each course instead of passing platters of food on the table, à *la française*. Without the clutter of multiple dishes, society dinners could boast elaborate centrepieces of the sort on Honoria's table.

Cross changed tactics and tried something he knew was closer to Mrs Burnham's heart.

'Tell me, Mrs Burnham. Which do you feel are superior – gowns from Worth or gowns from Pingat?'

She lit up at the question. 'Worth, Mr Cross, always Worth. In fact, I just received a trunk last week. We had visited the showroom in Paris in the spring to place the order, and I tell you, Mr Cross, we weren't disappointed.'

'That gown looks magnificent on you.' The expected response.

Mrs Burnham blushed. For the next twenty minutes, she spoke enthusiastically about her clothes, only stopping to offer an aside about how handsome Count Aleksandrov was.

The white-gloved footmen continued to serve the food and pour the alcoholic beverages. Finally, desserts of pudding, ices, Bavarian creams, petits fours, and glacés aux marrons were offered, along with a fruit-and-cheese course. By this time, Cross had given up trying to engage Mrs Burnham in conversation and had begun talking to Marmaduke Scott, who sat across the table.

Scott had made a fortune importing beef from the West in the new refrigerated railroad cars. Cross hoped the conversation would swing to possible architectural commissions, like a summer place in the Berkshires, where it was much cooler. These dinners were often a gold mine for new jobs. But Scott was in a foul mood.

'It took an hour to go four blocks in my carriage on Broadway this morning,' he growled, wolfing down strawberries drenched in sweet wine. 'Four blocks. Traffic crawled like a slug, I tell you. It's damn impossible to get anywhere in New York.'

'And the dust and the manure is shocking,' Mrs Burnham said.

'They said the elevated trains would reduce traffic by half. What a lot of nonsense. Traffic is ten times worse. We need new ways of travelling. Perhaps under the ground.'

'Exactly,' Mrs Burnham said. 'Years ago, I remember my father taking me for a ride on Mr Beach's underground railway on Broadway. It was so wonderful. Such a shame it went bankrupt.'

Cross's eyes widened, and the spoonful of Bavarian cream that was about to enter his mouth stopped in mid-air. Setting down his gold dessert spoon, he turned to Mrs Burnham and smiled.

'Elizabeth Burnham, you are an amazing, magnificent creature.'

CHAPTER TWENTY-SIX

'I assume this must be urgent, as you've summoned me down here at 2 a.m.' Kent was in evening dress and top hat, his expression frosty.

'I'm glad I didn't get you out of bed,' Cross said. He'd made the call when the gentlemen at the Lees' party had retired to the smoking room for brandy and cigars.

Kent frowned. 'Millicent and I had just walked in the door from a dinner party at Sherry's – very tired, mind you – when you called.'

They were standing in the shadows of the huge U.S. Post Office, south of City Hall on the east side of Broadway. There was barely a breeze, but the night air felt good after the hot day.

'I designed Fidelity National across the street,' Cross said, pointing to a narrow, six-storey brick building, its huge, arched entry supported by polished granite columns.

'A very handsome bank, I'm sure. But unfortunately, I experienced a recent mishap robbing a bank in the daytime,' Kent said. 'It's made me cautious.'

'It was you who tried to blow the vault at Manhattan Merchants & Trust,' Cross said, shocked in spite of himself.

'With very poor results. Houses of society people are more lucrative – and less of a risk.'

'Suppose you robbed a bank over a weekend.'

'Please continue, Mr Cross.'

'Back in '70, a man named Alfred Beach, the editor of *Scientific American*, had a new idea for public transportation. His train travelled not aboveground, but below,' Cross said.

'I remember. He built an experimental underground tunnel with his own money so the Tweed Ring wouldn't find out.'

'For an underground pneumatic railway, propelled by blasts of compressed air.'

'Where was it?'

Cross pointed directly in front of them, at Broadway. 'There. In front of my bank.'

Kent walked to the kerb and looked down at the cobblestone street. It was brightly illuminated by the electric street lights.

'It's a ten-foot-wide, brick-lined tunnel that went one block, along Broadway from Murray Street on your left to Warren Street on your right. After the panic in '73, Beach couldn't get financing to continue it and went bust. He rented the thing out as a wine cellar and shooting gallery. Then he gave up and sealed it in '74.'

'So it's still down there,' Kent said with a smile.

'There's a sealed plate around the corner on Warren Street where the entrance was. Come on.'

At this hour, Cross thought they'd be alone, but the area was thick with streetwalkers. They walked to the west side of Broadway and past the bank.

'Where's the vault?' Kent asked.

'In the basement towards the front of the building – in line with the bottom of the tunnel.'

As they walked, the whores called out in low voices, 'Fifty cents, fifty cents for a fine time.' Most of the women were poorly dressed hags. Drink, opium, and violence had eaten away any trace of beauty they'd once possessed. But their vulgarity and coarseness were what most offended Cross. New York had a strict hierarchy of whoredom, from the first-class parlour houses in the West Twenties to the streetwalkers at Broadway and Twenty-Fourth, who almost resembled fashionable ladies and brought their clients to respectable quarters to transact business. Then there were these disgusting creatures at the bottom. Only the most depraved and desperate were out this late.

A gap-toothed wench in a torn and soiled dress brazenly confronted Kent.

'Fifty cents for a handsome gentleman like you. What do you say?' she croaked.

With astonishing speed and viciousness, Kent struck her on the head with his cane. She dropped to the pavement, crying out in pain. Kent grabbed the gold head of the cane, pulling out a long blade, and held it against her throat. 'Stay away from me, you filthy bitch,' he snarled.

Wide-eyed and shaking with fright, the whore crawled away from him, holding the side of her head.

Kent sheathed the blade and continued walking. 'How wide did you say the tunnel was?' he asked. He spoke casually, as though he'd just shooed away a gnat.

'Not more than ten feet in diameter. There was only one set of tracks. The air blew the train in one direction and then sucked it back.'

Turning the corner at Warren Street, they saw the iron plate set in the street. Kent bent and poked at it with his cane. 'You're right. This is likely where the station was.'

Rising, he walked quickly around the corner back to Broadway. This time, the whores who saw him coming gave him a wide berth. Kent stopped in front of the bank and smiled at Cross, rubbing the head of his cane with his white-gloved fingers.

'Yes, Mr Cross, this has great possibilities. I must look into it more closely. Preparation, preparation, preparation. As always, the key to this game of ours. You'll be hearing from me.' He turned to leave.

'Kent.'

Kent stopped.

Cross walked up to him, closer, and closer again. Their faces were six inches apart. 'Fidelity National handles big accounts. Edison Electric, Atlantic & Pacific Steamship, B. Altman. The owners were on the bank board that hired me, so I know. There's a good bit of money in there.'

'And I'm sure it'll go far in reducing your son's debt. Goodnight, Mr Cross.'

Honoria Lee laid her head on Count Aleksandrov's shoulder, toying with the soft hair on his chest. 'Sergei, you're wonderful,' she cooed.

'And you, my love, are more passionate than any woman in Saint Petersburg.'

'I have everything in life a woman would want – money, houses, clothes – except passion,' Mrs Lee said forlornly.

'A woman of your quality needs passion, every night.'

'Ha. Avery Lee knows what a six per cent return on a Pennsylvania Railroad bond will bring, but he knows nothing about passion.'

Aleksandrov laughed. 'Mr Lee is a good provider. That's what matters most.'

'Oh, I suppose.' Mrs Lee raised herself up to look at the clock on the fireplace mantel. 'It's almost 5 a.m., my dear. You must get back to your room before the servants are about.'

Aleksandrov kissed her on the cheek and rose from the bed,

reaching for his robe. He opened the bedroom door a crack to check the hallway, waved, and was gone.

The electric lights were off in the long carpeted corridor, but daylight was creeping in through the windows. Aleksandrov stopped at a door and opened it. Before going in, he took off his leather slippers.

From their breathing, he could tell the Tartletons were sleeping soundly. The guests of honour were housed in a magnificent room with an adjoining sitting parlour. Aleksandrov smiled at the sight of the couple. They probably hadn't slept in the same bed in years, but their hosts had been afraid of offending them by providing separate rooms.

Aleksandrov crept silently to the dresser where Sir Henry's handsome leather wallet sat. Opening it, he found several hundred American dollars, of which he borrowed three-quarters. Rich men like this never kept track of their cash. He spotted the lady's dressing table and quietly slid open the drawers until he found Lady Deidre's jewel case. With an expert's eye, he laid aside the choicest piece, an emerald-and-pearl necklace, and slipped a small ruby brooch inset with tiny diamonds into the pocket of his robe.

Smiling, Aleksandrov left the bedroom.

CHAPTER TWENTY-SEVEN

'On arriving at the ball, the guests will find you standing on your mother's right. She will do the introducing. Then you will dance the German with the gentleman *she* selects to lead.'

'Yes, Granny.'

Julia and Granny were walking along Broadway together. They would always be together from this point on, for Julia's coming-out meant that she needed a chaperone. And, to her horror, her mother had designated Granny, not a maiden aunt, for this grave responsibility. Granny had taken up her duties with an enthusiasm bordering on mania. Her granddaughter's well-being and social worth were at stake; the task was not to be left to an amateur.

'A chaperone is the guardian angel of a well-bred girl,' Granny declared. 'She must always be by her side.'

Julia had a very difficult time concealing her anguish.

A widow in her seventies, Granny lived alone in a three-storey brownstone house overlooking Madison Square. It was the heart of what Julia called Knickerbocker Land. When she wasn't at the Cross house interfering in the family's lives, Granny spent her days sitting at the tall window in the front parlour, surrounded by at least a dozen cats, watching the world go by. It was like staring at an aquarium, a source of constant fascination for her.

This morning, Julia had told her mother she was to meet Lavinia Stewart on West Thirty-Second Street to look at a crystal punch bowl at Fernbach's. This wasn't quite true. First, she had an appointment with John Nolan. Then she would see the punch bowl. Granny's accompaniment threw her plans into disarray. There was no possible way of getting rid of her.

'Above all,' Granny said, 'never paint your cheeks. Complexion comes from within.'

'I promise I won't.'

They passed shopfronts stocked with every kind of product, protected from the hot August sun by striped awnings. The streets brimmed with the usual flood of carriages, horse-drawn trolleys, and wagons. The stench of horse manure and urine was particularly pungent for so early in the day.

'It is perfectly correct for you to refuse an offer of a dance with a man, but you *must* then sit that dance out. Never accept another offer for the same dance. It *just* isn't done.'

Julia ignored that, as she'd done for all the advice she'd been given for the last eight blocks, consumed by the question of what to do about her rendezvous with Nolan. Reluctant to stand him up, she decided to steer her grandmother in the right direction and then improvise.

'Granny, let's turn at Thirtieth. I want to see something in a shop window.'

This didn't interrupt Granny's discourse in the least. She continued to lecture on about taking cold baths every morning. Julia saw a hat shop window on the north-west corner of Sixth Street under the elevated railroad and crossed the street. Above, a train thundered past, and Granny stopped talking for almost ten seconds. She had never ridden on an elevated train and she never would, she exclaimed when it was gone. They threaded their way through the crowds to the shop, and Julia pretended to be interested in its wares, sweeping the streets with her eyes.

'Excuse me, ma'am. I believe you dropped this.' A young man handed Granny her rose-coloured velvet purse with a smile.

'My goodness, yes,' Granny exclaimed, bewildered. 'I can't understand how I lost it. It was tucked in my handbag.'

'Why, Mr Nolan, how good to see you again,' Julia said cheerfully.

Confused, Granny turned her head from Julia to Nolan and back to Julia. 'You know this man, Julia?' It was her sworn duty to keep Julia from making improper acquaintances.

'Of course. You remember the Nolans on East Twenty-Sixth Street. Very close friends with the Roosevelts,' Julia said with a big smile, shooting a wink at Nolan. 'Their son, Theodore, is going to run for mayor.'

Once Granny heard a familiar Knickerbocker name like Roosevelt, she began to calm down.

'Young John here was with me at Doddsworth Dancing Academy. In fact, that's where you met him, Granny. You said that you'd never seen a young boy dance a more elegant German. You must remember.'

Granny looked at the boy. Julia knew she was thinking that he *was* quite handsome and well dressed.

'Thank you so much, Mr Nolan. You came around at exactly the right time. There were four hundred dollars in that little purse,' Granny said in a surprisingly friendly voice.

Julia saw Nolan frown. 'Mr Nolan, this is my grandmother, Mrs Arabella Rutherford.'

Recovering, he shook Granny's hand. 'A great pleasure, ma'am.'

'We're just doing some shopping,' said Julia.

174

'For Miss Cross's coming-out ball,' Granny added proudly.

'A ball for Miss Cross? How nice. Please, let me escort you. So many wonderful things to buy in this district. It would be an honour to carry your parcels.'

'Indeed, yes, I love to shop here,' Granny gushed. Julia could see she was falling for Nolan's charm and good looks.

'What's your favourite thing in the world, Mrs Rutherford? Something you don't have enough of, I mean?'

'Cats.'

'You're a cat lover! So am I,' Nolan said. 'It just so happens that I know where there's the most incredible collection of cats – and all for sale.'

'Really?' There was obvious pleasure in Granny's voice. Without any children left in her house, cats had become her surrogates, offering endless unconditional love. She'd had scores of them over the years and lavished attention on them. It was such a paradox to Julia: Granny, so rock hard and uncompromising in her feelings toward humans, was so loving and affectionate to her cats. In her will, her surviving animals were due a sizable bequest. Her cats would have a higher yearly income than ninety-nine per cent of New York.

'The place is just on the next block, on Thirty-First Street. Would you like to see?'

'Oh, yes.'

'Tell me more about the plans for Miss Cross's ball.'

As they walked, Granny rattled off the details, down to the pattern on the Dresden china settings. Nolan listened with great curiosity, peppering her with questions. They stopped in front of an ordinary-looking brownstone building, and Nolan led the way in.

The first thing Julia noticed was the odd smell. Not noxious, but almost alluring – rich and smoky. Instead of the usual layout of rooms off the central hallway, there were cubicles furnished with small plush sofas. Each one held a little round table and an oriental rug. Very respectable-looking men and women lay inside, smoking what looked like a pipe. The windows were shuttered from within, making the interior very dark. But throughout there were dozens and dozens of cats of all different colours and sizes, perched on tables and the arms of sofas, sleeping on the cushions, pacing the hallway.

'My goodness, so many beautiful cats,' Granny exclaimed and began to walk around, petting and caressing the cats. Granny was so distracted that she didn't seem to notice the people lying about.

A smiling Chinaman wearing a blue-and-gold quilted jacket with shiny black pantaloons approached. 'Lady like kitties,' he said.

To Julia's astonishment, Granny returned the smile and nodded. As far as Julia knew, she had always found anything different from Knickerbocker society vulgar and disgusting. Yet she treated the Chinaman as though he was a Van Rensselaer.

'Oh, yes. Are any for sale?'

'All kitties for sale. Which one you like?'

'Oh dear, there's too many to choose. That calico is amazing, and that tortie! Adorable.'

'No hurry. You sit here.' The Chinaman pointed to a sofa. He began to gather cats and arrange them like throw pillows. 'You sit, lady, here. I bring you *Li Yuen*. That "Fountain of Beauty" in English.'

Granny perched primly on the sofa and began to caress the cats, which purred loudly as they rubbed against her. 'They're so friendly,' she said with glee.

At Julia's side, Nolan beamed with pride.

Instead of bringing tea, which Julia had thought Fountain of Beauty was, the Chinaman brought her aunt a long ivory pipe, a little box, and what looked like a lamp.

'This *yen tsiang*,' he said, pointing to the pipe, and then holding up the box. 'This *yen hop*.' He pointed to himself. 'And I Wah Kee.'

He took a tiny blob of what looked like grease from the *yen hop*, put it in the jade bowl of the pipe, and lit the lamp. Then he placed the pipe in Granny's hand, motioning her to hold the pipe bowl over the lamp and inhale.

'Granny, you really shouldn't be doing this,' said Julia, alarmed.

'Fiddlesticks, Julia,' snapped Granny. 'My Uncle Hector was in the opium trade with Warren Delano. Made a fortune. Warren's daughter, Sarah, married James Roosevelt up in Hyde Park a few years back, and I was at the wedding. Uncle Hector told me the smoke had definite medicinal qualities. It might be just the thing for my lumbago.'

Granny lay back on the sofa and calmly inhaled, then coughed.

'Take in slow, hold, let out slow,' tutored Wah Kee, giving her a solicitous smile.

'Besides,' Granny continued, a stern gaze fixed on her granddaughter, 'this is good manners. Like smoking a peace pipe in an Indian village. It's a token of this yellow devil's gratitude for buying his cats.'

Granny looked over at the cubicle directly across from her. 'Isn't that the mother of your schoolmate, Ellen Bentley?'

Indeed, a woman in a royal-blue princess dress, puffing away on a sofa, was Ellen's mother. She seemed to be in a state of hazy bliss, her eyelids drifting down with each inhale.

Closing her eyes, Granny continued to smoke. The cats snuggled up around her.

'It's almost noon, Miss Cross,' Nolan whispered in Julia's ear. 'The cockfight will be starting soon. If we leave now, we can make it. Remember, the bird that won for you last time, General Sherman, is fighting.'

Julia nodded and moved towards her grandmother, extending a hand to bring the elderly woman to her feet. Granny looked up, annoyed, a glassy look in her eyes.

'My child, I am not ready to leave, and I won't be rushed into making a decision as to which cats I want. If you must run an errand, I shall allow Mr Nolan to accompany you. You did say he's a close friend of Theodore Roosevelt's family?'

Julia nodded and whispered to Nolan, 'Wah Kee will look after her, won't he?'

The Chinaman nodded. 'Lady be fine, Mr Johnnie. You go. She buy cats – two dollar for cat. Good price.'

'Don't worry,' Nolan said to Julia. 'We'll be back in an hour.'

CHAPTER TWENTY-EIGHT

George rested his head against the window of the train. Only five minutes out from Grand Central Station, he was struck by how fast the buildings disappeared. An empty landscape met his gaze, vacant lots punctuating the grid of streets. A few isolated brick buildings stood alone, as if they had sprung up from the earth like weeds. The builders, it seemed, were patiently waiting for development to flow north to their doors and increase the value of their property.

Each of the twelve children in his class had a window seat. Their small faces were pressed against the windows, peering out eagerly. None of them, George knew, had ever taken a train ride out of the city. Their world had been a ten-block radius, filled with tenements packed cheek by jowl onto the filthy, crowded streets. It was as if they were on a rocket to the moon. The smallest detail fascinated the children, and it delighted George to see them so excited.

Many of the lots had jumbles of run-down shanties on them, with open fires and chickens, cows, and goats milling around. The children pointed out the animals to one another, laughing happily.

'Look, a castle!' cried Fred Enman.

The vacant blocks had given way to the open countryside of northern Manhattan, which was dotted with farm buildings and the occasional estate and imposing mansion, some of which looked like medieval castles.

Fifteen minutes later, the train crossed the Harlem River into the Bronx.

'Fordham Station. Next station, Fordham Station,' the conductor called.

The train slowed to a stop. George gathered his charges and jumped down to the platform. Joining the crowd of hundreds of race fans, the group climbed Kingsbridge Road up the long hill to the Jerome Park Racetrack. It was a beautiful August afternoon, warm but not hot. The children followed George and passed through the huge, double-arched main gate into a field with a racetrack, bordered on its far side by a hundred-yard-long, two-storey grandstand. It was filled to capacity on both tiers, with spectators crowding the rail in front of the building.

The children were stopping to point out anything that interested them. Like a cowboy herding cattle, George directed them across the track to the grass infield. He saw Jonah Kissel carefully gather up a fistful of the soft, reddish dirt and put it in his pocket.

The infield directly across from the grandstand was filled with every imaginable type of expensive carriage and coach. Top-hatted society gentlemen in black frock coats and grey trousers picnicked with attractive young women in brilliant princess dresses. Spread out on the lush, green grass were white linen tablecloths and huge wicker picnic baskets filled with cold food and bottles of chilled wine and champagne. All the teams had been unhitched, and some people ate on the roofs of their carriages to get a better view. The drivers ate off by themselves but within earshot of their masters.

Up on a bluff overlooking the track and grandstand was the clubhouse, the home of the American Jockey Club. It was a white wooden mansion with a red slate mansard roof. It offered luxurious hotel accommodation so that horse owners could entertain guests at lavish balls, put them up for the night, then have breakfast and watch the morning workouts. In the past, George had spent many a wondrous afternoon there.

'George, old boy! Come join us!,' yelled a young, red-haired man in a top hat, waving a champagne glass.

'Yes, please come, George,' pleaded his companion, a girl holding a yellow parasol.

Smiling, George tipped his hat and continued on with the children to a large empty area towards the south end of the infield. He put down his picnic basket and told the class to find seats on the grass.

As a child, he'd always taken grass for granted. He was amazed at the effect it had on the children. Whenever he took them to Central Park, they loved rolling around, yanking out clumps, even just touching it. Their world was confined to hard surfaces – stone pavements and cobblestone streets. Grass was a revelation.

Sandwiches, apples, and bottles of sarsaparilla were distributed. After passing out cookies, George pulled a deck of cards from his jacket pocket. With thirty minutes before post time, there was room for a lesson. Every outing, he assured Dr Bennett, had educational value – although he didn't tell him he was taking his students to the track. Dr Bennett would have had an apoplectic fit.

With a deft hand, George flashed a two of spades and placed a four of spades next to it.

'Now, how many spades do I have altogether?'

Hands shot up in the air, but Andy Clayton shouted out 'Six!' before anyone else could answer.

'You're supposed to be called on, you idiot,' snarled Ginny Talbot.

'Your turn, Ginny. If I have the nine of diamonds but take away four, I'll have . . . ?'

'Five!' she screamed with glee.

181

Nothing gave George more pleasure than seeing his class progress. Each day, they improved. The reformers had thought them underprivileged dolts, rendered hopeless by cruelty and neglect. But George knew better; he had unearthed bright minds.

'Let's go back to multiplication. There's a special kind of multiplication we use at the racetrack. It's called odds, and it's a way of predicting whether a horse will win. If you have a horse at three-to-one odds, and you place a two-dollar bet and it wins, then you multiply two with the three and you win six dollars.'

'Six whole dollars?' Davey Hill exclaimed.

'Indeed. But if you put down five dollars, how much would you win?'

'Fifteen?' Tom O'Hara said.

'Exactly. Tom, you have the makings of a mathematician,' George said with a smile. He glanced at his pocket watch and motioned Sarah Shulski forward. At fourteen, she was the oldest and most mature, the big sister to the group.

'Sarah, I have to see someone, but I'll be back in five minutes. Give them these peppermint sticks and keep an eye on them, will you?'

Sarah, a pretty, dark-haired Jewess, smiled and took the candy. George trotted off to an open-air, wood-framed pavilion on the inside rail of the track. People were crowded eight deep around the round structure, shouting at bookies who were furiously taking down bets on scraps of paper. George fought his way through the crowd to the pooling stand. A lanky man with a black waxed moustache waved and went down the staircase to meet him.

'Georgie, I ain't supposed to take bets from you unless it's just two dollars. Toby warned me if I did,' he said. On either side, people yelled and cursed at the bookie for ignoring them.

'A thousand dollars on Sam Brown to win in the first, Jake.'

Jake looked at him in disbelief. 'Christ, Georgie, did you say a thousand?'

'A thousand on the nose.'

'He's a five-to-one shot in a mile and a furlong, Georgie.'

'Jimmy McLaughlin's still riding him, right? And he's the best jockey in America, right?'

'Well, yeah. But one thousand dollars? Toby told me not to take any more big bets from you. You're goin' to get my ass in trouble.'

'Write it down, Jake,' George said and walked away.

Returning to the class, he motioned them to follow. The children ran after him, laughing and shouting. He brought them up to the thick, white wooden rail lining the track. Most were so short that they had to look out from below it. The children screamed with delight as the horses for the first race were brought up to the starting line, about thirty yards to their left. The horses snorted and stomped and swung their heads up and down and side to side, impatient to run. One reared up, pitching its jockey off.

Heart in his throat, George watched Sam Brown approach the line. He was a two-year-old descendant of a sire in Pierre Lorillard's stable, the finest in America. With racing's best jockey aboard, George's tip from last night told him, the horse was due for a big win.

'I like the brown one,' shouted Andy.

'Nah, the grey one's gonna win,' Sam Mostel yelled.

'The one we want to win has the scarlet and black colours,' George said, pointing out the jet-black thoroughbred. 'Cheer with all your might for Sam Brown – that's his name.'

The official starter came alongside the horses, and the jockeys turned their heads in his direction. He raised his right hand, held it there for ten seconds, and then dropped his red flag to signal the start. A dozen horses thundered off, their hooves pounding the dirt track like drums. George could see McLaughlin guide Sam Brown immediately to the front. He meant to control the pace from the start and run the race on his terms.

When the horses flew by, the children went wild with excitement. Sam Brown roared down the track like a locomotive.

'Come on, Sammy!' screamed Andy.

As the field rounded into the final turn for the home stretch, the black thoroughbred led by three lengths. A wonderful feeling of elation seemed to lift George a finger's breadth above the infield grass. Then, ever so slowly, Sam Brown slowed down. It looked as if he were running in reverse. Buckstone caught up and passed him, and George's heart sank like a rock.

But fifty yards from the finish, Sam Brown put on a burst of speed and surged ahead to win by half a length. Crazy with joy, George picked up Sam Mostel and swung him through the air like a rag doll. Seeing their teacher's elation, the class exploded with delight, jumping up and down and hugging one another.

'Wait here with them, Sarah. I'll be right back!' George shouted as he ran off.

As Jake counted out the winnings into George's hand, George slipped a hundred-dollar bill into his pocket. He'd celebrate his good luck by taking the children to a nice dinner and a show. Giving the bookie a smile, George said, 'Put the rest on Night Train to win in.'

A hand clamped onto the back of his neck, squeezing like a vice. George thought his head was going to be ripped from his shoulders. Twisting around, he saw Mike Donovan, a red-haired giant, towering above him. Donovan snatched the cash from George's hand with a grim smile.

'Now you only owe Harrigan three thousand, Georgie.'

CHAPTER TWENTY-NINE

'Tell Mrs O'Shea what a fine meal that was. No one does salmon à la reine better.'

As Cross would be away on Sunday, his family ate together that Saturday night. He looked around the dinner table at his family, a perfect portrait of warm domestic bliss. Only he knew the terrible danger they were in. Each of them had their own sword of Damocles, dangling by the thinnest of threads over their heads, and only he could prevent Kent from snapping them.

Despite the dread welling in his chest, Cross tried to put on a cheerful face.

'I bet you're looking forward to the Giants game, Charlie.'

'It's Tuesday afternoon. You said you'd be back on Monday,' Charlie said with a worried expression. 'Uncle Robert is going.'

'I'll be back Monday afternoon at the latest. It's just a short trip to Albany to see about a museum project,' Cross said. He turned to his daughter and smiled. 'I haven't read your novel in ages, Julia.' He was immensely proud of her love for literature and real talent for writing. To his relief, she wasn't growing up to be an empty-headed socialite.

'I'm afraid I haven't done much writing lately,' Julia said. 'I haven't had the time.' She bit her lip and added, 'And, in fact, I may have come across a new subject.'

'With all these preparations for the ball, of course she hasn't had the time,' Helen said, ignoring Julia's latter comment.

Cross smiled. He knew his wife thought her daughter's literary aspirations a serious impediment to a successful marriage.

'Well then, I'm off. Everyone come give the papa bear a kiss goodbye so I can catch my train.'

Julia and Charlie jumped up and ran to their father, hugging and kissing him. Helen sat where she was, hands folded in her lap.

In the hallway, Cross picked up his leather bag and went out to hail a carriage. But instead of telling the driver to take him to Grand Central Station, he asked for the Union League Club. He smoked and read the papers until Culver picked him up.

Preparations for the robbery had taken three long weeks. The robbers would tunnel twenty-five feet from the side of the underground tunnel to the basement wall of Fidelity National, break through, crack the vault, and loot the safety deposit boxes. Cross was not expected to do any digging, but his presence would be required when they reached the basement wall.

The corner of Warren Street and Broadway was deserted when the carriage pulled up to the iron plate in the street. The whores had gone to wherever it was the poor wretches lived – in the cellars or alleys. There would be no prying eyes tonight.

Cross and Culver knelt on the floor of the carriage. Culver removed a false panel, took an iron bar with a hook at its end, reached down, and pulled up the plate. *A clever way to bring the digging equipment into the tunnel without being noticed*, Cross thought.

'Down ya go, Mr Cross,' Culver said.

Below the plate were stone steps. Cross descended slowly. To his amazement, he found himself in an opulent waiting room, fitted out like a luxury hotel lobby, with a cut-glass chandelier, wood panelling, and a marble floor. An empty stone fountain stood in its centre. Except for a layer of dust, the room looked exactly as it must have when Beach opened his underground railway.

A rough man in an expensive suit and derby was waiting.

'I'm Dago Frank,' he said, not extending his hand.

Cross nodded and followed him to the far end of the waiting room, where the pneumatic tunnel began.

Frank held up his lantern. There stood the abandoned tubular train car, which had been pushed through the tunnel by the huge blower fan. They entered the car's front door, then walked down the ten-foot aisle flanked by plush leather bench seats and out through the rear. Even in the swaying light of the lantern, Cross noted how well engineered the tunnel was. A perfect cylinder constructed of painted white brick, it showed no sign of deterioration or leaking water. Beach, he knew, had invented a flexible hydraulic shield that could cut through the earth without cave-ins. Kent would not have that luxury tonight. He'd have to tunnel through the sandy soil by hand and shore up the sides and top with planks. The whole job had been planned to the letter, only it still could be doomed by a cave-in.

After walking about forty yards, Cross saw light ahead. The men had broken through the brick wall of the Beach tunnel and begun excavating. He stopped by the opening and peered in. The tunnel was already twenty feet long. His first impression was that Kent had hired real coal miners to do the excavation, but then he recognised the regular gang, hard at work. Even Brady was there. The twelve-man team consisted of diggers with picks and shovels, haulers who took away the dirt in small wheelbarrows, and men who shored the tunnel. Instead of their customary suits, Kent's men were dressed in work clothes and covered with dirt. Their efficiency reminded Cross of an ant colony he'd had as a boy.

Kent emerged out of the shadows, dressed in his usual elegant attire, twirling his cane.

'Just a few more feet and we'll hit the basement wall, Mr Cross.'

'Then you have four feet of solid brick foundation to get through,' Cross said.

'We have the tools we need. Your drawings were very helpful. May I offer you some food and drink?'

In spite of himself, Cross was hungry. He followed Kent down the tunnel to a pile of wooden boxes containing sandwiches and bottles of sarsaparilla. 'Clever not to provide alcohol on the job,' he said with a smile.

'Some of my men are too fond of it, and it can impair their judgement,' Kent said, picking out a sandwich for himself. He sat on the box and ate.

'Remember our discussion,' Cross said. 'Tonight's proceeds should forgive my debt.'

'I certainly do. And as I said, it's a possibility.'

'I want to be present when you do the accounting.'

Kent did not answer.

They ate and drank in silence. More than an hour passed. Cross listened as the picks beat against the brick foundation wall. He looked to the right and saw a small wooden box with red Xs painted on the top and sides. His heart sank. Kent was going to try nitro again.

Without thinking, Cross asked, 'Why does a man like you do this sort of thing? You certainly don't need the money.'

Kent smiled. He didn't seem at all offended by the question. 'Mr Cross, you can't imagine the feeling of exhilaration I get when committing a robbery. Whether it's cracking a bank vault or stealing valuables from a house, there's a sense of intense ecstasy, a sensation like no other.' He paused, grinning from ear to ear.

'The excitement comes from the fact that at any second, I might be caught. I love that feeling more than any other. You're right; I don't need the money. But I *want* that feeling.'

Cross looked at him incredulously. He'd never met a man like this before. 'Is it true that you studied to be a doctor?'

'I *am* a doctor. Graduated from Columbia University College of Physicians and Surgeons.'

'But how—'

'Whether we like it or not, our lives are dictated by pure circumstance, Mr Cross. One night, there was a knock on my office door. A man told me his friend was badly hurt. When I grabbed my bag and went with him, I found a man shot through the gut and bleeding to death. I saved his life. His name was Ben McGarrigle. At the time, he was one of the most feared underworld bosses in the city. In gratitude, he paid me ten times my usual fee, took me under his wing, and treated me like a son. He was more of a father to me than my real one in Baltimore. With his help, I descended into the underworld. It's a separate universe, Mr Cross. It has its own rules and values, and it doesn't have to answer to anyone. I admired that. But I didn't give up my privileged life in society. I didn't have to. I simply took on a secret life. And after a time, I gave up my practice and went into a more lucrative line of work – crime. I've never regretted it. You see, there was another thing I found out about myself. Instead of saving life, I like taking it away.'

Culver approached, out of breath, but with a smile on his face.

'We've broken through.'

CHAPTER THIRTY

The gang gathered around the jagged opening in the brick wall, and the first two men passed through, holding lanterns. All the men were in a boisterous mood, laughing and talking among themselves.

While some banks housed their vaults in full view on the banking floor, most preferred to hide them in the lower bowels of the building, where they would be harder to rob. The safe itself was some forty feet into the basement in its own room, fronted by an ornate iron gate Cross had designed. Beside it was a room lined with safety deposit boxes. There was no alarm system installed. Fidelity National hadn't thought they'd need one. They were too cheap to even hire a watchman. The police came by to check the front door while on their night rounds.

Two more men stepped inside the hole in the basement wall as Kent and Cross approached.

'Make way for Mr Kent,' came the command.

As the men began to part, a voice from within the darkness of the basement yelled out, 'Hands up. You're under arrest. Stay where you are.'

The voice hit them like a thunderbolt. Cross and Kent froze, as did the rest of the gang. In an instant, the basement was flooded by another source of light – the electric lights on the walls and ceiling, illuminating the space in stark tones.

'Pinkertons!' someone cried out in panic.

'That's right, gentlemen, and you're under arrest.'

The voice hit Cross in the stomach like a prize fighter's punch, almost knocking the wind out of him. Robert had a rich, deep baritone like that. Cross crouched and looked through the mass of men to see his brother, standing in the basement, holding a revolver.

'Damn you. I said hands up!' Robert Cross roared.

Kent's men stood frozen in place. Cross felt like he was about to pass out. Staggering backward, he leant against the tunnel wall to keep himself from falling. Then he began running like a madman. As he pumped his legs and struggled to breathe, he kept thinking about explaining the tawdry story to his brother from inside a jail cell.

Back in Beach's tunnel, he turned right and sped to the nitro box. He removed his handkerchief and tied it around his face. Carefully lifting the lid, he saw that the box was packed with cotton. Fishing his hand around in the stuff, he found the glass vial of nitro. Cradling it in the wad of cotton like a newborn, he ran back into the tunnel, towards the basement of the bank.

As he ran, he heard shots ring out. Kent and his gang were pressed against the wood shoring of the tunnel walls, guns drawn. One man was down, holding his leg and screaming in pain.

'Put your guns down or I'll give you this nitro!' Cross screamed in a raspy voice he prayed his brother wouldn't recognise.

His words were met by dead silence.

Cross dropped the wad of cotton and walked to the opening, holding the vial above his head.

'You men, get out of there,' he commanded the gang members already inside the basement.

191

The men obeyed. Robert, along with the other Pinkertons, lowered his gun and backed slowly away.

'Stay where you are or I'll throw this!' Cross shouted. The Pinkertons didn't move.

Cross stayed where he was too. Behind him, the entire gang inched out of the tunnel. Two men picked up the wounded robber and dragged him out.

Cross started backing down the tunnel. Under his voice, to no one in particular, he said, 'Cave it in.'

As men on either side yanked out the wall shoring, Cross turned and ran. The ceiling came down hard; in an instant, tons of yellowish-brown earth filled the opening. Safely beyond the cave-in's range, Cross carefully set the nitro vial on the soft dirt, happy to leave it behind.

Kent met him at the intersection with Beach's tunnel. 'They'll be waiting for us at Warren Street. Come this way,' he yelled.

Instead of going north, the gang ran to the south. Cross heard shouting from the railway tunnel; far in the distance, he saw men with lanterns running towards them. Brady and Coogan stopped running. As if reading each other's minds, each man grabbed handfuls of the dozens of canvas sacks meant to transport the money, piled them in the middle of the tunnel, and threw four lanterns onto the stack. There was the whoosh of spreading flames, and a wall of fire blocked the entire tunnel diameter.

At the Murray Street end of the tunnel, Dago Frank pulled open a heavy iron hatch on the right wall. Men flew into the opening like rats jumping into a ship's porthole. The passageway opened up into a tiny service alley. One by one, the men disappeared into the darkness.

'You tipped off the Pinkertons, you son of a bitch.'

Cross couldn't believe this was happening. As the gang had

scattered into the night three hours earlier, Brady had collared him and dragged him into a carriage. Throughout the fifteen-minute trip to McGlory's, as Cross lay helpless on the floor of the carriage, Brady pummelled him with his fists.

Cross was now standing on a chair, a wire noose around his neck. Instead of being hailed as a hero for his quick thinking, the gang seemed ready to kill him for being a traitor.

'Don't lie to us, you shit. You told them!' Brady screamed.

Kent wasn't watching. Calmly smoking a Havana, he was bandaging the leg of Bill Crabb. The white gauze was wrapped neatly and tied off with a sure hand. 'Haven't lost my touch,' Kent said to himself, smiling.

'Who else have you told?' Brady had his foot on the rickety wooden chair. With each outburst, he shook the chair until it was about to topple over – and then stopped.

'Goddamn you, I didn't tell a soul!' Cross was red in the face with anger. 'Why the hell would I do that? One of you betrayed us, can't you see that?'

'Bullshit. No one ever informs. Ever,' Brady hissed.

'The police could've picked up one of your men. Maybe he turned on you.'

'The men waiting for us were Pinkertons, not the police,' Kent said in a quiet voice.

'I'm telling you: I didn't say a word to anyone. Why would I do that?' Cross pleaded.

Brady began to shake the chair again.

Cross was breathing heavily, his heart pounding like a drum. At any second, Kent would announce that his brother, the Pinkerton, was one of the men waiting for them, and his fate would be sealed. Brady would yank out the chair with glee.

'They'd catch the gang in one shot, and you'd be in the

clear,' said Coogan, looking up at Cross, his hands on his hips.

'And suppose just one member of the gang wasn't down there. He'd find out I was the turncoat and kill my whole family in front of me,' Cross said.

Kent laughed. 'Mr Cross, you're beginning to understand how we think in this line of work.'

'Good God, man, you'd be sitting in the Tombs right now if it weren't for me. I saved you. Where's your goddamn gratitude?' A wall of silence met his question. 'There's a traitor. Goddamn it, don't you see? All of us are at risk.'

'None of my men is a traitor – they know what the consequences would be,' Kent said. He circled the chair, smoking his cigar, deep in thought. 'All right. I'll give you a second chance, Mr Cross. We lost a good deal of money tonight, so you'll have to make it up to us. Find another house. No more banks, not for a while.'

'But there's a traitor. No matter what move we make, the Pinkertons will be on to us.'

'Then from now on, we will be more cautious. You'll only deal with me,' Kent said and nodded to Brady, who, with a disappointed expression, stepped up on the chair, removed the noose, and shoved Cross to the floor.

CHAPTER THIRTY-ONE

'You're back so early.'

Cross's and Helen's separate but adjoining bedrooms allowed Cross to come in at all hours of the night without waking his wife. It also ensured that she kept out of his private life. But they shared a spacious bathroom, specially designed by Cross, with all the latest plumbing features, including the Deeco flushing toilet.

It was just past midnight. The going-over Brady had given Cross in the carriage had produced a noticeable swelling on his right cheekbone. He was patting it with a wet washcloth when Helen slammed open the door.

'What on earth happened to you, John?' she cried in an almost hysterical voice that made Cross cringe.

'I fell from the carriage on the way home, Helen. That's all.'

She came forward and studied his face. Some of Brady's other handiwork had resulted in small, angry red blotches.

'No, you've been in a fight.' Helen's eyes widened in horror. Men in society attacked with insults and cutting sarcasm, never their fists. Physical brutality was something ruffians on the Lower East Side did to one another, or to their wives and children. She put her hand over mouth, looking at her husband as though he had contracted leprosy.

Cross grew angrier by the second – at Helen and at the fact that he hadn't thought to design them separate bathrooms.

'Damn it, Helen, I'm fine. Leave me the hell alone,' he said.

But Helen stood her ground. She placed her hand under his chin, rotating his head side to side. 'No, John. Someone beat the hell out of you.'

Instead of shouting at her, Cross stomped away to the other side of the bathroom, fighting the rage welling in his gut. Helen followed.

'Tell me what happened.'

'Nothing. I was set upon by robbers. That's all.'

Unexpectedly, Helen reached around Cross's side and felt for her husband's wallet. 'They did all this to you, but they didn't take your wallet?'

'I . . . I got away from them.'

'All those men attacked you, and you escaped?'

'I just told you what happened,' snapped Cross, his back still facing her. 'You will listen to me.'

'Tell me what *really* happened, John,' Helen said.

Despite his anger, Cross was touched by her concern. He bent his head, eyes on the black-and-white-tiled floor.

In his fraternity of society gentlemen, a man who faced a crisis or financial disaster would never tell his wife. Even if he went dead broke, his wife and family would know nothing – until the day the bank came to repossess the house and throw the children out into the street. The reasons for such silence would be the gentleman's sense of shame and the general perception of society ladies as overly emotional, useless dolts. A gentleman would confide in his friends at the club, his valet, or his favourite bartender, never his wife. The only woman to whom a man might tell his tale of woe was his mistress.

But in this matter, there was no one in whom Cross might confide, no one to turn to. He was hopelessly alone. Every day, he woke with a sense of dread – this would be his family's last day on earth; something would go wrong and force Kent to kill them. The pressure sometimes seemed unbearable. He didn't know how much longer he could stand it. And there was no way out. If he went to the police, his family would be dead within the hour. Griffith's frozen head had taught him that.

Robert's new involvement put the Crosses in even greater danger. Once Kent discovered who his brother was, he'd be out for blood. Cross had thought of confiding in Robert, but that would almost certainly mean his death. The fact that he was a Pinkerton wouldn't deter Kent.

He was lost, and he was alone. He looked into Helen's eyes, and the urge to tell her was overpowering.

Helen knew something was terribly wrong. She instinctively knew her husband's moods and feelings. 'Please tell me,' she whispered.

Cross closed his eyes. At first, the words wouldn't come out. Was he doing the right thing, or was he condemning Helen to death? 'We're in great trouble, my dear.'

'When you have bad news, it's best to get it out quickly,' Helen said.

'George has a gambling problem,' Cross said. 'He owes thousands to a man who threatened to kill him if he didn't pay.'

Helen stepped backwards, pressing her body against the sink. She gripped the edge of the marble counter until her knuckles turned white. 'How much?'

'More than forty thousand dollars.'

Helen gasped and covered her face with her hands.

'When George couldn't pay, these men came to me to make good on his debt.'

'But we don't have that kind of money!'

'They knew that. They wanted me to help them rob the houses and businesses of my clients.'

Helen looked at him in astonishment. 'We have no choice but to go to the police, John. They can arrest these criminals, and then we'll be safe.'

'I tried, but it didn't work. I know this beyond a shadow of a doubt: if I go to the police, all of us – you, me, George, Julia, Charlie, even your mother – all of us will be dead. These people aren't bluffing, Helen. They're cold-blooded murderers.'

Helen shook her head violently from side to side, her eyes filling with tears. 'No, I won't let anyone hurt my family. Aunt Caroline can help. She knows powerful people, people who can help us. I'm going to call her right now.'

Helen ran from the bathroom into her bedroom, but Cross was on her in a flash. He grabbed her from behind, threw her on the bed, and pinned her down by her shoulders. 'If you call Caroline – or Robert or anyone – we're dead!' he shouted, his face pressed close to hers. 'Do you hear me? Dead!'

She looked into his eyes with a pleading, helpless look and asked in a low voice, 'Then what can we do, John? What can we possibly do?'

Cross released Helen and sat next to her on the bed. 'Until I can think of some other way out, I have no choice but to do what they say.'

Helen lay on the bed for a few moments, her body shaking with sobs. Then, as if gathering her will, she sat up and put her arms around Cross's waist. She pulled him close, settling her head against his shoulder. 'Until *we* can think of some other way out,' she said.

Cross smiled and kissed her on the cheek. 'I've had a long day, Helen. I need to get some sleep. Tomorrow, I must find a new place to rob.' He raked his fingers through his hair. 'I confess, though: I'm drawing a blank.'

Helen's eyes met his, and he saw in her gaze a flash of unexpected excitement. 'Remember the Greenes on Fifth and Sixty-Fifth? They're up in the Berkshires for the month, and, John, Edith Greene just bought a tiara with a diamond the size of an almond!'

CHAPTER THIRTY-TWO

'Did your shot hit the robber, Uncle Robert?'

Annoyed that Charlie was more interested in Robert's account of the bank robbery than the baseball game, Cross said, 'What did you think about that putout Dude Esterbrook just made at third, Charlie?'

'Sorry, Father, I missed it. Did any Pinkertons get shot, Uncle Robert?'

It was a perfect, sunny day at the Polo Grounds. Cross had kept his promise to go to the game with his son and brother, to please Charlie – and to get information from Robert.

The crowd cheered like mad as Smiling Mickey Welch struck out the Detroit batter to end the inning. It was an important game: the Giants were two behind the Detroit Wolverines, so if they won that game and the next, they'd be tied for first. The three-year-old stadium, directly across from the north-east corner of Central Park, stretched from 110th to 112th Streets and was filled to capacity with ten thousand rowdy fans. Along 112th Street, people stood atop their carriages, straining to see. As yet, very few buildings had been constructed so far up Fifth Avenue. The few taller ones near the ballpark also had spectators on their roofs.

'Did you see that fastball Welch threw?'

'I wasn't watching . . . Did any of your men get hurt, Uncle Robert?' Charlie repeated.

'No, Charlie, none of our men were hurt. One fellow sucked in too much smoke when the gang set a fire in the tunnel, but he's all right now.'

'Charlie, your uncle is here to enjoy the game. He doesn't want to keep talking about the robbery. Look, Ewing's the first batter up,' Cross said, winking at his brother.

'But it's so exciting. *My* uncle stopped a bank robbery. I can't wait to tell my friends.'

'Turn around and watch the game,' Cross said, exasperated. Charlie did as he was told and was soon caught up in the action. Ewing, the catcher, rapped a single to right, and the crowd roared. Chip Ward advanced him to second on a bunt, and a single by Dorgan, the right fielder, sent Ewing home for a 1-0 lead. The Giants protected the lead with great fielding and scored again in the sixth on a three-run homer.

But soon Detroit had two men on. The crowd fell quiet. Could their star pitcher, Mickey Welch, throw his way out of the jam?

In the momentary lull, Cross slipped a veiled question to his brother. 'I'm glad you're all right, Robert. That must have been a close call.'

'It didn't turn out the way I'd hoped,' Robert said. 'We had them dead to rights, John, but every single one got away.'

'Were you able to see who they were?'

'No one I recognised. We're going through the rogue's gallery to see if any turn up. But I'm not optimistic. The clever bastard who saved them wore a mask. The one threatening to throw the nitro, I mean. If he hadn't had the nerve to do that, they'd all be in jail.'

'Was it really nitroglycerine?'

'Indeed. Luckily, we found the vial in the tunnel before anyone stepped on it. It would have blown the underground railway tunnel to bits and taken us along too.'

'A daring robbery.'

'It was a brilliant piece of planning. Would've worked like a dream if we hadn't gotten a tip.'

Cross stiffened in his seat.

The next batter up hammered the ball, bouncing it off the McCann's Celebrated Hats billboard in the centrefield bleachers for a three-run homer. The crowd inside the stadium groaned. But several pitches later, Welch finally got the third out with a strike.

'Charlie, go down and get yourself a pretzel,' Cross said, handing his son a nickel.

'I don't want a pretzel.'

'Well, go get something else you like,' he snapped.

'How about a beer?' Robert said. He and Charlie burst out laughing. Cross glared ruefully at his son as he ran off to the concession counter under the stands.

'Who tipped you off?' Cross asked in a matter-of-fact voice, looking straight ahead at the field. 'One of the gang?'

'I don't know. Someone telephoned on Saturday afternoon and told us about the robbery.'

Robert sounded evasive. Cross wondered if his brother was keeping the information close to the vest for professional reasons. Until he discovered the informant's identity, Cross knew he was in danger at every moment.

Connor, Ewing, and Ward all grounded out, and the Wolverines came up for their last at bat. Charlie returned with a bag of popcorn in time to see Welch get three quick outs to retire the side, and the game was over.

'Great game, huh, Charlie?' Robert said, clapping the boy on the back. 'We win tomorrow, and we're tied for first! Let's do this again next week. What do you say?'

He's so happy to be with family, Cross thought. The joy fairly radiated off of him. When he'd come to dinner for the first time, Robert had enjoyed himself immensely, chattering on with Helen, Julia, and Charlie, interested in every detail of their lives. He seemed to want to stay for ever. Robert had since gone with them to social events and spent many quiet evenings at their home. Cross's children and wife were even pestering him to have Robert come and live with them.

Charlie had liked his uncle from the beginning, but the robbery had sent Robert's stock soaring. He beamed up at him and said, 'They play Boston next week. The Giants will beat the shit out of them.'

'Charlie,' Cross scolded.

Swear words had become a more frequent part of his son's vocabulary in recent weeks. Cross didn't know where Charlie picked it up. Probably the footman of that Mackay boy he'd been playing with.

'Let's look at the schedule by the ticket window,' Robert said.

At 109th Street, they tried to hail a carriage with little success. While they waited, Cross asked his brother about his rooms at the Benedick, an apartment house designed by Charlie McKim. They were most satisfactory, Robert said.

'It's good you've found a nice place to live. You can relax, perhaps get your mind off the robbery,' Cross said.

Robert smiled at him. 'Little Brother, I'm obsessed with the robbery. And I guarantee you: I will catch that bastard with the nitro.'

CHAPTER THIRTY-THREE

The failure of the bank robbery had bitterly disappointed Cross. He knew he should be grateful for their skin-of-the-teeth escape from Robert and the Pinkertons, but he'd been counting on the take from the job to wipe out his son's debt. Without it, he needed new victims. And as Helen had suggested, the Greene mansion on Fifth Avenue and Sixty-Fifth Street was perfect. Not only were the Greenes rich and away for the summer, but they also weren't former clients.

The time would come, Cross knew, when Robert would discover that his brother had designed both the Cook mansion and the bank. He'd start asking questions. Henceforth, Cross's own clients had to be avoided in favour of his architect friends' rich clients. There was a good selection: McKim, White, and another successful colleague, Bruce Price, had a slew of them. The Greenes had been clients of James Ware, an architect Cross knew from the New York chapter of the American Institute of Architects. Having made a fortune in steamships that plied the Gulf of Mexico, Andrew Greene was another classic parvenu, come to New York to buy his way into society. For his part, Ware was a talented architect who'd achieved national fame by winning a design competition for a new tenement model that allowed more light and air into the units. The tenements in the Lower East Side were unbelievably foul, inhumane hovels. Ware's design was nicknamed 'the dumb-bell plan', because its squeezed-in form resembled an exercise dumb-bell.

Cross called Ware to see if he could look at the plans. He was going to do some tenement work, he told him, and he greatly admired the dumb-bell design. Architects loved to be flattered, and Ware enthusiastically agreed. Cross used the same ruse on Ware's draftsman as he had on Hardenbergh's, and paired with Helen's personal knowledge of the Greenes' wealth, he determined where everything of value was located in the house.

But at every moment, Cross was cautious. Someone was watching – and waiting to tip off the Pinkertons again. Cross had reconnoitred the Greene mansion in the middle of the night and insisted that Kent not tell his gang the next target until right before the job. Not wanting to repeat the violence of the Cook robbery, Cross took great care in determining that no servants had been left behind.

On a sultry August night, Kent and his men cleaned out the Greene house. They stole Belgian and Irish linens, Gorham silver, and seventeenth-century Sèvres china. Helen told Cross that the wives of parvenus loved to show off their jewellery to fellow society ladies, so she knew where Mrs Greene's jewels were hidden. The Crosses had been there just a month prior. Mrs Greene's prized tiara and the rest of her valuables were hidden in a secret compartment below the stone hearth of a fireplace in her bedroom. A long piece of marble was cleverly hinged so it blended in with the rest of the stone, unseen. By just tapping on it, it popped up like a jack-in-the-box, revealing a deep-purple, velvet-lined box. Cross thanked God for his wife's powers of observation. The hiding place wasn't shown on the drawings, and they never would have found it.

When Kent's men opened the compartment, it was like lifting the lid of Captain Kidd's treasure chest. Even the usually cool and calm Kent almost fainted when he saw the flash of gems and metals.

Every stitch of Mr and Mrs Greene's clothing was taken, including their silk underwear. This time, Kent made sure he had larger wagons to haul away the huge Meissonier paintings of epic Napoleonic battle scenes. Not one bottle of vintage wine was left in the wine racks. Every one of Mr Greene's rare black-and-red Ancient Greek vases was taken. To his delight, in Greene's immense, wood-panelled library, Cross discovered four priceless tapestries made at Gobelin, the official design studio of the French kings; along with three exquisite Persian rugs, these found a place in Kent's wagons. Cross had a solid knowledge of antique furniture, and he directed Kent's gang to take away the choicest seventeenth- and eighteenth-century French pieces.

Helen also knew that Mr Greene's secret safe was located in the back of his medicine cabinet. His wife bragged that no thief would look there. Kent's men took his horde of cash and negotiable bonds, plus all his imported French cologne.

Strangely, Cross found he was enjoying himself. Walking about and barking orders gave him a power he'd never experienced before, a feeling of indescribable elation, and he liked it. In a way, he thought, architects were well-paid servants of the rich, complying with their every whim, no matter how stupid. They had to bow and scrape to get jobs and be paid. Clients often compromised Cross's design with ridiculous demands, catering to the momentary whims of their wives. How many times had Cross wanted to tell them to go to hell? But he didn't have the guts. He just smiled and took it.

This night was different. This night, he was in command.

Cross was not alone. Hidden in the shadows of the trees on Sixty-Fifth Street, Helen watched the loot from the Greene mansion being carted off. Seeing the robbery gave her an unexpected feeling of exhilaration, like drinking three glasses of champagne one after the other.

Walking north to Sixty-Sixth Street and over to Madison Avenue to hail a carriage home, Helen skipped along the pavement like a ten-year-old. She hadn't felt this alive in years.

Despite the rich haul, Cross discovered when he met with Kent that the debt had been reduced by only ten thousand dollars. Without losing his temper, he detailed the incredible value of the tapestries and the jewellery. Kent laughed in his face. If they'd stolen Michelangelo's *David*, he said, it'd still be sold at only a millionth of its true cost.

'This wasn't an auction at Christie's, Mr Cross,' he added.

Cross demanded to know where his debt stood. A man with a head for figures, Kent scratched out some numbers on a scrap of paper and handed it to Cross, whose jaw dropped.

'Christ Almighty, man. Still twenty-six thousand dollars?'

'You keep forgetting the fifteen per cent weekly interest,' Kent said contemptuously. 'I'd have thought an architect would better understand numbers. So tell me: What's the next job?'

There was no use arguing. Cross knew that when Helen heard about the amount of the outstanding debt, she would fly into a rage and want to confront Kent, but he'd convince her that to do so would be madness. To ensure her safety, Kent could never know she was aware of their business arrangement.

Besides, Cross thought, *Kent is being tough on the debt because he still believes that I informed on them*. If he told Kent it had been an anonymous tip, the man would ask who'd given Cross that information and grow even more suspicious.

In the days after the robbery, there was no mention of the

crime in the papers. Greene, like Cook, wanted no publicity about the burglary of his home. The Pinkertons, and probably Robert, would be on this case as well, but Cross had no choice. He had to continue. He had to get out from under George's debt.

After meeting with Kent, he was in a foul temper. Instead of going home, he walked to the Union League Club on the corner of Fifth Avenue and Thirty-Ninth Street. As he approached the building, he felt some of the weight on his shoulders lessen, and he smiled. His entry hadn't won the design competition, but he admired the domestic quality of Peabody & Stearns's Queen Anne building. It was much nicer than the renovated house of the rival Knickerbocker Club. *A club should have a homey feel*, Cross thought. After all, it was a gentleman's home away from home.

Built of beautiful, red, pressed brick and Belleville brownstone, the building featured a huge dormer window with a Tiffany glass oculus on the Fifth Avenue side. Cross entered and went directly to the reading room, the main social space on the second floor. It stretched the length of the Fifth Avenue façade and was also called the 'ogling room', as it allowed members to sit and watch the young female passers-by. Cross settled into a large leather armchair and stared out of the window. Members came and went, some using the adjacent smoking rooms or the bowling alley in the basement. Some had just finished dinner in the main dining room on the fourth floor and settled into a favourite chair in the reading room.

Many of the men, Cross knew, rarely went home. They lived in various bedrooms in a separate wing of the building. The club was their inner sanctum and was never violated by a woman's presence. Even the highest quality ladies of the evening were not allowed. The furniture was arranged in groups, allowing men to do what they loved most while in a club: bond in male comradeship and bonhomie. With servants fetching glasses of brandy and cigars, the members chattered on like the women they sought to avoid.

'It was Shelby's idea,' said a portly, middle-aged man with a brush moustache.

'And a grand one. A private banquet for our horses! It's never been done before,' said another man.

'Robertson will bring Storm Cloud.'

'What a horse. Paid twenty thousand for the animal, but he's paid off twice as much in purses,' said a scrawny man holding a glass of brandy and a cigar.

'I saw him run at Brighton Beach just last week. Won by eight lengths.'

'We've picked a place on West Forty-Ninth. The dinner will be catered by Delmonico's – canvasback duck and quail, oysters, roast sirloin.'

'Blue Day, who you'll recall won the Westminster Derby at Jerome Park, is coming. And Buckshot, Lemon Drop – the finest horseflesh in the land will be there.'

Though he pretended to look out the window, Cross was listening with great interest.

CHAPTER THIRTY-FOUR

Helen made sure to put the jewellery box back exactly as she'd found it.

With a contented smile on her beautiful face, she continued to survey Mrs Elizabeth Ogden's dressing table for items of exceptional value. Finding nothing else, she turned her attention to the dressing room, which was the size of a parlour at the Crosses'. With an expert's eye, Helen assessed the quality of Mrs Ogden's gowns. The absolute finest, but she had expected no less. Mrs Ogden's husband owned the biggest copper-mining company in America.

There was a joint in the cedar-lined closet wall behind the gowns, barely visible unless one looked closely. Pushing the clothes aside, Helen found a secret door, which opened by a recessed brass latch. Inside was a lead-walled room filled with racks of beautiful Russian sable and mink furs. Running her hands over them and pressing them against her cheek was a most wonderful sensation.

Leaving the dressing room, Helen moved to the enormous Tudor four-poster bed, which had been imported from Dottington Hall in England, took out her little red leather notebook and a gold pencil, and catalogued her findings. She was not nervous or scared, nor did she feel the slightest guilt about going through another society woman's possessions.

At first, she'd only cared about helping John steal enough to pay down her son's debt. Like a tigress protecting her cubs, she told herself, a mother must do anything for her children. Her family, the centre of her existence, would not be harmed. But another feeling was competing with her biological instinct – she *enjoyed* doing this. She loved the intense thrill of the robberies. Though she was forbidden from accompanying her husband on jobs, it gave her an enormous sense of excitement to help plan them.

In the wake of John's devastating news about George, Helen's visits to the guests who would attend Julia's upcoming ball had taken on new meaning. Among the fifty families that remained to be seen, there would be many nice things for 'future acquisition'. To Helen, a good Knickerbocker Episcopalian, the seventh commandment no longer had meaning.

It had been perhaps fifteen minutes since she had excused herself to go to the bathroom. Not an excessive amount of time, given the difficulty of lifting one's long dresses up around the waist and lowering the many layers of underwear. Many women resigned themselves to suffering and postponed going.

Smiling, Helen rose from the bed and walked downstairs to rejoin the tea.

'Will you be going to the opera this season, Miss Cross? *Faust* will be the first production at the Metropolitan,' Alfred Wharton asked, balancing a cup and saucer expertly on his knee.

'Yes, Mr Wharton, I plan to attend,' Julia said.

This was no idle chit-chat. Julia did enjoy the opera, especially the Italian productions. But for her, opera-going would be different. When she sat in Aunt Caroline's box in the Diamond

Horseshoe tier at the Met, she saw with great disgust that society women attended not to appreciate the music but to show off their latest Parisian gowns and jewellery. Going to the opera on Thursdays was the most important event of the social season, which began in mid-November and ran until mid-February. The Met's huge gold-and-white auditorium glittered with the flash of diamond tiaras, earrings, and chokers.

Julia thought the worst thing was that no society person ever arrived on time. They always came in the middle of the first act. When Aunt Caroline arrived, not one person paid attention to the performance, craning their necks instead to see what she was wearing. The audience talked constantly and left for supper before the end of the second act. When Julia told Caroline that one day she hoped to attend an opera from beginning to end, her aunt laughed uncontrollably.

'We have a box in the second parterre,' Wharton said. 'Perhaps after your coming-out, my family can have the pleasure of your company in our box.'

The Whartons were among the old society people who'd made the switch to the Met. When the parvenus couldn't get boxes at the Academy of Music, society's old opera house on Fourteenth Street, the Vanderbilts, Whitneys, and Morgans decided to build their own on the corner of Broadway and Thirty-Ninth Street. The Academy of Music couldn't compete and had made the switch from opera to musicals. The Knickerbockers, with Aunt Caroline leading the way, decamped with the 'new people' to the luxury boxes of the Met.

'That's very kind of you, Mr Wharton. I'd like that very much.' This was Julia's fifth visit to an at-home tea. Society ladies like Elizabeth Ogden sent out cards with 'Thursdays in August, tea at four o'clock' handwritten in the corner. On that day of the week, they would accept visitors. Attending these teas was an informal way of introducing Julia and allowing her to practise her social skills. She had also had one at-home tea at her house. Because the men were working, the guests were predominately female. A few fellows, like Wharton, took time off specifically to see Julia. She was fast becoming the most admired debutante of the season. That day, at least two dozen visitors filled the Ogdens' opulent parlour.

'We're going to the Thalia to see that new Gilbert and Sullivan production, *The Mikado*. They say it's first-rate,' Wharton said.

Granny, sitting next to Julia and waiting to intercept an improper advance, interrupted.

'While Miss Cross cannot go out without a chaperone, perhaps you and she will happen to attend the same performance.' Julia smiled at her grandmother, knowing she had to protect Julia yet steer her toward acceptable Knickerbocker men. Wharton was handsome, wealthy, and without a stain of scandal – a very good catch.

'Yes,' Wharton said enthusiastically, 'I could let you know in advance when we're going.'

'What are you studying at Yale, Mr Wharton?' Julia asked. She wanted to know if he was a serious scholar or the usual society college boy, who drank all the time and never opened a book.

'Palaeontology, Miss Cross. The study of dinosaurs at the Peabody Museum of Natural History.'

This so impressed Julia that she put down her cup of tea.

'I'm just back from a summer expedition in the south-west,' Wharton continued. 'We found eight new species of dinosaur bones and twelve tons of vertebrate fossils.'

'How exciting, Mr Wharton! I'd like to see those.'

Wharton was pleased to have found something to spark Julia's interest. It gave him an advantage over the other handsome young suitors in attendance. 'One day in the autumn, you must come up to New Haven, and I can show you.'

'This will be my last year at Miss Spence's,' Julia said proudly. 'Then I'm off to Vassar.' Holding her breath, she awaited his reaction. Would Wharton frown at the prospect of a girl going to college, or would he be supportive?

'That's wonderful, Miss Cross. What will you study?'

Wharton has possibilities, Julia thought, smiling. 'English literature.'

'And become a teacher?'

'No, a writer. In fact, I'm working on a novel. A young girl, born in the lowest and cruellest depths of poverty in the Bowery, rises up and becomes a doctor.'

'How fascinating.'

'I'm doing research for the book now.'

Granny smiled at Julia, the signal that she should get up and mingle with the rest of the guests. But before Julia could rise from her chair, Helen approached, a tall young man with chestnut hair at her side.

'Mr Van Cortlandt, this is my daughter, Julia.'

'A great pleasure, Miss Cross,' said the young man.

'Mr Van Cortlandt. You know Mr Wharton?' Julia asked, knowing full well that all the children of the Knickerbockers knew one another. They went to the same dancing and riding schools, to the same prep schools.

'Hello, Wharton. How are your beloved dinosaur bones doing? The fellows at Yale call Wharton here "Bonehead", Miss Cross,' said Van Cortlandt, laughing heartily at his joke.

Julia scowled at him. 'Mr Wharton will be a famous scientist one day,' she said indignantly.

Granny shot Helen a withering look, and Helen smoothly

redirected the conversation to another guest at Julia's right, a handsome gentleman named John Beekman.

'Julia, Mr Beekman has just graduated from West Point. He's going to join General Miles's staff in Arizona and will help hunt down that Apache savage Geronimo,' Helen said.

John beamed with pride. 'Since he escaped from the reservation at San Carlos, Miss Cross, Geronimo's killed a dozen Americans and hundreds of Mexicans. We're going into the mountains to bring him back, dead or alive.'

'It sounds *so* dangerous. The *Tribune* has been full of stories about that heathen Indian,' Helen said in a hushed voice.

'He's a killer, Mrs Cross. No doubt about that.'

'Geronimo fights because he refuses to accept America's occupation of the West. Not to mention the terrible conditions on the reservation,' Julia said and took a sip of tea.

A moment of awkward silence ensued. Only the sound of Julia's spoon stirring sugar into her tea could be heard. Hours seemed to pass before anyone dared to speak.

'Julia . . . reads the newspapers daily,' said a very embarrassed Helen.

John Beekman stared into his teacup.

'Will you gentlemen excuse us for a moment?' Helen said, giving them a radiant smile. In the hall, she grabbed the back of her daughter's white princess dress, pulling it so tight that Julia gasped for breath. The talking-to was finished within a minute, and then they were back in the parlour. Julia was steered back toward Van Cortlandt, then on to Charles Whitney and Frederick MacKay.

When the tea concluded two hours later, Julia threw herself on the recamier in the parlour at home and looked resentfully at her mother.

'When do I have to pay a call after that shindig?'

'Don't use slang, Julia. And how many times have I told you? A guest does not pay a call after a tea.'

Julia looked at her mother curiously. She sounded deeply annoyed. Julia had noticed that in the past weeks, Helen had taken far less pleasure in these calls than she had when they'd started. She'd become testy and irritated too, and sometimes Julia would see her staring off into space. But when she asked if anything was wrong, her mother put on a cheerful face and insisted everything was fine.

Granny sat down next to Julia and whispered, 'I'm surprised Mrs Ogden didn't invite that nice Mr Nolan today.'

Julia was at a loss for words. 'I . . . I think he had a business engagement.'

'Such a shame. You know, dear, the next time we go shopping, I was hoping we could go back to Wah Kee's to look at more cats.'

CHAPTER THIRTY-FIVE

At around 7 p.m., twenty wagons, each transporting a single horse, pulled off West Forty-Ninth Street into an alley beside an L-shaped, five-storey, cast-iron-fronted warehouse.

One by one, the beautifully groomed horses, which had been saddled and tacked up, were led to a freight lift at the end of the alley. The lift took two horses and two stable boys at a time up to the fourth floor.

The doors opened on a bizarre sight. The empty warehouse floor had been transformed into a rural scene, as if transposed from the Long Island countryside. The wood plank floor was completely carpeted with real green turf. Attached to the ten-foot-high ceiling was a twenty-foot-diameter dome constructed of plaster. Its underside was painted dark blue and festooned with strings of tiny twinkling electric lights, creating the impression of a night sky. The columns of the space had been altered to resemble pine trees. A forest had been created using huge potted trees and mature shrubbery. Dozens of real birds flew from tree to tree.

Directly under the dome was a circular, white wood plank fence with twenty separate hitching posts, each with its own trough of hay and water. After the horses were led from the lift, servants dressed as jockeys fitted them with special trays attached to the front of the saddle and a pair of saddlebags that contained champagne bottles in ice buckets. Off to the side stood a group of distinguished middle-aged men, all dressed in cutaway coats, white ties, and gloves. They smoked and talked among themselves.

One by one, each gentleman mounted his horse and walked it to its assigned hitching post. Soon twenty horses circled the fence. Between every second horse, servants placed a small carpeted staircase. When everyone was in place, a six-piece band began to play 'Camptown Races.' One of the men on horseback raised his hand and spoke.

'My fellow horsemen. Welcome to the First Annual Horseback Banquet. Tonight we honour the greatest and finest racehorses in the entire world.'

The men applauded, roaring with delight. The horses were too busy eating from their troughs to take notice.

'Let the festivities commence!' the master of ceremonies yelled.

Twenty servants carrying platters of food rushed to each of the horsemen, climbed the little staircases, and placed food on the special trays. Each guest pulled out a champagne bottle and popped it open, producing a twenty-gun salute of flying corks. In place of glasses, they sipped the champagne through long rubber tubes. As the band played on, the gentlemen ate and drank with gusto. Twenty more stable boys with small shovels carried out the clean-up from behind when required. Smoking, laughing, joking, and bragging about their steeds, a spirit of goodwill and fellowship spun around the circle like a ring of fire. In the general gaiety, the stench of gallons of urine soaking into the turf wasn't noticed.

After a modest eight-course dinner, a dessert of chocolate-covered strawberries with whipped cream was delivered. Then the master of ceremonies raised his hand.

'Gentlemen, may I present Amos and his Dancing Darkies!'
Into the inner circle came three white men in blackface, dressed in
white evening clothes and top hats, carrying banjos. The performers
bowed and began to strut around the circle. The crowd cheered like
mad. 'Better than real coons!' someone yelled out.

More champagne was placed in the saddlebags as the evening
wore on. After three bottles, Clarence Post fell off Eclipse onto the
turf and had to be reseated.

Out of respect for their beloved horses, the banquet ended after
three hours.

'You here for Mr Robertson?'

'Yeah, what about you?'

The drivers of the wagons stood in the dark night, waiting for
the festivities to end and the horses to be loaded. They were in
a rotten mood. Upstairs, the horses ate to their hearts' content.
Down in the alley, no one had had the courtesy to offer the men
refreshments.

'I'm waitin' on Mr Shelby. Hey, how 'bout a drink while we
wait?'

'I never refuse a free drink.'

Lefty Montgomery pulled out a flask and poured two shots.

'How about those whores out there on Forty-Ninth?' he said,
nodding towards the street. 'Wish I didn't have to work tonight.'

The driver followed his gaze to the parade of streetwalkers. 'That
one in the purple dress looks mighty good.' He knocked back the
shot in a single gulp. 'Thanks,' he said, grimacing at the strong taste.

Ten seconds later, the driver fell to the ground in a heap.
Montgomery looked around; the coast was clear. He quickly pushed
the man's body off the bench, onto the floor of the wagon. There was
no better knockout drop man in New York than Lefty Montgomery,

a master at sneaking chloral hydrate into a drink in a fraction of a second. He'd had twenty years' experience knocking victims out, robbing and stripping them, and dumping them in alleys. He believed using chloral hydrate was an art. A fifty-grain dose was best for knocking out a burly man the size of the driver. Too much would paralyse the heart and lungs, and you'd have a corpse on your hands.

As the horses were led off the freight lift, Montgomery hopped onto the driver's seat and reached down to put on his victim's hat. Taking the reins, he waited five minutes, until he heard the horse being loaded in the back of the wagon by Mr Robertson's groom. From behind, there came the sound of a scuffle. Pig McGurk, who'd been hiding in the hay bin inside the stall, came out, chloroformed the boy, and dumped him in the wagon. Three sharp knocks sounded. Montgomery snapped the reins to get the two dray horses moving.

At an abandoned building off West Nineteenth Street and Eleventh Avenue, the men dumped the two unconscious bodies in a basement and then proceeded to South Street on the East Side. The wagon was met at the pier by Cross and Kent. Montgomery backed in towards the gangplank, and McGurk flung open the rear doors and led the horse out by its bridle.

Cross was delighted to see the wagon. He had been so angry at Kent's refusal to reduce the debt, and then the idea for this robbery had fallen into his lap purely by accident. It was a quick and easy way to make a big killing. It didn't have the usual risks of breaking into a building or needing elaborate planning. He thought of it all by himself. The job had a wonderful simplicity to it – just wait for the horse to be loaded in the wagon for you, then drive off.

Cross took two steps towards the horse – and froze.

'That isn't Storm Cloud!' he shouted. Kent ran up beside him.

'What the hell are you talking about?'

'This is a chestnut, not a bay, and it has a blaze on its head.

Storm Cloud doesn't have a blaze,' Cross said, panicked. He went to the side of the wagon and examined the coat of arms painted on its side: two crossed golden sabres on a circle of blue. 'It's the right wagon. Goddamn it, they must have loaded the wrong horse.'

'It's still a first-rate thoroughbred. What does it matter?' Montgomery snarled.

'It matters to my buyer,' Kent said. 'He's paying an arm and a leg for Storm Cloud – and only him.'

Cross and Kent looked at each other and seemed to read each other's minds.

'We have to search the other wagons. It's only been fifteen minutes. They're likely still on the street.' Kent turned and called for his men, who were milling about the pier.

'Most of the stables are in Jersey, so they'll be heading for the Hoboken ferry,' Cross said. On either side, pairs of gang members got into carriages or mounted horses and tore off into the night. 'He's got socks on his two front legs!' Cross yelled after them.

'Five hundred to the men who find him!' Kent shouted.

An elderly man, his face weathered to the texture of leather, walked up to Kent. 'This ship leaves at the tide in two hours and waits for no one,' he growled.

In a smooth movement, Kent whipped his blade from his cane and held the tip to the man's throat. 'Rest assured, Captain,' he said softly. 'Our cargo will be aboard by then.'

'Might as well load this one,' Cross said, gesturing to the chestnut.

Kent ran his gloved hand across the horse's muzzle. 'He's beautiful. My children will love him. It's time they learnt to ride.'

From a carriage a block away, Helen watched in amazement as men ran in all directions from the dock.

* * *

As McGurk held a pistol to the driver's forehead, Montgomery yanked open the door of the horse transport.

'Shit, it ain't him,' he barked, imagining his share of the five hundred flying away as if on wings. The two men hopped into their carriage and sped off.

At King and Greenwich Streets, a masked man pulled the driver and groom off their seats onto the street; another ran to the back of the wagon and unlatched the door.

In the darkness, a dappled grey with a mouthful of hay turned to look at the visitor. With a huff, he went back to eating his meal.

'That's my boy!' shouted Flannigan, peering under the horse's belly to see its two front white socks. A block from the Hoboken ferry slip, he'd found his prize. He danced a crude Irish jig as he went back to the front of the wagon and signalled Jenkins to begin pistol-whipping the driver. He took care of the groom, and they dragged the unconscious bodies into a doorway off of Barclay Street and West Broadway.

CHAPTER THIRTY-SIX

'This is a very special transaction I'm offering, Mr Springer. To buy gold bullion at this price is most unusual. But you're an astute businessman who knows a good opportunity.'

George Cross watched as Herbert Springer, a prosperous grain merchant from Toledo, Ohio, ran his hand over the gold bar on the sitting room table. The initials *US* were stamped on the top and bottom. As Springer picked it up to look more closely, it gleamed in the sunlight streaming through the window of his room at the Grand Hotel.

Springer had come to the city for a week to attend the National Grain Dealers Association convention, held at Chickering Hall on Fifth Avenue. The night before, George, posing as a Mr George Candler, had shown him the pleasures and sights of the Tenderloin. The appreciative Springer was more than willing to listen to his investment pitch.

'Gold is a rock-solid investment in times like these, Mr Springer. It will *always* rise in price,' George said.

'Indeed, Mr Candler. But you understand that I need to verify the quality of the metal,' Springer said, setting the bar back down.

'Of course. That's why Mr Bertram Johnson, chief assayer of

the Manhattan Guaranty & Trust Company, has joined us today.'

Mr Johnson, a plump gentleman with wire-rimmed spectacles, smiled and bowed from the waist. From a leather bag on the table, he removed a glass vial of clear solution and an empty steel cup. Impressed, Springer stepped aside and let him get to work. Johnson took the dropper out of the vial, paused, and explained in a professorial manner, 'This, sir, is nitric acid, the test for true gold.' He put a drop on the gold bar. 'If the solution turns green, it means this is gold-plated. If there's no reaction, it's true, one hundred per cent gold.'

Springer's eyes were glued to the bar. When he saw no reaction, he broke into a wide grin.

'I assure you, Mr Springer, that all the bullion is of this quality,' George said.

'Very well then. You're right, Mr Candler, you can't go wrong with gold. Silver is for pansy-picking fops.' Springer pulled out a cigar and picked up the heavy bar. He paced the sitting room, tossing the gold into the air and catching it with one hand. A strapping man in his forties, he did it with ease. But on the third try, the bar slipped from his hand and landed on the stone hearth of the fireplace. Springer stooped to retrieve it – and froze.

He looked at George with cold eyes. Slowly, he pointed to a greyish gash on the edge of the bar. Taking his penknife, he started to scratch away at another part of the bar, scraping off a film of gold to reveal a dark grey surface. At the spot where the solution had been applied, he found a quarter-inch plug of solid gold.

'You blackguard! This a goddamn lead bar,' Springer cried, dropping the bar to the wood floor with a thump.

George stood paralysed with fear as Springer pulled a derringer from his frock coat pocket.

'You thought I was some dumbass hick you could swindle,' he said in a hurt voice, raising his arm to aim the weapon.

'Yes, as a matter of fact, I did,' George said. With the agility of the former athlete he was, he scooped up the bar in a fluid motion and smashed Springer on the head with it.

The businessman tumbled to the ground and lay still. 'Let's get the hell out of here, George,' Johnson yelled, grabbing his bag.

George took a step toward the door – then halted. He went back to Springer and took his wallet.

He and Johnson were out on the street in less than a minute. 'Don't run. Walk,' George hissed. The two men paced up Broadway and turned right on Thirty-First Street. They walked eight blocks along Sixth Avenue before slipping into a saloon. George downed two mugs of beer, his throat as dry as a bale of cotton.

'Christ, that was close, George,' Johnson said. 'What are you going to do now?'

George was counting the money in the wallet. 'Only four hundred,' he said dejectedly.

'How much are you down?'

'Four thousand. I could've gotten that for the one bar,' George said, rubbing his hands up and down his face.

'At least we still have the bar. But we'll have to get it re-plated.'

'That bar's been good to us, Henry. It's paid off eight thousand by now.'

'Still. It's best to lie low for a while. You're going to have to give them something soon, Georgie, or they'll come looking for you again.'

George ignored Henry's words. Staring into space, he muttered under his breath, 'With this four hundred, I can get even tonight. I know I can.'

CHAPTER THIRTY-SEVEN

'I believe the first dance is mine, Mrs Cross.'

'Don't be such an ass, Wilberforce, I've called for the first dance.'

Horace Wilberforce and Clinton Collingwood stood forehead to forehead with looks of rage on their red, leathery faces.

Helen Cross inserted her long, white-gloved arm between the pot bellies of her two admirers, but they paid no mind. They still glared at each other, seconds away from launching into combat like two elks locking antlers in mating season.

In a quiet, soothing voice, Helen said, 'Mr Wilberforce has the first dance, but you may have the next one, Mr Collingwood.'

Collingwood snorted and stepped back, angry at Wilberforce's smug look. The full orchestra in the balcony of the great ballroom struck up a Strauss waltz. Helen took Wilberforce's plump, gloved hand and glided effortlessly on to the dance floor. The old man beamed with joy as though he had been transformed into the young man he had been in 1858. The couple spun gracefully across the beautiful, black marble floor of the ballroom with all eyes fastened on Helen in her white, low-cut ballgown. When Helen spotted her husband standing by himself, near one of the gilded cast-iron columns that held up the horseshoe-shaped balcony, she smiled, and he walked out of the room.

Out in the high-ceilinged foyer, Cross ran into his friend, Bruce Price.

'Not leaving so soon, old boy,' admonished Price in a pretend scolding.

'Just wanted to get a smoke and gaze at the ocean from the piazza of your magnificent building.'

Price smiled at the compliment.

'This may be your best work of all. What a palace. There's never been a hotel like this,' said Cross with genuine feeling. He always admired – and at the same time was jealous of – Price's tremendous talent. The man never failed to do something innovative in each of his buildings, and that was the true mark of artistic genius. Cross tried to do the same in his commissions but never pulled it off. His projects always turned out to be a rehash of a previous design. He needed to break through that creative wall to do something special.

Cross pulled out his gold cigarette case as Price turned and entered the wide double doors to the ballroom. 'I'll be right back. Catch up with you inside.'

Though Newport was the centre of the summer season, there were important events held elsewhere. All of society's elite were at the charity ball at the new Oceanside Hotel in Long Branch, New Jersey. It was an invitation no one would turn down. The hotel, through the tobacco heir Pierre Lorillard's patronage, had become fashionable very quickly. Cross wasn't lying when he said no other hotel was like it. It was massive, stretching along the beach for two hundred yards at least. But instead of housing hundreds of small rooms, the hotel offered only fifty, all huge suites. The owner's strategy was shrewd, like the Metropolitan Opera's, which kept its elite seating to a minimum to drive up demand. Along the entire rear of the building was a deep porch where one could enjoy the views and walk on a wooden bridge over the dunes to the private beach. Servants in cutaway coats would serve guests on the sand, bringing buckets of champagne and iced platters of Blue Point oysters.

The hotel was also unusual in its method of construction. Instead of being built of wood with a shingled exterior, it was made entirely of stone, giving it a strong, massive stature rising up out of the sand dunes like a fortress. No hurricane would ever budge it from its place. Its sense of majesty made it seem very elite and special to the rich – a place they *had* to visit.

Cross puffed away on his cigarette as he walked down the thickly carpeted hallway flanked by panelled walls of African mahogany with onyx wainscoting. At the end of the long hall, he turned around to see if anyway else was about. But with the ball going on, the rest of the hotel was completely deserted. He put out his cigarette in an ashtray on a side table and walked to a door located just before the window in the end wall of the hallway. Through the door was a service room where there was an open dumb waiter. In his white tails, Cross hopped into the dumb waiter, sat down cross-legged, and pushed the switch to send it up. It rose along iron rails in its wooden enclosed shaft, slowly passing identical service rooms on each floor. At the fourth floor, it came to a stop, but instead of getting off, Cross stood up and gave a low whistle. Above him was an opening in the ceiling, and Culver's head appeared. He reached down to Cross to help pull him up into the opening.

Aside from being a great work of design, Price's hotel had included an engineering innovation that no hotel had ever employed. All other hotels followed the same layout – a central corridor on each floor, lined on both sides with rooms about fifteen feet in depth. The Oceanside used huge, wood and iron roof trusses that spanned its stone walls for a distance of seventy feet, allowing the rooms to measure over thirty feet and giving them a palatial feel. No one had ever before used such colossal trusses, other than for the roofs of great railroad sheds.

Cross stood with eight other members of Kent's gang. In front of them were row after row of the great timber trusses, giant triangles latticed with iron and wood struts. Directly below them was the ceiling of the fourth floor, which was attached to the bottoms of the trusses. And that was where the top-floor luxury suites were located – brimming with expensive jewels, clothing, and cash. All the gang had to do was walk along and break through the ceiling into each suite. Instead of plaster ceilings, the rooms had ornate pressed metal. By just tapping on the ceiling panels from above, they could quietly remove a section and lower themselves down into the room. No messy plaster and lath to deal with, and no risk of being seen entering from the corridor.

'This will be a snap, Mr Engineer,' said Culver, slapping Cross on the back. After each successful robbery, Cross had been more and more accepted into the gang until he was pretty much considered one of the fellows – except by Brady, who mercifully wasn't present tonight.

'I'm actually an architect, Mr Culver. There's a big difference.'

Cross was trembling with excitement, not only because of the potential take, but also because he alone would direct this robbery. Millicent, Kent's beloved wife, was quite ill, and Kent wouldn't leave her bedside, so he'd entrusted the entire operation to Cross. Kent really had no choice. The job was planned for the night of the gala ball and couldn't be postponed. Cross had to prove he was up to the task. When Helen had smiled at him from the dance floor, that was the signal that every top-floor guest was in the ballroom. The men who were carrying canvas bags and small hammers took their positions so they were lined up over the rooms and waited for Cross's cue. From the floor plans, Cross knew how the rooms were spaced out and where each man should stand. He felt like a general about to give the command to attack. Cross took a breath, grinned, and waved his troops into battle.

'Nice and easy. You just tap and the ceiling comes loose,' reminded Cross.

Using the wooden end of the hammers, they lightly tapped and pushed down the metal ceiling panels and, like rabbits hopping into their burrows, dropped down into the rooms using narrow rope ladders tied to the trusses. Cross followed Culver down and went along with him as he scooped up every piece of clothing and grabbed objects off dressing room tables. Each room had a small safe that Cross thought would be invulnerable, but with a pry bar, Culver made easy work of it and emptied the safe out. The rooms were luxuriously decorated with beautiful rugs, chandeliers, and French period furniture. Bedrooms flanked a massive sitting room. Cross went over to one of the huge picture windows to look at the ocean and smiled.

'All done,' whispered Culver, who started climbing up the ladder. Two men were left above to pull up the bulging bags from below. Cross followed him, and they hit another room. Soon the truss space was filled with bags. Down the gang went into room after room. Cross grew tired of following Culver down and waited for him above, hoisting up the bag of loot. There were a dozen suites and, by Cross's count, four more to go. The truss space was pitch-black, so Cross was shocked when it was suddenly filled with bright light. He was confused, and his eyes opened wide in panic. The other men froze in place. They looked around, expecting to see police shining lanterns at them with guns drawn. But Cross finally discovered the source of light. It was coming from one of the ceilings they had lifted – the lights were on in a room below.

Cross crept over, knelt by the hole, and cautiously peeked into it. His head jerked back in fear as he heard voices.

'Edith, I couldn't keep my eyes off you. I want you so badly,' a man cried.

'Gerald, we can't do this – it's madness. We'll be missed,' said a woman, not very convincingly.

'The hell with them. They're too busy dancing. It'll be an hour before they notice we're gone.'

There was a brief silence and a woman's low moan.

'Take me to the bedroom,' cried the woman.

'No, here,' ordered the man.

With great care, Cross had decided where in the ceiling to enter, so rope ladders would be off to the side in the sitting rooms, away from the entries. But this ladder seemed to be not more than ten feet away from the couple. It would be seen immediately if either one of them glanced upward. Cross slowly raised the ladder and tucked it up safely in the truss space.

'I want to kiss every square inch of your body,' commanded the man.

'Do it,' pleaded the woman. 'But be careful of my gown – it's a Pingat.'

'I'll buy you ten gowns. I'm going to rip this off your body. I want you naked.'

The woman gave out another low, passionate moan.

All of a sudden, Cross recognised the voices – it was Gerald Davenport and Edith Trevelyan, who were both married, but not to each other. To his knowledge, they had never even spoken. Cross was temporarily transfixed by this discovery of infidelity. He knew that many married individuals cheated on their spouses in his set but was amazed that these two were lovers. Who could have imagined it? Although Helen had probably known all along.

The other men had come up from below and were standing around him. Cross propped his arms on both sides of the opening and slowly lowered his head through. Not more than ten feet away were two completely naked people, fornicating with incredible animal energy. True to his word, Davenport couldn't wait and had taken Edith right on one of the matching sitting room sofas. Sounds of such intense passion came floating up and out of the opening that Cross was embarrassed. His gang members were mesmerised.

Cross kept watching, but out of the corner of his eye, he saw something move under the opposite sofa. He pulled himself up and started taking an inventory of the gang. 'Where's Culver?' he hissed.

The other men shook their heads.

In horror, Cross looked down and saw movement again under the sofa across from the lovers. He looked back at the couple, who had increased the vigour and intensity of their lovemaking and seemed to be in no hurry to finish. Cross began to panic. He could imagine Kent berating him for fouling up the job. It might be an hour before the two of them called it quits, and that would be an unbearable wait for Cross. He just couldn't chance it; he had to stick to the timetable he'd set. The longer they were up there, the greater the possibility of being detected. In a low voice, he ordered the men to begin to bring down the bags on the dumb waiter. Cross lowered his head again and saw Culver peeking out from under the sofa and up at the ceiling. Cross looked over at the couple to make sure they were still preoccupied, then waved at Culver to get his attention. A decision had to be made quickly. Should they wait it out until they finished and returned to the ball? But that could take some time, and when they were putting their clothes back on, would they spot Culver?

Cross gestured to Culver to come up. Culver's eyes were full of fear at this command, and he glanced over at the man and woman. He suddenly slithered out and crawled on his hands and knees across the Oriental rug, holding the bag of loot on his back like Santa Claus. Cross lowered the rope ladder through the hole, and Culver scampered up like hounds were on his tail. Up in the truss space, he was breathing heavily and calmed himself by taking a long swig from a small, amber-coloured bottle.

Cross and Culver went down the dumb waiter to the basement where two bound and chloroformed hotel servants lay motionless on the stone floor. After helping Culver out through the basement door with the bag, Cross returned to the ballroom and asked Sybil Davenport, Gerald's wife, to dance.

CHAPTER THIRTY-EIGHT

'This place is one giant treasure chest,' Helen exclaimed. She had been in incredibly high spirits since the Oceanside heist last week. It delighted Helen that all of New York society was in an outrage over the robbery. That's all they talked about. She couldn't wait to plan the next job. It became her consuming passion, even more important than Julia's coming-out ball.

On a table before them lay a map of Newport. Helen had marked the houses with the greatest potential for loot with red Xs. The marks concentrated on either side of Bellevue Avenue, the main thoroughfare for the town's richest neighbourhood.

For ten weeks in the summer, this narrow stretch of land overlooking the Atlantic Ocean became New York society's social Mecca. At a staggering cost, balls, dinner parties, yachting fetes, and concerts were thrown, each family trying to outshine the other. Bellevue, Daily, and Ocean Avenues were jammed with a promenade of magnificent carriages, carrying beautiful women who wanted to be seen and admired while their husbands raced yachts and played polo. Aunt Caroline's mansion, Beechwood, recently renovated by Richard Morris Hunt at a cost of two million dollars, was the brightest star in Newport's social firmament. During the summer season, Helen and John had a standing invitation to stay there anytime they wanted.

'How about Watts-Sherman? He's a banker,' Cross said. 'Remember, I worked on that house for Richardson. I may still have a set of plans.'

Helen smiled at her husband. 'Of course I remember. You were a young architect, so happy to be learning from the master. Those were happy days. Lean, but happy.'

'True. I was just getting started, but you know, those were some of the best days for us. George had just been born. Do you remember? I didn't think I'd like having a child, but I was wrong. It was a joy.'

'We'd take him along the Cliff Walk to that little beach near the point. He'd get knocked down by the waves, but he'd always get up and run back in,' Helen said, smiling.

'George was always headstrong,' Cross said. 'But those were wonderful times.' He placed his hand on his wife's. 'What do you think?'

'Watts-Sherman's place has nothing special. There are more lucrative targets.'

Cross smiled. Helen's tenacity amazed him. She could have been a general or an admiral, planning a battle.

'Kingscote, Château-sur-Mer . . . What about the Belmonts' place – By-the-Sea?'

'Maybe Beechwood?' Cross asked, knowing what his wife's response would be.

'Blood is thicker than water, sir. Aunt Caroline is off limits. She's family,' Helen said, giving his hand a little slap and laughing.

'The problem is the servants. These places can have up to a dozen, and they're always there. It's too many to tie up or lock in the wine cellar,' Cross said. Helen nodded. 'What about Isaac

235

Bell?' he continued. 'I can get the drawings from Stanny.'

'No, too poor,' Helen said. She ran her finger along the red marks, pausing to take inventory of each house. It had amazed Cross to discover that his wife had a near photographic memory when it came to valuable objects, recalling where every priceless vase or necklace was located. Her reconnaissance of Julia's coming-out guests' homes had been quite impressive.

'The Millards are a possibility. So are the Christies. The Van Alens' house is all by itself, and he's always in London on business. Do you know, he actually keeps his horses on the first floor and lives above them!' Helen said, amused by this eccentricity.

'No more horses for me,' Cross said. 'Too damn much trouble.'

At that moment, Helen's bedroom door swung open. Charlie dashed in, grinning.

'It seems you've forgotten the rule about knocking,' Cross said.

'I didn't know that applied to me.'

'It especially applies to you.'

Sucking on a lemon stick, Charlie sidled up to the table and looked at the map.

'What's going on here?' he asked with mock curiosity.

'We're marking all the places in Newport to which we've been invited this summer,' Helen said.

'Great guns, you're popular. Glad I don't have to go. So dull.'

'We certainly don't want to bore you. That's why you're staying behind with Mrs Johnston,' his father said, patting him on the shoulder.

'I'm most grateful,' said Charlie. 'Now, do you want to see my dancing steps?'

Though his parents were plainly preoccupied, they nodded. If they indulged him, they might get rid of him more quickly.

Charlie started to hum a tune, and with dainty, nimble steps, he performed a little dance. When he was finished, Cross and Helen politely applauded. Charlie was smiling from ear to ear – not because his parents were pleased with his performance, but because the dance he'd made up on the spot had been a success.

'I'll need one dollar for next week's lesson,' he said brightly.

'I thought it was always fifty cents,' protested his father.

'Special double session. We're learning the latest mazurka.'

Cross doled out the money, and Charlie skipped out of the room. Next week, he'd demonstrate his progress in art class by showing them some drawings his classmate, Fred Truscott, would provide him for five cents apiece.

The Crosses returned to the map. The logistics of the job greatly depended on the location of the house, so they paid particular attention to the entry and exit points. Helen wrote the names of potential victims on a sheet of paper. She went down the list, giving her husband the pros and cons of each. When the cons outweighed the pros, she crossed off the name.

'John, the Van Duncans have this unusual staircase just for the use of the servants,' Helen noted with excitement. 'So Henry and Lily don't have to run into the servants in the hallways, they had an inner stair built so the help can get into the rooms through secret doors. The staircase is entered from the basement and leads all the way up to the fourth floor. We get in there, and we can clean out the place when they are having a dinner party.'

Helen's beautiful face lit up at the thought. Cross had never seen his wife look so radiant.

'But Henry's had some financial setbacks lately, so they're not nearly as rich as they used to be,' Helen said and crossed the Van Duncans' name off the list.

As they worked, Cross marvelled at the ways in which his wife had surprised him. After he'd told her about Kent, she had thrown herself into the project with incredible energy. He'd thought she would fold under the heartbreak, but to his amazement – and admiration – she'd displayed an iron will. Cross felt he had no choice but to tell Helen that Robert was assigned to investigate the robberies, but she showed no panic at all. In fact, at dinners with her brother-in-law, she carefully probed to find out what he was up to. From the typical, cloistered society woman, content to dedicate her life to household responsibilities and children, she'd undergone a remarkable transformation.

Unlike her husband, though, Helen never condemned George for causing their calamity. *She doesn't understand the shadowy side of our son*, Cross thought. *Neither do I, as a matter of fact.* Father and son had avoided each other since their confrontation in the carriage, unsure of what to say.

Helen spoke of nothing but the planning of the robberies whenever they were alone together. For the first time in years, they spent evenings in the same room, selecting potential targets and weighing the merits of each job. They hadn't talked so much in the last decade. Cross had a new regard for his wife, for the clarity of her analytical thought. He actually enjoyed her company. Helen's mind, he realised, was razor sharp.

She already knew where the owners would be on a certain day throughout the summer; the Newport social calendar was set in stone weeks before the season began. Some would be sailing yachts far out on the ocean; others would spend the afternoon at a polo match and attend a party after. Next to the names of the most likely victims, Helen made an inventory of assets that could be taken. The more she spoke, the more mesmerised Cross became. He could imagine her as the head of a giant company, barking orders to a board of directors.

Each name on the list reminded the Crosses of parties they had attended or gossip they had heard. As the evening wore on, they spent more time reminiscing than planning the robbery.

'Old man Ogden thought he had me trapped, but since you designed his house, I knew where the dumb waiter was. I escaped his grasp and down I went. He spent an hour searching for me upstairs. You know, that dumb waiter of Ogden's could be quite useful if we decided to hit them, a wonderful way to get all the loot down – just like at Oceanside.' Helen was laughing uncontrollably, and Cross couldn't help joining in.

Abruptly, though, he stopped and looked at his wife's face. It was lovelier at forty than it had ever been before. He reached out and put his hand on the back of her slender neck. Gently, he pulled her towards him. Giving her a long, passionate kiss, he whispered, 'I've been quite the fool.' With his arm around her waist, he led her to her bed.

In the darkness, Cross gazed at his wife's naked body as she walked to the bathroom. She *was* like Helen of Troy, with the sort of beautiful body one saw on statues from antiquity – perfectly conceived, without the tiniest flaw. Her long black hair cascaded down her back, swaying as she walked.

When she returned, Helen snuggled up against Cross's chest. He wrapped his arm around her, pulling her close as he drifted into a wonderfully peaceful sleep.

He awakened abruptly to a cry from his wife.

'My God, what have I done?' Helen sat up in the bed.

Alarmed and disoriented, Cross sat up too.

'The Goelets. I completely forgot about the Goelets. *They'll* be our next job,' Helen said triumphantly.

CHAPTER THIRTY-NINE

'Hurry the hell up, Charlie, or we'll be late.'

Charlie had had to take the unfamiliar Ninth Avenue Elevated Railroad to meet Eddie, and it had taken longer to get across town than he'd thought. His friend was impatiently waiting at the bottom of the stairs at Cortlandt Street. He grabbed Charlie's arm and pulled him in the direction of the West Side piers.

Crossing West Street, Charlie saw hundreds of screaming boys crowded around a pier where a white steamboat was moored. A fast-moving stream of boys was running up the gangplank onto the ship. Once aboard, they raced around the decks, shouting and waving to the boys still on the pier.

'What the hell's this?' Charlie shouted above the din. Cursing had become second nature to him, a fact he took great pride in, as it allowed him to blend with the rest of Eddie's set.

'It's the annual newsboys' picnic. They're taking us on a boat ride up the Hudson River to the Palisades,' Eddie yelled, waving to friends already on board.

Together, he and Charlie squirmed their way to the front of the crowd and sprinted up the gangplank, butting up against the backs of the boys ahead of them.

'Come on. Get your asses movin'!' Eddie screamed, pushing them forward.

One boy fell on his face, and Eddie and Charlie hurtled over him. On board, they raced to the bow of the boat.

'The rich people feel sorry for the newsies, so they try to do somethin' nice for us,' Eddie said, climbing onto the ship's railing and spreading out his arms for balance. 'Same do-gooders who built the lodging houses, so we don't have to be out on the street. But you know you'll never get me in one of those joints.'

'They'll send your ass out west to work on a farm, right?'

'That's right, Charlie, my boy. Eddie Mooney ain't gonna be no farmer with cow shit on his shoes. I'll step in the horse shit on the streets of Manhattan any day.'

The boat was fully loaded, hundreds of crazed, filthy newsboys racing back and forth on the decks like wild animals let out of cages at the zoo. The children were delirious with excitement and impossible to control. The crew members, dressed in smart, navy-blue uniforms with red piping on the sleeves and legs, were cursing and yelling at their new passengers, but corralling them was an impossible task, and they quickly gave up. Soon, every painted cork life preserver was around a dirty neck, and the restroom was a pigsty, the toilets impossibly backed up. When the newsies discovered the steel staircase to the bridge and started their ascent, the captain, a nautical-looking elderly man in a double-breasted tunic with gold buttons, ordered the door to the bridge barred.

The *Blue Angel* cast off, the engine thrown into reverse as it backed away from the pier.

'Come on,' Eddie shouted to Charlie. 'They're going to give out candy.'

At the stern, a table was set up. Well-dressed, middle-aged men were arranging brown paper bags on its surface, but the newsboys descended like locusts, grabbing the bags as fast as the men could set them out.

'One to a boy. One to a boy,' screamed one of the benefactors.

The bags contained abundant amounts of wrapped caramels, bonbons, and a variety of hard candies, which were immediately stuffed into salivating mouths. When their stomachs no longer had room, the boys did what came naturally: they threw candy at one another. Once the first boy began flinging sweets about, another followed suit. In an instant, three hundred newsboys were pelting one another and the crew with projectiles. The crew, outgunned and helpless, retreated below decks, locking the hatches behind them. They were paid to be sailors, they huffed, not attendants in a zoo.

The captain and helmsman, captive on the bridge, watched the spectacle in horror. As the boat steamed slowly north, the frenzy increased. The children seemed mad with delight.

In an attempt to entertain them, the Society for the Prevention of Cruelty to Children, which had officially sponsored the excursion, had hired a small brass band. The society believed that the unfortunate children had never been exposed to music, though in fact every boy present likely frequented saloons and heard music daily. Undaunted, the musicians set up on the lower deck at the bow; in the belief that the show must go on, they played stirring military marches, which only seemed to intensify the madness spinning about them. Soon the newsies turned on them too, bombarding them with candy. With its wide-mouthed horn, the tuba was a favourite target. It soon filled with candy, making it impossible to play. Charlie caught the percussionist in the back of the head with a peppermint ball. The band had no choice but to retreat.

Finally, the captain could take no more abuse. He charged from the bridge like a wounded rhino and made his way below deck to a private cabin. Entering, he was amazed by an incongruous sight: society ladies and gentlemen from the Society for the Prevention of Cruelty to Children, having tea.

'So nice of you to take the time to accompany us today, Mr Cross,' Mrs Isabella Beekman was saying as she poured tea into George's cup. 'Captain, George recently graduated from Harvard and is teaching at the Children's Aid Society school this summer. His students have made wonderful progress.'

George, who had been shanghaied into coming by Dr Caldwell, gave a meek smile and took a sip of his tea.

Cap in hand, the captain walked up to a distinguished matron in a hat bedecked with artificial flowers.

'Mrs Beekman, do you have any idea what those little beasts are doing to my boat?'

The woman took a long sip of tea and patted her lips with a linen napkin. 'I do hope the children are enjoying themselves. Those poor unfortunates deserve some pleasure in their lives,' she said.

Around the table, her companions nodded earnestly.

'Madame, I'm turning this boat around. We are going back to Manhattan.'

'You shall do nothing of the sort,' Mrs Beekman said. Her voice implied that the captain was a feeble-minded Irish servant of the very lowest sort. 'You have been paid to land us at the picnic grounds at the foot of the Palisades and then take us back. *That's* what you'll do, sir.'

'I'll land you and leave these animals there,' the captain thundered.

'That would be a mistake indeed, sir. Do you know of my family?'

Reminded of the Beekmans' sway, the captain cowered like a beaten dog and left the cabin.

At the Palisades, each boy received a large lunch box as he disembarked. Inside was a thick roast beef sandwich with pickles, two hard-boiled eggs, a generous slice of chocolate cake, a bottle of sarsaparilla, and an apple. The newsboys' hunger had returned, and the food was devoured in minutes, save the apples. They became handy projectiles as the boys cavorted happily across the picnic grounds. The hot summer air was full of delicious red missiles.

Like many of the boys, Eddie had no interest in games. With Charlie at his side, he was eager to explore the woods. Eddie prowled about with great interest. It was a completely alien world to him. He had been to Central Park, of course, but always to steal purses, and he didn't have much time to enjoy nature.

The captain, who had raised the gangplank so that the boys would be forced to stay ashore, ordered the crew to feed river water through a fire hose to wash off the decks. If need be, he vowed, he'd turn the hose on the boys on the return trip.

From the upper deck of the bow, Mrs Beekman and her fellow members of the Society watched the fun the boys were having with great pleasure.

'Remember that we are child savers,' Mrs Beekman said. 'Though I maintain that these wretches would be better off with farm families, breathing the good, clean country air of the Midwest.'

'But some have parents. They'd never see them again,' a dissenting voice murmured.

'You call those vile creatures *parents*? A cat would make a better mother or father,' Mrs Beekman said, voice dripping with disdain.

After two hours, the steamboat's whistle blew, signalling the return to the boat. To the crew's relief, gorging themselves and running around had worn the boys out. Most stood at the ship railings and quietly watched the Palisades to the west and Manhattan to the east slip by. A few even fell asleep on the decks.

As the gangplank was lowered, Mrs Beekman and other Society members gathered at the top of the gangway to hand out an informative pamphlet entitled 'God Loves a Clean and Moral Boy'. It was forced into the newsies' hands before they could descend the gangplank.

'Here. I think this will do you some real good, Charlie Cross.'

Charlie's heart dropped like a stone. He looked up and saw his big brother standing above him, a very amused look on his face.

'Let's have a talk onshore, Little Brother,' said George.

CHAPTER FORTY

'John. So good to see you, old man,' Stanford White bellowed. 'I was wondering when you and Helen would make it up to Newport.'

'With Helen preparing for Julia's coming-out ball and all the work that's come into the office of late, it's been hard to get away,' Cross said.

'I'm eager to see your design for the theatre.'

'You'll see it in *American Architect and Building News* next month,' Cross said.

'John Cross here is one of the city's best architects, Bob,' White said to the tall man standing next to him. 'You know Robert Goelet, John?'

'Yes, we've met several times,' Cross said, nodding to Goelet.

'Mr Cross, always a pleasure,' Goelet said. 'Quite a crowd tonight, eh?'

The horseshoe-shaped porch at the rear of the Newport Casino was packed with women, whose vibrant summer gowns stood in stark contrast to the black evening wear of the men. The casino, on Bellevue Avenue, was the social centre of the Newport summer season. It had been designed by Charlie McKim for James Gordon Bennett Jr., owner of the *New York Herald*. Bennett's friend had gotten kicked out of the Newport Reading Room, the resort's former social centre, after Bennett dared him to ride a horse inside. Outraged, Bennett bought land and built his own club. It was a wonderfully creative building covered in wood shingles, its porch clad in a screen of lattice and spindles. White, who'd decorated the rooms, added a domed clock tower. Lawn tennis courts were added shortly after the building was completed, and McKim included a sizable theatre on the second floor.

Tonight, there was to be a performance by a well-known tenor from Italy.

'Stanny designed a wonderful house for you, Mr Goelet,' Cross said.

After the Astors, the Goelets were the biggest landlords in New York, collecting millions in rent. Goelet and his brother, Ogden, had inherited the business from their father and uncle. Of late, real estate had become the most lucrative business in the city. If he'd known how valuable the land would become, John Jacob Astor was fond of saying, he would have bought up the entire island of Manhattan.

Two years before, Stanny had done a huge shingled house for Robert Goelet on Narragansett Avenue, near the cliff overlooking the Atlantic. The project cost more than eighty thousand dollars. The house's rear façade, facing the ocean, had a porch that stretched the width of the house, supported by the slender, Japanese-inspired columns Stanny so admired.

'We love Southside. Sitting on the porch, seeing the sun rise over the ocean . . . it's my favourite place in the world,' Goelet said, smiling at Stanny.

To create a house in which a client loved to spend his time – that was one of the best things about being an architect. It wasn't just four walls and a roof; it was a home and a refuge, a place where one might feel safe from the unfairness and cruelty of the world. Cross wished he could design a country house of his own. He could escape there and take his family with them, spiriting him away from harm.

It was seven o'clock. The crowd began to make its way towards the theatre. Cross excused himself and went to look for Helen. He found her in the cafe, surrounded as usual by male admirers. One of them, a distinguished man with an aquiline nose and a mane of swept-back hair, he'd seen somewhere before.

'John, you remember Count Aleksandrov?'

'Of course. We met at Honoria's party. How are you, Count?'

'In the presence of such beauty, I always feel elated,' the count said in heavily accented English, nodding towards Helen.

Cross smiled at the compliment. Then he excused himself and pulled Helen aside.

'Remember, you've got just two hours,' she said urgently. 'Once the performance is over, I don't know if I'll be able to hold Goelet here until you get back.'

'If anyone asks where I am, tell them I hate Italian opera and went out for a smoke,' Cross said. He knew no one would miss him. The men would kill for the honour of sitting next to Helen and be glad that he was out of the way.

'The necklace with eight hundred pearls is in the safe under the floorboards, in her private study on the second floor in front of the bay window,' Helen reminded him. 'You have to lift the rug. And Goelet's ninth-century gold chalice is behind a panel on the fourth bookshelf from the top in his library.'

Cross nodded. Then he drifted to the rear of the crowd filing into the theatre. As the last person entered, he slipped down the stairs to the entry hall and left. Walking two blocks north, Cross turned into an alley where a boy held the reins of a bay. Giving him

248

a dollar, Cross mounted and headed east, making his way through backstreets until he came to Narragansett Avenue. As he rode, he couldn't help wondering if – or when – the informant would strike again. Would he be riding into a trap? Would he find the Pinkertons and his brother waiting for him?

No. He had to put his fears out of his mind and concentrate on the task ahead.

Finally, he reached a large house on the right. There, the road dead-ended at the cliff. Tying the horse up behind a large holly bush, Cross opened the saddle bag and pulled out a folded sheet of paper. He checked his pocket watch – 7:15 p.m. – and walked up the drive.

As he reached the front porch, Kent emerged from the front door. 'Such a nice summer house. I'll keep the details in mind when you design one for me,' he said, puffing away on his Havana.

Cross cursed him under his breath but gave only a strained smile. 'What about those servants?'

'Fast asleep. Montgomery has sprinkled his fairy dust,' Kent said.

Though it wouldn't have bothered his conscience, Kent had thought killing six to eight servants too time-consuming. Another method had to be employed to get them out of the way. Luckily, the large houses always needed extra help in the summer. By lying through his teeth, Montgomery secured a job as a gardener's assistant for the week before the robbery. He showed himself a hard and dedicated worker and was quickly accepted into the Goelet household. His fellow servants liked his jovial personality. Mrs Hopkins, the widowed head housekeeper, had already taken a fancy to him.

Two hours earlier, as the servants prepared to have their tea, Montgomery kindly offered to help – and put an expert dose of chloral hydrate in the pot. In the servants' dining hall, Cross saw all seven fast asleep, heads resting on the long oak table. They looked like schoolchildren, fallen asleep atop their desks. The head butler was snoring so loudly that Cross burst out laughing. Shaking his head, he walked back to the twenty-four-foot-high entry hall White had designed. Kent's men had already begun to work. Priceless Japanese and Chinese pottery was snatched up and bagged. Paintings came off the walls. With a blueprint he'd secured from White's office, Cross directed them to a secret compartment behind a wall in Goelet's dressing room that held jewellery, rare coins, and stacks of cash. His wife's closets were cleaned out, as well as the china and silver service. Helen's keen eye led them to the floor safe, where Mrs Goelet kept her priceless necklace, and to the gold chalice.

Watching the buzz of activity, that same incredible sense of exhilaration swept over Cross like an ocean wave. He felt as if he were walking on air, floating a foot above the floor.

He strolled through the house, as much to admire Stanny's interior decoration skills as to supervise the men. On each successive job, Stanny outdid himself – a hard thing for an architect to accomplish. But Stanny had yet to reach his artistic zenith. While Cross didn't like robbing a friend's client, he knew from conversations with Robert that he had to pick different marks. Mansions in the city were no longer safe. That made Newport the next most lucrative target.

The men were working their way through the eight bedrooms on the second floor. As Montgomery opened a wide, panelled oak door, a deafening explosion rang out, and he fell to the hall carpet, clutching his right leg.

'I've been shot!' he cried and launched into a tirade of expletives. Dozens of tiny bloodstains appeared on his light grey

Brooks Brothers trousers. His leg, the gang realised as they clustered around, had been blasted by buckshot.

Another blast exploded above their heads, and the men dived to the floor.

From inside the bedroom, an angry, high-pitched voice called out, 'General Jackson, the British have commenced the attack! They're advancing in force against the earthworks.'

Another blast followed. The men scattered to either side of the bedroom door, trying to see inside. Kent joined them. In the dim light streaming through the bedroom shutters, he could make out a withered old man, sitting on the bed, reloading a double-barrelled shotgun.

'We have them on the run,' the old man shouted. 'The bastards are falling back.' He raised the shotgun and unloaded both barrels at the door.

Cross came up behind Kent. 'What the hell is going on? This racket's going to alarm the neighbours.'

Kent frowned at him. 'It's a family member, I believe, who thinks he's under attack.'

'General Jackson, the fog is lifting. We can pick them off like squirrels!'

Cross peeked in. 'The old fool thinks he's back with Stonewall Jackson?'

'Not Stonewall – Andrew Jackson. At the Battle of New Orleans, if I'm not mistaken.'

Cross was dumbfounded. 'What should we do?'

'You men finish up – and don't forget that tapestry in the library!' Kent yelled.

Another blast boomed forth. Cross and Kent ducked behind the wall, exchanging uneasy glances. Then Kent got down on his hands and knees and crawled into the bedroom.

'Cease fire, cease fire! The Redcoats are retreating. We've got them on the run, boys!' Kent yelled with great dramatic effect, as if he were on a stage. Cautiously, he made his way to the side of the bed, stood up, and slapped the old man on the shoulder.

'Good work, good work. We've won. I'm proud of you, son.'

The old man laughed, waving the shotgun above his bald, wrinkled head.

'We did it, General. We thumped those goddamn Britishers.' Kent smiled and gently removed the gun from the old man's hands. Gently, he eased him back against the pillow. 'You've had a rough day, son. Take a rest.'

The old man smiled and closed his eyes. 'We did it, sir,' he mumbled. 'We whooped the hell out of 'em.'

A bottle of soothing syrup stood on the nightstand. Kent picked it up and examined its contents. Seeing that it contained cocaine and had an eighty per cent alcohol content, he gave the old man three tablespoons.

'Sweet dreams, soldier.'

Kent set the gun under the bed and left the bedroom. In the hallway, he met Cross, who was shouting orders, trying to get the men out. Montgomery was being helped down the stairs, still cursing his head off.

The house had a corner turret. Cross ran to one of its tall windows and looked down Narragansett Avenue.

'Gather the rest of the loot and get the hell out of here!' he yelled. 'It's the police!'

Galloping down the street were two black-helmeted constables. If it had been a workingman's house instead of a millionaire's, Cross thought, the police would have taken hours to respond to the call.

'Let 'em in the front door, and I'll take care of 'em,' Brady said.

Kent turned to face him. 'Get downstairs, lock the front doors, and rip out the telephone,' he commanded.

Cross ran into the hallway. 'Come on, goddamn it, get a move on. We haven't got much time.' From a window in the entry hall, he saw the two policemen tethering their horses at the hitching post.

'Everybody out. Now!' yelled Kent.

Men dragging long, white canvas bags ran past him to the rear of the house.

The constables started knocking on the front door in a polite but insistent manner. One tried the doorknob.

'This is the police! Open up!' One of the constables finally lost patience and pounded his fist on the glass-and-wood door.

Knowing that the transport of so much loot through Newport would attract unwanted attention, Kent had devised an ingenious scheme. Goelet's backyard overlooked the ocean. It was easy to move the booty down the steep cliff path to the rocky beach, where three rowing boats were waiting, ready to take the loot to a small steamship anchored out beyond the breaking waves. Kent's men bounded out of the back door and down the path to the beach.

The police were shouting and pounding with all their might on the door.

With the police at the front door, Cross and Kent ran down the hallway to the rear servants' staircase that led to the kitchen. Suddenly, Kent stopped and faced the wall on his left.

'My God, that's a manuscript from 900 A.D.! A Muslim work from *Spain*. Look!'

On the wall were four framed, illuminated manuscript pages, done in gold and silver with brilliant purple and red.

'These are priceless!' shouted Kent, as he began to take them off the walls.

Cross stood in shock for a second, then ran to the top of the main staircase and saw only one constable trying to force the door. He knew the other had headed for the back door. The constable smashed the leaded glass of the door and reached his hand in to unlock the door.

'Christ almighty, Kent, we have to go!' screamed Cross, grabbing Kent by his sleeve. He had the four framed manuscript pages under his arm. Cross could hear the policeman running through the first floor like a crazed man, in and out of every room. When they got down the servants' staircase, they heard the other policeman break through the back door, and they retreated up the stairs.

Kent knew the severity of their predicament. Cross watched with horror as Kent pulled a small pistol from the side pocket of his linen suit.

'No,' hissed Cross, who looked about the hallway and yanked Kent by his lapels into a bedroom. He pulled him to what looked like a closet protruding from the wall. Opening the door, he shoved Kent in and followed behind. In a second, they were sliding down a corkscrew slide made up of polished sheet metal. Around and around they slid until they crashed into a door at its bottom. It opened up to the side yard, and out they ran to the beach path.

'What the hell was that?' asked Kent in amazement.

'Goelet's aunt is scared of burning to death in a fire, so he had Stanford White put in a spiral fire escape slide just for her. It's compact and better-looking than sticking a staircase on the side of the house,' huffed Cross as they ran.

At the path at the top of the cliff, he halted while Kent ran down, still clinging to his precious manuscripts. Cross saw that two rowing boats were almost to the steamship. The last one was waiting for Kent on the beach. Luckily, the ocean was calm.

With the police inside the house, Cross circled around to the front yard and back to his horse. He was mentally and physically exhausted but managed to ride back to the casino without pitching off. He slipped into the rear of the theatre as the audience rose to give the Italian howler a standing ovation. The crowd filed down into the courtyard, where Cross found his wife standing with the Goelets and a crowd of other guests.

'I hope you enjoyed tonight's performance, John,' said Helen in a soft, mocking tone.

'I did. The evening was an unqualified success. We must do this again.'

'Oh, and John,' Helen said. 'Mr Goelet has invited us back to his home for a late dinner.'

'How kind. I've been dying to see the house.'

CHAPTER FORTY-ONE

'You red devil, you'll never have me!'

'You'll be the first of all my wives in my lodge, white woman!'

'Never, you beast!'

'But first you must be made to obey!'

As the war-bonneted warrior chief hefted his tomahawk, ready to rain down a crushing blow upon the scantily clad white maiden, an explosion sounded outside the log cabin. Through the windows came the roar and crackle of reddish-yellow flames.

A bugle call rang out, followed by a volley of ear-splitting gunshots. The Indians inside the log cabin ran to the windows, pointed their Winchesters, and fired.

'Holy shit, Eddie, they're using real bullets!' Charlie screamed.

Amid the chaos of the attack, the Indian chief leered at the white girl, lowered his weapon, and ripped her white lace bodice, exposing a plump, pink breast. The girl screamed, cowering back.

'He's going to fuck her right there!' yelled Eddie.

The audience was in a frenzy, screaming and cursing the Indian for what he was about to do. The girl fainted, dropping limply to the floor, and people gasped, realising that the redskin would easily have his way with her.

'Leave her alone, you red shit!' someone in the audience screamed.

Then the tide seemed to turn. The Indians at the windows began to fall like tenpins, grasping their chests where the bullets had pierced them. More explosions followed.

With an evil smirk, the chief knelt over the helpless girl and lowered her dress to her waist.

'Ya dirty Injun bastard, don't you touch her!' bellowed a woman wearing a floppy hat ringed with fake yellow flowers.

With a resounding crash, the crude wooden door of the log cabin slammed open, and a young cavalry officer with flowing blonde hair thrust his way inside. Seeing the chief, his eyes widened in shock, and he lunged forward, ramming his sober through the Indian. The chief staggered back, holding his hands over his wound, and dropped to the floor. The crowd went mad with joy, cheering and clapping.

More cavalry soldiers poured in, killing off the rest of the Indians. The officer lifted up the white maiden and embraced her. The men at the bar at the rear of the Baxter Street Playhouse raised their schooners of beer in honour of the brave soldiers, throwing amber-coloured foam in all directions. The crowd rose to its feet, giving the heroes a standing ovation.

The actors proudly took their bows. When the one who played the chief took off his headdress and bowed, the audience hissed and cursed the actor, who smiled broadly. It was proof he'd given a convincing performance.

In the midst of the crowd, George, Charlie, and Eddie clapped and screamed their heads off. George had never had so much fun at the Metropolitan Opera House. He was always bored to death and couldn't understand a word of the German or Italian being spouted by the singers. Not that it mattered. The opera was merely a place for society women to show off their gowns and jewellery, and they gabbed through the entirety of the performance.

Since he'd started teaching on the Lower East Side, George had made it a habit to attend musicals and theatre near the sleazy dumps where he gambled. It was wonderfully refreshing to see something so improper and salacious. The plays were always the same: a villain punished for his evil deeds, a nearly nude heroine rescued by a handsome hero.

As the audience filed out, George smiled down at Charlie and Eddie as they chattered away excitedly about the play. He had taken them to four others, but *The Savage's Lust* was definitely the most exciting. The use of special effects was unparalleled, and while most heroines were in a state of perpetual undress, this menaced maiden exceeded the others by a long shot. It would be a very popular production indeed.

Out in the street, they followed their established after-theatre ritual and headed for a restaurant.

'I tell you, they were using real bullets. Don't you think so, George?' Charlie asked.

'Sure sounded like the real thing.'

They tore into plates of beefsteak and fried potatoes. As they ate, George couldn't stop smiling at his brother. He was very pleased that Charlie had found a new world for himself, a universe free of the deadening Knickerbocker propriety they'd been brought up in. Charlie was so happy. Eddie, George had learnt, was a good and loyal friend. In a way, it made George envious. He had no such person in his life.

'Her tits were popping out of that dress, did you see?' Eddie exclaimed. 'We should go back tomorrow tonight!'

Perhaps we will, George thought.

CHAPTER FORTY-TWO

Nolan sat in his armchair, staring at the invitation he'd lifted from Julia's handbag at the cockfight.

Mr & Mrs John Cross
request the pleasure of introducing their daughter
Julia Claire Cross
to

_____

Monday evening, September 24th, at half past nine
at the residence of Mr William B. Astor JJ
424 Fifth Avenue

From a side table drawer, he pulled out a pen and ink pot. In careful, flowing cursive, he wrote 'John Evan Nolan' on the blank line. He blew on the ink until it dried.

Walking over to the window, Nolan looked out on to Morton Street. He liked where he lived. Greenwich Village was quiet. He was far from the bustle of the Tenderloin and the filth of the Five

Points and the Bowery, where most of his fellow gang members resided. Having a nice, well-furnished flat was a point of pride for him. It might have been the home of a college man or a law clerk.

Although his parents had cast him out into the streets at the age of nine, Nolan had developed a middle-class sense of thriftiness in contrast to the 'live today, gone tomorrow' philosophy of the netherworld he inhabited. He had been brought up in a savage and unforgiving jungle where only the strong and wily survived. Death from violence and disease always lurked around the corner, choosing its victims with cruel randomness. At twenty-two, Nolan had seen scores of men and women die before the age of thirty. To them, such constant threat meant enjoying the moment and never thinking about the future. A dollar made was a dollar instantly spent – on drink, food, gambling, or whores.

Such a life was not for Nolan. He had vowed to save his money. Of the eight hundred dollars he'd recently stolen, three hundred went to the gang, leaving him a five-hundred-dollar share. Eighty per cent, or four hundred dollars, went immediately into his account at the Emigrant Savings Bank on Chambers Street. Even if he only came away from a job with ten dollars, eight went into the bank. For six years, he had faithfully built up his fortune. The gang chided him constantly for his frugality, even accusing him of having Jew blood, which he always angrily denied – to their delight. But one hundred dollars was more than enough for the basic necessities and for entertainment, which he enjoyed as much as the next crook. On a good day, he could bring in at least one hundred dollars for himself, or what a bank clerk made in a month.

Nolan went to the table in the centre of the parlour and picked up a slim, leather-bound volume. As he settled into his armchair, his black cat, Jupiter, settled in his lap. Nolan opened the book to the title page: *The Book of New York Social Etiquette – A Description of Our Customs as Taught & Practised by the Superior Families of New York City, by Humphrey L. Oglander.*

The introduction read, 'As to the unfortunates who have been reared at remote distances from the centres of civilisation, there is nothing left for them to do but to make a careful study of unquestionable authority in those matters of etiquette that prevail among the most refined people.' Nolan had no argument with this statement. While the world of the Bowery and the Five Points was separated by only two miles from Fifth Avenue and Twenty-Third Street, it might as well have been as distant as Mars.

Nolan moved on to the first chapter, 'The Young Man Who Desires to Enter Society'. It proved a good primer on the basics, including attire for a ball: black broadcloth dress coat, white waistcoat, pantaloons, faultless linen, and a white cravat. No jewellery except plain finger rings, and one's nails must be beautifully cut and trimmed, 'like Lord Byron's'. White gloves were essential, as they prevented perspiration from ruining the back of a lady's gown.

Nolan read every chapter carefully, pausing on 'A Young Lady's Entrance into Society'. But chapter ten, 'Giving and Attending Parties, Balls, and Germans', was the most informative. First were the instructions on eating properly: the napkin in your lap, never tucked in at the collar; the fork always in the right hand, except when cutting meat. Above all, never bring the knife into contact with the lips. When arriving, a girl and her parents must stand near the entrance of the drawing room, where she is introduced to the guests. A gentleman bows to them, but not excessively.

The dinner at a debutante's coming-out ball comes first, with dancing to follow, but ending no later than 1 a.m. A gentleman can only ask the girl for one dance. After the dance is over, he brings her back to where her mother is sitting. He may converse with her for only a minute or two. He then continues to dance with the other ladies who have him reserved on their dance cards. A gentleman never smokes in the presence of ladies but retreats to a library or smoking room in the house.

It was almost eight o'clock when Nolan finished. It was a lot to absorb in one sitting, but there was time to reread it before the ball.

He'd just finished fixing himself something to eat when he heard a knock at the door.

'Hello, Bernie,' he said, greeting a small, florid-faced man in his sixties.

'Johnny, my lad. Are you ready for your lesson?' the man asked in a refined British accent.

'Let's start,' Nolan said, waving him in. 'Want a drink?'

'Best to wait on that until after our lesson, son,' he replied with a chuckle and a wink.

Bernard Covington, formerly of Birmingham, had been head butler in some of England's finest homes. Because New York society idolised anything English, he'd had his pick of jobs in the city and chose the Pembroke-Joneses, one of the richest families.

But Bernie had the curse. While cleaning up after dinner parties, he would drain every glass on the table, drinking any molecule of wine, claret, hock, or sherry left in them. At first, his master ignored his habit. Only when Bernie was found dead drunk in the wine cellar, surrounded by empty wine bottles of priceless vintage, was he given the sack. The scandal of his dismissal prevented him from landing another job, and he embarked on a new career as a con man. With his British accent and gentlemanly manner, he'd fooled many a country bumpkin into buying fake stock certificates.

'Now, the first dance will be a quadrille, and we've already gone over that. Then a waltz, a polka, and a mazurka. Do you remember the steps for the mazurka?'

The two men clasped hands and danced the correct steps while Bernie hummed a tune.

'Good boy. Now, at a debutante's ball, there may be what they call a German, which is a circle dance led by a leader and his partner. The leader will motion for a few couples to join in what they call a *tour de valse* around the ballroom. When it's finished, he'll motion for two more couples and so on until everyone has danced. The ball will end with *les bouquets*. For that, they bring a flower cart filled with favours. After each *tour de valse*, a couple picks a favour and offers it to a new partner. It continues until everyone has danced and everyone has a favour.'

Bernie laughed at the perplexed look on Nolan's face and slapped him hard on the back. 'You're right, lad, it's confusing, but I'll teach you. *And* give you some good tips. With all those people, it's going to get hot as hell in the ballroom. Take extra starched collars and exchange the sweaty ones for fresh in the bathroom.'

The lesson continued on into the night, with Bernie demonstrating steps for more dances in the German. Finally he flopped onto the sofa.

'All right, lad, I'm ready for that drink.'

CHAPTER FORTY-THREE

Cross and Helen had been waiting for this day for weeks.

He'd received a call from Kent that morning, asking him to come down to McGlory's at 7 p.m. He knew that Kent was going to tell him the debt was paid after the Goelet job. His family was out of danger. He would never have to see Kent again. The relief was so strong he could almost taste it.

The last months had seemed like a nightmare from which Cross couldn't wake up. What he had been forced to do was reprehensible, but he'd had no choice. And the people he'd helped rob were so rich that they could replace the stolen goods within a week.

But his mind always returned to the image of the Cook's servant girl. Staring out the window of the carriage, unseeing, he chastised himself for being squeamish. This was the price that had to be paid for saving his family. Would he rather see Charlie or George murdered?

At Hester Street, the usual evening depravity was underway. A man lay in the gutter; a filthy stray dog licked eagerly at his face. Whores leant out of doorways, hectoring passers-by. Cross passed through the noise and chaos of McGlory's concert saloon, ignoring the tarts who pressed him to drink with them. He made his way down to the basement corridor. The parade of fake cripples and blind men was beginning to assemble. Without knocking, Cross went into the gang's room and found Kent, Brady, and Coogan seated around the table.

Kent raised his hand in welcome. 'Please sit, Mr Cross,' he said, gesturing to the chair directly across from him.

Cross smiled and sat. On the way there, he'd decided he would control the conversation.

'I suppose my debt, including the interest payments, has finally been satisfied?' he said, using a formal, stentorian voice to show Kent that he meant business.

'Except for a thousand or two, which I forgave out of appreciation for your fine efforts.'

'Then if you and I are finished with our business, I'll bid you farewell, Mr Kent,' Cross said, beginning to rise from his seat. 'I can't honestly say I enjoyed it, but it's been an experience. I think it's best we never meet again.'

'Finished? It's just starting. Mr Cross, we're going to make more money together. Lots more,' Kent said, rising to his feet and pointing enthusiastically with his gold cane.

'Like hell we are.'

'I'm afraid you've been under a misapprehension, Mr Cross.'

'What the hell do you mean?' The smiles on the faces of all three men horrified him.

'In the brief time you've worked for us, you've been a gold mine for our organisation. We've never cleared so much revenue.'

'I'm glad to have helped. But our business is finished.'

'You don't understand. We've decided to let you into our organisation on a permanent basis. We'll give you a seven per cent cut of the take. That's very generous. And it's a great deal of money. Far more than you'd make in a year as an architect.'

The three men stood beaming, proud as hell to have bestowed such an honour on Cross.

'Damn you, I don't want to be part of your gang!' Cross cried.

'Organisation, Mr Cross,' Kent said.

'He don't seem to be very appreciative of this offer, does he?' Coogan said.

'No, he doesn't,' Brady said. 'I don't think you really have a choice, Cross.'

'You'd be more of a consultant, really. You'll be able to continue your architecture practice. A man as talented as you should be allowed to create. I wasn't joking about having you design a summer home for me,' Kent said, smiling at Cross.

Cross felt his knees weaken beneath him. He took hold of the back of the chair. 'You said once I repaid the debt, I was out,' he whispered.

'I might have misled you. I'm sorry. But you're just too damn valuable to let go, Mr Cross.'

'You've got a real talent for this line of work,' Coogan added.

'You'll make us all rich,' Brady said.

'And I suppose I have no say in the matter.'

'Of course you do. All those in favour of Mr Cross joining our organisation, raise your hands,' Kent said. He, Coogan, and Brady raised their hands. 'There you have it. Three to one – democracy in action.'

Cross sat in the chair, eyes fixed on the floor.

'You see, Mr Cross, in our world, once you're in, you can never leave. No retirement. That's the rule. And if you try to break it, you must be punished – severely.' Kent's tone was that a pastor might use with a wayward congregant.

'You mean my family.'

Brady walked up to him and stooped, bringing his eyes level

266

with Cross's. 'Every Tuesday,' he said, 'Helen goes to Arnold Constable. Anything can happen to her on the way. She gets in the way of a runaway carriage. Maybe she falls under a horse car and gets trampled to death.' He pulled out a length of piano wire and wrapped it around his hand, critically examining its length.

'Julia and Charlie go back to school in a few weeks,' said Coogan.

'And then there's George. Poor hapless boy,' Brady said. At his words, Coogan burst out laughing. 'But we don't have to worry about George. Someone else will wind up killing him.'

Cross jerked his head toward Coogan but said nothing. He had a vague idea of what he was referring to but didn't want to think about it. Things were going badly enough. It was Kent who broke the silence.

'I'm glad we've come to an understanding. Let's drink to our new partner, gentlemen.'

CHAPTER FORTY-FOUR

Nolan stood at the back of the room with his best friend, Pickle Nose Johnson, an expert forger. Their gang, the East Side Cowboys, rarely held official meetings. The leader, Spike Milligan, detested all authority. He ran the gang in a very autocratic manner and preferred to meet members individually. Nolan thought it must be a serious matter for them to gather like this in the rear of the gang's saloon, the Bucket of Blood.

As one of the finest pickpockets in New York City, Nolan was highly regarded by the gang. Milligan liked him because he was respectful and a good, consistent earner. He never tried to cheat the gang out of its share either. In return, the gang provided protection from other gangs that might intrude on Nolan's territory, the Ladies' Mile. Fourteenth to Twenty-Third Streets offered a rich hunting ground, with many silk purses just waiting to be picked. Christmastime was the most lucrative season, but the area was a temptation year-round.

The Cowboys, who numbered around sixty, sat knocking back shots of Irish whisky and draining schooners of beer. Lunch had been set out; they devoured sandwiches of rye bread, liverwurst, and salami slathered with brown mustard. Times were good for gangs in New York. The docks were full of good things to steal, and out-of-town hicks were flocking to town, ready to be robbed. The Cowboys couldn't have been happier.

Milligan walked to the front of the room, and the noise instantly ceased.

'Boys, somethin's been bothering the hell outta me,' he announced. Milligan was a barrel-chested man with flaming red hair and a long pointy nose. He squinted accusingly at his men. 'I don't like it when another gang gets rich and we don't. It jest ain't fair.'

The men in the room murmured in agreement.

'There've been some real big heists in the last couple of months. You all heard about the Cook and Greene houses gettin' knocked off.' Milligan paused for dramatic effect, then growled contemptuously, 'I know it was Kent's Gents that did those jobs. I just heard that they stole some valuable horses from some rich bastards too. Those three jobs took in what we clear in a whole goddamn year!' He slammed his big fist down onto the table, upsetting a schooner of beer.

The gang put down their drinks and sandwiches and started talking among themselves. Nolan stayed silent, his mind whirling. He knew that Milligan hated Gentleman Jim Kent. Milligan hated everyone who was better bred, better educated, and smarter than he. His hatred was also fuelled by his unshakable belief that street crime was the province of the poverty-stricken underclass, not college-educated swells who smoked Cuban cigars and ate at Delmonico's. It was this crossing of class lines that upset Milligan most.

'Now,' Milligan shouted, silencing the crowd. 'I found out that they have an inside man who set those jobs up. I don't know his name yet, but they call him the Engineer.'

The gang all seemed to think this was less than sporting.

'We have to find this man and make him an offer to join up with us. Pay 'im more than that cheapskate Kent,' Milligan said. 'Every man has his price, and we'll learn his.'

'What if he won't switch sides?' a man shouted.

Milligan smiled and shook his head. 'Well, we can't allow the competition to have an unfair advantage, can we?'

CHAPTER FORTY-FIVE

Cross knew what an animal felt like when it was caught in a steel trap. No matter how hard he struggled, short of chewing off his own leg, he couldn't get free.

A week had passed since he'd been forcibly made a permanent member of Kent's Gents. Until he thought of a way out, he had to cooperate. That meant planning the next job.

When he'd returned home after his meeting with Kent, he'd found Helen waiting up to celebrate the end of their indenture. She had baked a Lady Baltimore cake, his favourite dessert. When he told her it wasn't over, Helen had almost fallen to her knees, as if she were physically crushed by the news. Nothing had changed, she said; her children and husband were still in danger. There was no end in sight.

But instead of weeping, she'd sat in an armchair and stared out into space, almost as if she were in a trance. Cross had stared at her, unsure what to think.

After a few minutes, she'd stood and said in a calm, determined voice, 'The Whitmans will be away in Long Branch for two weeks, starting on Tuesday.'

If he could ignore his unwanted partnership with Kent, times couldn't have been better for Cross. He'd been getting so much new work that he'd had to hire three more draftsmen. He was at the height of his career, yet his predicament cancelled out any happiness he might have felt.

One of his new commissions was a theatre on Longacre Square. It was a prestigious job, but since he'd never designed a theatre, Cross began doing research, attending numerous shows. Instead of sitting and enjoying the performances, he paid close attention to the seating, the interior detailing, the staging logistics, bathrooms, and circulation. At the end of a show, he waited, watching how the patrons exited. He noted sight lines, measured how wide the seats were and how much leg room there was. Every night for a week, he'd attended the theatre by himself. He was glad for the immersive nature of the experience. It took his mind off his problems.

Tonight, he was walking home from a revival of *The Telephone Girl* at the Casino Theatre on the corner of Broadway and Thirty-Ninth Street. The building, designed by his friend Francis Kimball, was only four years old and offered the city's most up-to-date theatre design. Kimball had given him a set of drawings to study and had asked the owner to let Cross walk around backstage. It was a beautiful building, done in a Moorish style that gave it exotic appeal. The theatre, which sat thirteen hundred, had a six-storey, domed tower anchoring the corner. Still, its most novel feature was a roof garden, the first in the city. The garden served as a separate space, had seating to serve alcohol and food, and offered a small stage for entertainment. It was lit by thousands of electric lights and packed every night. Cross hoped he could design something half as good.

It was late September. The nights were finally getting cooler. Cross took his time, smoking and enjoying the evening. In his mind, he worked out the basic shape of his theatre on its midblock site. He wanted a dramatic entry with a long canopy to protect theatregoers from the weather as they waited for their carriages. *It should be bigger than the one at the Academy of Music*, he thought.

'Excuse me, sir. Can I get a light?'

A rough man in an ill-fitting green suit stood next to Cross. Jolted out of his reverie, Cross said, 'Certainly,' and pulled out a box of matches. Smiling, he lit the man's cigar.

'Beautiful night, isn't it?' said the man.

Cross was anxious to be on his way but didn't want to be rude. With a sigh, he answered. 'Yes, but fall will be here soon. I prefer the cooler weather.'

'Me too. It's been hotter than a nigger's ass this summer, hasn't it?'

'Yes, there were some hot days.' Cross nodded goodbye and started to walk on.

'Hey, don't I know you?'

'No, I don't think we've ever met,' said Cross over his shoulder.

'Sure, sure, you work for Gentleman Jim Kent, don't you?'

Cross stopped dead in his tracks and turned to look at the man. He knew every face in Kent's gang, but he had never seen this man before.

A sense of panic enveloped Cross. How did this piece of scum know about him? It was no good to pretend ignorance. 'How the hell did you know that?' he snarled.

'Oh, I hear things.'

'Like what?'

'Like you're called the Engineer.'

Cross was about to correct the man but stopped. 'What else have you heard?'

'That you're a smart fellow. An expert planner who knows where the big money is.'

Cross smiled. 'I'm afraid you're mistaken, my good man.'

'Nope, that's who you are.'

'What do you want of me?' Cross blurted. He was tired of beating around the bush. 'Out with it, damn it.'

'You're short-changing yourself, working for Kent. You could do better. I know a way you could make a lot more money. And work for people you can trust – not a murdering shit like Kent.'

The puzzle pieces of this mysterious encounter were slowly fitting into place. Cross was being recruited by a rival gang. Which meant someone else knew what he'd been doing.

Oddly, in a roundabout way, he was flattered by the offer. He remembered working in the office of H. H. Richardson when an architect from Stephen Hatch's office approaching him, asking him to jump ship. Hatch had done many prominent buildings in the city, including Bryant's Opera House. Cross, then a young man not long out of the École des Beaux-Arts, had been flattered to be asked to join his firm. The promises of more pay and design responsibility were tempting, and he gave the proposition a great deal of consideration. But in the end, he stayed with Richardson, wanting to learn from a master.

This was different. Richardson wouldn't have had him murdered for leaving. There could be only one response.

'Thank whoever sent you for the offer, but I'm staying put,' he said.

'Just think about it,' the man urged. 'And take this. Little token of our esteem.'

The man placed a very expensive pearl-and-gold tie stud in his hand. Cross didn't protest; he didn't want to insult the man and risk a beating – or worse. *Who had the stud once belonged to?* he wondered. Maybe someone he knew.

'Thank you. But—'

'Just think about it,' the man repeated. 'We'll talk again.'

CHAPTER FORTY-SIX

'Jesus Christ, Georgie! You did it! We're in the clear!'

On the edge of the green felt of the faro table lay nine thousand dollars in greenbacks. Kitty had lost control, hugging and kissing George ecstatically. She grabbed a handful of bills, closed her eyes, and rubbed them against her high, rouged cheekbone. No perfume had a sweeter smell. The crowd around the table was cheering the way people had cheered when George hit the winning home run at the Polo Grounds.

George was floating somewhere in the stratosphere. He'd chased this feeling for so long. Kitty began gathering the stacks of bills and placing them in the envelope the house attendant handed her. With the money tucked safely inside his frock coat pocket, George took Kitty by the arm, bowed to the adoring crowd, and walked out of Benfield's.

On Forty-Sixth Street, Kitty gave him a long, passionate kiss, not giving a damn what the passers-by thought. George patted the bulge on his left side, smiling down at her.

'I knew I'd hit a lucky streak. Mathematics all comes down to probabilities,' he said.

'We're going straight to Mallory to pay him off,' Kitty said, looking George square in the eye.

'We have more than enough,' George said. 'We should go get you a special gift first and celebrate at Sherry's.'

'After.'

'Then let's get a carriage,' George shouted with glee, grabbing her arm. Across the street, a conveyance was discharging a passenger. But as they got closer, someone else commandeered it. George looked up and down Forty-Sixth Street but saw no other carriages.

'We'll go down to Forty-Second and get one.'

As they walked down Sixth Avenue, they passed a large toy shop with huge, plate glass windows. George stopped in his tracks. Without saying a word, he tugged Kitty's arm, drawing her inside.

'Why are we here?' she asked, casting him a puzzled look.

'I want to share my good luck with the children at school,' he said, already perusing the shelves. 'The girls would love china dolls, and the boys like cast-iron toys – like that locomotive there.'

Overhearing his wish, the proprietor appeared with a hearty, 'May I help you, sir?'

Though she was annoyed by the detour, Kitty decided not to make a fuss. Playing the good sport, she inspected the wide variety of dolls, ready to make some selections and get the hell out. George examined the trains and horses. As he mulled his choices, his eye stopped on a blue bicycle leaning against the wall of the shop. It was one of the new safety bikes and had equally sized wheels instead of the huge front wheel that made older models almost impossible to ride. The new design had spawned a bicycling craze all over America. It was the best gift one could get.

'How much is that bicycle?' he asked.

'Twenty-five dollars, sir, and they come in a range of colours,' the proprietor said, rubbing his delicate white hands together.

George stared at the bicycle and then grinned. 'I want fifteen of them,' he said.

'George! No!'

The proprietor frowned at Kitty's protest but beamed a smile at George. 'Certainly, sir. We only have four in stock here, but there are many more in our warehouse on Murray Street.'

'Get me a variety of colours. The address is 112 East Broadway,' George said, counting out the money.

'They'll be there tomorrow,' said the very happy shop owner.

'For God's sake, George, you can't give everyone a bicycle,' Kitty said. 'It's too extravagant. What will Dr Caldwell say?'

'Dr Caldwell can go straight to hell. His family was rich, and he never wanted for anything,' George said bitterly.

The proprietor pressed the receipt into George's hand before Kitty could change his mind.

'That's enough, then,' she said firmly. 'Don't buy anything else.'

Irritated, George thrust the envelope toward Kitty. 'You hold the money then.'

On the street, though, Kitty saw the happiness radiating from George. He was smiling from ear to ear. She wasn't going to chastise him again, she resolved. After all, it was only a tiny portion of the money.

Instead of hailing a carriage, they walked down Sixth Avenue. Catching hold of his arm, Kitty matched George's brisk pace along the pavement. Occasionally, she looked up at his handsome face. He smiled at her but said nothing. It was a beautiful summer afternoon, with a warm breeze sweeping the avenue. Kitty felt so happy, as if her heart might burst.

As they neared the corner of Thirty-Eighth Street and Sixth Avenue, George came to a halt. He turned west and walked a few doors to a wide brownstone with forest-green canvas awnings on every window. Kitty knew this address. She took a step back, heart sinking in her breast.

'Please give me my money,' George said gently.

Kitty looked at him incredulously.

'I need my money,' he repeated.

'I'm not going to give it to you,' she said, shaking her head.

George's eyes narrowed. 'You don't understand.'

'Don't understand what?' Kitty asked, looking not at him but at a porter across the street, sweeping off a stoop in slow, steady strokes.

'My good luck is bound to go on. I have to take advantage of it. It's like a strong wind behind a ship. You don't fold your sails – you keep going as far as you can, because you never know when the wind might die.'

'That's nonsense, George. We're taking the money to Mallory,' Kitty said, looking unflinchingly into George's eyes. 'It's taken us too long to get this. You can't blow it now.'

'Trust me,' George said soothingly, extending his hand. 'I can double this.'

'No, goddamn it.'

George's face grew dark, and he swallowed hard. He moved closer.

'Please, George, for God's sake, don't do this,' Kitty pleaded, tears welling in her eyes. 'Let's get away from here. We'll have a wonderful dinner after we see Mallory, maybe go to a show.'

'Now,' he commanded loudly.

'There's no way in hell I'm going to let you do this,' she said defiantly, holding the purse behind her back.

George's blue eyes seemed full of fire as he lunged at her. Kitty backed away, but he caught her by the arm, which she tried with all her might to keep locked behind her back. George jerked her around, putting her back to him.

'No, no, don't do this,' she yelled. Passers-by noticed the

commotion but did nothing to intervene. Kitty was sobbing, tears running down her cheeks. 'Don't you know you're going to lose?' she cried.

This enraged George. He easily twisted her arm until the purse fell to the pavement. Picking it up, he removed the envelope and handed the purse back, smiling amiably.

'There's nothing to worry about, my love. You'll see.' George began to climb the high stoop of the brownstone, the fire still burning in his blue eyes. 'Come along.'

Kitty sprang forward, grabbing his pant leg. She fell onto the stoop and sat on the bottom step, holding George's leg in a bear hug. He tried to wriggle free, but she clung tightly to him. Furious, he took hold of her hand, roughly yanked it away, and resumed his ascent. Kitty collapsed into hysterics, lying flat on the step, bawling her eyes out. This was George's sickness, taking over his mind and soul. He was powerless to prevent it. And so was she.

A group of people paused to ask if they could help, but Kitty waved them away. She lay there for fifteen minutes, then sat up and wiped the tears that had streamed down her face like rivers, destroying her powder and rouge. Still sobbing, she stood and looked up at the glass-and-wood doors of the brownstone building. She didn't want to be there when George came out.

Slowly, Kitty walked away.

CHAPTER FORTY-SEVEN

'It's interesting. You never mentioned that you designed Cook's house . . . and the Fidelity National Bank.'

Cross sat across from his brother at a table in the Park Restaurant on East Sixty-First Street. He and Robert had gotten into the habit of lunching together once a week. They also went to ball games and the theatre and sometimes took walks together in Central Park. For the first time in their lives, they lived near each other, and they were developing a deeper personal connection, even discussing their feelings about their parents, especially their father, and growing up in society. Cross felt a sense of relief and comfort when he confided in his brother about the past. He knew Robert felt the same way.

He wasn't shocked by Robert's question. He'd been expecting it. He was only surprised that it took so long in coming.

'I thought I told you I'd designed Cook's place.'

'No, I would've remembered that.'

'Mmm, thought I did. I don't think I mentioned the bank.'

'Quite a coincidence.'

Cross held his hands above his head and widened his eyes. 'I confess! I robbed them both,' he wailed. He stuck out his hands, as if to receive handcuffs.

Robert roared with laughter. Around the restaurant, curious patrons looked up from their meals.

'I've designed lots of buildings in the city over the years,' Cross added. 'So many that I sometimes forget about them.'

'There've been other big robberies of mansions.'

'Not my clients.'

'No, but the places were cleaned out in the same manner, probably by the same gang.'

'What are the Pinkertons going to do?'

'We've set up a network of informants that covers Fifth Avenue and the Upper East Side. They'll keep watch for us at night. And after so many massive robberies, the rich are running scared. They've hired watchmen to patrol their properties, whether they're at home or away.'

'And the banks?'

'We met with the New York City Commercial Bankers' Association to convince the cheap bastards to hire guards. I think most of them will. But we have people keeping an eye on some of the bigger ones nonetheless.'

Cross took a sip of his coffee and a bite of apple pie.

'You've got a real crime wave on your hands,' he observed. 'No more help from your informant?'

As Robert paused, Cross watched carefully, trying to read his brother's reaction. If only he knew the man's name! The identity of the informant tormented Cross.

'Not a peep. And that's not the whole of it. Some prize racehorses have been stolen too. That's upset the hell out of the parvenus – more than the robberies even. You can rob his mansion, kidnap his wife and children, but you never steal a man's horse.' Robert gave a barking laugh. 'It isn't sporting.'

'That's incredible. Any news about the horses?'

'They're probably somewhere in Europe. Their identities

would never be discovered over there. We'll never find them.'

Cross finished his dessert, called for the check, and lit a cigarette.

'As if the crime wave wasn't enough, we have to coordinate gold bullion shipments for Kidder, Peabody & Co., the big Wall Street investment company.'

'They handle gold?'

'They act as brokers on gold exports out of the country. To countries like Spain or Italy. Say, how's George getting along? I never see him. Whenever I ask him out, he's busy.' Robert sounded disappointed.

Cross's family had truly become the centre of his brother's life, Cross thought. To his dismay, Helen had even been playing matchmaker for his brother, introducing him to an assortment of wealthy widows and young heiresses. Robert played along good-naturedly, placating his sister-in-law by socialising. He'd even been to a tea at their house that Aunt Caroline attended. To Cross's surprise, the fact that Robert was a Pinkerton didn't bother her. She seemed to be very proud of him and steered several eligible ladies his way herself.

'I never see him either. George lives his own life. It upsets Helen.'

'Oh, he just wants to be on his own. You should be proud. He'll be a brilliant professor.'

'Yes. I should be,' Cross said, voice barely audible. He still hadn't been able to force himself to find out whether George was gambling again. He was a coward. Whatever the truth, he didn't want to face it. A father wants to believe he can trust his son.

'And Charlie. What a special kid! You should be proud of him too.'

Over the summer, Charlie had become an expert at stripping naked at a run and jumping off the pier into the East River. The most exciting part was leaping off the edge and being suspended in mid-air – it felt like he was flying – before crashing into the cold water of the river. On a hot day, it was as refreshing as a drink of cold beer, which he greatly enjoyed thanks to Eddie's tutelage.

It was a warm September day, one of the few Charlie had left before school resumed. He was determined to fill every remaining minute with fun. The rotting pier off Cherry Street was filled with skinny naked boys, either diving or pushing one another into the river. Charlie sprinted along beside Eddie, and together they flew off the pier and hit the water, just missing a floating hog carcass. The East River sported a continuous parade of dead creatures through its currents, including the occasional human body. The water was filthy with oil slicks, dead rats, floating rubbish, and human and horse faeces, but the cold water felt so good that one ignored such minor distractions.

'How about some rat wrangling today?' Eddie asked, his head bobbing up and down in the dark waters. 'We can get thirteen cents a head.'

'We should try that warehouse on Thirty-Second Street. You can hear them squirming around from the pavement,' Charlie said, trying to float on his back. A partially decomposed horse drifted by a few feet away.

'Then let's get going.' They swam back to the pier and hoisted themselves up. Some boys were lying in the sun on the pier; others were soaping themselves down and then diving in to rinse off in the filthy water. This was the only time they got anything close to a bath.

After dressing, the boys stopped off at Eddie's to get the mailbag and club. It was a good haul, about eighty rats, exceptionally energetic and fast. The bag was heavy to pull, and Charlie had to continually beat the vermin about the head to prevent them from escaping. Despite his best efforts, three squeezed out, causing a woman on West Twenty-Ninth Street to scream.

'I hope one bites ya on yer tit,' Eddie yelled after her.

At the rat pit, Eddie haggled with Nardello over the price, calling him a dirty wop until he relented and agreed to thirteen cents.

'I got a tip for ya,' said Nardello as they readied themselves to leave. 'We got a new dog named Mustard. A ten-to-one shot, but I seen 'em. He's a killer – can do fifty in eight minutes. You got time to lay down a bet. The action starts in five minutes.'

Eddie and Charlie looked at each other and smiled, doing the math in their heads. They went in through the back door to the amphitheatre, which was filled to capacity. After Eddie placed two bets, they found seats in the second row from the bottom. The crowd was noisy and happy, impatient for the games to begin. Mustard was tugging hard on his leash, almost yanking his handler's shoulder out of its socket. His colouring looked like any fox terrier's: brown and black, with no sign of the yellowish colour indicated by his name.

The chute opened, and the rats came flying into the arena in their usual frenzy. The crowd roared with delight as Mustard went to work, tearing into the rats with glee. It almost seemed as if he were smiling. With astonishing speed, he killed rat after rat, flinging the dirty grey carcasses through the air onto the dirt floor of the arena. At seven minutes in, he'd finished off an astounding forty-eight rats. He'd have gotten more than fifty kills if he hadn't run out of victims. Most people threw down their betting chits in disgust, defeated by the long odds.

Ecstatic, Charlie was hugging Eddie when he looked to his right. At the end of the row, he saw his sister, Julia. At that exact moment, Julia saw him. Looks of utter bewilderment gave way, slowly, to smiles. They both burst out laughing.

An instant later, Charlie ran up to Julia and hugged her.

CHAPTER FORTY-EIGHT

'When Rome was just a swamp, children, the ancient Egyptians were beginning their greatest period. They built the mightiest and richest empire in the world, the New Kingdom, along the great Nile River.'

'Is that how they got this diamond?' Henry Kent asked.

The Kent family stood in front of the glass case housing the Pharaoh Blue Diamond, a huge gem with a mysterious blue-green glow. On loan to the Manhattan Institute of Science and Technology from the Alexandria Museum of Antiquities, thousands of New Yorkers had stood in lines that summer to see it. But because Kent was a member of the board of trustees, he and his family didn't have to wait in line.

'What a marvellous colour,' said Millicent with awe. 'It could hypnotise you.'

'It's so big,' gushed Bill Kent.

'Maybe the biggest in the whole world,' Kent said, affectionately mussing his son's hair.

Cross looked up into the night sky. Thick storm clouds were gathering; he heard thunder rumbling in the distance. Normally,

285

a downpour would be just the thing to cool off after an unusually hot autumn day. But later, at 2 a.m., on the roof of the Manhattan Institute of Science and Technology, it wouldn't be welcome at all.

A week earlier, Kent had summoned Cross to a meeting and given him the plans for the building. As a trustee, Kent had been given a set of construction drawings when the Institute was built five years before. It was the first time since they had started working together that Kent had actually set up a job, and to his bemusement, Cross realised that instead of being relieved, he was miffed.

By setting up a job himself, Cross could foresee the dozens of ways the theft might foul up and get him arrested. Before a robbery, along with studying the drawings, Cross would prepare himself by standing near the building and just looking at it for at least an hour. Using his imagination, Cross transported himself inside and conducted the robbery step-by-step, then asked himself what could possibly go wrong at each step. Would a lantern be seen from across the street? He studied the entry point and envisioned the escape route. Was there enough cover at the exit, or could the neighbours see them leaving the building? Right off, he could see a few negatives about tonight's project – like what if someone had insomnia in the ten-storey apartment building behind them, looked out of their window, and saw men on the roof at two in the morning?

But with Kent running the show, Cross had no control over how the job was run. And there was another thing that bothered him. He *wanted* to plan the jobs. It gave him a sense of satisfaction and enjoyment – and Kent had taken that pleasure away.

For all his acumen, though, Kent couldn't read the drawings. He relied on Cross to figure out a way of getting the coveted prize: the Pharaoh Blue Diamond. When Kent told him about the job, Cross thought he'd gone mad. Stealing such a famous gem? It was

286

crazy. But trying to talk Kent out of it was useless; he had no choice but to cooperate.

'Always steal in a way that's admired, Mr Cross,' Kent had told him sanguinely.

Because of the enormous value of the diamond and its provenance in another country, armed guards sat in a carriage directly opposite the institute twenty-four hours a day. The rear of the building, on Forty-Sixth Street, was watched as well. Such a guard was easy to get around, though. The institute was a hundred-foot-wide, four-storey, marble structure that sat mid-block, flanked by buildings of about the same height. The gang would enter a building two doors down, go up to its roof, and cross over to the institute.

Kent, Brady, Cross, Culver, and another gang member named Lacey were standing on the flat tar roof. Next to them was a fifty-foot-long pitched skylight. Kent, not Cross, had decided this would be the easiest entry point, though not the safest. The skylight was twenty feet above the gallery floor.

Carefully, Cross opened one of the skylight's pivoting glass panels. He fastened the hooked end of a rope ladder to the edge of the opening and lowered it to the floor below. Based on the drawings, Cross knew exactly how long the ladder had to be.

Lacey, a lithe bantamweight, climbed down with the agility of a circus acrobat. On the gallery floor, he steadied the ladder for the others to descend. Cross made his way down slowly, causing Brady to curse him viciously. The ladder swayed back and forth, and Cross had to hold on for dear life. The others followed with little difficulty, which embarrassed him.

The institute was a science and technology museum. Tall glass cases containing all manner of scientific and archaeological displays lined the walls. Down the centre of the gallery stood long display tables topped with flat glass.

Lighting a match, Kent looked at his pocket watch. 'Right on schedule, gentlemen. We need to be on the third floor,' he said, nodding at Cross, who knew the layout by memory and led the way.

In pitch-darkness, they waited in an alcove off the hallway. Down the hall came a flickering light, moving slowly towards them. The men backed into the alcove as a rotund night watchman of about sixty passed by, carrying a newspaper. He shuffled to the end of the hallway and opened a door.

'Good old Collins. You could set your watch by his bowel movements,' Kent whispered.

Culver walked to the door. From a canvas sack, he pulled out a flat iron bar and wedged it into both sides of the doorjamb. 'He's not goin' anywhere for a while,' he whispered, rejoining the group.

Cross led the men down to the second floor and through a corridor to the south side of the building. 'We're going to drop down from here into the main heating duct that's hidden in the south wall of the gem room on the first floor,' he said over his shoulder. 'And then pop out the heating grille near the floor, and we're in.'

From the drawings, he knew the building had a new kind of heating system in place. Instead of sending the heat from a huge cast-iron furnace in the basement through the building by gravity via floor gratings, the furnace used sheet metal ductwork to transfer heat. These ducts were big enough for a man to fit through. When he got to a point down the corridor, Cross stopped in his tracks. He walked farther down the hall and then back again.

'I was positive the duct opening was here. This is where we were supposed to enter the main duct and go down,' he said.

The men looked at him but said nothing. Sighing, Culver lit a small kerosene lantern and handed it over. A circular pattern of yellowish light washed the walls of the corridor.

'Where the hell did it go?' Cross asked no one in particular. He turned to Kent. 'When did you get those drawings?'

'Before we started construction,' Kent said, annoyed.

'But were any changes made?'

Kent thought for a moment. 'Well, yes. The damn architect came in with a cost so far over budget that we had to make some cuts.'

'Did you ever get a set of revised drawings?'

'That was the only set I got.'

'Then those weren't the final drawings,' snapped Cross. 'They don't show what was actually built. I'll wager the heating system was changed back to a gravity system to save money – which means there's no goddamn ductwork.'

'So what?' growled Brady.

'So what? That was how we were getting into the gem room – through the ducts,' Cross said.

His revelation was met by silence. All of them knew they were stuck, and Cross knew that they expected him to think up a solution, even though this wasn't his fault.

Running his hand through his hair, he leant back against the white plaster wall. Minutes passed like hours as he racked his brain for an answer. As he paced back and forth, he inadvertently swung the lantern up, shining the light onto the ceiling.

'Come on. We're going to the first floor,' he announced.

The institute had a large interior room on the first floor used exclusively for special exhibits. It was there that the diamond was kept. Trying to breach its double bronze-fronted doors would have been useless; they were as strong as the doors to a bank. Blowing them with nitro would bring the guards in from the street.

Cross led them into a room to the left of the exhibit hall.

He lifted the lantern towards the ceiling. 'See that truss?'

Above them was a five-foot-deep iron truss that spanned the entire width of the building. It was one of six supporting the load of the second floor, like a very wide ladder laid on its side, with diagonals connecting the rails. Its ironwork was exquisitely crafted and had beautiful ornamentation on every segment. Because this was a museum devoted to science and technology, the architect had deliberately exposed the trusses to show the engineering structure.

'We're going to get up there, walk along the bottom edge, break through where the truss intersects the wall, and get inside the gem room. There's only a thin infill around the truss penetration there.' Cross spoke like a general barking out orders for battle. He would not brook any dissent. 'Mr Lacey, there has to be a ladder in the basement. Mr Culver, we'll need that axe and length of rope you brought along.'

The men did exactly as they were told.

A ladder was placed against the wall, and Cross climbed up, then carefully inched along the edge of the truss, holding on to the struts. Where the truss intersected the wall, he chopped a small hole in the plaster infill, inserted the saw, and began to cut a hole the height of the truss. Plaster dust showered down. Having cut a rectangular shape barely wide enough for a man to fit through, he pulled it out and let it fall to the floor.

'All right, follow me,' he commanded.

One by one, the four men climbed the ladder onto the truss. Because the bottom edge was only six inches wide and it was almost fifteen feet down to the marble floor, they crept along cautiously to the opening Cross had cut.

Somehow, Cross was experiencing no fear at all, only that wonderful sense of exhilaration he got while thieving. He was a circus acrobat on a high wire, no net beneath him. His confidence seemed to propel him along like a steam engine.

They were in the gem room. Cross took the lantern from Culver, lowering it towards the floor. Below them was the Pharaoh Diamond, enclosed in a small glass box on a tall, stone pedestal in the centre of the exhibition room. The multifaceted gem caught the light of the lantern, throwing off a brilliant iridescence. The men turned to one another, smiling and nodding in appreciation.

'She's a beauty,' whispered Culver. 'A real beauty.'

'The glass case is fastened to the top of the pedestal. We'll have to unscrew it,' Kent said, eyes fixed on his prize.

Without being told, Lacey tied a length of thick ship's rope to one of the struts of the truss. With a screwdriver in his pocket, he began to shimmy down towards the floor. *He must have been handpicked for this assignment,* Cross thought. He was nimble and quick, unlike the generally stout, heavyset members of the gang.

Lacey was almost to the end of the rope, which dangled about two feet above the floor. Cross's heart leapt into his throat.

'Stop!' he yelled. 'Don't go any farther.'

'What the hell is your problem?' Brady said, grabbing him roughly by the shoulder and almost making him lose his balance.

Cross crouched on the bottom of the truss and lowered the lantern as far as he could, staring at the floor. 'Something's wrong,' he said, swinging the lantern back and forth. 'Don't drop down yet.'

An annoyed Lacey stayed where he was, about three feet from the end of the rope.

'The floor doesn't look right,' Cross murmured.

'What the hell do you mean?' Kent asked.

'A marble floor wouldn't reflect light like that. Look: it's almost as if it's wet.'

And indeed, the men saw an odd reflective sheen coming off the floor, which had a kind of rippled texture. Cross swung the lantern, trying to throw more light.

'There,' he said, pointing. Beneath the spot where he had cut through the wall, he could see tiny fragments of plaster bobbing gently up and down.

'It's covered with water. Why the hell did they do that?' Brady hissed.

Lacey looked down and laughed derisively. 'Yeah, it's water, but it's barely an inch deep. It ain't like I'm gonna drown.' He resumed his descent.

Above, Cross walked the length of the truss to the opposite wall, lowering the lantern as much as he could. He stopped abruptly and turned back towards the gang.

'Lacey, if you don't want to die, get back up here. Now!'

CHAPTER FORTY-NINE

'See that?'

The men, including Lacey, had inched across the truss until they were next to Cross. He pointed down to the bottom of the wall. In the dim light thrown by the lantern, they saw a thick wire protruding from the wall and extending about a foot onto the marble floor.

'What the hell is that?' Kent demanded. Cross knew he was greatly upset by the delay.

'It's an electric wire,' Cross said.

'So?'

Electricity was a fairly new phenomenon. It had been less than a decade since Edison's invention of the lightbulb. New York was rapidly replacing gaslight with electric, stringing miles of wire along the streets. As an architect, Cross knew about the other properties of this new medium.

'When you insert a live electrical wire into water,' he explained, speaking slowly, as if they were five-year-olds, 'and step into that water, you will be electrocuted.'

The four gang members stared down at the floor in astonishment.

'It's to discourage people like us from stealing the diamond.'

'Shit,' was the only reply.

'My guess is that they flood the floor with a half inch of water at closing time and then unplug a hole to drain it out in the morning.'

Lacey looked at Cross with new appreciation and clung more tightly to the struts of the truss.

'They say Edison's come up with a new way to execute people using electric current. Supposed to be more humane than hangin',' said Culver.

'I'll take hangin' any day,' Brady said.

The men looked at the diamond. They had come too far to give up. Even more slowly, they edged back to the centre of the room, directly above the gem.

'Move the rope so it'll hang right over the pedestal,' Kent ordered.

Everyone knew what he was going to say next.

'Down you go, Mr Lacey. Stay off the floor, and you'll be just fine.'

Staring down at the floor, Lacey swallowed hard.

'Don't worry. I'll include some hazard pay in your cut,' Kent said, patting his shoulder.

'Better tie a big knot at the end so his feet can rest on something,' Cross said. He'd been lucky in his entry point. The truss he had chosen to follow was close to the centre of the room. Still, Lacey would have to reach over a few feet to get the diamond. In the flickering light of the lantern, Cross could see rivulets of sweat travelling down Lacey's forehead.

The rope was ready. Lacey paused for a few seconds to build up his nerve and then started down. They could all see how scared he was. He looked straight ahead and stopped once to wipe sweat from his eyes.

When he got to the level of the pedestal, he was too far away to reach over to the glass.

'How are you doing, Mr Lacey?' Kent called.

'Just fine, sir.' But even as the words left Lacey's lips, his sweaty hands slipped on the rope. Down he went – but he grabbed and held on at the last possible moment. The toe of his fashionable black shoe stopped two inches above the surface of the water.

In unison, all four men watching above exhaled an audible sigh of relief.

Lacey looked up at his companions, smiled wanly, and said nothing. He climbed back to the right height and began to sway his body side to side, slowly gaining momentum. After four swings, he made it, wrapping his legs around the pedestal. Using just his arms, he pulled himself up the rope until he could stand atop the stone column. The pedestal was about three feet square, with the six-inch square glass box sitting on its centre. Lacey had plenty of room to stand.

Wrapping the rope securely across his chest, Lacey took out the screwdriver and went to work removing the glass case. The four screws at the corners came out easily. Cross was thrilled, his body bursting with excitement as he watched. *It's that feeling of absolute ecstasy Kent once described*, he thought, casting the criminal mastermind a sideways glance.

Tilting the glass box on its left edge, Lacey placed his hand beneath it to get the diamond, which sat on a small purple velvet cushion. Without hesitation, he grabbed it. At that instant, the handles on the bronze doors to the room made a slight rattling sound, as though someone was jiggling them. In the dead silence of the exhibition room, the noise had the effect of a pistol shot, and Lacey was so startled that he lost hold of the diamond. It dropped onto the pedestal top, bounced, and rolled towards the edge. Lacey fell to his knees and lunged for it as it dropped off the pedestal, snatching it in mid-air. But in doing so, he lost his balance and pitched to the side. The men above watched, wide-eyed with terror.

With lightning-quick reflexes, Lacey grabbed the rope with one hand, swinging to and fro like a zoo monkey. Then he placed the diamond in his jacket pocket, gasping for air as if someone had him by the throat. It took almost a minute for him to compose himself. Then he said, looking over at the doors, 'I thought the watchman couldn't get out of the john.'

'That wasn't him. The guards stationed outside probably came in and checked the doors,' Kent said. 'They've likely gone back to their posts.'

'I sure as hell hope so,' Lacey said and began to climb the rope. At the truss, Brady and Culver hoisted him up by the armpits. Lacey handed the diamond to Kent, who barely looked at it for fear of dropping it. Quickly, he stuck it in his trouser pocket.

The men walked along the truss to the opening in the wall. On the way back up to the fourth-floor gallery, Culver checked the bathroom.

'He hasn't finished taking his shit,' he said with a big smile.

This time, Cross scampered up the rope ladder like a squirrel. Culver, who had been steadying the ladder as they climbed, was last to ascend. About ten feet off the floor, he tried to shift the sack of tools he was carrying from one shoulder to the other and lost his grip. As he tried desperately to grab for the sack, his feet slipped off the rope rungs of the ladder.

In a sickening instant, Culver plummeted to the floor. Instead of falling straight down, he came off the ladder at an angle, crashing onto one of the display tables in the centre of the gallery. At the sound, the men, who were waiting on the roof in the midst of a downpour, rushed back to the skylight window. Beneath them, they saw Culver writhing in pain on top of the smashed display table. Its legs had splayed out from the force of his body's impact, and glass was scattered everywhere.

Brady started down the ladder in an instant, cursing viciously under his breath. But when he had descended just halfway, the electric lights in the gallery snapped on.

'What the devil's going on here?' a voice shouted from the end of the gallery.

Brady froze in terror, seeing a bearded man in his mid-thirties walking towards him.

'Who the hell are you?' the man cried. He dashed to the foot of the rope ladder and looked up at Brady, then squinted at the other men poking their heads through the skylight.

'It's Dilts, one of the museum curators,' whispered Kent. Kent was too slow to pull away from the opening, and Dilts caught a glimpse of a familiar face. 'Mr Kent?'

Brady jumped the last six feet to the floor.

Dilts had turned his attention to Culver, who was moaning in pain. The destroyed table had displayed Stone Age tools, which were strewn about the floor. Brady picked up a long club carved from the bone of some prehistoric beast.

'Don't do it, Brady! Don't do it!' Cross screamed at the top of his lungs.

But Brady brought the weight of the club down on the skull of the curator with savage fury. As he beat the man about the head, Cross was reminded of a Neanderthal caveman, pummelling an animal. Finally, he stopped, satisfied his prey was dead. Throwing the club aside, he helped Culver to his feet and, with great difficulty, hauled him up the ladder. Lacey descended halfway to assist.

On the roof, Brady walked up to Cross. A mere inch of space separated their faces.

'There was no choice, swell,' he said.

CHAPTER FIFTY

'Mr. Wharton, so good of you to come tonight. May I present my daughter, Julia?'

Julia Cross stood to the right of her mother and Caroline Astor, greeting the guests at her coming-out ball in the Astors' ballroom at Thirty-Fourth Street and Fifth Avenue. Her father, George, and Granny stood immediately behind them.

In a Worth gown made of white satin, the plunging neckline embroidered with pearls interspersed with tiny diamonds, Julia was radiant. A magnificent pearl necklace graced her long, slender neck. Men's eyes widened in amazement when they saw her, and Aunt Caroline beamed with pride. Twenty eligible bachelors might well propose to her before the evening ended.

'You look lovely tonight, Miss Cross,' Alfred Wharton gushed.

'Thank you, Mr Wharton. We *must* talk about your dinosaurs tonight.'

Wharton blushed, uttered something unintelligible, then moved on.

'Lieutenant Beekman, may I present my daughter, Julia?'

'Miss Cross, I got special leave to be here tonight.' The handsome man in his dress uniform gave a low bow.

'I'm sorry I took you away from Geronimo and the Apaches.'

'That's quite all right. He surrendered at the beginning of September.'

'Well, then I'm sorry you didn't get the chance to shoot him.' Helen shot Julia a wicked look and smiled at Beekman, who bowed and moved on.

Stephen Van Cortlandt stepped up and bowed to Helen. Her face lit up at the sight of this exceptionally rich Knickerbocker. 'May I present my daughter, Julia?'

'Miss Cross, if you don't save a dance for me, *I'll* be cross,' said Van Cortlandt, chuckling at his own joke.

'I didn't think it was possible. There's a woman here as beautiful as Helen Cross.' Robert Cross smiled broadly, holding out his hand to Julia. He cut an impressive figure and was turning the heads of many women in the ballroom.

'And they say all Pinkertons are roughnecks,' Aunt Caroline said. 'You were born to wear evening dress, Robert.'

'Remember, Aunt Caroline, I *am* part Livingston,' Robert said, giving her a wink. 'And don't you dare tell me, young lady, that there's no room on your dance card for me. If you do, I'll arrest you.' He used a deep, authoritative voice that made Julia laugh.

'Maybe you can catch the thief of the Pharaoh Blue too,' Aunt Caroline said with a laugh. 'That's all people are talking about tonight. In the wake of the loss, I hear Egypt wants most desperately to declare war on the United States.'

'Don't worry, Robert. No police work is required tonight, regardless of what Aunt Caroline says. We've chosen you to have the first dance,' Helen said, giving Caroline an affectionate smile.

Robert flashed a smile at his brother too, acknowledging the great honour he'd been given.

'Good evening, Mrs Cross.'

Helen smiled at the very handsome, dashing young man in front of her and knitted her brow, trying to remember the gentleman's name.

'John Nolan!' Granny, who was standing a few feet behind, blurted out. She bulled her way between Aunt Caroline and Helen and greeted him heartily. When the others saw that the young man had Granny's seal of approval, smiles broke out all around – except for Julia. Her mouth hung open; her breathing was shallow. Seeing Nolan there – and seeing how good he looked in a white tie and cutaway coat – sent her into a mild state of shock.

'The Nolans, you know, are very close friends of the Roosevelts – and John is also a good friend of mine, I'm proud to say,' Granny gushed. Caroline still had a confused look on her face. Granny spoke to her in a testy whisper. 'Calm yourself, Caroline. I introduced Mr Nolan to Julia.'

Though she was still unable to recall putting his name on the invitation list, Helen extended her hand and said, 'Mr Nolan, may I present my daughter, Julia?'

'Miss Cross, I knew you were a beautiful woman, but tonight, in that gown, your beauty is increased a hundredfold,' he said.

After a few seconds, the still-astonished Julia recovered herself enough to form words. 'Mr Nolan! How . . . good of you to come. I'm overjoyed to see you here tonight. I have a space for the fourth dance. May I?' she asked, taking up the little vellum card attached to her white-gloved wrist by a blue ribbon.

'With the greatest pleasure,' Nolan said.

Julia, openly breaking the rule of filling in her dance card in the reception line, wrote down Nolan's name.

'And I'd like to introduce you to my father, Mr John Cross, and my brother, George,' she said.

Both came forward, smiled, and heartily shook the young man's hand. As Nolan bowed, Julia saw Granny come forward and take him by the arm.

'That darling Wah Kee has sold me the most beautiful *yen tsiang*, made of the most exquisite ivory with gold fittings. Even the *ow* is pure gold! He tells me it's much easier to clean, but then I never have to clean anything. Wah Kee always does it for me. Such a gentleman.'

'I'm pleased to hear it. When will you and Miss Cross be visiting my neck of the woods next?'

'Saturday morning. Julia must procure a few things for school. With the autumn term at Miss Spence's starting soon, I'll be coming down on my own.'

'How wonderful. I hope you will do me the honour of letting me take you out for tea or lunch, Mrs Rutherford.'

'You can be sure of that, Mr Nolan. Now, I want you to mingle with the guests and enjoy yourself tonight. I can see that you've already caught the eye of many young ladies,' Granny said, giving him a gentle push towards the glittering assemblage before returning to the reception line with a smile.

'That Mr Nolan is a fine-looking gentleman,' Caroline whispered.

'Indeed. But then, he *is* one of us,' added Granny.

Julia kept glancing about for Nolan as she received new guests. The Astors' huge ballroom could easily hold four hundred, and only about half that number had been invited, but it still made it difficult for her to see. Julia finally spotted him strolling along the perimeter of the space, admiring the paintings that hung cheek by jowl on the silk brocade walls and were stacked up to the moulding that marked the base of the high, coved ceiling. As he walked, he flashed his magnetic smile at the ladies, old and young alike, who chattered among themselves about who this charming man might be.

To see him in this world was thrillingly anomalous. For the last three months, their shared universe had consisted of the Tenderloin and the Bowery, of gambling houses, opium dens, and ratting contests, of enticing depravity in all its many forms. Now there he was, amid the richest people in America, in the house of the leader of New York high society, and he didn't look a bit out of place. In fact, she thought him the handsomest fellow in the room.

The last of the guests was received, and dinner was announced. Per custom, John Cross escorted Aunt Caroline into the dining room first, followed by George and Julia, who sat at her father's left hand. Helen was the last to enter, on the arm of William Backhouse Astor II.

Caroline had spared no expense for her relative's coming-out dinner. The twelve courses were eaten on gold service at a black walnut table covered with white embroidered Irish lace over red velvet. Instead of placing high, obstructing ornaments down the length of the table, Caroline had selected a low epergne of orchids, which allowed easy conversation. Mrs Astor's liveried servants brought out the food, à la russe, beginning with oysters on the half shell and soup à la reine accompanied by sherry.

Nolan escorted Olivia Scott-Jones, the young daughter of one of Helen's closest friends. They sat two-thirds of the way down the table from Julia. Throughout the meal, Julia kept looking over at the pair, who were talking and laughing with each other and the nearby guests. She wondered what Nolan was talking about that so engaged them. Their own conversations always centred on the sins of the Tenderloin. Was he talking to Olivia about that? The thought made her jealous – that was the world *they* shared.

As she peered down the table, Julia suddenly realised how easy it was to converse with Nolan on any topic – especially in contrast to a bore like Stephen Van Cortlandt. With her last year at Miss Spence's about to begin, it would be hard to get down to the Tenderloin as often, and this made her sad. She watched in fascination as Nolan correctly used every one of the ten pieces of silverware and five goblets at his place setting. Smoothly, he placed his finger on the rim of the champagne glass to signal to the servant that he wanted no more wine. *His manners*, Julia thought, *are impeccable.*

After a dessert of puddings – tutti-frutti ice cream, and fruit, with coffee and liqueurs on the side – the guests rose from their seats to enter the ballroom. The orchestra opened with a quadrille, and Robert led Julia in the first dance. Men in identical white tie and women in a virtual rainbow of beautiful gowns swirled about the ballroom. Julia barely paid attention to her second dance partner, Sir Geoffrey Maitland, so intent was she on watching Nolan waltz with Olivia Scott-Jones. She even stepped on Maitland's foot – and gave only the hastiest of apologies.

Nolan danced the polka and a gallop effortlessly with his next two partners. Finally it was time for the fourth dance on Julia's card.

'Mr Nolan, I wouldn't have been more surprised if Grover Cleveland himself had attended my ball,' Julia said, eyes sparkling.

Nolan laughed. Putting his white-gloved hand on the small of her back, he pulled her a shade closer.

'I knew you'd be shocked, Miss Cross, to see me out of my element.'

'On the contrary, you don't seem to be out of your element at all.'

'I always wanted to see what your world was like,' Nolan said, looking up at the huge crystal chandelier that swung above the ballroom.

As they pranced along in a mazurka, Julia looked up into Nolan's dark blue eyes, and an odd feeling of bewilderment and exultant happiness surged through her. It was an unknown sensation, and it made her feel both confused and elated.

To her disappointment, the dance inevitably ended, and Nolan escorted her back to where Granny, her official chaperone for the evening, sat with several other dowagers in black lace gowns. After a brief rest, Julia danced with the next partner on her card, Alfred Wharton.

Normally, a gentleman could only dance with a woman to whom he'd been formally introduced or who he knew before the ball. Tonight, however, Granny had introduced Nolan to a score of young women. With his good looks and Granny's imprimatur, Nolan kept busy dancing until the German, for which he partnered with Lavinia Stewart to expertly dance the *tour de valse* around the ballroom's shiny parquet floor.

During a pause in the German, Julia sat next to Granny to rest. The heat generated by two hundred people in heavy gowns and wool evening wear made the ballroom feel like Equatorial Africa. Somehow, Julia noted, Nolan's collar stayed fresh and stiff. Staring across the ballroom at him, she decided to try something a bit untoward. In society ballrooms, men and women used a time-honoured system to send covert messages without attracting the notice of a chaperone. A quick opening and folding of a woman's fan told a man she wasn't interested in him. Dropping her gloves signalled that she was in love. An experienced debutante from Miss Spence's had tutored Julia on the subject.

Eyes fixed on Nolan, she held her fan in front of her face with her right hand. Nolan, who had been watching her from across the ballroom, grasped her meaning instantly: she meant for him to follow her. Rising from her seat, Julia whispered to Granny that she needed to go to the ladies' room. Nolan met her in the drawing room off the central entry hall. Julia took hold of his hand but said nothing. Nolan smiled, bent down, and kissed her. At the touch of his lips, Julia was propelled into a magical world she could hardly bear to leave. She kept her lips pressed to his for almost half a minute, gently absorbing the smell and feel of him.

Nolan ran his hand through Julia's hair and looked into her eyes. 'Your grandmother said you'd be coming down on Saturday.'

'Just in time for the cockfights at Rocky's.'

'We can't miss that,' replied Nolan with a smile.

'But I need to ask you a favour.'

'Anything.'

'There's a gentleman here tonight named Van Cortlandt. I'm going to accidentally bump into him, and if you could relieve him of his wallet, I'd be most appreciative.'

'You'll be my stall?' Nolan said.

'Exactly. And on Saturday, we bet the proceeds on General Sherman.'

CHAPTER FIFTY-ONE

'Gentlemen, why don't we take our cigars and brandy to the main hall?'

Pierre Lorillard V led the way out of the dining room. He was proud of the new house Bruce Price had designed for him in Tuxedo Park, New York, an up-and-coming luxury retreat in the Ramapo Mountains that his father, Lorillard IV, had just created. Cross, a weekend guest, told Lorillard how much he liked the house, but in honesty, he didn't like it at all. A hipped-roof house with an awkwardly placed conical tower, it was nowhere near as good as other cottages Price had designed. Those previous designs had simple, powerful geometries. This one was fussy and conventional, with unnecessary Adamesque decoration on the exterior. It was almost as if the young Lorillard and his wife had strong-armed Price into doing a particular type of design. In cases of a flop, Cross *never* blamed the architect.

Still, Tuxedo Park was a special place, thirteen thousand acres full of winding roads and picturesque landscaping. To great acclaim, Price, Lorillard's favourite architect, had also designed the clubhouse, stables, and many of the first cottages. A fence topped with barbed wire surrounded the development, ensuring that New

York society had another exclusive summer watering hole at which they might escape the heat.

Price and Cross were good friends, and Lorillard had already thrown work Cross's way in the city. Moreover, Helen wanted to see Tuxedo Park, which had only opened in May. With all these factors weighing on him, Cross had accepted an invitation to visit. He knew or recognised a few other weekend guests, including the handsome Russian count he and Helen had seen in Newport a few weeks before.

And Cross liked Lorillard, whom he didn't find pompous or overbearing in the way of so many scions to great fortunes. Lorillard had an endearing passion for horses, which he could discuss for hours. His family, which ran an immensely successful tobacco company, had perhaps the greatest racing stables in America. Their horses had even won the Belmont Stakes and the Epsom Derby in England.

'So where do you keep your fabulous horses, Pierre?' Cross asked.

'In New Jersey, in Rancocas,' he said. 'Not enough room here. But I may bring a few up.'

The main hall connected directly to a veranda that stretched the width of the house's rear. The men drifted out onto it and gazed out at the setting sun.

'I think my father is prouder of Tuxedo than anything else,' Lorillard said. 'He carved this land out of virgin forest. It's a great feeling to create something that will live on after you. Architecture must be the same, eh?'

'That's true,' Cross said thoughtfully. 'You leave something behind for people to use.'

Helen and the other wives came out onto the veranda. Although the French thought it a barbaric habit, the English and Americans

307

split off male and female guests after dinner. The women had been chattering away in the reception room. Emily, Pierre's wife, approached Cross.

'I'm so glad you were able to bring your wife along this weekend, John. She's enchanting,' Emily said. She wore a magnificent choker of diamonds and an emerald-green gown. 'I think Helen is more beautiful than Jennie Jerome, Lord Randolph Churchill's wife.'

'That's quite a compliment,' Cross said, smiling at Helen.

The guests returned to the hall, where chairs had been set up for an informal piano recital. Cross found the performance quite enjoyable. The programme consisted of popular music instead of the usual classical tripe. Refreshments and light food were served afterwards, and the evening continued on until about 1 a.m., when Lorillard and his wife bade their company goodnight, signalling the evening was over.

The guest rooms weren't luxurious, but they were comfortable and each boasted the latest amenity in country houses: a private bathroom. The October nights were cooler, especially in the mountains, and the fireplaces were lit. In silence, Cross and Helen undressed and prepared for bed. But at about three in the morning, Cross lifted his head from his pillow to look over at Helen. She was wide awake, staring at the pressed metal ceiling.

He touched her shoulder. She turned on her side to face him, smiled, and stroked his cheek. 'Good luck, my dear,' she whispered.

Cross grasped her hand and then slowly rose from the bed. He put on his robe and slippers, checked the time on his pocket watch, and made his way down the curving stair tower to the main hall. He unlocked the glass door to the veranda and waited.

About five minutes later, two figures appeared in the shadows. Cross opened the door to let them in. In walked Brady with a much shorter man.

'You know Chops Connolly, don't you, Cross?'

He nodded hello, and Chops grunted back.

'So, where is it?'

'In the main parlour,' Cross whispered.

'Lead the way, Mr Engineer,' said Brady.

Last week, Bruce Price had shown Cross his drawings of all the Tuxedo houses, including Lorillard's. He'd told Price that the Kent and Van Buren designs were particular masterpieces, and in any profession, one needed to learn from a master, which delighted Price.

As he'd examined the drawings, Cross's eye had caught on the ingenious way Price had hidden Lorillard's safe in the wainscoting of the parlour rather than the usual place in the master bedroom. He quietly opened the door – and froze.

At the far end of the room, Count Aleksandrov was looking behind the paintings on the plaster walls. The men watched in silence as the Russian moved from one painting to another.

'Who the fuck are you?' Brady hissed.

The count whirled, eyes widening in shock. Then he recovered his nerve and stood erect. 'I am Count Aleksandrov. I was looking for something to read,' he said indignantly.

Brady smiled at Chops. 'I didn't know they put books behind paintings, did you, Chops?'

'No. Far's I know, they used to put them on bookshelves.'

'Mr Cross,' the count said in disbelief. 'What are you doing here?'

'You two know each other, eh?' Brady said, amused. With unhurried strides, he walked up to the count and took the small leather satchel from his hand. Opening it, he found small tools and lengths of wire. 'A very professional burglar's kit.'

Clinging to his aristocratic bearing, the count looked straight ahead and said nothing. Cross felt almost embarrassed for him.

'I'm sorry to say that you've interfered with our plans tonight, *Count*,' Brady said.

'Ah. If you gentlemen will excuse me, I'll be getting back to my room.' He began to walk away, but Brady grabbed his arm. Cross was afraid the count would start yelling and wake the house; after all, Aleksandrov could easily say he'd come downstairs and found them robbing the place. He was an aristocrat – those in New York society would believe anything he said. And how would Cross explain his presence? It would be awkward at best.

'If we could have *one* more moment of your time, Count,' Brady said in a solicitous tone. In a lightning-quick movement that stunned Cross, the man looped a length of piano wire around the count's neck. He pulled the ends tight. The count's eyes bulged, his face turned blue, and a low gurgling sound came from his lips, then he slumped to the Persian carpet, his eyes staring emptily up at the wood-beamed ceiling.

'So, where's the safe?' Brady asked nonchalantly, putting the piano wire back in his side pocket.

In a state of shock, Cross didn't immediately answer.

Angrily, Brady asked a second time. Without taking his eyes off the dead body, Cross pointed to the wainscoting on the right of the fireplace. 'Push down on the top moulding and slide the middle panel to the right,' he said.

Was he going to faint? Cross felt his head spinning. This was the third man he'd seen murdered before his eyes, but that didn't make it any easier to stomach. He stumbled to the wall, putting out a hand to brace himself. Brady smirked, delighting at Cross's squeamishness.

Chops had his own bag of tools, including a doctor's stethoscope to listen to the movement of the lock's tumblers. He went to work on the safe and had it open in twenty minutes. They removed Emily Lorillard's extensive jewellery collection, which included her wedding gift, an antique gold necklace from the Spanish court of Philip II, and a large amount of cash.

Sniffing, Brady prodded the dead count with his boot.

'A great turn, the count here showing up. They'll think he stole the goods and lit out. All we have to do is make him disappear. To make sure, though, let's leave a little evidence behind.'

He took the count's monogrammed cigarette case and dropped it on the rug.

'We'll need your help to get him to the fence, Mr Engineer. He's too fuckin' big for me and Chops to carry.'

CHAPTER FIFTY-TWO

'Damn, Julia, you don't bet on a bird in a cockfight because you like the colour of its feathers,' moaned Charlie as they exited the Red Rat, a gaming establishment on Ludlow Street.

Julia frowned at her brother. 'It's not like it was your money lost, little boy.'

'I know,' Charlie said proudly, looking over at Eddie. 'My bird won.'

'Stop wasting your time teachin' her strategy, Charlie. A woman thinks how she thinks, and ya can't do nothin' about it,' Eddie said.

'Thank you, Mr Expert on Women,' Julia said, smirking.

Eddie rolled his eyes at Charlie and John Nolan, who laughed.

'And don't lecture me on betting, you little beast,' Julia continued, growing more incensed. 'I'm far, far ahead of you in the ratting ring. I've had six straight winners!'

Charlie bent his head in shame and said nothing. She was right: he'd been on an unlucky streak. It could happen to the best of them. That's what George had said. He'd gone with him and Eddie to the cockfights and had also lost a lot, but it didn't stop him from gambling. In fact, it seemed to make his brother gamble even more.

The group strolled leisurely along Ludlow, taking in the cacophony and bustle of the streets. It was a hot, humid day for October, and the air stank with the smell of rotted food.

Just ahead of them, a bouncer heaved a drunk into the gutter, cursing violently. They walked by as though nothing had happened.

'Where are you supposed to be this afternoon?' Julia asked.

'Science class at the Museum of Natural History. What about you?'

'The library with Jocelyn Van der Meer. Remember that, mind? Last time you got the story mixed up, and Mother was suspicious.'

Charlie scowled at his sister and muttered something under his breath to Eddie.

'We have time before the dogfight. Why not pop into Hannigan's here for a sandwich?' suggested Nolan, gesturing to a small nearby restaurant. His hope of avoiding a sibling free-for-all was realised. Everyone agreed to his plan, filed into Hannigan's, and found a table.

While they waited for their food, Nolan looked surreptitiously at Julia. She was engaged in animated conversation with Charlie and Eddie about the upcoming fight and whether Mustard should be their bet. He smiled at her, and she returned the smile. Her happiness made him happy. So did her presence. Since running into Charlie at the ratting match, she'd wanted to do things with her brother – albeit occasionally. They did love to argue. But Nolan knew Julia loved the fact that Charlie had a secret life like hers.

What they were doing was forbidden, which made it fun and exciting. Julia and Charlie had been raised in a world of suffocating social rules, in which being different was the worst conceivable crime. She had explained all of this repeatedly to Nolan. All their lives, they'd been told what to do to conform:

what to wear, what to eat, how to dance, and above all, with whom to associate. Now, the Cross siblings had dared to travel into a taboo world. If anyone found out about their journey, the consequences would be dire.

Is it a fair price to pay for the excitement and feeling of freedom? Nolan wondered.

Looking at Julia, he knew the answer. Every second was worth it.

CHAPTER FIFTY-THREE

Cross did his best thinking when he was walking. Earlier that afternoon, he'd looked at an empty lot on East Sixty-Fourth Street between Fifth and Madison Avenues. A new client had purchased it to build a house. Instead of being narrow and deep, it had a fifty-foot frontage, allowing a nice wide façade. Cross was pleased. It was a beautiful October day, and he'd decided to forgo a carriage and take the long walk back to the office.

But as he walked down Fifth Avenue past Central Park, Cross's mind shifted to the next robbery. This happened frequently, he'd found, when he was enjoying a musical at the theatre or eating his breakfast. Suddenly, he'd start pondering what to rob next.

It never mattered how successful the last robbery had been; Kent wanted a new job lined up within a week so that he might begin the planning. *Preparation. Preparation. Preparation.* The words echoed ceaselessly in Cross's head.

The target still couldn't be in the city. Last week, he'd accompanied Robert on a late-night stroll, and his brother had shown him first-hand the operatives lurking off Fifth Avenue. Between the pressure of Pinkerton surveillance and the stress of dealing with the murders he'd witnessed, Cross felt worn down.

Images of each man being killed flashed in his mind – Gordon being drowned, Dilts being bludgeoned to death, the count's eyes bulging out as he was strangled. Sometimes Cross felt like beating his head with his fists, so desperate was he to drive the images out.

With brute effort, Cross forced himself to consider the house design. A stylistic change was taking place in the city. The Queen Anne, once so popular, was on the way out. In its place came the understated classicism introduced by McKim, Mead & White's house on East Thirty-Third Street, which housed two bachelor brothers named Phoenix. Built of yellow brick with terracotta, what it omitted from its façade made it original. Instead of picturesque ornament, it was completely flat, the detailing limited to the terracotta panels. Such minimalism was the direction Cross was interested in going with his houses too, he decided.

'Well, Mr Engineer, have you decided to join us? I promise you won't be sorry,' said a jolly voice. The speaker stood directly next to him. Cross whirled, startled to see the man in the derby again. Amid the pressure from Kent to plan more jobs and the flurry of preparation for Julia's coming-out ball, he'd forgotten about him.

The man stood, smiling, hands on his hips. He wore the same ill-fitting, forest-green suit. Cross noticed his unusually thick eyebrows.

'So? What do ya say?'

Though he was annoyed that the man had crept up on him, Cross held his temper in check. He'd treat the man as he would an obstreperous ten-year-old, he decided, with patience and a patronising tone.

'It's kind of you to offer me this opportunity, but I have to refuse. I trust you'll understand?'

'Come on. Reconsider. You'll make a helluva lot more money working for us. Look what I brought you.'

This time his gloved hand held what looked like a gold Tiffany cigarette case.

'Again, that's extremely kind of you, but I can't accept.'

The man seemed to be at a loss for words. A frown replaced his broad grin. He placed the cigarette case in his pocket, removed his hat, and ran his hand through his hair. Looking down at the hexagonal stone pavers in the pavement, he seemed to be searching for something to say.

'And that's your final answer, huh?'

'Yes, I'm afraid it is,' Cross said, giving him a sympathetic smile.

A middle-aged couple passed by, talking quietly among themselves. The man watched them go and then shrugged his shoulders, face still composed and mild. 'I guess there's only one thing left to do,' he said and pulled a revolver from his inside pocket. 'Can't let the competition have an advantage over us. It's not good business.'

Before the man could point the gun, Cross had vaulted the stone wall that separated the park from Fifth Avenue and was running through the woods like a wild animal. He heard the man crashing through the undergrowth behind him. Like all the men of his social class, Cross never exercised. After fifty yards of sprinting, he felt as though he might pass out. His heart was pounding so hard he thought it would burst from his chest. Sweat drenched his clothes. But he didn't dare let up the pace. At any second, he expected a bullet to pierce the base of his skull.

He tore across the East Drive to a path at the edge of the pond and headed north along its bank. People in the park stopped and stared at the chase, stupefied, as Cross and his pursuer passed by

317

like blurs. Instead of continuing north, Cross took a hard left over the Gapstow Bridge, hoping to fool the man in the derby. But even when he crossed, he heard the footsteps pounding behind him. Running west along the footpath, he almost collided with a nanny pushing a pram. He turned north on the next path and slowed to look over his shoulder. The crack of a pistol report sounded. He felt more than heard a sharp-pitched hissing by his right ear.

With a burst of new-found energy, Cross flew up the path, running like a madman. Another hissing sound shot by his shoulder. He looked ahead and found that he was at the dairy, south of the Sixty-Fifth Street Transverse Road. A Gothic-style building of stone and wood, it had a gable-roofed open shed connected to it. Cross ran into the shed and hid behind the low stone wall that supported the corner columns on the far side.

A few seconds later, the man entered the shed. When he saw no one in the long, open space, he turned and went out. Cross waited a few minutes, struggling to catch his breath, and then stood up slowly and went around to the back of the adjoining stone building.

At the corner, he craned his neck, trying to see if the man was about. No one was in sight. He started to run off – then stopped and stared at the grassed area at the side of the stone building. A dark green shape in the shadows blended in with the grass. Cross crept forward.

Twenty feet away, he saw the man lying face down on the ground. He walked over and knelt beside him. The man's eyes were wide open, staring up into the cloudless blue sky . . . and a knife protruded from between his ribs. On the ground next to the body lay his derby and the revolver.

Cross looked around to see if anyone was watching. He saw no one.

* * *

From a grove of trees fifty yards away, Nolan watched Cross walk away. He looked down at his shaking hands.

In his heart, he knew he had done the right thing. Yes, he had betrayed his gang – his only family – but he loved Julia. He couldn't bear to see her hurt.

CHAPTER FIFTY-FOUR

Kent and Cross were standing on Hester Street when the bullet passed through the two-foot space between them, shattering the plate glass window of the saloon at their backs. A shard of glass ripped into a patron standing at the bar, who screamed. Startled, the horses of Kent's carriage bolted, pitching the driver onto the pavement. As he dived to the ground for cover, Kent saw a phaeton with two men in derbies speeding down Hester Street.

'Coogan!' he screamed. 'Get that goddamn carriage!'

Coogan, who had been keeping watch in the doorway of McGlory's, sprinted down the crowded pavement. Kent helped Cross stand. The architect was shaking with fear. A man not used to disrespect, let alone a murder attempt, Kent was seething with anger. It was unusual to see the calm, level-headed criminal mastermind in such a temper.

'Who the hell do they think they are?' he screamed in the direction of the would-be assassins. 'Are you all right, Mr Cross?'

For a fraction of a second, Cross was touched by his concern. Then he realised Kent only wanted to know whether his asset had been harmed. He had paid no attention to the anguished wailing of the injured man in the saloon.

'Yes, I'm fine,' he said shortly.

'Goddamn it, I'll find out who's behind this,' Kent growled.

An imaginary debate had been raging in Cross's mind. He had been unsure whether to tell Kent about the rival gang's offer and about what had happened at the Central Park Dairy. Because of the mysterious circumstances surrounding the man in the green suit's death, Cross thought it possible that one of Kent's men had been assigned to him as a kind of guardian angel. In that case, there would be no reason to tell Kent about the threats, because he probably already knew. To Cross, Kent already seemed like an underworld god, all knowing and all powerful. In his company, he felt protected from further harm. No, Cross had been far more worried about the traitor than rival gang attacks. But this changed the situation.

A pistol report rang out a few blocks away. It was a common sound in the Bowery, like the howling of an alley cat. No one on the street paid it any attention.

'There's something I must tell you,' Cross said cautiously.

Kent stood, expressionless.

'Two weeks ago, I was approached by one of your rivals. They asked me to leave you and join them. Of course, I turned the man down. Yesterday, I refused them again, and a man tried to kill me in Central Park. But someone killed him first.' Cross spoke in a contrite voice, like a little boy admitting to a misdeed.

Kent stared at him for a few seconds. Then he walked over and leant against the brick wall of the saloon. Taking out a cigar and lighting it, he looked at the pavement, then back at Cross, with a perplexed expression.

'I guess I should've told you right away,' Cross said, lowering his eyes.

Kent burst out laughing. The spasms of mirth seemed

uncontrollable, as if he couldn't stop. 'Yes, Mr Cross,' he said. 'That would've been helpful. But I admire your loyalty.'

'It wasn't loyalty. It was pure fear. You would've killed me for jumping ship.'

'In a second.'

Coogan raced up to them. 'They turned south on Mott. I got close enough to get a shot off, but I missed. Got a look at the fellow, though. Think it was Big Josh Hines from Milligan's gang.'

'What did the fellow who made you the offer look like?' Kent asked Cross.

'He wore a dark green suit and had these peculiar eyebrows, like caterpillars above his eyes.'

'Rip Murdock,' Coogan said with a grim smile. 'It's Milligan.'

'I hate wars. They're bad for business. But Milligan must be taught a lesson. A very hard one,' Kent said.

'Should I start with Hines?' Coogan asked.

'Mr Coogan, if you want to get rid of wasps, you don't kill them one by one. You find their nest and destroy it outright,' Kent said.

'I understand. You and Mr Cross will need someone to keep an eye on you until this business is finished. I'll see to that,' Coogan said and walked away.

'Now, Mr Cross, before we were so rudely interrupted, you were telling me about the next job.'

Still shaken by the shooting, Cross wanted to go home and hide under the bedcovers, not discuss another robbery.

'Another house in Manhattan? Or Tuxedo?' Kent seemed to have forgotten that less than five minutes ago, he'd been inches from death.

Cross shook his head, unsure whether to be amazed or terrified. 'Manhattan is out. There are too many Pinkertons around.'

'And how do you know that?'

Cross realised his mistake as soon as the words left his mouth. He couldn't stumble with his explanation; it had to be perfect. 'Cook, my old client. I ran into him at the Union League Club, and he told me. Tuxedo's tightly guarded now too.'

'What about another bank?'

The last jobs in Newport and Tuxedo Park had been rich hauls. Cross had thought Kent might be pleased enough to not insist on another job so soon. But success had made him greedy.

And true to his word, Kent had given him a seven per cent share. Unsure what else to do with it, Cross had deposited the money in a separate bank account.

'I'm looking into that,' Cross said, 'but I've got another possibility. A far bigger take.'

'I'm listening.'

CHAPTER FIFTY-FIVE

Nolan and Julia had just dropped Granny off at Wah Kee's for the afternoon. Julia's grandmother had grown fond of her granddaughter's handsome friend and allowed her to step out with him unchaperoned, opportunities that came chiefly when she was enjoying herself at Wah Kee's. Opium was a miracle cure, she told her granddaughter. After ten years of daily pain, her lumbago had vanished. Her visits increased to three times a week. They always escorted Granny home, a dreamy, elated expression on her face.

Still, Julia worried that her grandmother would buy more cats from Wah Kee. The animals were overrunning her brownstone home and had already caused two servants to quit. There were dozens of them, and they had taken over the house.

But the risk was worth it. Julia loved to walk the streets of the Tenderloin and the Bowery with Nolan; their perambulations had become her consuming preoccupation. Charles Dickens, whom she greatly admired, walked for miles through London every day. She wanted to do the same thing, she told Nolan, to observe life and take in the details – the more sordid, the better.

'I can supply you with sordidness to last a lifetime,' Nolan said with a mock evil leer.

But after hearing so much about Dickens – and without telling Julia – he'd purchased a second-hand copy of *Oliver Twist*, which he read and enjoyed. The description of the pickpockets rang entirely true. Fagin was his favourite character and reminded him of his mentor, Crazy Ned. Now Nolan was reading *Nicholas Nickleby*.

Instead of rat baiting or the cockfights, Nolan chose to escort Julia to a gambling den on West Thirty-Eighth Street called Cantwell's. New York City had a wide variety of gambling establishments that catered to all classes of society, and Julia was interested in all of them. She and Nolan had even been to a gambling den in Chinatown. In contrast, Cantwell's was high-class. Its four large rooms were each devoted to a specific game: roulette, faro, dice, and poker.

Nolan would never allow Julia to bet her own money, and he always put down her bet. Every gambling joint cheated, no matter how classy it seemed. In the end, the house always won. But Nolan was a friend of the owner of Cantwell's. He gave a nod to the croupier, and Julia's number hit again and again. She shrieked with laughter at every win, which pleased Nolan immensely. Caught up in her excitement, the other patrons at the table eagerly placed bets too – just as the house wanted. Nolan had taken Julia to other joints where he knew the dealers, and she had won at faro and dice. But Julia always quit while she was ahead, unwilling to tempt fate.

After stopping, she stayed at the wheel to watch the other gamblers. The spinning of the wheel and the way the little white ivory ball bounced crazily around mesmerised her. She offered breathless encouragement to the players and heartfelt sympathy when they lost.

From the dice room came the sound of cheering. At first, it was low in volume, but it got louder and louder. The roar was only interrupted when the player was about to roll the dice. Then came wild applause and laughter: he or she had won.

'Someone's lucky today,' Julia said to Nolan.

There was a lull in the cheering. A lone voice shouted out, 'Mathematicians have a special connection to the number seven. You'll see!'

Julia turned abruptly from the roulette table and rushed out of the room. Alarmed, Nolan followed. The dice room was packed like a sardine can, and Julia found herself blocked by the crowd at the doorway. With bulldog determination, she squeezed past the dozens of wildly cheering spectators. A heavy haze of cigar smoke floated over the heads of the onlookers like a great storm cloud. Julia peeked between the bodies at the front to see her brother, George, standing at the head of the table, throwing the dice. He had a kind of crazed expression on his face, a hazy smile, as if he were in a drug-induced delirium. Julia had never seen that look on him before and barely recognised him.

'That's my brother,' she said in a voice that hardly sounded like her own, as Nolan stopped next to her.

Two more rolls of the dice brought two more wins. The applause grew yet more raucous. George seemed oblivious to the attention, carefully stacking his chips in neat piles, lost in his own private world.

In front of Julia, an elegant woman in a red-and-purple walking outfit leant over to the man next to her.

'I think he's up to eight thousand,' she said, as excited as if they were her own winnings.

'More like nine,' the man said.

Three more passes brought three more wins. The crowd was in a frenzy. The gambling in the other rooms had ceased. The players were crowding into the room to see what the furore was about. Julia stood there, amid the noise and the chaos, and stared at her brother. Nolan watched her, baffled.

The noise had died down, the crowd anxiously awaiting the next throw.

'It has to be more than ten thousand,' said the man. George paused, looking down at his horde of chips. He picked up a few, jiggled them in his hand, and then put them back on their stack. With both hands, he began carefully taking each tall stack and placing it on the green felt of the dice table. First one, then another and another. They reminded Julia of white towers, forming the outer walls of some medieval fortification.

A stunned silence swept the room. Not a single sound was uttered. When every chip was down, George picked up the dice in his right fist and stared down the length of the table. Julia wanted to leap forward and plead with her brother, but she remained frozen in place. The fashionable women in the crowd grabbed the arms of their escorts, squeezing them harder and harder as the tension mounted. The well-dressed men were wide-eyed. The longer George took, the more unbearable the wait became.

With a quick flick of his wrist, the dice went careening down the table, bouncing off the green felt of the barrier wall. Every person in the room held his or her breath as the white cubes came to a rest.

'Two,' cried out the croupier. A loud collective moan filled the room. The two black dots stared back at George like tiny eyes. The good cheer and bonhomie vanished in a second, and the crowd dispersed quickly, not wanting to catch George's ill luck. He stood, a lone figure at the head of the table. Another player, a man with grey mutton chop sideburns and a large belly, stepped up beside George and held the dice, ready for the next throw.

As she watched her brother, a feeling of crushing despair descended upon her. She grabbed Nolan's hand and rushed out of the building.

CHAPTER FIFTY-SIX

Cross had spent the afternoon arguing with a client over the cost of marble, the prospect of the next robbery hovering perpetually in the back of his mind. He felt dog-tired, as if the weight of the world was pressing down on him.

Not seeing any carriages, he decided to walk to the Grand Central stop of the Third Avenue Elevated Railroad and take the train home. It was late afternoon. Crowds of people filed up the iron stairs for their evening commute. The usual ragged newsboys were hawking their papers. Alongside them, food vendors sold everything from gingerbread cakes to roasted ears of corn. An Italian in a greasy-looking derby sold sausages.

Physically and emotionally drained, Cross trudged up the stairs.

'Extra! Extra! Russian count robs the rich and is murdered!' cried a newsboy standing on the landing of the stairs above.

The announcement sent a jolt through Cross. They must have found the count's body in Tuxedo. Brady had left some jewellery on his body, bait to convince the police that he'd robbed the Lorillards. Apparently, they'd bitten.

'Russian mastermind steals rare jewel! Read all about it in *The Sun*!' the boy screamed.

Amazing. The yellow press was blaming Aleksandrov for the other robberies, including the Pharaoh Blue. It was ridiculous and implausible – and perfectly fine with Cross.

He approached the newsboy, eager to get a paper – and paused, startled. Most of the newsies were filthy urchins in rags, but this child was well dressed and clean. He took another look and almost stumbled down the stairs in shock. His son, Charlie, was peddling papers!

'Extra, extra! Read all about it! Russian count robs the rich and is murdered!'

Stunned by the sight of his son, Cross regained his composure. Instead of confronting Charlie, he slipped down the opposite side of the staircase and back on to the street. Concealing himself behind one of the iron columns that supported the station above, he stared at Charlie. The boy handed out papers and took the money expertly, making change for a dollar and screaming out the lurid headline all the while. Cross couldn't decide if he was more surprised by the fact that Charlie was there or by how well the boy did the job. He had never seen Charlie do a single practical thing in his life. With servants filling their house, there was no call for it.

An unwitting smile spread across Cross's face as he watched his son work. Unaccountably, he felt a real sense of pride in his boy.

Soon Charlie was out of papers and began to count his day's earnings. A very ragged urchin approached him. From the way they smiled and laughed together, it was plain that they were friends. They ran up the next flight of stairs, and Cross followed. The boys boarded a downtown train, and Cross did the same, sitting at the very end of the car to avoid being seen. At this time of day, it was crowded. He had to stand to keep an eye on Charlie. Once he ducked down, afraid the boy was looking his way.

At Grand Street, the boys got off and made their way to the street. Following them proved more difficult than Cross had anticipated. Instead of heading to their destination in a direct line, they stopped to look in shop windows or pick up junk in the gutter, to throw a rock at a rat and buy candy from a Chinese vendor. Cross had to duck into doorways and peek around corners. Squawking, an old woman chased him away with a broom.

He watched the boys approach a pushcart that sold fruit. The urchin kept the vendor busy while Charlie stole pears and peaches, stuffing them into a burlap bag he pulled out of his trouser pocket. The boys continued on to a street bordering the East River. It was a dirty, ramshackle neighbourhood full of abandoned buildings. Whores stood in doorways, croaking out come-ons to men walking. Flies blanketed a rotting cat in the gutter. The pavements were strewn with rubbish.

Charlie and the urchin turned into an alleyway beside an abandoned warehouse. Cross ran across the street and craned his head around the corner, watching as the boys crawled through a window opening. He followed, finding himself in an old boiler room.

'Not a bad day, Charlie, my boy, not bad at all,' the urchin was saying proudly.

'We should do some wrangling tomorrow,' Charlie said.

From the shadows, Cross watched as the urchin unlocked a padlock on one of the huge boilers, climbed inside, and shut the door. Amazed, Cross hurried over to the door. Through the joints, he could see that the boys had lit candles or a lantern. He stood, listening to them talk about their plans for the morrow. Charlie would meet the urchin at nine at the pier.

So this is where Charlie learnt to curse, Cross thought, amused, as expletives tumbled from his son's mouth.

In one smooth move, he swung open the boiler hatch. Two surprised boys stared back at him, faces illumined by the flickering candlelight.

'Charlie, you must introduce me to your friend – or is this your dancing instructor? And are you gentlemen free for supper tonight? I saw a charming restaurant on my way down here.'

CHAPTER FIFTY-SEVEN

'Just think, Freddie. Two thousand dollars cash in your pocket.'

'You're asking me to take quite a risk, George.'

'Fletcher's in on it,' he lied. 'We need you.'

Fred Watkins, George Cross's teammate from Harvard, was a pitcher for the Boston Beaneaters of the National League. He'd had an outstanding collegiate career, and when he'd graduated, Boston had signed him immediately. He was now an average pitcher on a fifth-place team trailing Chicago by thirty games. The season was in its final two weeks, and Boston was in town to play the Giants. George had finally hit a winning streak at faro, but he still owed a packet to a fellow named Hurley, the owner of Handsome Harry's on Baxter Street. Hurley's men had caught up with George two days prior, and he'd pleaded for one last chance before they made good on their promise to kill him. With his back against the wall, he had decided to do something he'd tried and failed with Kent: fix a game.

If all went well, Watkins would throw the game, and the Giants would win this afternoon.

'You're the pitcher, Freddie. You control the game; you know that.' George sat on Freddie's bed in the Windsor Hotel.

'Come on, Freddie, be a sport,' Kitty said. 'Help us out – and help yourself too. You don't get paid shit for being a ballplayer.'

Kitty had insisted that George bring her along in an attempt to seal the deal. He'd been working on Freddie for the last two days, but the pitcher still hadn't committed. He was scheduled for the 2 p.m. game at the Polo Grounds, and time was running out.

'The Giants are in third place,' Freddie said. 'They're far better than us.'

'Then we need you just in case you start winning,' George pointed out.

'Think of all the things you could do with two thousand. You're a Harvard man. You can get a tip from your brother at Kidder, Peabody & Co. and invest it,' Kitty said.

Freddie went over to the window and looked out at the traffic on Fifth Avenue.

'The way I'm pitching, I don't know how long the majors will keep me around.' His voice sounded distant; he spoke to no one in particular. 'Sure, the money would come in handy. But it's a big risk.'

Kitty looked at George, frowning. It was 11 a.m.

After the incident on the steps outside the gambling hall, Kitty had sworn to stop helping George, but that resolution lasted less than a week. Just as George was compelled to gamble, Kitty was compelled to help him. She just couldn't stop herself. *Maybe that's what love does to a person*, she reasoned. *It makes them act in a foolish manner and do things that are bound to come to no good.* But good or no, she and George were both under a spell too powerful to resist. And if George didn't immediately come up with the money for Hurley, it wouldn't be a beating and a warning. He'd get a bullet in the head. It was their last chance.

'George, why don't you meet me at the baseball ground? Freddie and I can talk things over,' Kitty said. She nodded discreetly at the little table in the middle of the room. George got off the bed, placed five one-hundred-dollar bills on the table, and left.

After seven innings, the score was Boston 4-0, and George was getting worried.

Sitting three rows behind him were Piker Shaw and Gyp Sullivan, Hurley's collectors. The two men were laughing and rooting loudly for Boston; they wanted Freddie's team to win so that they could kill George after the game, before they went out for dinner.

In her own special way, Kitty thought she had convinced Freddie to cooperate. Her eyes darted repeatedly to Hurley's men. A scowl marred her pretty face.

From his time as a ballplayer, George could see that Freddie was trying to lose. But every time a Giant made contact, the ball wound up in a Boston glove. A strong wind blowing in from centre field was making long fly balls, which normally would have been home runs, into long outs at the foot of the fence. Freddie practically lobbed the ball over the plate and still the Giants couldn't get a hit. When they did get men on, they promptly batted into double plays, stranding men on base. Freddie tried walking batters, but they got stranded too.

As if caught up in the spirit of the day, the Boston infielders – normally mediocre fielders – made spectacular plays to deny the Giants hits. Hanson, the third baseman, made a diving grab and snagged a ball that would have driven in two runs. George felt tension building in his temples. He massaged his head, unable to look at Kitty.

At the top of the eighth, Boston came up to bat and pounded two hits down the right field line, putting men on first and third with no outs. George's heart sank. But the reliever, Jack Singleton, bore down and struck out the side, finally giving the fans at the Polo Grounds something to cheer about. And in the bottom of the eighth, with Freddie's help, the Giants' bats came alive. Connor led off with a double to left centre. Esterbrook smashed a home run over the fence in right centre. The ball flew so far that it landed at the foot of the A. G. Spalding Sporting Goods sign. Keefe singled, and O'Rourke brought him home with a double. The score was 4-3. With no outs, it looked like a cinch for Freddie to get two more runs, but the next three batters popped up, grounded out, and fouled out.

Boston was up, and Morrill, their home-run hitter, drove the ball to the left field fence. George gasped, clutching at Kitty's hand, but the wind kept the ball in. Wise walked but was forced out at second in a double play. The bottom of the ninth had arrived.

Freddie had one chance left to lose the game.

Dorgan led off. Though Freddie lobbed him the ball, he popped up. Gerhardt followed with a ground out. George was down to the last out. People were heading for the exits. Shaw and Sullivan leant forward, ready to ensure that their target wouldn't slip away with the crowd.

Freddie delivered four straight balls, miles out of the strike zone, to walk Johnson. Callahan came up to the plate and fouled off the next two pitches.

'It's time to go, Georgie,' Shaw said, placing a beefy hand on his shoulder.

Callahan fouled off two more pitches, prolonging George's agony. Shaw yanked the boy from his seat, pulling him into the aisle.

'Time to go,' he repeated.

On the field, Callahan swung and missed. Ten thousand people let out a collective groan. As Kitty watched helplessly, Shaw dragged George by his collar up the stairs.

But then the umpire signalled. A foul tip, dropped by the catcher. A few seconds later, the crowd started screaming wildly. George broke loose from Sullivan's grasp and ran back to the seats. His heart leapt as he saw a white orb defying the wind, sailing into dead centre, and bouncing off the billboard for McCann's Celebrated Hats of the Bowery. The Giants had won on a two-run homer. Kitty threw herself into George's arms, kissing him passionately. Amid the thousands of fans yelling and jumping for joy, Shaw and Sullivan turned and stomped away, looks of disgust written large on their faces.

'I'll see you later at my place,' Kitty yelled over the din. 'You see, I promised Freddie a bonus if he lost.'

CHAPTER FIFTY-EIGHT

Impossible as it seemed, no one knew anything about the robberies. The only word Robert heard on the street was a mad rumour about the 'Engineer' who had supposedly masterminded the crimes. Usually criminals were like gossipy women, blabbing about anything and everything they'd heard. This time, there was almost total silence. In all his years as a Pinkerton, Robert had never seen such a thing. People were too scared to talk.

Following the lead of the newspapers, the public had eagerly blamed the larcenous Russian count for the robberies. Robert knew this was nonsense. The count wasn't even a real royal; he was an accomplished con artist who'd fooled the gullible rich into thinking he was of the aristocratic class. The idea that such a petty criminal had stolen the Pharaoh Blue was laughable. The man behind all this was the Engineer.

Walking west on Grand Street to the Second Avenue Elevated Railroad, he saw his nephew, George, come around the corner at Allen Street and enter a ramshackle two-storey house. Robert was shocked. Seeing George in such a squalid setting was like seeing a handsome prince walking through a pigsty. Without hesitating, Robert followed George to the house. It was one of New York's vilest gambling dens, a disgusting dive where the lowest of the low went to throw away their money. *Probably a brace house*, Robert thought, casting a critical eye about him. Those unscrupulous dens offered a fixed game twenty-four hours a day.

In the next instant, and to his amazement, he saw his niece following her brother. Julia was about a block behind and had a tall, handsome young man at her side. Robert could see that they didn't want George to notice them. After George went into the dive, they waited a minute or two and then followed.

Aside from the scum of the street, clerks from businesses and brokerage houses might visit the house during their lunchtimes. For a few seconds, Robert debated whether he should follow. In a cramped little dump of this sort, the risk of being seen by George or Julia was too great.

And he didn't need to enter to picture the interior. Robert knew all about these places. A narrow, dimly lit corridor would lead to a smoke-filled room with a faro table, its usual set-up of thirteen cards in parallel rows glued down on a greasy, enamelled oil cloth. At the table would be the mechanic, or dealer, with his assistant taking cards from a brass box that was always rigged. On the other side of the table stood the suckers, placing their bets on the glued-down cards.

The den had no amenities, which meant it was also a snap house, a place that rented space to individual gamblers. These men set up their own games in exchange for a ten per cent cut. A roulette game and a chuck-a-luck dice game were probably going on in the back.

Robert walked across the street and stood in the doorway of a used clothing dealer's shop. He lit a cigarette and waited. Watching a building was an art; one couldn't get distracted and miss the suspect's exit. He was an expert, keeping one eye on the door of the gambling den and the other on the parade of characters passing by. The streets of New York were an endlessly fascinating kaleidoscope, packed with an incredible variety of people. On any given day, Robert would see Hebrews who looked like they'd stepped out of Russia, inscrutable Chinese men with long pigtails, and Greeks with jet-black hair and pointy noses. It was so different from Buffalo, where there were only white people who looked like him.

A beautiful, swarthy Italian girl carrying a huge basket of laundry on her head smiled as she passed. The street was a river of traffic, choked with delivery wagons, carriages, and dray carts. In this part of Manhattan, nobody gave a damn about whether the streets were clean; manure, piss, and rotting rubbish carpeted the surface.

After ten minutes, Julia and her companion rushed out of the dive. His niece looked shaken; her face was white with shock, and her hands were clenched into fists. The sight troubled Robert, but he held to his post. Her companion was familiar – perhaps from Julia's coming-out ball? – and looked as though he would protect her in such a rotten neighbourhood.

An hour passed. Robert grew hungry but didn't abandon his post. He snapped his fingers at a woman peddling hot, spiced gingerbread. It would tide him over until supper.

Finally, George emerged. From the expression on his nephew's face, Robert could tell what had happened. George leant against the brick wall of the building and lit a cigarette. After five minutes of staring down at the dirty pavement, he walked off.

Robert waited until George was down the block and around the corner. Then he went across the street into the dive. He walked into the faro parlour and stood at the rear, behind some men watching the game.

The dealer was talking to his assistant when Robert walked over.

'That young, well-dressed fellow in the blue suit that was just here – does he come here often?'

'What the hell does it matter to you?' the dealer snarled.

Robert grabbed the man by his collar, slammed his head down on the faro table, and held his Pinkerton shield in front of his face. 'I'm sure that's an excellent bit of cheating you do with that needle squeeze on your dealing box. The police might be interested in a demonstration. Or perhaps you can answer my question instead.'

'His name's George Cross,' the man squeaked. 'Society swell. He gambles all over the Bowery and the Five Points. He was up three thousand today, but he pissed it all away. Poor bastard never knows when to quit, so he's always in hock.'

'Where does he get his money?'

'Don't know. He's got a few cons on the side. A whore gives him money sometimes. But he keeps coming back to lose.'

Robert let the man off the table with a shove. 'Lose?' he sneered. 'You mean win.'

The dealer started to laugh. 'These fools *want* to lose. That's why we love 'em.'

CHAPTER FIFTY-NINE

Brownie Snead's left hook caught Whitey Samuels square in the jaw and bounced him off the brick wall onto the hard-packed dirt of the cellar like a rubber ball. With the agility of a cancan dancer, Brownie kicked Whitey underneath the jaw. As Whitey rose to all fours, Brownie kicked him in the stomach. Still, the tough old bastard wouldn't go down.

Nolan had ten dollars on Brownie and was impatient to end the thing. But Whitey rammed his fist into Brownie's groin, sending him to the floor where he rolled about in agony.

'Ain't none of those sissy Marquess of Queensberry rules here like they got in England!' Pickle Nose Johnson yelled.

The East Side Cowboys were in the cellar of the Bucket of Blood, enjoying what they called 'a free and easy', a bare knuckles brawl with no ring and no rules. They drank and ate as they watched, gathered around tables in an open space at the rear of the cellar.

Back on his feet, Whitey delivered the coup de grâce, stomping on the fallen Brownie's face three times. Finally, Brownie lay still. The gang groaned: Brownie had been the overwhelming favourite. Conversation resumed. No one attended to the downed fighter.

Nolan took a sip of rye and dealt cards to the other men at his table, readying for a game of hearts.

'How ya makin' out with that society girl?' Pickle Nose asked. 'Miss Julia's mighty pretty.'

'She's gone back to school, but I see her in the afternoons and on weekends,' Nolan said, examining his cards. He'd begun playing soon after being thrown out on the street. The cards had taught him his numbers and how to add and subtract. From an early age, he'd also learnt about cheating. Nolan knew every trick – trimmed and marked cards, making two cards stick together, hold outs for concealing cards in sleeves and vests, even tiny mirrors used to read the cards of opponents. These were advantage tools and were advertised in the newspapers and sold on the Bowery.

Pickle Nose, he saw, was cheating at that very moment by palming an ace of hearts he would tuck up in his sleeve. But Nolan could cheat so well that he was able to counteract any moves against him. He'd even instructed Julia in some of the techniques, which delighted her. The game of whist was fashionable in her set, and Nolan had given her pointers on how to gain an advantage. Society played the game for money; now that she had come out, Julia was allowed to join in. Under his tutelage, she wiped out her opponents. This pleased Nolan greatly. She regularly took the proceeds and bet them on ratting contests, which she consistently won. The girl had an innate talent for picking winners, which her brother Charlie greatly resented.

Milligan came in and began making the rounds, greeting his men, telling jokes, and topping off drinks. Brownie was conscious and sitting at a table, knocking back shots to ease his aches and pains. Whitey had collected his earnings and left.

The door to the room opened again. A mousy man wearing spectacles stuck his head in. 'I've got a beer delivery for Mr Spike

Milligan,' he said. His voice was loud and silenced the room.

Annoyed, Milligan walked up to the man. 'Goddamn it, jackass, I'm not a saloon keeper. Deliver it upstairs to the owner,' he snarled.

The delivery man, who looked like he'd been cursed and insulted often in his line of work, smiled and waved his hand in a friendly way. 'No, sir. This is a special order from Mr Croker.'

Milligan's face lit up. He looked at his men, who nodded and smiled in approval. Richard Croker was the Grand Sachem, or boss, of Tammany Hall. He was an Irish roughneck who'd used his fists to rise from the gutter and earn appointments as coroner and fire commissioner, positions for which he was completely unqualified. When Honest John Kelly had retired as Tammany boss two years before, Croker had been heir apparent. He held political power in New York with an iron fist. The New York City election for mayor was next month, and Croker expected the gangs to do what they did best – get out the vote for his candidate.

The delivery man rolled a huge keg on a hand truck to the front of the room. Staring at it, Milligan seemed to glow with pride.

'Boys,' he said, pointing to the keg. 'This is a token of Mr Croker's appreciation for how we've helped him in past elections. *And* it's a reminder of what we have to do next month. Mr Croker wants Abraham Hewitt as the next mayor, not that fuckin' socialist shit Henry George or that fancy-ass Theodore Roosevelt. We have to bring out the vote for Tammany.'

Nolan laughed. Milligan would get a person to vote – and then vote six more times. He was a master at getting bums, cripples, and beggars to turn up at different polling places in the various precincts. An array of costumes was provided to disguise repeat voters. In the last mayoral race, one man had voted fourteen times.

'Mr Croker says the greatest political crime is ingratitude, and the Cowboys ain't gonna be ungrateful. Let's do our part and not let him down,' Milligan called.

The gang cheered and whooped in response.

The delivery man handed Milligan the tap for the keg and shook his hand heartily in Tammany solidarity. But outside the open door, he paused. 'Mr Kent hopes you enjoy the lager. And by the way, he's voting for Roosevelt!' he shouted. Drawing a Colt, the delivery man fired at the keg and slammed the door behind him.

There was an ear-splitting explosion, and an orange-red fireball engulfed the room. The men sitting closest to the keg were blown to atoms. Pieces of bodies shot into the walls and ceiling with the velocity of bullets. Shards of glass and wood penetrated skulls and torsos. The entire room filled with flames and sulphur-smelling smoke. Men screamed in agony as they burnt to death. In what seemed like seconds, the wood beams holding the floor above creaked and began to give way. The first floor, filled to capacity with saloon patrons, came crashing down into the cellar.

Then the noise stopped, replaced by a silence punctuated only by low moans. The room was so thick with smoke and dust that a man could not see his hand in front of his face.

Nolan felt a crushing pressure on his stomach. He opened his eyes but saw only a thick, black cloud pressing down upon him.

He could only think of Julia.

CHAPTER SIXTY

'The vault for the silver and linens was well concealed. So was the safe that held the jewellery. Who knew their exact location?'

'The servants,' William Cook said. 'Myself, my wife . . . and the architect who designed it, of course.'

'Yes, the architect,' Robert Cross said softly. He knew very well who that was.

'Have you recovered anything?' William Cook asked. Soon after the theft, he and his wife had replaced everything they had lost with even more expensive items, including a rare Dresden china service. It was the insult of the robbery that offended him, not the loss of money.

'Two salad forks have turned up in Philadelphia, but that's all, I'm afraid.'

'It was that Russian son of a bitch, that phony bastard who stole the diamond. That's who did this! Three times, I hosted him in my house. Well, I learnt my lesson. No one will ever rob me again. I've installed one of those newfangled telegraphic alarms. It's connected straight to the police precinct.'

After Cook left his office, Robert sat, looking at the architectural drawings Fidelity National had lent him. He saw how close the sub-basement vault was to Broadway and the abandoned Beach tunnel. It was an extremely well planned robbery, nothing like the usual poor attempts by the none-too-bright criminals to which he was accustomed.

His colleague, Pemberton, was hunched over his desk nearby, poring over a report.

'You've worked here in the city for a while, haven't you, Pemberton?' The white-haired man looked up and smiled.

'About a million years. Since '76.'

'Remember George Leslie?'

'Couldn't forget him. Called that fellow the king of the bank robbers.'

'Wasn't he some sort of engineer or architect?'

'Something like that. Came from a well-off family back in Ohio and studied engineering at the University of Cincinnati, I think. Good with building plans. Definitely the brains of the outfit.'

Robert stared out of the window, watching the traffic on Broadway. Then he picked up the telephone, rang up Greene, and got the name of the architect who'd built his city mansion. Flipping through the New York City directory, he jotted down addresses and telephone numbers.

'Mr Ware. So nice of you to let me come by on such short notice,' Robert said.

'Anything to help you find the bastards who robbed Mr Greene,' James Ware said, showing Robert into the conference room where his architectural drawings were laid out. 'I hope this is what you're looking for,' he said. 'It's a complete set of the house on Sixty-Fifth.'

'Thank you. I understand that you came up with a very innovative design for a tenement house. Won a competition, in fact.'

Ware beamed at the recognition. Robert could tell he was proud of his design.

'Why, yes. The whole idea was to produce a humane design,

to let these poor wretches have more light and air. Perhaps even running water and indoor toilets.'

'It's an important step. Those unfortunates live in the most disgusting conditions. Like animals, really,' Robert said.

'Indeed. The way those landlords convert old houses into rookeries and stuff a dozen families in them is downright criminal, but the law protects them. Then they build appalling tenements. No windows except at the front and back.' Ware's voice was rising with emotion. 'More than five hundred people per *acre* live down there.'

'Exactly what I'm saying. Animals in the zoo are treated better. By the way, Mr Ware, where were you on the night of the robbery?' Robert said casually.

'I was in Boston that week,' Ware said. 'When I heard about the robbery, I was outraged.'

'Such a beautiful house you designed. Did you and Mr Greene part on good terms? Did he pay your full fee, I mean?'

'Why, thank you, Mr Cross. And yes, he paid to the penny, even for the extra design work.'

'Thank you so much for your time, Mr Ware. I must be going now, but I should say how much I admire men like you. My brother John's an architect in the city, you know.'

Ware's face lit up in recognition. 'Oh, I'm a good friend of John's. Please tell him I said hello.'

'I will. And thank you again.'

'John's a talented man, but he always wants to learn more. That's the sign of a great architect. He's even been up here to look over my drawings,' Ware said, the pride evident in his voice.

Robert stopped and turned. 'Oh . . . recently?'

'Perhaps a month ago. Wanted to look at my tenement design because he said he was going to design one.'

* * *

347

Robert walked down Madison Avenue and turned east on Twenty-Eighth Street. In a small restaurant, he ordered coffee and a ham sandwich. Taking out a notebook, he turned to the page listing his current cases. Unlike most men he knew, he enjoyed his work. Every case was a challenge that he eagerly anticipated solving. He could never leave his work behind at the office; he spent hours every evening working on his cases.

When he'd first come to work at the Pinkerton Agency, Robert had been amazed by the evil that dwelt in men and women alike. Before that, he had never known any truly bad people, people capable of committing heinous acts of violence and cruelty. Those kinds of humans soon became part of his everyday life, and instead of being revolted, he was fascinated by them. He admired their great ingenuity in committing crimes. Greed, it seemed, was the root of evil in ninety-nine per cent of his cases. The pursuit of money was never-ending, like water cascading over Niagara Falls – wives poisoning husbands to inherit their fortune, children killing parents for the insurance money, clerks embezzling funds under their bosses' noses.

The cases Robert had been assigned since transferring to New York were without question the most challenging he'd ever faced. The fact that the robberies had been carried out by one gang was exciting as hell, and though the escape in the tunnel at Fidelity National still angered and depressed him, it had made him all the more zealous in hunting the criminals down.

Robert ran his finger down the list to the latest case he had been assigned: a robbery in Newport. The local police had had no luck and, under pressure from the victim, had asked the Pinkertons to take over. He finished his coffee and paid his bill. Taking Madison Avenue south, he walked to Seventeenth Street and turned right. He came to 9 West Seventeenth Street, a narrow brick building that looked like a residence. Going up the path to the arched entry, he knocked and announced himself. A porter led him to a small waiting room furnished with overstuffed leather chairs, where a lanky man with thinning hair and spectacles greeted him.

'I'm pleased to meet you, Mr Cross. Mr Goelet said that we were to offer you our every assistance. Come into my office where we can talk privately.'

'Thank you, sir. I have only a few questions. Do you know which architect designed Mr Goelet's house in Newport?'

'Oh, that would be Mr Stanford White of McKim, Mead & White. In fact, he did this little house here too, as the Goelet family's business headquarters. It's almost like a home, wouldn't you say?'

'Indeed,' Robert said, his eyes distant. 'It's quite charming.'

'Thank you for your time, Mr White.'

'Call me Stanny, Rob,' the red-headed architect bellowed. 'It's been a pleasure to meet you. Anything I can do to help catch those bastards, you let me know. And be sure to tell John I said hello. You must both come to my club for drinks some evening.'

'I'd like that,' Robert said. 'And I'll be sure to tell my brother you said hello.'

Solving a crime, he thought as he walked down Fifth Avenue, was like putting together one of those giant puzzles that were so popular these days. When the hundreds of pieces were first dumped out, it seemed impossible to fit them all together to form a detailed Adirondacks landscape or a Biblical scene. But slowly, piece by piece, the image became visible.

The pieces in this puzzle had started to fall into place. But instead of the accustomed feeling of elation, Robert was very troubled.

CHAPTER SIXTY-ONE

When Nolan opened his eyes, he saw a gleaming sky of pure white. The brightness was so intense his eyes began to water.

'It's about time you woke up, Rip Van Winkle,' a man's voice called.

With great difficulty, Nolan lifted his head. He saw Dunn, a member of his gang, waving at him from a row of beds across a centre aisle.

At that moment, he realised he was in a hospital ward, not the afterlife. The dozens of beds were filled with male patients, some covered in bandages, some not. Above him was a ceiling of pure-white plaster, with suspended electric lights bouncing illumination off it.

All Nolan could think of in that moment was how incredibly clean and bright the huge room was. Then he felt something on his face. When he lifted his arm from underneath the white sheets, a terrific pain shot up his right side. Wincing and touching his face, he discovered that there was a bandage covering his left temple and part of his forehead.

'Didn't think you'd ever wake up.'

'Where the hell are we?'

'New York Hospital on Fifteenth Street.'

'Christ, what happened?'

'Kent sent us a beer keg full of gunpowder and blew the shit out of the room in the Bucket of Blood. Don't ya remember?'

'I remember the keg being brought in . . . but after that, it's a blank.'

'I bet. You've been out almost two days. They shot ya up with a gallon of morphine.'

'Where are the rest of the guys?'

'*We* are the rest of the guys. Everyone else's dead, the poor bastards.'

Ignoring the intense pain, Nolan raised himself up on his elbows.

'Everyone?' he asked incredulously.

'Except Swanson and a couple others who weren't there. Everyone else was wiped out: Milligan, Johnson, Pickle Nose, Brinkerhoff.'

'Pickle Nose?'

'The only way they knew it was him was that big honker of his. They had to scrape bodies off the walls. Some people who were on the first floor when it collapsed bought it too.'

'Pickle Nose . . . dead.'

'I was at the far end of the room getting a deck of cards when the explosion went off. Still got thrown against the wall and broke my fuckin' leg.'

Nolan began touching his torso, flinching in pain.

'I heard the doc say a couple ribs are broken, and ya got a big gash on your skull. Still, you're pretty fuckin' lucky to be alive. Good thing you was standing towards the back of the room.'

Nolan collapsed back against his pillow and started sobbing. He couldn't help himself. Though they were dishonest, ignorant scum, the members of his gang were the only family he'd ever had. He'd grown up with most of the men and had come to have great affection for them. They'd relied on each other in times of trouble. Pickle Nose had been like an older brother: he'd looked out for Nolan and taught him the ways of the street. Nolan would not have survived without his help. Pug Johnson had helped him refine his pickpocketing skills. As a sign of respect, Milligan, who had treated Nolan like a son, had let him keep a large percentage of his earnings.

Nolan could barely remember his real family. What he did recall was the shouting, beatings, and near starvation doled out by his drunken father. Sometimes, he'd thought that getting kicked out into the street was the best thing that could have happened to him. All those good men who'd sheltered him were gone, never to be seen again. And it was his fault. He had brought his fate on by killing Murdock before the man could murder John Cross.

What had he done? He had acted impulsively for the love of a girl – the blood of more than a score of men stained his hands. The thought crushed Nolan. As he stared up at the ceiling, an anger deep within his chest ignited and began to burn. Gangs in New York frequently skirmished with one another, but Kent's act of revenge – murdering so many men in cold blood – was reprehensible.

'Kent's a fuckin' animal. He deserves to die,' Nolan said, his voice cracking.

Dunn was distracted by movement near the door. 'Here she is. Hello, my beauty,' he yelled.

'Good to see you, Mr Dunn.'

The sight of Julia at the foot of his bed filled Nolan with joy. In an instant, his anger drained away. He tried to lean forward to greet her but fell back.

'This little girl's been here three times today, waiting for you to wake up.'

Julia knelt by the bed, took Nolan's hand, and kissed it.

'John, I was so worried you wouldn't wake up. Oh God, it's so good to see you.' She choked out the words between sobs.

Nolan ran his fingers through her hair but said nothing. For the time, her mere presence eased his pain. 'What day is it?' he asked softly.

'It's noon on Tuesday.'

'Shouldn't you be in school?' he asked, still stroking her hair.

Julia raised her head and smiled. 'I played hooky today. When I went looking for you at the Bucket of Blood – or what's left of it – they told me what happened. But don't worry, I won't get in trouble – I already forged the excuse note, just like you taught me.'

CHAPTER SIXTY-TWO

'There's a lot of building going on in the city. Business must be good, John.'

'Best it's ever been. There's the theatre, the hospital, a few office buildings,' Cross said. He wasn't a man who boasted, but as always, Robert's praise was uniquely affirming.

'I've noticed quite a few tenements getting built too. Doing any of that sort of work?'

'Sadly, no. But I'd like to try my hand at a tenement project. There's a lot of room for improvement when it comes to their design.'

The two brothers were finishing dinner at Sherry's. In the last few months, Cross had never missed a dinner or a lunch with Robert. His reasons were twofold. He loved the company – and he wanted to know what the Pinkertons were up to. Were there any leads on his robberies? What about the informant who'd spoilt the bank job? It was odd that he hadn't struck again. The thought of that betrayal was a constant torment to Cross.

Adding to his dilemma, Robert's dragnet of informants throughout the city had made robbing the wealthy almost impossible and lining up robberies for Kent yet more difficult. Seeing no way out of his predicament, Cross and Helen had continued to wrack their brains for possible targets.

'You know, I saw an incredible house going up on Madison Avenue right behind Saint Pat's. U-shaped thing done in brownstone,' Robert said, taking a forkful of apple pie.

'That's for Henry Villard, the president of the Northern Pacific Railroad. He's related to Charlie McKim, a close friend of mine, who did the design. It's actually not one house but six separate dwellings arranged around an entry courtyard.'

'Six? It looks like one big mansion.'

'That's the genius of it. The design's based on an Italian Renaissance precedent, the Palazzo della Cancelleria in Rome, but the details have been simplified. Pilasters were eliminated, and the window surrounds were reversed . . .'

Cross stopped. His brother was grinning from ear to ear, a sure sign that Cross was boring the socks off him. He burst out laughing, as did Robert.

'I'm so sorry. Once I start talking about architecture, you know I can't shut my mouth,' Cross said apologetically.

'You're passionate about your work. It's a wonderful thing. I'm passionate about mine too. I want to solve every case and bring every criminal to justice,' Robert said, his gaze steady on Cross.

'Any progress on the robberies – Cook and the bank and all that?'

'Not much, I'm afraid. Very cunning crimes usually take time to solve. But I'll get them. I've got a damn big caseload too, along with routine duties like protecting businesses.' Robert finished his coffee and stared out at the flow of traffic on Fifth Avenue. 'McKim, Mead & White did Villard's place? Isn't that Stanford White's firm?' Robert asked finally.

'Why yes, he did the interior design for the houses. Stanny's a very good friend of mine. He was at Julia's coming-out ball. Tall fellow with red hair. Hands down the best architect in the city. An incredible talent.'

'I think I remember him,' Robert said. He paused, then added, 'He must have a lot of rich clients, like the ones who have the big houses along the cliff in Newport.'

'The richest of the rich. Although Aunt Caroline doesn't use him much.'

'Did you go up to Newport to see the old girl this summer?'

'We went up for a week. But she was in the Berkshires.'

'Did you go to the casino? I hear they have good concerts.'

'Helen dragged me to one.'

'I hear Tuxedo is the place to be nowadays. Lorillard's built himself a whole town up there.'

'Yes, a colleague of mine, Bruce Price, designed the cottages and the clubhouse. It's quite the place.'

'Didn't he do the Oceanside Hotel in Long Branch?'

Cross paused and took a sip of coffee. It gave him a few seconds to size up the situation. He shifted around in his seat and dabbed his mouth with the linen napkin while repeating in his mind the entire conversation he and his brother had had up to this moment. Each word his brother spoke threw up a red flag – tenement, White, Newport, cliff, concert, Price, Tuxedo, and Oceanside.

'Yes, Price did the hotel at Oceanside, where that big robbery took place a few weeks ago.'

'Yep, the place was wiped out during a charity ball. Unbelievable,' said Robert.

'Came through the metal ceiling on the top floor, they said,' added Cross.

'It was ingenious. Word on the street is that a mastermind named the Engineer planned all these jobs.'

A spoonful of peas in vinaigrette sauce was about to enter Cross's mouth when they slid off the utensil, bouncing against his shirt and waistcoat. 'Damn,' uttered Cross, who, with a flustered expression, looked across the table at his brother.

'I see your table manners haven't much improved since you were ten,' said Robert with a laugh.

Trying to wipe out the tiny stains on his bright-white shirt front, Cross replied, 'Really, they call him the Engineer?'

'He's greatly admired by the underworld. Almost like a mythical hero.'

Cross smiled feebly.

'Maybe Price is the Engineer. Lorillard's house was robbed, you know, and he designed it,' said Robert, rapping his knuckles on the white tablecloth.

'I thought that fake Russian count did that.' Cross knew Robert didn't know he was there that night. To protect their privacy, Lorillard wouldn't reveal the rest of his guest list that weekend. A society gentleman would never embarrass his guests in that manner. In their world, it just wasn't done.

Robert laughed so loud that the other patrons turned to look at him. 'No, it wasn't him.'

'But it can't be Price, old boy.'

'And why not?'

'He's not an engineer; he's an architect. World of difference,' said Cross, grinning. 'One's an artist and the other's not.' Robert let out another explosive laugh.

The conversation was making Cross uncomfortable, so he decided to change the subject to something he knew Robert enjoyed talking about.

'How about dinner tomorrow night, then we'll all go to the theatre?'

'Wonderful. Will George be there? I never see him any more. How is the boy doing?'

'We forced him to come to supper last Saturday,' Cross said, sighing. 'He's still teaching down in the Bowery. He'll keep at it until the autumn term starts. He really loves those children. Urchins, every one of them.'

'He seems to have turned his back on society. It must drive Helen mad. I'm sure she's picked out at least a dozen suitable wives for him,' Robert said with a smile.

Cross nodded. 'I've told her time and again to leave him alone, but she won't listen.'

'What does he do to occupy his spare time?'

'I'm afraid it's a mystery.' And it was. Cross had no idea what George was doing with his days outside of teaching – secretly, he didn't want to know.

'Does he like the ladies, polo, horse racing . . . gambling?'

Cross wondered whether his brother saw him react ever so slightly to the last word, like the twitch of a cat's ear or a leaf on a branch moving in the breeze. He realised that his brother knew the truth – and was setting a trap into which he was walking blindly. It was like those tiger traps in India he had read about, in which a deep hole is covered with grass and brush that blends in with the ground cover. He had always tried to be on his guard when he was around Robert for fear of revealing something, but somehow he had grown careless. He was one step away from falling into that hole.

'He inherited Helen's looks, so I imagine he's popular with the girls. He probably hangs about with the men from Harvard. There are a lot of them in the city.'

'I'd like to ring him up and ask him out to supper if he's not too busy,' said Robert.

'George is very fond of you. I'm sure he'd like that.'

'Ah, to be young again. I envy him,' Robert said, signalling the waiter for the bill. Before John could protest, he added, 'Please, let me take care of it.'

As Robert walked up Fifth Avenue, his head was bent in sadness. The police and newspapers had held back the fact that the top floor of the Oceanside Hotel was robbed from above the ceiling. He knew his brother had been at the ball that night.

CHAPTER SIXTY-THREE

'Eight thousand? You owe eight thousand? But just this morning, it was fifteen hundred.' Kitty fell to her knees on the carpet of her parlour and put her hands over her face, trying to stifle her sobs.

George stood above her in silence, his head bowed.

'I can't do this, George,' she moaned. 'I just can't. Every day, you risk being beaten to a pulp or killed. I can't go through it any more.'

'Kitty, this is the last time. I swear. I'll never—'

'Do you know how many times you've told me that? A million!' Kitty cried, her eyes blazing with passion. 'And each time I believed you with all my heart. Because I love you with all my heart. But no more, George. No more. You're killing me.'

'Please . . .'

'Every day, we scramble for money. It never ends, and it's tearing me apart. One day, they're going to find your body in the river. I don't want to be there for that.'

'You know I've tried, Kitty. You know that.'

'And it's damn useless. You're powerless, George. You're like a drunk who promises with every sip that this will be his last drink. This sickness has hold of you, and I can't do anything about it.' Kitty's voice had gone soft. George had never heard her sound so defeated. 'I'm watching the only person I've loved in my entire life destroy himself.'

'Kitty, I love you. I do. Together we can beat this. We can't give up.'

Kitty stood and looked into George's face. He tried to put his arms around her, but she pushed him away. 'No. It's over. I won't do this to myself, not any longer. They say if you love someone enough, you can forgive anything, endure anything, but that's not true,' said Kitty. It was as if her entire being had been drained out of her body, and all that was left was a shell.

'You've said that before, darling.'

'This time I mean it. It's really over. I want you to leave.' Kitty spoke firmly, despite the tears welling in her eyes. 'I can't see you again, George. Not ever.'

George stood before her, as still as if he'd been turned to stone. 'Please go, George,' Kitty said in a soft, defeated voice.

When he didn't respond, Kitty couldn't help herself. She started sobbing violently and pushed him towards the door. He tried to resist, but she kept pushing him. 'Get out, damn you. Get out!'

George turned and walked out the door. Kitty slammed it behind him. The sound seemed to echo in his ears for a long time. In spite of himself, he waited in the corridor, hoping she would fling open the door and come after him.

Time passed. All he could hear was Kitty, sobbing softly on the other side of the door.

Alone, George walked slowly down the black iron staircase to the street.

CHAPTER SIXTY-FOUR

The workmen grunted and cursed under their breath as they transferred gold bars into the wagon. By itself, a single bar wasn't heavy – perhaps five pounds. But the continuous loading was exhausting. Having performed this task countless times over the years, the thought of stealing a bar no longer entered the men's minds. They might as well have been loading bricks.

After the last bar was in the wagon, the men retired to a room in the corner of the cavernous warehouse for coffee and sandwiches. The driver and armed guards would be there in twenty minutes to take the gold to the pier. At 5 a.m., before traffic choked the Manhattan streets, they would leave the warehouse on Eleventh Street and First Avenue.

The driver and guards arrived, locked the rear double doors, and started their journey to the pier at Front and Spruce Streets on the Lower East Side. There, the gold would be loaded on a ship bound for Belgium. Instead of an armoured wagon, the investment house of Kidder, Peabody & Co. were taking the precaution of transporting gold bullion in an old converted beer wagon, pulled by four dappled grey horses. The set-up was meant to avoid unwanted attention. A Pinkerton guard with a revolver sat on top behind the driver, and another guard driving a small milk delivery cart rode ahead. Rather than uniforms, the men wore work clothes.

It was a cool late October morning, and as they clip-clopped slowly through the streets, people emerged onto the pavements to prepare for the business day. Men brought out stands of groceries, cranked open awnings over plate glass windows, and set out barrels of goods. As they rode, the men silently scanned the streets, looking for any possible sign of trouble. They had made the trip three times a year for many years, always varying their route. Every time, the early morning scene was the same. As usual, no one paid any attention to their passage.

They crossed Houston Street and turned east onto Stanton Street. Up ahead, before the corner of Columbia Street, a large masonry warehouse was under construction. Rickety-looking wooden scaffolding had been erected up to the fourth storey, where brick was being laid. On the street in front of the building, construction workers in overalls were milling about, getting ready to start the day.

Just as the wagons passed in front of the building, a low creaking sound could be heard, gradually intensifying in pitch. The drivers frantically looked about for the source of the sound and – to their amazement – saw a section of the scaffolding plunging down towards them. With a terrific crash, the brick-laden wooden structure smashed onto the pavement, spilling into the street in front of them. The horses screamed and reared, trying to bolt. The drivers barely kept them under control.

Suddenly, and from both sides, men carrying lengths of lead pipe appeared. The construction workers joined them as they leapt onto the wagons, striking the guards viciously. The driver of the beer wagon's skull was split open like a melon, and his guard was battered until he fell off the wagon. The milk cart's driver was yanked from his seat and beaten savagely on the pavement. As if in a piece of well-rehearsed choreography, the assailants dragged the bodies into the warehouse. Two men jumped into the driver's seat of the beer wagon and whipped the horses forward on to the south pavement, around the debris. The wagon turned south, travelling at top speed, bouncing along Columbia Street and turning west onto Delancey Street. Slowing to match the pace of traffic, it continued on to Kenmare Street and then Broome Street. At Hudson and Laight Streets, it came to the huge Saint John's Terminal, the freight station built by Commodore Vanderbilt for his New York Central Railroad. Fifty feet tall and constructed of brick and granite, a loading platform ran the entire length of the massive structure, allowing the transfer of goods from wagons to the trains that entered the building.

The driver steered the wagon into one of the forty-foot-wide arched openings and drove up a wide wooden ramp right into an open freight car that was coupled to the many other cars of the New York Central train. By yanking the reins hard to the left, the horses were forced to turn the wagon in a tight radius into the car, where the conveyance came to a halt.

As soon as the wagon was in place, Kent, Cross, Brady, and Culver ran up to the freight car and looked in. The horses were nervous and disorientated, stomping about and causing the wagon to rock back and forth.

'Get these goddamn horses off here!' yelled Brady to the drivers. 'Fast!'

The men jumped down and began to unharness the team, working at top speed.

'This train leaves in ten minutes,' Kent said, looking at his pocket watch. 'Let's check the goods. Bring a lantern; it's pitch-black in there.'

The four men walked up the ramp into the car and went to the back of the wagon. With a crowbar, Brady pried open the double doors. Culver went in first with the lantern.

'Holy shit!' Culver yelled.

'A big haul, eh, Mr Culver?' Kent said.

'Look!' Culver sounded incredulous.

Standing next to a pallet stacked high with gold bars was George Cross.

CHAPTER SIXTY-FIVE

The men stood, looking in amazement at George, who stared wide-eyed at his father.

'George, for God's sake, what are you doing here?' Cross said, absolutely astonished.

Kent burst out laughing. 'The same thing we're doing here, Mr Cross. Stealing the gold. *Our* gold, I should say.'

George jumped out of the wagon and walked up to his father. He swallowed hard before he spoke. 'Is this true?'

No words emerged from Cross's mouth. He was in shock.

'What are you doing here, Father?' George asked.

'Your father happens to be my partner, George,' Kent said, smiling. The irony of the situation seemed to please him no end.

George looked at his father, who had turned away from him. Slowly, he walked around and looked his father straight in the face. It was dark at the end of the freight car, and Culver held the lantern high, throwing spooky shadows that danced on the walls.

'But why?' George whispered.

'He was going to kill you if you didn't pay your gambling debts, son. I couldn't let that happen. So I paid off what you owed by planning robberies for him.'

'And he does it extremely well,' Kent said, lighting up a cigar.

George rubbed his hands over his face and walked slowly away.

'It's too bad, Georgie. Some of this gold might've paid off your current debts . . . which I understand are considerable,' Kent said, turning to smile at Brady and Culver.

Cross looked up at his son, his expression anguished.

George nodded, resigned. 'An old classmate who works at Kidder, Peabody & Co. told me about their gold bullion shipments. After the gold was loaded and the workers left, I snuck into the back and hid. The plan was to fill a satchel with bars and break out the back while the wagon was moving.'

'Oh Christ, George,' Cross said.

'I couldn't come to you for help. I was too damn ashamed . . . and anyway, you didn't have that kind of money.'

'You kept on gambling after I begged you not to,' Cross whispered. 'Why?'

His father looked like he was shrinking, being crushed to the floor by the weight of this revelation. George wanted to shrink himself, to collapse to the size of an insect and crawl away. Kent, who was enjoying every second of the confrontation, started laughing.

'You don't understand, Father. You can't just walk away from it. I couldn't help myself, and I—'

'Don't feed me that hogwash. You knew you had to stop, and you didn't. Goddamn it, do you know the calamity you've caused? Three people are dead because of you!' Cross grabbed his son by the lapels. But he didn't shake or hit him. Tears filled his eyes, and he placed his head against George's chest and sobbed.

The wagon lurched forward as the horses were led out of the freight car.

George placed his hand on his father's shoulder. 'I'm very

sorry I got you involved in all this. If I'd known, I would've let this bastard kill me,' George said, staring coldly at Kent, who just grinned at him.

'I'm glad I didn't, George. Without you, I never would have met your father and made all this money.'

Cross scowled at Kent.

'Sorry to interrupt this tender family reunion, gentlemen, but this train is about to leave the station,' Kent said.

Brady shut the wagon doors and led the way out. The men followed him down the ramp to the concrete platform. The drivers removed the ramp, and one of them shut the freight car door. Two minutes later, the wheels of the freight cars began to squeak and squeal as the train crept slowly along the track.

'Next stop will be Peekskill. Peekskill, New York,' Culver said, mimicking a railroad conductor's announcement.

'A quiet little town. The perfect place to unload gold,' Kent said, patting the side of the car as it moved out, 'and take it to the foundry, where we can melt it down and recast it into something a little less conspicuous.'

Ignoring Cross and his son, the men parted company and started to walk out to Hudson Street.

'I'll see you at McGlory's at nine,' Kent said to Brady and Culver.

'Stand where you are. You're under arrest!' a clear voice shouted. Kent and his men halted, still deep within the shadows of the loading platform. Ten men stood across Hudson Street, pointing shotguns at them.

'I told you to stand where you are. And put your hands up!' Culver, Coogan, and the driver pulled revolvers and began firing. Blasts from shotguns returned their fire. The other driver took off down the street.

In seconds, the space was so filled with white gun smoke that neither side could see the other. Cross rushed to the edge of the opening. Between gaps in the smoke, he made out his brother reloading a shotgun across the street. To his right, Culver took a blast to the chest and fell down heavily. The driver came to his aid but was hit in the head. Cross could hear Coogan firing away; the reverberation of the pistol reports inside the loading dock was deafening.

He ran back to George, who stood next to the moving train, frozen with fear.

'Follow me!' Cross yelled. He grabbed his son by the sleeve and led him in the opposite direction of the train. 'We have to get on the other side,' he whispered.

Gathering his strength, Cross ran along the side of the train and grabbed the brakeman's ladder. In a tremendous effort, he swung himself up between the cars, onto the coupling, and jumped off on to the other side of the platform. George did the same. Cross then pointed to a stair enclosure in the rear wall. Running as fast as they could, he and George made it up to the attic space. Exposed iron roof trusses were lined up, one after another. Cross and his son ran to the south, hopping over the bottom chords of the trusses until they came to another staircase at the end of the building. A door at the bottom led directly out the rear, onto Varick Street. At the corner of West Broadway and Grand Street, soaked with sweat and breathing heavily, they hailed a hansom.

'You know your buildings,' George said.

'You're damn right I do.'

Dragging Culver's limp form, Kent, Brady, and Coogan had hitched a ride on the rear platform of one of the cars as it pulled out of the terminal. At West and Morton Streets, they jumped off and ran. Two blocks away, they turned and saw that the train had stopped.

Kent and Coogan, who held Culver by the arms, laid him down gently on the dirt of a side alley. Blood was pouring from his chest. Kent worked frantically to stem the bleeding with his jacket, but it was hopeless. Culver's eyes rolled backwards, showing their whites. He was gone.

Kent let out a groan, dropping his head onto Culver's chest. 'The sons of bitches killed him,' he said, beside himself with anger.

'Christ, that was a close call,' Brady growled.

'And they're taking my gold, goddamn it!' Kent yelled.

Coogan bent and met Kent's eyes. His face was grim.

'Just before the shooting began, Burgess, one of the drivers, said a Pinkerton named Robert Cross was yelling at us. Man had arrested him once in Buffalo.'

Kent froze. 'Cross?'

CHAPTER SIXTY-SIX

'So, Cross's brother is a Pinkerton.' Oddly, Kent seemed more amused than angry.

'A Pinkerton who killed Culver and took our gold!' Brady said.

'It was Cross who tipped them off this morning. It had to be,' Kent said. 'I thought he was the traitor after the bank job, but I wasn't sure. Now . . .'

'I told you Cross was the snitch from the very beginning, but you never believed me,' Brady said. He sounded hurt.

Kent walked to the window of his apartment at the Dakota and looked out at the park. He never tired of the view, that vast expanse of green, with people and carriages coming and going. It was like living in the country without having to leave the city. When he was upset, it always had a calming effect on him.

Grimly, he tied his red silk dressing gown more tightly around his waist and sat down on the sofa. Millicent, his wife, appeared at the sliding doors of the library.

'Dinner at eight. Chicken à la Maryland, your favourite,' she said.

Kent smiled and raised his hand in a gesture of approval.

'Will Mr Brady be staying for dinner?'

'I'm afraid not, dear. He has some urgent business to attend to.'

Millicent nodded, waved goodbye to Brady, and left quietly.

'Cross has played us for fools. He knew I wouldn't let him go, so he bided his time and sold us out to his brother,' Kent said bitterly. 'That's how he knew about the gold shipment.'

'Cross has to die,' Brady said. He stood before Kent, posture stiff with determination.

'Along with his entire family,' Kent said, looking up at Brady to make sure he understood his orders. 'That's what I promised him would happen if he betrayed us – and I never break a promise.'

'It'll be my pleasure.'

'It's a shame, though. We had a very lucrative run with Mr Cross. From a business standpoint, I'll be sorry to see him go. But you know, Mr Brady, even if he didn't tip them off, with a Pinkerton for a brother, he's still too big a risk to keep on.'

'What *about* his brother?'

'I'm afraid he's become a liability as well.'

'I wanted to thank you for your information about the gold robbery. Kidder, Peabody & Co. was most generous with their reward. It's far more than Fidelity National Bank paid for your information. And it's in gold, waiting for you in the usual location.'

'I'm glad to hear that. Gold is the sovereign of sovereigns.' The voice emerged from the darkness some fifty feet away.

'If you could please provide me with more details about the robbery, I'd be very grateful. Who was involved, for instance.'

'I'd be glad to. Come forward, and we'll talk about it.'

Robert Cross stood in the Stygian darkness of a storage pier that stretched out over the East River. He couldn't see a thing, but he knew the source of the voice was directly in front of him. Standing very still, he tried to discern whether there was anyone else on the pier. He could hear only the sound of the river, beating steadily against the pier's wooden pilings below.

Slowly, Robert walked forward, waiting for his eyes to adjust to the dark. His feet kept shuffling through puddles, bumping into piles of trash and pieces of timber. He kept his hand on the trigger of his revolver – just in case his informant turned uncooperative. About twenty feet away, he could make out the outline of a figure.

The voice spoke again. 'I can give you their names and tell you where to find them – for more gold, of course.'

Robert paused, straining his eyes to get a better view of the man. The fellow remained indistinguishable, a mere black outline against the greater blackness of the pier. Robert inched forward, splashing inadvertently into a puddle. He felt a sudden jolt; it rocked his entire body as if he'd been hit in the chest with a two-by-four. But he didn't fall down. He stood, stunned, as a strange sensation rushed through him.

Finally, he fell face first into the puddle. His lifeless eyes stayed open, as wide as if he'd seen a terrifying sight.

From out of the shadows, Ned Brady appeared. He walked to an electric panel on the wall from which a long length of wire extended into the puddle and pulled the short metal lever up. Bending over Robert's body, he reached down to his neck and felt for a pulse. Nothing.

'Amazing thing, electricity,' Brady said. His words echoed in the silence of the pier.

He picked up the body by the armpits and dragged it to the end of the warehouse, dropping it with a dull thud. Brady pulled up a trapdoor in the wood floor. Below the opening, the current of the East River flowed past in a muffled hush. Occasionally, a dead rat or piece of rubbish passed by.

Brady was truly sorry to see the Pinkerton go. He had been

a very lucrative source of extra income. Kent had constantly brushed off Brady's requests for a bigger cut on the jobs, refusing to acknowledge the value of his skills or his long service to the organisation. But far more than that indignity, Brady loathed being bossed around by an upper-class swell, especially in front of the other men. Kent was rich and educated, so *of course* he always knew better. Brady hated Kent's guts, but he'd kept his volcanic temper in check and bided his time for an opportunity for revenge. And it had paid off handsomely – at least for a while.

With some difficulty, Brady lifted the body and dropped it into the opening. There was the barest sound of a splash. The Pinkerton's body was silently caught up by the rush of water, and in a second, it was gone.

CHAPTER SIXTY-SEVEN

'You know he means to kill us all.'

'Yes, George, I'm aware of that,' Cross said, his voice devoid of emotion as he ran his hand through his brother's matted hair.

Robert was laid out on a marble morgue slab in the basement of police headquarters at 300 Mulberry Street. The expressionless coroner stood behind Cross and his son. One could tell that he'd silently watched the grieving relatives of the dead hundreds, if not thousands, of times before.

'I remember when I told him that I wanted to be an architect, but our father wouldn't hear of it. Father said I should go into business and become rich, so *I* could boss the architects around. Robert told me that was nonsense, that I should follow my heart and go to Paris to study like I wanted.'

'He was such a good man. I wish he'd come to New York earlier.' George shook his head, placing his hand on his father's shoulder. 'Uncle Robert loved being part of the family.'

The coroner edged closer to Cross and said in a quiet voice, 'Sir, may I ask you to identify the body?'

'This is Robert Cross, my brother,' Cross said heavily.

Nodding, the doctor stretched the white sheet over Robert's

head. As Cross and George turned away, an attendant handed them a sack containing Robert's personal effects and his Smith and Wesson 38-calibre pocket revolver.

'What should we do, Father? Tell the Pinkertons?' George asked, nodding towards the glass doors of the room. On the other side stood half a dozen of Robert's colleagues, all of whom had angry, vengeful looks on their faces. No one murdered a Pinkerton and got away with it.

Cross turned to look at them. 'No. This is a family matter now. I must take care of this myself, George.'

George blocked his path, staring incredulously at his father. 'You can't take on Kent. He may seem like a gentleman, but he's an animal.'

'I know that all too well,' Cross said, images of the three murders he'd witnessed flashing vividly through his mind. 'That's why he must be dealt with very quickly.'

'But you can't do it yourself,' George said. 'You're no match for him and his men.'

'I have no choice. I can't stand by and let him murder the rest of my family.'

'Then let me help. Please, Father. I caused Uncle Robert's death – I caused all this trouble. This is my fault. You must let me help. You can't do this alone.'

With her face just inches from his, Helen said in a barely audible voice, 'It wasn't an accident, was it, John?'

Cross walked to the parlour window. Outside, a fruit wagon trudged slowly up Madison Avenue. The driver's head was bent over, as if he'd fallen asleep at his post. His brown nag also looked as if it was sleepwalking.

Without turning to face Helen, he said, 'No. Robert was

murdered.' Helen took a step back, grabbing at the heavy, olive-green velvet curtains that shrouded the tall windows. She said nothing for almost a minute. Then she placed her hand on her husband's.

Cross put his arm around her waist and drew her close. He was proud of Helen for standing up so well to the news. He'd told her immediately after he returned from the morgue. From their experiences in the past few months, he knew she wouldn't collapse to the floor in a faint or fly into hysterics. Rather, and as he expected, a steely calm came over her.

Travelling home in the carriage, Cross had realised that he'd never experienced the tragic, unexpected loss of a loved one. His parents and relatives had died of natural causes after a long life, which wasn't the same thing. No one he knew well had died in the Civil War, perished of a disease, or died in an accident. He wondered whether the insulated, elite world of New York society had enveloped him and his family, their cocoon of privilege protecting them from the cruelties of the world, at the hands of which average people always seemed to suffer. The grinding poverty, disease, and filth that plagued the residents of the Lower East Side and the Bowery, just two miles away, was something one occasionally read about in the newspapers. An unemployed labourer kills himself and his family because he doesn't want them to starve to death in their squalid tenement apartment. A homesick Irish housemaid is worked to death; she can't bear life any more and drowns herself in the lake at Central Park. Almost every week, a person was run down in the street by a runaway horse or wagon. But the victims were never of the society set. People in his world seemed immune to the random cruelties of life – until now.

He'd looked at George then, sitting next to him in the carriage. Though losing Robert ripped his insides out, secretly he was glad that it hadn't been George – or any of his children. That loss would have been too much to bear. Just the thought made him feel ill.

And it made what he had to do next all the more urgent. He couldn't lose any more of his family.

'You know what you have to do,' Helen said, as if reading his mind. There was not a trace of emotion in her voice.

Cross stared at her for a few seconds, amazed at the fury in her beautiful dark eyes. It was almost as if flames were shooting out from them.

'I have to think this out – and quickly.'

'No. *We* have to think this out,' she said.

He smiled at her. She buried her head in his chest and hugged him tightly.

'We can't fail at this, John.'

Cross knocked lightly on Charlie's door. Entering, he saw that his son's eyes were red and swollen. The boy had been crying since he'd heard the news from his mother. Across the hall, he could hear Julia sobbing in her room. Cross sat on the bed and put his arm around Charlie, who buried his head in his father's chest.

After a few minutes, Cross spoke. 'Charlie, I need you and Eddie to do a little detective work for me this afternoon.'

Sniffling bravely, Charlie looked up into his father's eyes and nodded.

'I want you to follow some people and find out where they live.'

CHAPTER SIXTY-EIGHT

Cross waited an hour after the lights went out in the front apartment. Only then did he make his way to 181 Mott Street. It was almost 2 a.m. and raining. The street was deserted, save a few rats scurrying about in the gutter.

As he approached the building, he couldn't help noticing how nice its façade was. *An inescapable professional habit*, he thought wryly. There was elegant Queen Anne detailing on the brickwork, quite unlike the usual tenement design, and three glass-and-wood doors. The centre one offered entry to the tenement. Cross looked across the street at George, who stood in the doorway of the Italian grocery at 178 Mott Street. George looked from side to side down the street and nodded. The coast was clear.

Once inside, Cross hefted the burlap sack he carried and walked down the centre hallway to the main staircase in the middle of the building. One of the new dumb-bell-style tenements, the building was pinched in the centre to channel light and air into the interior apartments. Cross climbed the marble steps quietly, listening for the sound of anyone descending. On the third floor, he walked to the two bathrooms located opposite the stairs. Indoor plumbing and running water were another innovation in the new design. Previously, one either went to a backyard outhouse or used a chamber pot that had to be emptied into the gutter.

Cross pushed open both lavatory doors. Neither was in use. The layout was the same on every floor, he knew: two bathrooms and two one-room apartments in the front and rear. He walked silently down the hall to the front right apartment. At the entry, he put his ear to the door and listened for almost a minute, then walked back down the hall and stopped by the gaslight mounted on the wall. Standing on tiptoe, he shut off the gas jet. Pulling a large coil of narrow-diameter rubber hose from the sack, Cross fastened one end to the gas nozzle, then began to unravel the coil and carry it back to the apartment door. Kneeling, he bent the end of the stiff hose into an arc and slid about six feet of it slowly into the gap at the bottom of the door.

After inserting the hose, he walked along the hallway, pushing its length flush against the baseboard, where it wouldn't be noticed. From the sack, he pulled out long strips of rag and began stuffing them tightly in the gaps around the door. It took almost five minutes. When he finished, he turned the gas jet on as far as it could go and returned to the staircase, checking the bathrooms again before he descended.

Back in the street, he met George in the doorway.

'No one's come in or out,' George whispered.

Cross buttoned his jacket against the cold and leant on the door of the grocers. They waited in silence. Having discovered each other's secrets, a wall of shame separated father and son. They had not discussed what had happened since the confrontation at the gold wagon. It was too painful, and Robert's death had made it yet more unbearable. It seemed there was nothing to say.

After about half an hour, Cross checked his pocket watch.

'I think we can go,' he said.

'Maybe we should wait a bit longer,' George said worriedly.

'No, I think it will be all right,' Cross said, taking his son's arm and guiding him out onto the pavement.

'How'd you know where the bedroom was?' George asked.

'Nick Gillesheimer did the building. He's a friend of mine, and he showed me the drawings.'

They were almost to Kenmare Street when they heard an ear-splitting explosion. Cross and his son spun and saw a fireball shoot out of the front right apartment windows on the third floor. A second later, a figure dived out of the window, engulfed in flames, screaming its lungs out. The body landed on the pavement with a dull thud and lay there, burning away like a pile of kindling.

'That's a shame,' Cross said, shaking his head. 'I'd wanted it to look like suicide. A nice peaceful death in one's sleep.'

Scores of people were running out of the buildings that surrounded 181 Mott Street. They watched the body burn in silence. Finally someone brought a blanket to douse the flames.

Fire bells began ringing off in the distance.

'Mr Coogan must have woken up and wanted a smoke,' Cross said with a smile.

CHAPTER SIXTY-NINE

It was almost 5 a.m. Except for those who had to leave early for work, the city was still asleep. Only two other people waited with Cross and George on the uptown platform of the Third Avenue Elevated's Grand Street station.

Cross, who hadn't slept in more than twenty-four hours, felt wired, as with electricity, alive with unending energy. His senses seemed hypersensitive, attuned to everything around him, like a wolf sniffing the air before a hunt. In the past hour, the weather had become rainy and misty, but Cross took no notice of the raw cold.

Shrouded by a cloud of steam, the train chugged into the station, its wheels squealing to a stop on the iron rails. Cross walked alongside the train until he found an empty carriage and signalled for George to get on. They found seats on the right-hand side of the car. The track hugged the east side of the Bowery, less than twenty feet from the face of the brick buildings that housed apartments and now-shuttered shops. Most of the windows on the second, third, and fourth floors were dark.

At the intersections of Broome, Delancey, Rivington, and Stanton Streets, they passed the electric street lights, which threw off a brilliant glow that illumined the inside of the train. When the train reached Houston Street, Cross and George got off and went down to the lower level. They crossed to the downtown side and waited about five minutes for a train, which they rode back to Grand Street. Again, they crossed back to the uptown platform, catching a train that was about to leave the station.

People had started stirring, opening up the shopfronts on the street below. Lights flickered on in the apartments. Cross and his son looked out of the window, but still they said nothing. The train clattered noisily along the elevated tracks, moving at about ten miles an hour. When a workman in a faded grey shirt and baggy black trousers entered the car, they moved to the next carriage, which was completely empty.

The train approached Delancey Street. Cross raised the wooden window sash and stuck his head out. Satisfied, he gave his son a nod. George looked about the car and returned the nod. When the train was at the intersection of the Bowery and Rivington, Cross twisted his entire body through the window opening until his rear end was perched on the sill. Grasping the frame with his left hand, he pulled his brother's Smith and Wesson from his jacket pocket with his right. As the train reached the middle of the block, Cross extended his body as far as he could and fired off six quick shots into a lit window directly opposite. There was the sound of breaking glass and a woman screaming. The train chugged past, and Cross pulled himself into the car. He sat back down on the cushioned seat and placed the revolver in his right jacket pocket.

George calmly shut the window and looked around the carriage. They still had it to themselves. At Houston Street, they got off the train. This time, they descended to the street. It was 5:45 a.m., and many of the Bowery residents were starting their day. Cross and

George passed shopkeepers setting out tables and barrels of goods, and men and women hurrying to get to work on time. At Lafayette and Great Jones Streets, they hailed a hansom cab.

Still, they did not speak.

As dawn broke in an apartment on the Bowery between Rivington and Stanton Streets, a woman screamed desperately, tugging with all her might at the bullet-riddled body of Ned Brady.

Kent's right-hand man slumped, lifeless, over the kitchen table. A pool of blood spread slowly towards his mug of coffee and the piece of cornmeal bread he always liked to have for breakfast.

CHAPTER SEVENTY

'He's not coming.'

'He's only ten minutes late.'

'Ten minutes? Kent's never ten *seconds* late. Punctuality is an obsession for him,' George said, leaning back against the trunk of an oak. The leaves on the trees in Central Park were almost gone, and the dead few that remained offered Cross and his son no protection from the cold drizzle. Even in the greatcoats they'd picked up from Cross's house on the way, George couldn't stop shivering.

'We should wait,' Cross said impatiently.

'No!' George was almost shouting. 'There's something wrong. He never misses his carriage ride in the morning, not even if it's snowing and sleeting.'

Cross fingered the pistol in his coat pocket. It felt as cold as ice. He pulled his black leather gloves from his other pocket and put them on.

George looked up at the Dakota, its four massive towers looming above the park. 'Wait here,' he said and bolted off.

'George, for God's sake! What are you doing?' Cross shouted after him. But his son had disappeared into the underbrush.

Cautiously, Cross edged out from behind the oak and looked

down the carriage path, peering through the rainy mist. In the distance, the track broke away from the Seventy-Second Street Transverse Road and curved east through the trees. He expected to see Kent's gleaming black-and-maroon phaeton gliding around the bend. But the path remained empty, shrouded in grey fog. Cross went back to the tree and positioned himself so his head was barely visible behind the trunk.

He lit a cigarette and blew clouds of smoke, watching them drift up into the sky. The cold, damp weather made them look thicker and puffier. What amazed him most in the last twelve hours was how good he felt about himself. He wasn't wracked by guilt or shame over what he'd done but rather felt a sense of pride. Ever since he'd hired a substitute in the Civil War, Cross had been dogged by the feeling that he was a coward, too scared to do his duty for his country. But he knew he wasn't a coward. He stood up and defended his family from harm without any reservation or fear. There was no hesitating. His wife and children meant everything to him, far more than designing great buildings. And he'd gotten revenge for the killing of his brother, though he couldn't shed the responsibility of getting Robert murdered. He'd have to bear that himself. There was just one more thing to do.

Five minutes later, George appeared, sprinting down the carriage path. 'He's not coming,' he gasped, out of breath from his run.

'How can you be sure?'

'I talked to the doorman at the Dakota. He knows me. He said that Kent is a guest at the statue unveiling today.'

'So that's what all the fuss is about. I couldn't understand why there were so many carriages heading downtown so early in the day. They've come for the parade,' Cross said, mind whirling.

Lost in his sorrow over Robert's death and terror over the danger confronting his family, he'd entirely forgotten the unveiling of the new Liberty statue on Bedloe's Island. For weeks, New York had been buzzing about the recently erected copper statue of a woman, holding a torch aloft, a gift to America from the people of France. No one had ever seen anything so colossal. Liberty's nose alone was five feet long.

It had taken a long time to raise the money for the statue's base and pedestal, but when Joseph Pulitzer, publisher of *The World*, sponsored a fund, thousands of nickels and dimes poured in. His friend, Richard Morris Hunt, had done the design. Thousands would march down Fifth Avenue in a parade. Then President Cleveland would go to the island and unveil the statue. An armada of ships in the harbour would sound their horns and shoot off guns when the sheet was at last pulled from the statue's face.

'We've no choice but to wait. He'll be here for his usual ride tomorrow,' George said, lighting a cigarette.

'Christ, George, we can't take that chance. He may already know about Brady and Coogan. If so, he'll have sent someone to come after us in their place. We can't dally!'

'There must be fifty thousand people downtown for the parade. Finding Kent will be like looking for a needle in a haystack,' George protested.

'I'm sure he had enough pull to win himself a seat on the reviewing stand. He's on the island,' Cross said, pacing back and forth across the carriage path.

'Then we'll come back to the Dakota this evening.'

'I won't take that chance. Come, let's cut through the park. I need time to think.'

They walked in silence through the cold drizzle. A fog had descended. A mere fifty yards ahead, nothing could be seen but a thick, grey curtain of mist. While Cross tried to determine his next move, horrifying images of what he might find at home flashed before his eyes. The dead bodies of Helen, Julia, and Charlie – perhaps Colleen and Mrs Johnston too. Kent was more than capable of such a thing. He would enjoy it.

They crossed the Mall to Bethesda Terrace. Not a soul was about. Even the birds seemed to have disappeared. Finally, they reached East Drive and headed south.

'Do you hear music?' George asked. His head was tilted up, as if he were looking for musical notes dancing in the air around him.

Cross stopped to listen. 'Yes, it's "Hail, Columbia." It seems to be coming from the end of the park. I suppose that's where the parade will start.'

'Listen,' George said with a smile. 'Can you hear the cheering?'

They hastened their pace and arrived ten minutes later at the south-eastern edge of the park, where an incredible sight met their eyes. Before them in the rain and fog, Fifth Avenue was filled from gutter to gutter with a rolling tide of soldiers in blue, marching in perfect unison down the street. White-gloved officers in cocked hats and gold trim led them. Bayonets on rifles swayed above the ranks like waves of wheat. Marching bands rang out stirring songs like 'My Country, Tis of Thee' and the 'Battle Hymn of the Republic'. Each troop had a contingent of drummers, which beat time to the music and established the march cadence.

'Here! The parade starts here!' Cross shouted over the din, pointing to the side streets above Fifty-Ninth Street. Waiting columns of troops seamlessly blended into the flow. Cross was so excited by the magnificent sight that he momentarily forgot the grave danger they were in. The pavements were filled with humanity; people hung out of windows and leant from balconies, screaming with joy and waving like mad. Even behind the cornices of flat-roofed buildings, masses of people gathered. Above the packed pavements, boys had climbed street light poles to get an unobstructed look. Soaked American flags and French tricolours decorated the fronts of the buildings. The cheering was non-stop, a continuous rumble of thunder.

Cross and George fought their way south through the crowd on the west side of Fifth Avenue, but it was like trying to move a mountain out of their way. When they glimpsed a momentary gap in the flow of troops, they dashed across the street to the other side.

'Let's go down Madison Avenue!' Cross shouted, tugging at the sleeve of his son's greatcoat. 'It'll be easier.'

'You sure that was your father?'

'And my big brother. They passed right underneath us when they went to cross the street,' Charlie said.

'I hope he has more work for us.' Eddie was smiling from ear to ear. He patted the ten-dollar bill in his trouser pocket, as if to make sure it was still there.

Eddie Mooney and Charlie had found a choice viewing position by shimmying up an electric street light pole at Fifty-Fifth Street and Fifth Avenue. When President Cleveland had passed by in his open carriage, he'd looked up at them and waved. Eddie was sure of it.

They heard a loud clanging sound below. A New York City policeman was banging his long wooden club on the metal pole.

'Get your asses down from there, ya goddamn brats!' yelled the florid-faced cop.

'Fuck off,' said Charlie, kicking his foot out and knocking the cop's helmet off his head. Frustrated and unable to climb the pole after the boys, the officer grabbed his helmet and stomped away.

Compared to the cacophony of Fifth Avenue, Madison Avenue was as quiet and deserted as a tomb. Cross and George walked rapidly.

But at Thirtieth Street, they were shocked to see the parade had come east from Fifth Avenue to pass directly in front of Cross's house. Thousands were perched on rooftops and hanging out of windows, screaming and cheering.

'What the hell's going on?' George yelled.

After a moment's puzzlement, Cross grasped the reason for the detour.

'Fifth Avenue is unpaved from Thirtieth Street to Twenty-Sixth Street, remember? They didn't want to march through that muddy slop.'

They walked down the west side of Madison Avenue to Thirtieth Street. In the distance, Cross saw the parade turning onto Twenty-Sixth Street at the top of Madison Square and heading back to Fifth Avenue.

Suddenly, he saw Julia at the rear of the crowd between Thirtieth and Twenty-Ninth Streets. George spotted her too.

'Goddamn it,' Cross swore, his face going dark with rage. 'I told your mother not to let the children out of the house today on any account! Why is Julia in the street? She can see the parade very well from her own parlour.'

Beside his sister appeared a tall young man, a bandage covering his right cheek. He handed Julia a brown men's wallet, which the girl quickly slid into her purse.

'Isn't that the man from Julia's coming-out ball?'

'Yes, I think his name was Nolan,' George said.

Nolan walked away from Julia, melding into the crowd. After a minute, he returned with another wallet. No one on the pavement noticed. They were facing away, busy cheering the parade as it passed by.

George and Cross looked at each other in astonishment. Then a smile came over Cross's face. 'It seems our Mr Nolan has a very interesting occupation.'

As Julia and Nolan walked south on Madison Avenue, George and his father rushed across the street to their house. The front path was filled with cheering strangers. Helen was at the front parlour window, watching the parade. When they came into the parlour, she rushed to her husband.

'Did you . . .'

'He wasn't there,' Cross said. 'He went to that damned dedication on the island where they're unveiling the statue. I just saw Julia out in the street. Didn't I tell you to keep them inside? And where the hell is Charlie?'

'Oh God, John. I tried to mind him, but Charlie slipped out of the house early this morning. He must have gone before anyone was awake. And then that lovely Mr Nolan came, and he was so solicitous. I didn't see the harm in letting Julia watch with him down the street.'

Though he was furious, Cross kept his temper in check. 'They could be dead by now, Helen.'

'It'll be all right. No one will find Charlie in this throng,' George said, putting his hand on his mother's shoulder. 'And I'm sure Mother is right: Julia's safe with Nolan.'

Cross went to the window. It was surreal to see a flood of soldiers marching straight towards his house, then turning on a dime to the left. Madison Avenue above the Square was always so sedate and quiet. The scene in front of him was jarring. He stood for almost a minute, mind whirling.

'Helen,' he said. 'Do you know anyone who's going to the dedication?'

'Yes, a few people. They got invitations. It's a special blue card that allows the bearer and a guest to board the steamer to the island.'

Cross turned back to look at the parade.

'So you can't go unless you have one of those cards?'

'They won't let anyone on the island without one,' Helen said.

Deep in thought, Cross paced back across the parlour, lit a cigarette, and inhaled deeply.

'George, go down to the street and get Julia,' he said.

CHAPTER SEVENTY-ONE

'*You* robbed all those places? *You* stole the Blue Pharaoh Diamond?'

'Yes,' Cross said calmly.

Julia stood before her father, her mouth open in disbelief, her eyes fixed on the scarlet-and-green rug in the centre of the parlour. Cross knew the words 'this can't be true' were ringing through her mind.

George and Helen sat on the sofa, while Nolan stood by the fireplace. The room was silent, save for the cheering of the crowds outside.

'You're a criminal?'

'Yes.'

'And I've helped him. So that makes me a criminal as well,' Helen said.

Julia turned to her mother, stunned. Her beauty and poise seemed so at odds with the word, with the very idea of a criminal. 'But why would you do such a thing?'

'To save me,' George said gravely. 'To keep me from getting killed for not paying my gambling debts.' He stood and took a few steps towards his sister but stopped.

'I had no choice, Julia,' Cross said.

Julia looked at her brother with withering disdain. 'This is all about your gambling? Our lives are in jeopardy because of you? You've destroyed our family for a pack of cards!'

Agitated, she began to pace in circles around the parlour table. Then without warning, she ran to George and began to beat her fists on his chest. Gently, Nolan pulled her away and helped settle her in an armchair. Julia was sobbing uncontrollably. Through her tears, she spat out her words into the room.

'Our prim and proper society family isn't what it seems, is it? We're all just hiding in secret worlds where we escaped to be happy, away from that harsh Knickerbocker code. A code we had to obey even if we didn't believe in it. But we all decided that we didn't want to let it govern every second of our lives. For just a little while, we wanted to be free of it. What would Aunt Caroline say about us?'

Cross chuckled drily. 'She'd drop dead from a heart attack.'

Revealing his life of crime to Julia was humiliating. At the same time, he was proud of her perceptiveness. She showed remarkable insight, especially for a seventeen-year-old.

'My father, mother, both my brothers – and me – we all lead double lives. We all fled the emotionally repressive world of our birth. Who could imagine such a thing?' Julia gave a wan smile, shaking her head.

George knelt in front of his sister. 'You can't understand, Julia. I'm so ashamed of what I've done, but I can't help myself. I tried to repay the debt.' George had tears in his eyes. 'Over and over, I tried to pay it.'

Julia swallowed her sobs and looked her brother squarely in the eyes. 'I was at Cantwell's the day you lost ten thousand dollars. I saw you at the Yellow Dragon too, and at O'Malley's.'

George looked at his sister in shock.

'You could've walked away so easily every time,' Julia said, great scorn in her voice.

'That's what you don't understand. I couldn't. A sickness has hold of me.'

'What absolute nonsense.'

'I know it seems so, but until you've stood in my shoes, you can't understand what it's like. I'm *compelled* to do it. Like a sorcerer's spell.' George went to the window and stood, silhouetted against the pane. 'There's no sense trying to explain it,' he said unhappily.

'You sicken me, George. It's one thing to destroy yourself. It's quite another to destroy your entire family! Because of you, we're all going to die, just like Uncle Robert. Charlie is only ten years old!'

'No one's going to die,' Cross said in a commanding voice. It was more of an order than a statement. 'Not if we work together.'

'Oh my goodness, I'm so clumsy. Please forgive me.'

A light but steady rain was falling, and the pier at Twenty-Third Street was clogged with black umbrellas. A short, elegantly dressed gentleman tipped his top hat to Julia and smiled.

'It's so crowded here,' Julia said breathlessly.

'No problem at all, miss. What miserable weather for the unveiling.'

'It's awful – so damp and cold. I should be home in front of a big fire in my parlour, drinking hot chocolate,' Julia said, batting her eyelashes.

'I wish I was home right now, but I was invited and must go,' the man said.

'Try to stay warm, then,' Julia said, waving and skipping away. She saw the disappointment on the man's face. Clearly, he wanted nothing more than to stay and talk to a pretty girl.

Making her way through the crowd, she met up with Nolan about ten yards away. 'Got it?' she asked.

Nolan pulled a blue card from his coat pocket. 'You're an expert stall,' he said and smiled at her proudly. Though the confrontation with her family had left Julia solemn, even sullen, the compliment brought a smile to her face.

'I've been trained by a master,' she said.

He took her by the arm and ducked under her umbrella. Together, they wormed their way through the crowd. By the railing, they met Cross, Helen, and George. Looking around surreptitiously, Nolan quickly slipped Cross the blue invitation.

'Thanks, John. We're very grateful. Now we must be on our way,' Cross said, patting Nolan on the shoulder.

'Good luck, Mr Cross. Be careful dealing with Kent. Even without his men, he's dangerous.' Cross saw the concern in the young man's face and was touched by it. 'Are you sure you don't want me to come with you? I'd do it gladly,' Nolan added.

Shaking his head, Cross shook his hand, smiling.

Beside them, Julia grabbed the sleeve of George's black greatcoat. 'I'm sorry for what I said. I didn't mean it.'

'No, Julia. When people get angry with one another, they say exactly what they feel. Then, later, they say they didn't mean it because they feel guilty. You meant it . . . and you were right,' George said, hugging his sister and kissing her cheek.

Cross looked squarely into his daughter's face. He saw how worried she was. 'I promise you, Julia, everything will be all right. I want to read a chapter of your book tonight. Have it ready for me, please.'

A gust of cold, damp air swept up the East River. Julia shivered and gave a weak wave, eyes fixed sadly on her parents and brother.

Bulling his way through the crowd, Cross led his wife and son to the gangplank, which was admitting passengers. It led up to a steamer that had been painted bright white with red trim for the special occasion. Its two funnels billowed forth thick, black smoke. Cross handed Helen the invitation. When they got to the foot of the gangplank, where a seaman was stationed, she waved it in front of his face.

'Here's my blue card. As you can see, I've brought an extra guest, my son. I hope you don't mind.' Helen gave the seaman her brightest, most charming smile.

'Ma'am, I ain't supposed to let but one guest on 'cause I—'

Helen moved closer, pouring on the charm. 'It's just my son, and it's such a special day – you won't tell, will you?'

The seaman, who was no more than eighteen, broke into a shy smile and unhooked the chain barring the gangway.

As he watched the Crosses board, Nolan turned to Julia. 'Your father's a brave man,' he said. 'Not many fathers would have the courage to do what he's about to.'

Julia wrapped her arm around Nolan's waist and snuggled against him. Together, they watched the steamer cast off. The thought that she might never see her father, mother, or brother alive again lingered in Julia's mind, but with great determination, she drove it away.

Fully loaded, the *Indomitable* reached the tip of the Battery. Cross and George could see thousands of cheering people lining the sea wall. But a thick mist had settled over the bay, and the Statue of Liberty Enlightening the World could not be seen. There was only a ghostly procession of navy ships, tugboats, yachts, and steamers plying the lead-coloured water and continuously blowing their steam whistles.

These ships comprised the two flotillas, which were sailing down the Hudson and East Rivers through the constant drizzle and mist. To the east, Cross heard a blast of artillery fire from Governor's Island, which was apparently a signal for the naval men-of-war to fire a salute. This marked the entry of President Grover Cleveland's ship into the bay. The other vessels blew their whistles even more frantically, as if to make up for the fact that they didn't have cannons to fire. The deafening noise made Cross's ears ring, and he retreated to the stateroom, which was full of people and cigar smoke. Out of the tightly packed crowd came Helen, smiling nervously. Despite their strained circumstances, she looked ravishing in her long, navy-blue coat with white rabbit-fur collar and sleeves. The matching hat, adorned with a long feather, was particularly captivating. All the men stared, and all the women were jealous.

'Senator Evarts is giving a speech first. When he finishes, Bartholdi, the sculptor, will yank a cord to pull the veil from Liberty's face,' Helen said in a low voice. 'Then President Cleveland will speak.'

The noise made it very hard to hear. Cross signalled that they should go out on deck. By the ship's rail, Helen continued. 'Kent and the other guests are already on the grandstand, waiting for the president. They're on the seaward side of the pedestal. Remember, the unveiling happens the minute Evarts finishes his speech. That's our chance.'

'We must make sure we're the last to leave the ship. That will give us leave to work our way to the grandstand,' Cross said to George.

Helen gasped. Cross, in a panic, looked up and down the deck. 'No. Up there,' she pointed.

A V-shaped opening had formed in the heavy grey mist. Towering above them appeared the statue.

'Good God,' cried George. 'It's incredible.'

Looking down at them was an enormous woman's head. She wore a spiked crown, and a portion of her raised arm and shoulder could be seen too. A tricolour veil hung from the crown, covering her eyes and nose and reminding Cross of veiled Arab women he'd seen in stereoscopic views of the Holy Land. The scale of the head was overwhelming. As a boy, Cross had read about the seven wonders of the ancient world. Among them was the Colossus of Rhodes, a gargantuan statue of a god straddling a harbour. *It must have been like this*, Cross thought, mesmerised. They'd been erecting Liberty for a year; it had been finished in April, but it had been only a speck in the bay. Not until one got close up could its enormity be comprehended.

'I heard that the model was Bartholdi's mistress,' said George with a sly smile.

'It has to be at least a hundred and fifty feet tall,' Cross said. Hunt's pedestal, as tall as a four-storey building, was beautiful in its own right, monumental without overpowering the statue. As the ship drew closer to Bedloe's Island, the presence of the copper-clad woman grew even more dramatic. All three Crosses stood, transfixed.

The *Indomitable*'s engines rumbled into reverse, and it expertly nudged up alongside the pier on the south side of the island. Cheering broke out among the excited passengers, who started filing out on to the deck. The Crosses' attention snapped back to the task at hand. The passengers spilt down the gangplank like water rushing into a trough, and Helen joined them. Cross and George hung back. About a hundred yards away, on top of the star-shaped base of the statue and hard against the pedestal, they could see a large grandstand, filled to capacity. Beside it was an elevated platform draped with the American and French flags, where the main speakers would talk. Looming above was the pedestal and the colossus.

Despite the urgency of their situation, Cross couldn't take his eyes off the statue. The tricolour veil was soaked with rain and plastered to the woman's face, allowing her features to be seen distinctly. A cord attached to the veil threaded through one of the openings of the crown, and Cross saw three men looking out.

CHAPTER SEVENTY-TWO

Cross and George stayed on the dock until the president and his party were almost to the grandstand. Cross had no idea where Helen might be. For the moment, it was unimportant. Exchanging looks with George, he and his son moved as one into the crowd.

They reached the left end of the structure and, for the first time, got a good look at the crowd. To Cross's disappointment, the guests were huddled under a sea of umbrellas, making it almost impossible to recognise individual faces.

'How the hell will we find him?' George whispered.

Cross was perplexed but said, 'Follow me.'

He and George walked underneath the grandstand behind the speakers' platform. It was all an open-bleacher arrangement, they discovered.

'He'll be sitting in the back half,' said Cross. He took off his right glove and placed his hand on the pistol in his pocket. Nodding to one another, father and son split up. Each man slowly walked under the rows of seats, looking up at the backs of the spectators.

When the president was seated, the festivities began. The Reverend Dr Richard Storrs delivered a mercifully short prayer. He was followed by the creator of the Suez Canal, the Frenchman

Ferdinand de Lesseps, who also kept his comments to a minimum. Then the main speaker, Senator Evarts, took the stand. As he droned on, George and Cross kept searching for Kent. The rows were at least a hundred feet long. Up and down they went, peering up at the exposed lower backs of the spectators. Rain dripped down from everywhere. Finally George signalled to his father, pointing to a spot above him.

Cross followed his son's gaze and saw a polished ebony cane with a distinctive serpentine gold inlay coiling up its shaft. He looked at George and nodded.

'We have a few more minutes before the speech is over,' he whispered, still holding the pistol in his pocket.

Evarts was discussing the assistance rendered by France to America during the Revolution when he decided to take a pause. Two seconds later, a roar went up from the crowd. The senator turned and saw that, to his horror, the veil had been removed from Lady Liberty's face. Bartholdi, along with the builders of the statue, had thought the pause meant the long-winded speech was over. They had yanked the cord, pulling the veil off and up through the large openings in the brim of the crown. At the same time, ships in the bay blasted steam whistles and horns, and the men-of-war opened up continuous cannon fire with their big guns.

The din was even louder than before, more deafening than the eruption of an earthquake. Great columns of smoke rose from the ships, blending into the fog. The flames from their guns sent yellow and scarlet flashes into the dark grey mist.

Cross was dumbfounded by the explosion of sound. It was supposed to provide cover for his pistol shot, but he was completely caught off guard. Pulling out his weapon, he fumbled and dropped it on the wet grass. He tried to pick it up but dropped it again. When he finally gained control, he hurriedly raised the pistol to take aim at Kent's back. But the crowd had gone wild with excitement and was rising to its feet. As Cross pulled the trigger, Kent stood too. The bullet whistled through the right leg of Kent's dark grey trousers and ripped a hole in the umbrella of a man directly in front of him. Though the report was drowned out by the racket, Kent instantly realised what had happened. He looked down and, through the grandstand, saw Cross and George gaping up at him. Then he bolted to the left.

Cross gave his son a panicked look and ran in the same direction, trying to catch a glimpse of the fleeing figure. Dropping his umbrella, Kent shoved past the people in his row. At the end of the grandstand, he jumped, taking a long fall to the sodden grass.

Just twenty feet ahead, Cross saw a figure drop to the ground, roll, and take off running, his top hat falling from his head. The speed with which Kent could run surprised him. In a second, the man had disappeared around the corner of the pedestal. Cross had no idea where he was headed; the island was basically barren, and the only wooded area was hundreds of yards away.

George shot past his father, just glimpsing Kent's leg as it flashed around the north-eastern corner of the pedestal. He followed and saw Kent slip in the entry on the north side. Panting, George waited for his father to catch up.

'He's gone inside,' he said to Cross, who was also gasping for breath, his chest heaving like a bellows.

'There're entries on all four sides of the pedestal. He'll probably try to go out another one and make a break for the pier,' Cross said.

'We have to go in and see,' said George.

They entered the base, but Kent was nowhere to be seen. Three men in cutaway coats and top hats came down a stairway and walked past with quizzical looks on their faces.

'He could be down here, hiding. You look around. I'll take the stairs. Meet me on the upper level,' Cross said. George ran off, and Cross began to climb. The pedestal contained one straight-run iron staircase with intermediate landings. At each one, Cross had to stop and catch his breath. Finally, he came to the spiral staircase in the statue itself and pulled out his pistol.

As he climbed, he observed its inner structure: it reminded Cross of a huge oil derrick supporting an intricate iron armature. The spiral stairway was dimly lit with electric bulbs that cast spooky shadows on the copper folds of the statue's toga.

He must have traversed more than a hundred steps before he realised the climb was a waste of time. Natural light was filtering down to him from above, however, and his curiosity got the better of him. Instead of turning back, Cross continued on. The closer he got to the top, the more light flooded the stairs. He was a dozen steps from the platform on the crown. It was a relief to enter a bright, wide open space after going around and around in the cramped dark. He could rest there before going down. Perhaps he might even spot Kent, running to the pier.

When he finally reached the iron-plate platform, his eyes were immediately drawn to the big, windowless openings that lined the brim of the statue's crown. As the dark grey mist swirled in front of them, damp wind blew through the five-foot-high gaps with unexpected force. Cross ran up the last few steps of the spiral staircase, rushed to one of them, and leant out. It was an exhilarating feeling to be up so high and feel the cold breeze on his face. The bay was still enveloped in a pea soup of fog, but he could see the ceremony going on directly below him. The people looked like ants. Cross braced his arms on the sides of the opening and stretched his body out as far as it could go. The sensation was incredible.

'So good to see you again, Mr Cross. I understand that we have business to discuss,' said a voice from the shadows.

Cross was so startled that he cried out. He felt like he might faint and pitch through the opening.

Kent stepped into the light. Dressed in a black sable coat, he was twirling his cane and smiling. 'I see that you've come today to dissolve our partnership. What a coincidence. I had the same idea.' He drew the long, thin sabre from his cane and started walking toward Cross, who staggered away from the opening. 'I'll be sorry to see you go,' he added. 'We've had a very lucrative run.'

Before Cross could reach for his pistol, Kent lunged forward and stabbed him in his left shoulder. He moved with the finesse of a Prussian swordsman. Cross watched in amazement as blood trickled onto the front of his greatcoat. He stumbled backwards and fell to the platform on top of the wet tricolour that had been yanked off the statue.

'That's a very handsome coat you have on. I didn't realise it was so thick,' Kent said. He raised the blade with both hands above his head, ready for the final thrust. Cross looked at him, accepting the inevitable.

As the blade commenced its downward arc, Cross bent his head, but then from the corner of his eye, he saw a pair of arms grab Kent's ankles and yank them out from under him. He fell flat on his face on top of Cross, who twisted his body to see George's head sticking out of the spiral stairway opening at the level of the platform. It almost looked like a decapitated head sitting on the floor. George clambered up the rest of the iron steps, but at the last instant, he stumbled, giving Kent time to stand up and raise the blade. As George advanced, Kent slashed him on the forehead, just above his left eyebrow. Stunned, George brought his hand to his forehead. His palm came away red.

Seeing the blood on his hand had the effect of setting a match to kerosene. George exploded with rage. He charged Kent, ramming his shoulder into his midsection as if he were tackling a football runner. Kent didn't have time to raise the blade again, and the sheer force of George's rush slammed into him, sending Kent's body out one of the tall openings that surrounded the crown. At the last second, George grabbed the side of the opening, preventing himself from falling out.

In shock, he watched as Kent plummeted through the air. Screaming, the criminal mastermind flailed his arms and legs wildly in panic until his body slammed down onto the statue's left shoulder, where the sculpted copper clasp fastened the woman's outer cloak.

Cross ran up to the adjacent opening and leant out. Kent's lifeless body rested face up on the shoulder of the statue. He lay with his head pointing downward, precariously perched on the raised clasp. The fall had plainly broken his back and neck. Kent's eyes stared sightlessly into the cloudy sky. The body slid a few inches downward, but the large metal fold of the cloak stopped it from falling any further.

Cold rainy wind sprayed their faces. Cross leant farther out and saw that Kent's body was positioned directly above the ceremony. Someone, probably President Cleveland, was speaking at the podium. The steam whistles of the boats in the bay could still be heard in the distance.

Cross pulled his son back through the opening. Blood was dripping into George's eye and running down his cheek.

'We have to get down from here, George. If Kent slides off and falls on top of the guests, people are going to come running up here. They'll be asking questions we don't want to answer.'

George pulled out a handkerchief and wiped his face. Looking down, he saw Kent's body slide a few more inches on the wet, slippery copper.

'Let's get the hell out of here,' he said.

They began a mad dash down the spiral staircase, their heavy footsteps echoing off the inside face of the copper cladding. Cross was dizzy from going around and around so many times. When he got to the bottom, he had to pause and steady himself. George grabbed him by the sleeve and led him down the stairs in the pedestal. At every step, they expected to meet policemen or soldiers coming up the stairs. But there was no one.

When they finally reached ground level, Cross thought his lungs were going to explode like overfilled balloons. When George tried to drag him along, he shook him off.

'We have to get back to the pier!' George yelled. He took hold of the collar of his father's coat and yanked him along. In less than a minute, they were outside the pedestal's north entry. Still, there was no one about. They made a wide circle to the south, avoiding the ongoing ceremony by walking out of sight below the base, keeping their eyes glued to the left shoulder of the statue. Cross could have sworn that the body had moved again.

When they approached the pier, they were surprised to find Helen waiting. In all the excitement, they'd forgotten about her. She beckoned to them, and they ran down the pier to meet her.

'There's a private launch leaving right now. I told them my husband took ill, and they said they'd give us a ride back to Manhattan,' she said in a commanding voice.

As one, George and Cross embraced her.

'It's over, Helen. Everything will be all right,' Cross whispered. He was sobbing.

Helen looked into her husband's eyes and caressed his cheek. He smiled at her.

'You were so brave, my dear,' he said tenderly. He took her in his arms and hugged her. Then she turned and gave George a long, tight hug too.

The launch slowly chugged across the water, threading its way through the maze of steamers, yachts, tugboats, and navy vessels in the foggy bay. Huddled together on a bench in the little foredeck, Cross wrapped his arms around Helen and held her close, nuzzling her sweet-smelling hair. After a few minutes, he rose and approached the pilot at the wheel of the launch.

'May I use your spyglass?' he asked.

'Of course, sir. That Liberty statue is a grand sight, isn't she?' asked the pilot, a rotund and swarthy Italian.

'She is indeed,' Cross said.

Through the glass, he saw that Kent's lifeless body still lay on the shoulder of the statue.

CHAPTER SEVENTY-THREE

'Look at this wonderful sunburst pattern – all done in gold thread. Doesn't it look marvellous against the dark green satin?' Helen, walking slowly past the rows of gowns, had stopped to pull one out for closer inspection. 'There are tiny pearls entwined in the embroidery. The House of Pingat always does such beautiful work.'

Satisfied with her selection, Helen handed the gown to her husband, who rolled it up and placed it in a long canvas bag. She continued walking and made six more selections.

Without saying a word to each other, she and Cross walked into Henry Linden-Travers's bedroom and entered his large, panelled dressing room. Cross made the selections, taking evening wear, cutaway coats, frock coats, waistcoats, and every pair of shoes and boots on the shoe rack. He then gathered every silk shirt and cravat. Everything went into another canvas bag.

Back in Mrs Linden-Travers's bedroom, they retrieved a bag of jewellery that must have weighed twenty pounds. Walking down the monumental main staircase, Helen smiled at her husband.

'Not a bad night,' she said happily.

'Yes. I might even call it a good night,' Cross said. Though weighed down by the bags, he managed to give his wife a kiss on the cheek.

Once their travails were over, Cross and Helen had realised that something was missing in their lives. Planning the robberies had brought them together in a way nothing else in their twenty-three years of marriage had ever done. And they made an excellent team. But best of all, they had both experienced the same sense of exhilaration Kent had described when Cross asked him why he was a criminal. It was a sense of ecstasy like no other.

Since Kent's death, whenever Cross designed a private residence or apartment building or bank, he couldn't help thinking about how he would rob it. At first, it was a parlour game, but after a time, it became a real plan that he and Helen put into action. Every other month, husband and wife planned and carried out a robbery. The anticipation was delightful. Though neither would admit it aloud, the robberies brought a renewed sense of love and commitment to their marriage. They were happy, deeply and purely happy.

On the first floor, the Crosses took a last turn around the parlour, just in case they had overlooked some item of value. When the social season ended in mid-February, the parvenus left New York for a warmer climate: Florida, California, even Italy. The Linden-Traverses were wintering in Saint Augustine. Their city mansion would be shut up for months. It was after 2 a.m., and the house was pitch-black. Cross and Helen used a small lantern for illumination.

In the main parlour, Helen picked up a gold cigarette case with a large ruby centred on its front and placed it in a bag. 'I think we have enough for tonight, don't you?' she said.

'Mmm, maybe a bit more,' Cross said, raising the lantern to look around.

After they had brought down Kent's Gents, Cross and Helen had worried that George would go back to his old ways, putting his life at risk with his debts. They sat George down for a lecture about the evils of gambling. At first, they believed his uncontrollable habit was a moral defect, as the reformers of the day claimed. Soon, though, they came to understand the nature of their son's problem. George suffered from a disease for which there was no vaccine or cure. He was unable to stop, no matter how hard he tried; the craving for gambling in any form – faro, horse racing, dice – was too powerful to fight.

But somehow, Robert's murder had changed things. Stunned by the murder of his uncle, George hadn't gambled in a year. His mother and father were relieved but continued to hold their breath. George was walking on a tightrope. The tiniest slip would cause him to fall back into his old habits. Merely handling a deck of cards could be fatal. No matter how guilty he felt about the heartbreak he'd caused, he might not be able to fight the urge.

Still, since he had taken up his teaching position at Saint David's, George had seemed content. He had even acquiesced to his Aunt Caroline's and his mother's matchmaking efforts and had begun to socialise with some girls of his own set. All the same, Helen and Cross squirrelled away some of their illicit earnings in a rainy day fund, fearful that a time when George was in danger would come again.

'Now I think we're finished,' said Cross. He extinguished the lantern, and together they walked down to the basement kitchen and out to the rear courtyard.

It was a crisp, cold March night. There wasn't a cloud in the sky, only a blanket of stars shimmering above them. Cross took a deep breath, savouring the quiet. A slight breeze rustled the naked branches of the trees in the Linden-Traverses' backyard. The fresh air was invigorating; beside him, Cross saw Helen with her head tipped back, smiling.

Slowly, he opened the wrought-iron gate and poked his head out, surveying East Eighty-Seventh Street. At the corner of Park Avenue, Eddie Mooney waved, the signal that it was safe to proceed. On Fifth Avenue, Charlie did the same.

From around the corner, a brougham slowly clip-clopped towards Cross. The driver, John Nolan, carefully and quietly backed it up to the gate. Behind the bench seat, a removable wall panel hid a compartment in which the goods could be stowed. Nolan smiled at Cross, who began handing him the canvas bags.

In the year that he'd spent getting to know him, Cross had grown fond of Nolan. To their mutual surprise, he didn't hold the boy's background or profession against him. In fact, with his good looks and poise, Nolan blended right into society. He'd even charmed Aunt Caroline, though she remained in utter ignorance as to his true identity. He and Julia continued to share each other's company while she was up in Poughkeepsie attending Vassar. For now, they were happy.

With the brougham loaded, Cross helped Helen up onto the seat next to Nolan, and they rattled off down Park Street. The few large houses amid the vacant lots in the neighbourhood were dark, hazy silhouettes against a bluish-black sky. At that hour, not a soul was on the streets.

That was what all their jobs were like. Not once had anyone stopped them. If they had, they would see only a well-to-do family returning home for the night. Charlie and Eddie had melted into the darkness; soon, Charlie would find his way home. Cross had offered Eddie money to find a real room, but the boy stubbornly refused to give up his boiler.

As they rode, Cross thought about how much their lives had changed in the past eighteen months. They weren't the same people. Julia was right: their lives had been a façade, hiding a secret. He smiled at the apt architectural metaphor. There were no secrets in his family any more.

Their double lives were known to each other, but not to the society world they still inhabited, a universe governed by unforgiving rules. But they would gladly take that risk; their clandestine life was liberating and exhilarating, and they refused to give it up. At the same time, they enjoyed the privileges of society. If it seemed hypocritical, so be it. He was proud that his family had challenged the Knickerbocker code. And Cross had no regrets about what he had done.

And he was a full-time architect again, designing some of the best buildings of his career, producing work that was truly creative and original, done in his own vision, no one else's. But every time his ego puffed up about his architecture, he'd stop himself and realise how it paled in comparison to what he'd done for his family.

At Madison Avenue and Thirtieth Street, Helen and Nolan disembarked. Cross waved to his wife as she went up the front path and then nodded to Nolan, who disappeared down the street. He gave the reins a snap and headed downtown.

Tonight, he would convince Bella Levine to take forty-five per cent on their goods.

ACKNOWLEDGEMENTS

What I said in the acknowledgments of my first novel still holds true. If you want to get a novel published, you must have people who absolutely believe in your work and stand behind you. Again, those two special people are my literary agent, Susan Ginsburg of Writers House, and Shana Drehs, editorial director of Sourcebooks Landmark. Susan gave me a great deal of valuable guidance and advice in the writing of my second novel, plus she's always teaching me how to navigate the turbulent waters of the publishing world. Working with Shana and Anna Michels showed me again how important an editor is in this whole process. An author thinks his or her manuscript is perfect but then realises an editor's insight can raise the book to a higher level, which is what they did. Thanks also to Susie Dunlop and Allison & Busby for bringing the book to UK readers.

Charles Belfoure
Westminster, MD